THE HARDER THEY FALL

THE DEADLY WOLDS MURDER MYSTERIES
BOOK 2

JACK CARTWRIGHT

CHESTNUT PRESS

ALSO BY JACK CARTWRIGHT

The DCI Cook Murder Mysteries

A Winter of Blood

A Secret to Die For

The Wild Fens Murder Mysteries

Secrets In Blood

One For Sorrow

In Cold Blood

Suffer In Silence

Dying To Tell

Never To Return

Lie Beside Me

Dance With Death

In Dead Water

One Deadly Night

Her Dying Mind

Into Death's Arms

No More Blood

Burden of Truth

Run From Evil

The Deadly Wolds Murder Mysteries

When The Storm Dies

The Harder They Fall

Until Death Do Us Part

THE HARDER THEY FALL

A Deadly Wolds Mystery

PROLOGUE

The sunset over St Leonard's Church must have been one of the most spectacular that Richard Hawkins had ever witnessed, certainly of those he remembered in the Lincolnshire Wolds, or even the UK. The sky seemed as though it had been painted specifically for the twelfth-century church, so the fading light could illuminate the moss on its old, olive-green stones, and the pink sky might highlight the rosy tints of its stained-glass windows. In fact, there was little doubt that St Leonard's had been created in harmony with the nature that surrounded it at such a time when devoted design was paramount to serving God.

Richard eased the car along the rugged, fence-lined track, beneath the skeletal trees that hid the most prominent aspect of the church from view – its church tower. Through the blooming spring branches, it rose into view, majestic yet modest, and he parked in its shadow.

A low whistle escaped Richard's lips, and as if in reply, his wife Sarah gasped aloud.

"Oh my," she said.

It wasn't that the church tower was any more impressive than any other. Built on the highest hill of the village of South Ormsby, nature contributed to much of its commanding presence. In fact, standing at about forty feet, the tower was smaller than many, and compared to Lincoln Cathedral, which they had passed less than an hour ago, St Leonard's paled in significance. But to Richard and Sarah Hawkins, the church was a grandiose masterpiece, a prominent symbol of their life together. He laughed once, then let it fade.

"This is where it all began, Sarah," he said. "Right here." He glanced over at her. "Who'd have thought, eh?"

There was no car park, just an area of flattened grass on the edge of the graveyard, which was filled with disjointed graves that stood at jaunty angles like broken teeth. Many were so old that the writing upon them was illegible. Who died there, why, and when, and who loved them? Information that had been lost to time.

Richard turned off the engine. For a while, they sat in silence, looking up at the setting of their most treasured memory. The clock of the tower was around the corner, on the north side, so neither could visualise how long it was they sat there. But that didn't matter. It just felt good to be back.

"It's just the same," Sarah said eventually, leaning forward to take in the church through the windscreen.

"It's been here for nine hundred years," Richard told her. "The twenty years since we last saw it are just a minute in its life."

"That's what I always loved about it," Sarah said. "That we're part of its history now."

Richard turned to face his wife and leaned over to kiss her cheek. "Happy anniversary, love."

She turned her head so that his kiss landed on her lips, and she stroked his face. He was greyer and chubbier, but still as rugged and handsome as the day she'd met him.

"You looked so smart," she said, straightening the collar of his quarter-zip jumper, "waiting for me at the end of that aisle."

"I'll never forget it," he said. "My heart stopped. It stopped," he reiterated, "seeing you walk towards me. Nothing could have prepared me for that sight, and nothing will ever take it away."

Sarah smiled warmly, then closed her eyes and laughed. "In that god-awful puffy-sleeved dress? I must've looked like Little Bo Beep."

"Hey," Richard said, pushing her arm playfully. "That's my wife you're talking about. You looked beautiful. Like Princess Di."

She laughed. "God help us."

Richard laughed, and then his face turned serious.

"And he did, didn't he?" he said. "He helped us along the way. Every step of it, in fact."

"He did," Sarah said, touching her heart, lips, and head the way she'd been taught as a little girl, in gratitude and faith. "We've been blessed."

They returned to their nostalgic silence, holding hands in the car's centre console. The sunset was fading now, and the swirled pink had deepened to a denser, twilight blue, slowly fading into a darkness that waited on the edge of the world. The old stone walls had begun to merge with the sky, becoming less and less defined, more and more shrouded in mystery. The bats had arrived. They flitted in front of the windscreen on their journey back up to the church tower.

Richard squinted at the graves once more, trying to read the names, but even writing became lost to time eventually, he reasoned. Nothing could last forever. Not even words.

He sighed.

"Maybe we could be buried here too?"

"Richard."

"What?"

"Don't talk like that." Sarah shuffled in her seat, like an uncomfortable bird rearranging its feathers. "You know I don't like to think about all that stuff."

"But it'd be fitting, wouldn't it?" He turned to his pouting wife. "See, my life began the day I married you here. It's only right it should end here too."

Her face softened. "For everything, there is a season," she said, "and a time for every matter under heaven. A time to be born, and a time to die. A time to plant, and a time to pluck up what is planted. A time to kill, and a time to heal." Richard *hummed* along to her quoting scripture as if it was a song he liked. "But our time isn't yet, Richard. Not for a long time, in fact."

At this, they sat for a while longer in silence, something anxious growing between them, a nervousness that they might be too late or too early. Richard checked his watch.

"Are we?" she asked. "On time?"

"Seven o'clock," he said, showing her his wrist for her to check. "Right on time."

Richard put his hands in his pocket, feigning a casual indifference but wanting to touch the folded letter in his pocket, as though reminding himself it was real. He fingered the corners of it, running his thumb along the envelope's edge until it caused a tiny paper cut. He winced and whipped his hand out of his pocket to examine the slice, and then suck at the seeping droplet of blood, and the irony taste filled his senses.

Sarah didn't notice, preoccupied as she was with her own thoughts. It was dark now, and he could sense her growing twitchy, scanning the graves, or the spaces between them, at least, through which anybody could stalk and head towards their car.

"It's probably a present," she said, repeating the same theory that she had argued the whole drive over from Norfolk. "An anniversary present from one of our old friends."

"Maybe Father Wassall," he said, just as he had last time.

"Yes," she said, nodding out the window, then adding quietly, "that would make sense."

"Or a party," Richard said, repeating his own theory. "It's our fortieth anniversary, after all. Something to celebrate."

"Ruby," Sarah said distractedly.

"Ruby," Richard said, taking her hand once more to touch the ruby ring which he had slipped onto her finger as she woke that morning. He kissed her fingers.

But Sarah barely reacted. She was uneasy. He could tell.

"What time is it now?" she asked.

Richard had only just looked at his watch but made a show about doing it again for Sarah's sake, as though he, for one, was not worried about the passing of time, about whatever they were here for, about being late. "Five past seven," he said, showing her his wrist again.

Sarah sighed and frowned. "What did it say again?"

Richard didn't need to pull the letter from his pocket. He had it memorised.

"*You're invited*," he read, but his monotone voice failed to capture the points of exclamation. "Seven o'clock. St Leonard's Church. Let's celebrate! "

"Right," Sarah said in a similar monotone. "Well, where are they then?" Richard could hear her voice developing that dangerous tone of haste that occurred when she was anxious or impatient. "I hate surprises, Richard."

"I know you do, love." He squeezed her hand, but it lay lifeless, cold with nerves. "Look, they're probably waiting inside for us."

"Yes," Sarah said, eying the graves again. It would be dark soon, the kind of dark one experiences only in the countryside – deep and dense. "Maybe."

"So, do you want to take a look?" Richard said, unbuckling his seat belt. "The door should be open."

He reached for the door handle, but she grabbed onto his arm, and he turned to find her fearful, her eyes wide. "What's got into you?" But before Sarah could say, before her lips had even parted, before she could arrange her fears into some semblance of order, a dark shape in his peripheral caught his eye through the glass sunroof.

He thought it was a bat at first, but the movement was wrong. It didn't dance in the sky, or flit between the trees.

It simply fell from the sky, growing larger with every fraction of a second until it landed with a violent crash onto the car bonnet, shattering the windscreen and rocking the suspension.

They sat for a moment, both silent and aghast at the wide and lifeless eyes that seemed to stare through them.

And smeared across the head, trickling from its eyes, ears, and lips was blood the colour of their fortieth anniversary – a bright, ruby red.

CHAPTER ONE

George Larson had lost the sunset's fading light and depended only on the measly, trickling glow that spilled into the front garden from the hallway lamp. The bats had joined him, dark flashes bursting in and out of the darkness.

Favouring the front garden to the rear, he enjoyed the clear view of the small road that ran between his house and St Margaret's Church across the way. In the short time since his arrival at Bag Enderby, he had learned the front to be the best spot from which to get to know his few neighbours, who strolled by with their dogs or idled past in their cars. With a couple of them, he had reached a single-nod level of recognition. Others, less so.

Ingratiating himself into the village was a slow progress.

Still, however much he had enjoyed the somewhat meditative task of sanding a headboard all afternoon, he could barely see the piece of wood between his knees anymore. He ran his palm along it once, but not a single splinter threatened to pierce his skin.

He stood and stretched his creaking back, then collected the smoothed oak and carried it inside the house. Tempted by the new brown leather sofa in the living room to his left, and the new decanter of whisky he had placed beside it, George headed upstairs, determined to finish his job for the day. He was not one to quit halfway through a project, regardless of his ageing body's complaints.

The spare bedroom, which had once belonged to Grace's parents, was slowly becoming lived-in. That had not exactly been the plan. George had intended to begin work in Grace's childhood bedroom, thus providing a base from which he could attack the rest of the house. But Ivy had stayed over in the spare room, what was it, five times now? She had even left a toothbrush in the ensuite. By accident or in preparation for the next time her husband's fractious mood became unbearable, George could not be sure.

Either way, Ivy needed a proper bed to sleep in, one that provided a good night's rest.

Having measured and cut the wood, and meticulously formed the tenon joints, of which he was particularly proud, George began slotting the pieces into place.

He replaced the old legs that had split over the past God knows how many decades and had been forced to replace a few of the slats, retaining as much of the old wood as he could. He had once heard that sympathetic restoration was as much about retaining the original as it was installing the new. The more a house or a piece of furniture is replaced, the more of its soul is lost. To that end, once the new headboard was in place, the bed was a hybrid of old and new, clenched together with tenons, biscuits, and dovetails.

The rest of the panels he had laboured over that day were to replace those few floorboards which had succumbed to damp, no doubt from the mysterious trickle of water that travelled from the attic to the living room walls downstairs. Though he had yet to trace its root.

Mostly, the work was just to keep George's mind occupied. Otherwise, he knew he could easily spend his weekends on his new sinkable sofa, sipping whisky, and likely investing in a TV to pass the time. But deep down, he knew that all he would do would be to get drunk and think of Grace, and that level of purpose was no way to spend his weekends. He had seen many a man spiral quickly into depression – drinking to forget or, more likely, to remember and regret.

He could not fix Grace. Nobody could. Perhaps there was nothing to fix. This was just who she was now, the woman she had evolved to be, changeable and irritated, forgetful, even of her own husband. It didn't matter that he visited, because she could not recognise the effort. All the visits served to achieve were to depress George, and warm him in equal measure.

But he *could* fix the house. Sometimes it felt that was all he was capable of doing. At least on the weekends. The working week offered its own distractions.

It was with that thought that George's phone rang. He pulled it from his pocket and nestled it between his ear and shoulder, while he inspected one of his joints.

"George Larson," he said, preoccupied with his handiwork.

"George?" said a familiar voice.

"Tim?"

"George, are you there? You're quiet."

"Tim," he repeated, pulling himself away from his woodwork and moving closer to the old sash window. "I'm here."

"There we go," he said with relief. "Hi, George. Sorry to call on a Saturday."

"Yup," was all George had to say. It was not exactly a surprise. In the few weeks since he had returned to the Wolds, his biggest investigation had taken place over a weekend. In his line of work, weekends were a privilege, not an expectation.

"We've had a call. A couple at St Leonard's church in South Ormsby They've found a body, well… "

"Well?" George said.

"Not exactly found. It, erm, landed on their car."

George frowned. He was not familiar with St Leonard's, but if it was anything like the church across the road from his house, the only way a body could fall on a car below would be by climbing the church tower.

"Suicide?" George said.

"Seems like it. But can you get on it?" Tim said. "They sounded somewhat frazzled. I've asked for some uniformed support, but you know how it is. They'll need some experience on the scene."

The Tim Long that George had worked with ten years ago would never have used the word frazzled. He had seen Tim drink local thugs beneath the table in return for a lead. The man had been behind a desk for too long, he thought.

"Sure," he said, and without a thank you or goodbye uttered by either man, George hung up.

Whether a sign of their age, or rank, or just that they were still getting used to the power dynamics of their new roles, George wasn't sure. It was an adjustment, Tim being his boss when they had worked side by side for years at the same level as sergeant. But times had changed. Life in the Wolds was different now than it had been ten years ago. George knew that better than anyone.

He flicked through his phone to his contact list, which was only five numbers long. This, he thought, was probably something to be embarrassed about, but George only found it freeing. One number was Grace's care home, one was Tim, and the other three were his team. What other numbers could he possibly need that he couldn't pull from an email, or a letter should the need arise?

He checked his watch. Seven-thirty. He didn't need to bring Ivy in on this. It was bath time in Mablethorpe, most likely. Time to prepare for the upcoming week, washing school uniforms, making sure Hattie and Theo had clean sports kits and their schoolbooks were ready.

Instead, he pressed Campbell's name. She answered before the third ring.

"Guv?"

"Campbell," George said, not one for titles, especially while still getting used to his new team, feeling out their potential. "I need you to meet me at St Leonard's Church in South Ormsby right away. Can you manage it?"

He was sure he heard a voice in the background, a woman's voice, stifled, as though Campbell had covered the speaker as soon as she had spoken, asking something like, "Who is it?" or "At this time?"

It was the kind of question Grace might have asked him once upon a Saturday evening.

Maybe the rest of his team had lives. Maybe it was just him who felt grateful for the call out, happy to have something to preoccupy his thoughts before another sleepless night, something other than memories of his wife's vacant eyes.

"Of course, Guv," she replied, hiding any hint of disappointment, if there was any.

"And pick up Byrne on the way, would you?" George added.

At this, more than anything, she failed to hide her disappointment. George could practically hear her eyes roll over the phone. "Yes, fine, Guv," she said. "What's the job?"

"A body's been found."

"At the church? Suicide or...?" She left the alternatives open for discussion.

"That's what we'll have to find out."

"My money's on suicide," she said.

"What makes you say that?" he replied, both curious and pushing the PC to explain herself.

"Well, you know, a church on a dark Saturday night. Feels like a place of significance for a lonely soul," she said, and George swore he heard the angry slamming of a door in the background. "Anyway, not much exciting happens in South Ormsby."

That was another reason he was grateful for the fresh faces on his team. Not only were they eager to please, but they knew the area well, much better than George and Ivy, who were more used to the coast by now.

"Indeed, the darkness shall not hide from you. But the night shines as the day. The darkness and the light are both alike to you. We enter darkness to pray as we close our eyes to focus and avoid distractions," he said.

"Is that another one of those bible sayings?" she asked, to which he laughed, and it felt good.

"Psalm 139:12," he told her. "I'll see you in twenty minutes."

CHAPTER TWO

The narrow country lanes wound like tarmac ribbons across the Wolds. Along the thatched-house-lined roads of Brinkhill, he drove, heading towards South Ormsby. The lanes were especially quiet even for a Saturday evening, with many locals enjoying a few pints at their local pub or huddled around the TV, perhaps preparing a family meal or planning to order a takeaway. George's life, he was aware, was not quite so cosy, spending his Saturday nights speeding through the dark towards a crime scene.

St Leonard's Church did not dominate the skyline or rise like some conspicuous, dramatic piece of architecture. Instead, it lay in the bosom of the Wolds, easy enough to pass by without noticing it was even there at all. In fact, George almost did drive straight past it; so small and innocuous was its rugged driveway. But he made the turn just in time and followed the bumpy road for a good fifty yards before glimpsing the twelfth-century stone between the trees, lit by his headlights.

The church wasn't majestic per se. Nor was it cute. It radiated a deep sense of history, older than the ash trees that surrounded it. The wooden side doors looked thick and solid, with rusting, black bolts that served better than any modern lock to keep no-good-doers off the premises—or perhaps to safeguard the church's secrets.And the gargoyles that penetrated the sky at the top of the church tower seemed to watch George's journey along the driveway with hollow and mischievous eyes.

Ruining the archaic aesthetic of the scene, however, were the fluorescent jackets of two recognisable police officers and the spinning lights that illuminated the timeless stonework with an artificial, blue glare.

Campbell and Byrne were talking to a couple who, George could only notice from afar, were even older than him, with slightly hunched postures and grey hair. The woman wore a heavy, navy coat over her shoulders that George assumed belonged to the man, who stood with his arm around her, wearing only a thin-knit jumper - the type he liked to wear over a crisp Tattersall shirt.

The driveway was narrow, a staple of the Wolds that George was growing used to. He pulled up behind the little convoy, which, aside from the liveried police car, comprised Campbell's silver Honda Civic and a blue Vauxhall Astra. George noted the number plate, coming up with a quick mnemonic to remember it. Even from this angle, he could see that the front of the Astra was deformed and sagged to one side. When he looked closer, he saw a huge crack in the corner of the windscreen that carried like splintered ice across the entire pane of glass.

Turning off his engine, George climbed wearily from the car. He wrapped his coat around him as he approached the scene, feeling the distinct lack of warmth post-sunset. It was March, and though spring was trying its best, the days were not warm enough to carry into the long nights.

The reason for the cracked windscreen and sagging bonnet became clear as he neared the Astra. A man's body lay across the front of it like a flattened spider. Without his torch, George could just about make out a dark coat and smart, black shoes that confirmed the victim as a male.

As George approached them, Campbell nudged Byrne, who was busy scribbling notes and then turned to face him. "Guv," she said, by way of welcome.

"Evening, Campbell," George said. "Byrne?"

He waited for the lad to finish his notetaking.

"Inspector Larson," he said. "I was just... "he said, then adapted to the glare from PC Campbell. "*We* were just taking a statement from Mr and Mrs Hawkins here."

The couple peered up at Larson with large, trauma-filled eyes. It was not that they were particularly short, just that George Larson was a tall man that many people looked up to.

"Detective Inspector Larson," he said, shaking each of their hands in turn.

"Richard Hawkins," mumbled the man in response. "This is my wife, Sarah."

Up close, Richard appeared to be well-put-together, wearing a blue and white chequered shirt beneath his sweater and navy trousers. He was of retirement age, like George. But unlike George, he seemed to be enjoying his freedom, judging by his bright eyes and healthy-looking skin. He wasn't a particularly handsome man, though that seemed the result of a lack of vanity more than any physical flaws. If he gave some thought to his bushy eyebrows and bought a decent shaver, George imagined he could be thought of as a silver fox. George smiled warmly enough to ease their tension, he hoped.

"You made the call, I presume?"

The five of them stood in the glare of headlights, from which George did his best to shield the mature couple.

It was Richard who spoke first. It seemed all Sarah Hawkins could do was swallow, whether the content was sickness or tears; George could not be sure. Sarah, too, was neither beautiful nor plain. She dressed modestly and respectfully without verging into vanity, demonstrated by her full head of grey hair that had been styled into hair-sprayed, tight curls. She wore a high-collar ankle-length dress in spring colours and a floral, leafy pattern beneath her husband's coat. George imagined she was the type of woman with a summer and winter wardrobe that she changed around about this time of year.

"It landed... "Richard started, swallowing his own sickness. "*He* landed on our car," he said and nodded at the damaged Astra for proof.

"I can see that," George said softly. "He fell from the church tower, I presume?"

He used the word *fell* cautiously, though they were all aware a better word would be jumped – or even pushed. He looked up at the tower in the darkness and turned back to see the couple's eyes looking up at it too, as though the tower itself was the murderer.

They both nodded.

"May I ask what you were doing here?" George asked, trying his best not to sound accusatory. "I mean, St Leonard's isn't exactly on the beaten track, is it?"

At this, to George's surprise, the couple smiled. Many of their reactions appeared to be in sync, he noticed. This was no surprise to George. He and Grace had been the same once, sharing a hive mind of sorts. It was what happened when couples were married for such a long time, at least happily married. No, the surprise came from the smiles themselves. What happy memory could they possibly be sharing in such a dark environment?

"We were married here," the man said, squeezing the woman's shoulders, who looked at him with loving eyes. "Forty years ago today,"

"Oh well, congratulations," George said, but the word felt strange on his lips. It felt inappropriate to congratulate anyone at that moment when a lifeless, mangled body lay not ten yards away. "So, you're from the area?" he asked.

"We were," Sarah finally spoke up, but offered little in the way of specifics.

"From Ketsby," Richard elaborated and squeezed his wife's

shoulders once more. "School sweethearts, weren't we, love?" Once more, she looked at him and smiled as though her husband was the only warmth in the cruel world that had just thrown a dead body onto the front of their car.

George watched them and felt a sudden ache for Grace. Of course, he and Grace would never be so brazen. They had never been ones to look deeply into the other's eyes in public or whisper sweet nothings to each other on the train. They had kept their distance, him reading a book, her doing the crossword, happy in each other's company without needing the whole world to know it. Still, he missed her. They should have been visiting the church they were married in together on their anniversary. But the date had come and gone months ago without Grace knowing.

George pulled himself back to the scene, his job, his focus, and away from thoughts of Grace.

"Did you see anybody around?" George asked. "Before or after the...incident."

"Nothing," Richard replied. "Saw nobody at all. Did we love?" He turned to his wife, who shook her head and stared at the ground.

"Byrne," George said, turning to the team's youngest PC. "Finish taking Mr and Mrs Hawkins' statements." Byrne rushed forward eagerly, notebook at the ready. Then George turned to the older couple. "Are you staying in the area?"

"Well," Richard said, "we weren't planning to. But now– "

"I think it's best to stay close for now," George explained. "We may need to ask further questions."

Richard opened his mouth to protest but seemed to decide against it and instead mumbled, "S'pose we have to get the car fixed now, at any rate."

"I suppose you do," George said, once more eyeing the damaged Astra. "We'll take your details and be in touch if we need anything. Where are you staying?"

"Ketsby," Richard said. "We got one of those internet bed and breakfasts."

"An Airbnb?"

"That's it. Though, there ain't no breakfast, is there, love?"

"No," his wife concurred dutifully. "No breakfast."

"Okay, PC Campbell will give you a lift to your accommodation," he said. "Try to get some rest, won't you? Forty years. That's an achievement." He shook his head to add weight to the statement. "You should be proud."

The Hawkins did not look particularly thrilled at continuing to be involved in the trauma that had already ruined their anniversary and would now hang over their entire holiday. But they nodded their gratitude.

George turned to Campbell and summoned her closer with a nod of his head. He lowered his voice and leaned in close. "We need CSI. I want the body identified and any work done asap. We need to let any family members know. Give Katy Southwell a call, would you?"

"Already done, Guv," she said. "She's on her way."

George nodded.

"Good," he said and headed to the front of the church.

"What are you doing, Guv?" she asked, pushing the line between efficiency and interference.

"I'm going to take a look inside," he explained.

But as he turned, he heard Sarah Hawkins's shaken voice call after him: "Inspector Larson?"

George turned to face her.

She bit her lip like a nervous schoolgirl. "Now I think of it," she continued. "We did see something. Someone, that is. Didn't we, love?" she nudged her husband.

"Aye, we did," he replied. "Well, we thought we did."

"Why didn't you say?"

"Oh, well, it's probably nothing. I thought I saw somebody

run from the church just a minute or so after...well... "She nodded at the body on their car. "You know?"

This was news to Byrne clearly, who flipped through the pages of his notebook looking for news of a person running from the scene in the statement he had taken so far.

George waited for her to elaborate, but she did not volunteer any more information.

"Well? Where did they go? What did they look like?" he asked.

"Like I said, I can't be sure. They just disappeared into the night," she said, pointing at the darkest patch of the night surrounding them, where the headlights could not reach. Sarah looked at her husband and hesitated as though unable to accurately describe what she saw. In return, he only frowned at her, out of confusion, George noted, or perhaps concern. "It was...a figure," she continued. "Like a shadow or, or a... "She stumbled over her words, but then her eyes grew large as she found the exact right phrasing. "No, I'll say it as I saw it," she said. "It was a demon."

CHAPTER THREE

George smiled kindly at Sarah Hawkins and nodded at Byrne to make a note before turning back towards the church, leaving the PC to take the Hawkins' full statements. He rounded the church tower's corner and looked up. George imagined the clock's face had been changed several times in its history. The current version was a somewhat modern feature of the church, black with gold hands that pointed to Roman numerals. A seven and an eleven: 7:55 p.m.

He headed towards the main entrance, keeping his eyes peeled for any elusive, *demon-like* figures. By God, he would have loved to have seen the look on Ivy's face at such a description. She had more academic experience of witness psychology than he did, not to mention far less patience than George.

But he knew well enough from experience that memories are not digital cameras. There is no playback button or recorded data. After all, it is the mind that interprets, not the eye.

He was glad he hadn't called her in for this. She'd be busy enough on a Saturday evening, keeping the peace between her and Jamie over the weekend. Certainly, Ivy had enough on her plate; George knew only too well. There was little he could do to aid her through her marriage, but he would avoid her working over-time if he could help it. Every little helped.

The north aspect of the church had its own spattering of illegible, wonky graves and psoriasis-like brickwork, ranging from olive-green stones to brown and black bricks that had stood the test of time. But on this side was the main entrance to the church. It was not one of the many old wooden doors that looked like they had been locked for centuries. This one was far more welcoming, with a little triangular porch and greeting sign on the wiry outer door.

George opened the outer door and immediately ducked his head at an oncoming object. It took a few seconds of panic and a light fluttering beside his face to realise he was not, in fact, being attacked, but he turned to watch a small sparrow flap its way into the night. The porch, he realised, was a cage of sorts to stop birds from becoming trapped inside the church, a small kindness to the local fauna.

Perhaps this was what Sarah Hawkins saw, he thought sarcastically, a little flying demon. But it did beg a more serious question. How long had the bird been in there? And if anybody had exited the church recently, would it not have flown out with them?

George walked through the birdcage entrance and pulled open the grand, heavy church door. He wondered how many other hands had opened this door, centuries of parishioners, good and evil alike, those seeking redemption or sanctuary. He was unsure of what it was he sought. But more often than not, in his line of work, it was truth he sought; a treasure that even the Almighty could not always convey.

The inside of the church was cold and dark, and his footsteps echoed on the stone floors he recognised as local Spilsby sandstone. The only source of light was the flickering of candles beneath a statue of Mary. George imagined that these symbols of hope burned day and night until time naturally snuffed their prayers out. Still, the candles only served to offer more erratic shadows in the church, their light dancing off the stone walls like ghostly puppets.

The church was not large, but it did have a sense of space to it, with high rafters and tall, stained-glass windows that made the walls seem at once imposing and transparent. Three rows of short pews were separated by stone pillars and arches that continued across the room to enclose the altar in the most shadowed corner at the back. George could only just make out the simple wooden cross that stood in the middle of it. Despite his religious upbringing, he was not a man to spend much time in churches. But even he could imagine the comfort of the ritual to come to this one every Sunday morning, to reflect on his past week and the one to come and consider whether he was being the best man he could be. Perhaps that was what the man outside on the Hawkins' car bonnet had been doing – reflecting on his life.

Well, whatever conclusion he had drawn, it clearly had not been a promising one.

It seemed, inside the church, that everything had its place – the altar for communion, the pulpit for speaking, the font for baptising, the pews for praying. For that reason, even in the gloom, it was easy enough for George to spot something that was out of place. And he could see that nothing was. Every door was closed. Every corner at a right angle.

At the back of the church stood a particularly old, wooden door with a dramatic, thick lock that required a key so perfectly key-shaped it verged on cartoonish. He tried the door. It was locked. Looking up, George could see from the curved wall above him that the door led to a staircase, presumably up to the church tower. He looked through the keyhole but saw only black.

Churches had a silence to them, which he rarely experienced anywhere else. So, when a voice called, "Guv," from the doorway and echoed throughout the room, George, usually not an easily startled man, jumped in surprise.

"Over here," he grumbled.

He turned to watch Campbell stepping towards him over the sandstone tiles.

"Sorry," she said, quieter this time, adapting her voice to the reverence of the church. "I'm going to take the Hawkins to their Airbnb now," she whispered.

She looked around the church with the same suspicion he had seen her use to eye a suspect, and she shivered, whether with cold or from the eerie, dark shadows George could not be sure.

"You never feel alone in a church, do you?" she said, almost to herself.

George, too, took a moment to assess the church, from the unmoving, life-size statues to the tombs on the floors beneath their feet, to the saints in the stained glass and their ever-watchful eyes.

"No," George said. "No, you don't, do you?"

"Have our uniformed friends close the place off to the public?"

"They have, guv," she replied. They'll be staying for the duration."

"Good. Have Byrne wait for Katy Southwell while you take the Hawkins to their Airbnb. Then, both of you get yourselves home. We'll wrap this up tomorrow. I'd like to find out how our victim managed to get up there in the first place."

"Victim, guv?"

"Yes, victim."

"It's a suicide, though, right?"

"He's still a victim, isn't he? He still suffered from depression, or who knows what?"

"Alright, guv," Campbell said, and with one last dubious look around, she left the church.

George took another moment to search for any more mistakes in the straight lines and order of the church, but finding nothing, he followed Campbell through the door. He breathed in the fresh air as his eyes adjusted to the moonlight, and he headed towards his car.

"Goodnight, guv," called Byrne, who stood alone, rubbing his hands, waiting for the CSI team.

George nodded in return and climbed into his car, performing a tight three-point turn in order to leave the way he had arrived. In his windscreen mirror, George watched Campbell follow his movements, a tired-looking Richard Hawkins in the passenger seat beside her and Sarah Hawkins, small and childlike, in the seat behind. But at the end of the road, where George turned right towards Bag Enderby, Campbell turned left towards Ketsby, leaving him alone on the empty road.

Only one car passed him on his way home – a small, red convertible. George especially took note of the vehicle because, in the winding, often rough, and sometimes flooded roads of the Wolds, a low-slung sports car did not seem the most practical of choices. A more common look in these parts was an SUV or a four-by-four.

George tutted at the bad habit of claiming small, country lanes as their own; the full-beam headlights, the reluctance to slow as they passed from which George felt a little shudder of mortality.

For some reason, the church had left him feeling somewhat spooked, and Campbell's words turned over in his mind. *You never feel alone in a church, do you?* For once, the prospect of solitude in his old, rickety house filled with its own haunting memories was not quite so appealing.

As if fate had answered his prayers, when he pulled up outside his house in Bag Enderby, the first thing he saw was Ivy's car in the driveway. She was sitting on his doorstep with a rare look of defeat on her face. And as George noted her puffy, red eyes in the glow of the moon that had escaped from behind a cloud, he heard Campbell's insightful words once more.

CHAPTER FOUR

When George awoke, he did the same thing he had done every morning for the past thirty years and reached for his wife's shape across from him in the bed. Lost in that dreamy space between sleep and wakefulness, he thought she might be there.

She wasn't, of course. In the ache of realisation, he groaned and turned his face into the pillow. He had tried many times to seek his wife's smell in the old bed sheets, but like her memory, Grace's flowery scent had succumbed to time.

George opened his eyes, reached for his glasses, and swung his legs from the bed lest he tumble into the pitfall of wasting countless minutes staring at the ceiling. Over the years they had shared, Grace had fine-tuned him. Little tweaks here and there, one of which was to take the time to fold his pyjamas each morning, a habit he was quite unable to break. He showered quickly, finishing with a blast of cold water to help him face reality.

As he dressed, he peered through the square window that looked out over the rolling hills and yellow fields dotted with hay bales and sheep. It was a calming view that had changed little for centuries - a reminder of how fragile and insignificant life was.

He wore a tie beneath a forest-green sweater vest, using the oval, gold-leaf mirror above the dresser to fix his collars; its aged, tarnished glass offering only a partial reflection. Wetting a comb, he brushed his thin, grey hair into a neat side-parting, then he kissed his hand and touched the photo on his bedside table of a young, carefree couple on their wedding day, before leaving the room.

George crossed the landing and looked across at the long window that dominated the front wall of the house, framing St Margaret's Church and the road outside with its ribbon-like curve. He remembered to skip the rotten third-from-the-top step he had yet to fix and headed downstairs, admiring how his new leather sofa had already improved the living room.

"Morning," George said, walking into the kitchen where Ivy was already brewing coffee. He had chosen to transport the old cafetiere from Mablethorpe the previous weekend, along with a few more home comforts, like his whisky decanter and glasses, his old bed sheets, a few proper coffee mugs, and a chequered table-cloth to cover the unsightly, scratched kitchen table he had inherited from Grace's parents, along with the house. It had been a small step towards making his house in Bag Enderby more of a home and letting go of his old life in Mablethorpe. But it would take time, he knew, and he needed to do so slowly. Some elements of his old life, such as Grace herself, he was far from willing to let go of anytime soon.

The transition would be his rehabilitation, and such endeavours could take years.

"Morning," Ivy mumbled in reply, and she looked to George as though she had not enjoyed the most restful of nights, even in the bed he had improved for her comfort. Although he doubted the bed had kept her awake.

She pushed down the cafetiere's plunger, poured coffee into two cups, and handed one to George without another word. George would have to be the one to initiate the conversation, as he was unsure how many nights Ivy could stay at his house without them properly discussing the true state of her marriage. After all, last night, she had gone straight to bed, leaving George to sip a whisky by the fireplace alone, pretending he couldn't hear her muffled sobs carrying through the walls from upstairs.

"Ivy," he started gently. "Do you want to tell me what happened– "

"Mmmm," she interrupted, swallowing her coffee. "So, what's the plan for today? Writing up the suicide?"

George sighed and set his coffee down to lean on the counter but decided to play along.

"You've been reading emails during the weekend," he said, knowing that unless she had spoken to Campbell or Byrne, that would be the only way she could have known.

"What else am I going to do? Scroll through TikTok?"

"Through what?"

"Never mind. So, was it? A suicide, I mean."

"All the signs are there," he replied. "Either that, or we need to put out a manhunt for the demon Sarah Hawkins saw." The comment failed to raise a smile from Ivy, and George guessed that little gem had yet to make it into written form. "Never mind."

"Sarah Hawkins was the woman in the car, right? Did she see something? Maybe she was in shock," Ivy said, dismissing Sarah Hawkins' vague statement just as George imagined she would have had she been in attendance. "It's common for witnesses to fill in the gaps with what their beliefs expect them to see."

She was right. George sipped his coffee, drinking it quickly. He knew better than most that the best thing for Ivy would be to get to work, to get her head into an investigation and out of her failing marriage. After all, that had been his plan since moving to the Wolds. Although, his marriage with Grace was not so much failing as fading.

"Come on," he said, pulling his coat from the back of a broken kitchen chair and performatively checking his watch. "Let's get going."

Ivy didn't argue. She sipped her own coffee as she headed into the living room to grab her coat from an old, rusted nail that George was temporarily using as a coat hook by the front door.

She did not bring her keys, choosing not to take her own car, from which George deduced that she would be in no rush to get home to Mablethorpe after work. Instead, together, they climbed into George's car. The drive to the station was a quiet one. Ivy clearly did not want to disclose any more than she already had about her husband Jamie, or why exactly she had spent the sixth night in three weeks at George's house instead of her own.

George at least could focus on navigating the narrow, winding roads he was only just getting used to after a month or so in the Wolds. It had taken him a while to get to know the smaller, local routes because so many of them had been flooded for so long. He took the Bridge Road that ran between Somersby and Salmonby, noting the turn-off for Somersby Road, where George had experienced his baptism of fire, investigating the cold case of Kelly Tucker. But that was all over now, and George had been surprised at how quickly he had moved on.

He didn't often wonder how the survivors of that ordeal were dealing with their grief. He supposed he had enough of his own personal issues to deal with without including those of strangers. After all, if George carried around the baggage of every investigation he had ever worked on, the weight would have dragged him under years ago.

But it was as he was about to pass an ambling tractor, peeking out to check for oncoming traffic, that a screaming police car with its blue lights spinning rushed past. George ducked back behind the tractor just in time. Even Ivy, who had been lost in her own world until now, winced at the rush. She turned to watch it disappear behind them with a disapproving glare.

But before she could comment, George's phone rang through the car's loudspeakers, and he pressed the green button on his dashboard to answer it.

"George?" came the voice on the other end.

"Morning, Tim," George said, trying to sound jovial.

"You're not near the station yet, are you?"

"Just on the Tetford Road," he explained. "About five minutes out."

"Good. Turn around. I need you at a scene in South Ormsby."

"South Ormsby," Ivy said without thinking. "That's where the church is, isn't it?"

"Sergeant Hart?" Tim said, sounding surprised over the line. "Is that you?"

George and Ivy locked eyes. Neither of them particularly wanted their superior to know any more about their personal lives than he had to.

"Oh...er, yes," she stumbled. "Morning, guv."

"Is this about the police car that just went screaming past, Tim?" George said.

"I think so, George. There's not much else happening," Tim replied. "According to the report, a delivery driver heard yelling coming from an old house. He thinks someone is trapped inside. Probably nothing, but seeing as you're over that way, and given last night's incident, check it out, would you?"

"Sure," George said, pulling into a farm entrance to turn the car around. The fastest way to South Ormsby was back the way they had come, but at least it was the opposite direction to which the tractor was heading.

"Must be the most action South Ormsby has seen in years," Ivy said as soon as Tim had given them the address and ended the call, and George was happy to hear intrigue in her voice. Anything – intrigue, curiosity, any of the emotions stirred by a potential investigation, even shock and disgust – was better than the quiet brooding she had exhibited that morning.

She typed the address into George's sat nav and he noticed that the house was not only in the same village at St Leonard's Church, but it was just down the road from it. Though, he reminded himself, that in a place as small as South Ormsby, nothing was far away from anything.

"Bit strange, isn't it?" Ivy said as the route established itself on the screen. She straightened into her seat, ready for action. "Coincidence?"

"I don't like the word coincidence," he replied thoughtfully and then winked at her. "I prefer to think of it as fate."

CHAPTER FIVE

For a few free moments, George and Ivy enjoyed the most agreeable silence they had all morning. She was no longer slumped against the window, but alert and ready. George saw so much of himself in her, he empathised with what she was going through. Not directly with her marriage issues. He and Grace had always worked through any issues they had. But the tendency to let the job overshadow any plaguing personal issues, deeming them far less severe than perhaps they actually had been.

The work was urgent and immediate, and there was no room for additional unpredictable emotions. It was the best distraction he knew.

And yet, the real world still turned alongside their work world, and as though to serve as a reminder, Ivy's phone rang. That was the thing George knew only too well. There was no running from it. Not really. It always, always caught up with you. And as soon as Ivy saw the name on the screen, her shoulders slumped once more.

Her hesitation suggested that she considered ignoring it. The way she let the phone lie on her lap for a few seconds. But then she shook her head, took a deep breath, and answered.

"Jamie," she said. "I'm at work. What is it?"

Well, they were on their way to work, sure. But George supposed that anytime Ivy was with George, she could pretend she was at work, even if it was not technically true.

"No," Ivy said in response to Jamie's reason for calling. "Absolutely not. We're not asking for her help again."

Even without hearing the other side of the conversation, it was easy enough to guess the gist. Hell, it would have been easy to guess just from the tone of Ivy's voice and the way her body seemed to tense in response, like a hedgehog curling into a ball, pawing its attacker off with a sharp claw. "Because she has her own life, Jamie. They're her grandchildren, not her kids. You can't expect her to drop everything just so you can work overtime."

From five years of knowing Ivy, George had come to know and like her mother. He'd met Val at children's birthday parties and local Mablethorpe events. She had even popped into their old coastal station on occasion. She was a lovely woman and a people-pleaser. The world needed kind people like her. But the fact remained that she would be seventy-odd by now, and even he could relate to not having the energy to regularly care for a couple of seven-year-olds.

"No, we don't need the money, Jamie," Ivy responded. "What we need is for you to look after your own bloody children and not work late every night because you don't want to go home."

This time, George did hear snippets of the voice on the other end, due to the rise in volume. Something about a pot and a kettle.

"Well, if you didn't ask me to leave the house every other night, I'd be there, wouldn't I?" George didn't hear a reply. Ivy clearly didn't either because she kept pushing. "Wouldn't I, Jamie? Then I could look after my own kids. But no, you want your space. How's that going for you? How's that space," she spat, "working out for you, is it, Jamie?"

She slapped the dashboard in frustration. All she had not said that morning, everything she had kept inside, was now being released. All George could do was focus on the road ahead and slow for the upcoming turn towards South Ormsby.

"God, do you know how bloody humiliating it is for me to turn up at my boss's house twice a week because my husband has kicked me out again? Do you know how traumatising that is for the kids? To see me leave and come back and leave again without knowing why or what's happening? If you even think–" "George heard the voice on the other end try to retaliate, but Ivy was having none of it, speaking over the response so that both voices were yelling their own one-sided conversation. It gave George the same kind of headache he got listening to experimental jazz. "If you even think about calling my mother again, Jamie, I swear to God–"

It was unpleasant enough for George to listen to. He did not like to think how it must be for Theo and Hattie to listen to these kinds of arguments every night.

"You can be the one to go to your boss, and you can ask to stay the night, and when that happens, don't bother coming home at all!"

She prodded violently at the red button to end the call and then settled for dropping the phone into the footwell instead while she breathed heavily and kicked at it with her feet.

George, meanwhile, pulled into Harden's Lane and followed the road until they rounded a corner to see a large, old house, where the sat nav declared that they had arrived at their destination. It was a solid building made of the same Spilsby sandstone George had recognised in the church. Before the large, oak front door were six shallow steps and a turreted brick wall across the front. Four evenly spaced windows marked the upstairs, and the downstairs might have mirrored it if not for the hexagonal conservatory that, judging by the Tiffany lamp and large writing desk in the window, served as a summer-cum-writing room.

Campbell and Byrne were already there, Campbell talking to a stranger by the police car and writing something in her notebook, and Byrne shielding his eyes to stare through the house's windows. George turned off the engine. He wasn't sure what to say. Thankfully, Ivy spoke up first.

"I'm sorry," she said, her breathing settling. "That you had to hear that."

"Ivy, you never have to apologise to me," George said, staring straight ahead through the windscreen, watching as Byrne noticed their arrival. "And you don't have to be embarrassed either." He turned to face Ivy, whose face was red, whether with shame or anger, George could not be sure, though he guessed it was a bit of both. "You're always welcome to stay with me."

Ivy took a deep breath and turned to meet him eye to eye. "Thanks, guv." Then she looked away again. "You know, I just... I don't know what to do."

"Is it still about the move?" he asked with a pang of guilt. She had, after all, followed George to the Wolds when she could have considered taking a job closer to home.

"If it was originally, it's not anymore. It's just falling apart. And to be honest, guv, I'm... "She trailed off, then tried again. "I'm... "

But still, she found the words too difficult to say.

"It's alright," George said, squeezing her hand once, knowing that to be the limit of Ivy's gratitude for touch. It seemed to help her somewhat, at least. She took a deep breath and spoke the words she clearly needed to get off her chest. But, for how long she had needed the relief, George could not know.

"To be honest, guv," she said. "I'm not sure I love him anymore."

He thought Ivy must have never imagined sitting outside a suspect house in South Ormsby doubting her love for her husband. But such was life. So rarely had things in George's own life gone the way he had expected them to. Through the windscreen, he watched Byrne look over, frown with confusion, and start towards the car.

"He doesn't want to be at home," Ivy continued, letting it all out now. "So now Mum's there all the time. And I love the kids. You know I do." She turned to him with big eyes beneath her fringe, begging for him to believe her, which he did. "But most of the time, I don't want to be there either. I feel dread," she said and clutched her stomach, "as soon as I walk through the door. It doesn't... It doesn't feel like home."

"Every marriage goes through rough patches," he said, somewhat unhelpfully. It was something one said in such a situation, but George knew they were empty words. He realised too late, also, what Ivy would ask next.

"Did you and Grace? Have rough patches, I mean?"

It was a personal question, but that was where they were. Their friendship had sailed past professional a while ago. George watched Byrne walk their way, looming like the coming of time, and he thought back over his own marriage, trying to find a rough patch to reassure Ivy but finding only minor spats and lovers' tiffs. Nothing especially significant.

"I'm sure we did. But it seems worse in the moment, doesn't it? And with time, you move on," he said.

Perhaps he suffered from his own type of amnesia, a romanticisation of his marriage, an inability to recall the bad times, only the good. And with that came its own load of suffering.

"But nothing this bad, right?" asked Ivy.

George had never doubted his love for Grace. Not for a single second. So, this time, he chose only to be honest. He could offer no help to Ivy by lying.

"No," he admitted. "I don't think so. The trick is not to dwell on the things the other does that irritate you, but to focus on the things they do that you like."

Rather than slumping into a downtrodden state, Ivy looked relieved, as though her instincts had been correct. As though the feeling of dread when she walked through her front door was not a feeling she had to continue to suffer. If it was not an integral part of marriage, then something was wrong. And if something was wrong, she could do something about fixing it.

She breathed aloud, like a bodybuilder before lifting a weight. "Alright then."

George smiled sadly. He did not relish witnessing the marriage problems of his friend and colleague, but he was glad she had opened up. He looked up at the house and then rolled his eyes. Turning to Ivy, he nodded out the windscreen and smirked at Byrne who continued to inch closer, a look of absolute confusion on his face at why they had not yet gotten out of the car. He waited until the young PC had tapped on George's driver window before asking Ivy his usual question.

"You ready for this?"

She looked past him at Byrne to shake her head with despair, then reached for her own door handle and offered George a convincing enough grin. "And if I said no?"

"Then I'd tell you to go home to talk to your husband."

She grinned again, and this time it was genuine.

"Well, then my answer is yes, guv,' she said. "I'm as ready as I'll ever be"

CHAPTER SIX

"Morning, Byrne," George said, climbing from his car. "What have we got then?"

George welcomed the cold, fresh air. Ivy's tension had made the air inside the car thick and stuffy. He buttoned his coat and started towards the man standing with Campbell beside the police car. On the other side of the wide driveway was a van blazoned with a bright orange logo that George recognised as a nationwide delivery service.

"A delivery driver, boss," he replied, looking between George and Ivy as though they were keeping a secret he should know. "Says he heard screaming from this house when he drove past."

"And DCI Long sent you, did he?"

"Yes, guv. We just got here five minutes ago."

"So that was you, was it?" George asked Byrne, who trotted at his side like a well-trained spaniel. "In the speeding police car we drove past earlier?"

"No, no," he said, holding up his hands. "Not me, boss." And like a telltale schoolboy, he pointed at Campbell, who stepped away from the delivery driver to greet George and Ivy.

"I should have you done for reckless driving, Campbell," Ivy said as she walked past, and from the look on her face, Campbell was not sure whether she was joking or not. Either way, George left Ivy to inspect the house and turned his attention to the delivery driver.

"DI George Larson," he said, shaking the man's hand, which felt rough-skinned and firm.

"Derek McGuinness." The man shook George's hand once, then continued to flick his eyes around impatiently. "Will this take long?" he asked. "I've still got a van load. I'm on a timeline, you know?"

"*You* called *us*, Mr McGuinness," George reminded him.

"Aye," he said, scratching at the stubble on his chin. He was in his mid-thirties, George guessed, with thick arms and a paunch most likely due to heavy drinking and a poor diet, exacerbated by his career. He wore a fleece that bore the same orange logo as the one on his van. His voice held the fluctuating remnants of an Irish accent. "Well, I was doing my morning run. Just dropped a delivery in Belchford and drove past here and, well, I heard a scream. I thought I'd hit something at first. So, I stopped, and well...that's when I heard it."

"It?"

"The scream. It was coming from in there," he said, nodding at the house. "Thought someone might be trapped."

"And what would give you that idea?"

"Well...someone was screaming."

"So?" challenged George. "You hear screaming all the time, don't you? Kids in the park, teenagers mucking around, couples fighting. Doesn't mean I call the police."

"Nah, there was something about it," he started, and George got the impression that Derek was repressing a shudder. "It was like a wild animal. A trapped wild animal. It was more of a... "He struggled for the right word. "More of a howl."

"A howl?" George asked while Campbell scribbled down the word beside him.

"Yes," Derek said, sure of his word choice. "A howl."

George nodded. "And what did you do, Mr McGuinness? When you heard this...*howl?*"

"Drove to the top of the hill," he said pointing to the hill George and Ivy had just driven down. "And I called you lot. Signal's crap down here."

"And then?"

"Then I waited for them two to arrive," he said, nodding at Byrne and Campbell, "and then we drove back down together, but I couldn't hear nothing anymore."

"Are you sure it wasn't the wind?" offered Byrne.

Derek turned on the young PC. "The wind?"

As if to confirm the folly of Byrne's question, the three men stood in silence for a few seconds, listening to the windless Sunday morning. Not a single leaf ruffled. Not a single branch swayed.

"You think I don't know the difference between the wind and a scream, lad?"

"No, I just– "

"Byrne, why don't you go help Sergeant Hart at the house?" George said.

The PC was about to answer back, then thought better of it and slouched off like a scolded pet.

"Guv," Ivy called across the driveway from the front door to the house. "It's open." She pushed the front door wide as though to confirm her statement. But George knew what she was really asking for. Permission to enter. He nodded once in confirmation. "Be verbal. Announce your presence," he said before turning his attention back to Derek McGuinness.

"You first, Byrne," he heard Ivy say, and George imagined the dramatic gulp the boy would perform before crossing the threshold.

"Mr McGuinness," George said, "do many deliveries around here, do you?"

Accentuating his point, the trill of birdsong filled the air, reminding them of their isolation.

There was no traffic noise, no nearby farm sounds, no passing hikers. It was a lonely road of a remote village with perhaps only this house on it. There were certainly no others in view.

"Not particularly," Derek said, unfazed. "I use this lane as a cut-through. Just means I don't get stuck behind any old biddies driving through the village."

"Have you ever dropped a package off here?" George gestured at the house they stood outside.

"No," he said quickly. "No, like I said, I drive past it now and then, but I always thought it was empty, to be honest. You get a lot of that out here, don't you?"

"A lot of what, Mr McGuinness?"

"You know, abandoned houses. Ageing population, rural depopulation, and all that. You know what I mean."

"Not particularly," George said. "From the area, are you?"

Derek laughed. "No. Don't get many McGuinness's in Lincolnshire. I'm from Carlow." At George's blank expression, he added, "Just south of Dublin." George stayed quiet again, reading that McGuinness was the kind of man who liked to fill a silence. "Look, I was just trying to help. You hear horror stories, don't you? Women getting kidnapped and imprisoned, and God knows what."

"Did it sound like a woman's voice, Mr McGuinness?"

In George's experience, people usually used higher-pitched synonyms for women – scream, shriek, wail – and lower-pitched words for men – shout, yell, howl. But Derek McGuinness had used both scream and howl.

Derek blinked as though he had not really thought about it. "I suppose I assumed," he said. "But now you mention it, it could've been a bloke, yeah." He moved from foot to foot like a restless toddler in need of the loo. "I'm not being funny," he said, even though George doubted that there was any trace of humour on his face. "But is this going to take long?" He pointed to his van. "I really have to get on."

For a moment, George considered searching the van, though he was not sure what for, and the only cause for delaying the man was his unease at running behind schedule. And he had been the one to call the attention of the police. Plus, George had no desire to make life harder for a man who was perhaps on one of those god-awful zero-hour contracts or faced fines for late deliveries.

"Very well," George said, stepping aside. "PC Campbell will take the rest of your statement and your details. We'll be in touch if we need any more information. Thanks for your time, Mr McGuinness." George started heading towards the house when a thought struck. "One more thing," he said, turning to face McGuinness again. "Why did you drive to the top of the road before calling us?"

Derek, who had tensed when George had turned around, visibly relaxed. "Oh. Well, it's like I said. Signal's crap."

He held up his phone, and even from a few steps away, George could see the lack of bars in the top-left corner of the screen. George nodded. He knew that without a signal, phones were unable to call 999. That was why the emergency services urged people like hikers and climbers to carry satellite phones - for when they got lost or injured in the depths of the countryside.

"You can't get through to anyone," McGuinness said. He met George's stare, and his Irish accent seemed to descend into a much stronger brogue as he reiterated, "I think it's what they call a dead zone."

"Perhaps you're right," George replied, and he turned to stare at the house, muttering to himself. "But let's hope you're not."

CHAPTER SEVEN

There were six long, shallow steps to the front door, which George climbed before he entered the house. The inside was tidy enough, but more unused than well-kept and minimally decorated. He walked through into the living room on the right, finding picture frames resting against walls, rolled rugs in corners beside unpacked boxes, and furniture that had still to be put together. Adjacent to the living room, on the other side of the hallway, a dining room with a long, polished table took pride of place. The far end of the table spilt into the space George had noticed outside – the summer-cum-writing room. He stepped up to the desk. It was an old, traditional bureau plate with ornate, curved legs that George imagined must have been bought from one of the antique stores in nearby Horncastle or possibly Alford. He ran his hand along the joins and grimaced as he recalled his own efforts the previous day. Tucked beneath the desk was a green leather captain's chair, worn through use but still with plenty of life left.

George pulled it out and sat down. Before him was a traditional black underwood typewriter. Although, he imagined it was only for show. The ribbon was frayed and there was no paper in the platen. A shiny, silver laptop in the corner of the desk confirmed his suspicions. But still, at such a gorgeous piece of furniture, with a 180-degree view of the wildflowers in the front garden, George imagined it would be a very pleasant place to write from. A very pleasant place indeed.

Somewhat reluctantly, he stood from the desk and walked through to the kitchen at the back of the house. This room, too, was unfinished but tidy, recently renovated in shades of teal green with a modern farmhouse décor. Unpacked boxes of the lesser-used kitchen appliances were stacked neatly in one corner. Still, it was lived in, George could see, from the plates drying beside the sink.

Throughout the house, the walls seemed to have been recently painted an agreeable off-white. It was a well-lit, traditional property, and its air of being a family home was strengthened by the distinct living, kitchen, and dining areas. Surrounded by countryside and with a large, wild garden, George imagined it would be a lovely place to grow up. Not too dissimilar to the Bag Enderby house.

Upstairs, however, told a very different story. George followed his nose, more than anything, to the first bedroom on the left off the landing.

Where a dusty, stale aroma had filled the air in his own house after being disused for so long, this house held a far different smell. The room stank of sweat and sickness, which greeted his senses like a foul hand smothering his face. He entered and took in the view. It was an absolute mess. The covers had been torn from the mattress and scrunched into one corner. Stains on the bedding suggested all kinds of bodily fluids had been released onto the bed. In one corner of the room, a collection of rotting food and cracked dishes had been piled in a heap. It was there that Ivy stood rummaging through various papers on the desk, making a clear effort to breathe through her mouth and not her nose.

"Wow," George said.

"I know," she agreed, scrunching her nose in disgust.

"Anything interesting?" George asked.

"Maybe," she said, throwing down the papers, which George could now see were random doodles and illegible drawings. He stepped closer. A few were of horned beasts and intense, flame-filled eyes. George picked one up. "And some of that... "she said, pointing at the bed coverings, "is still wet. Someone was here recently."

The contrast to downstairs was startling. He looked around for answers but could find none. "No bindings to suggest some-body has been kept here against their will."

"No lock either," Ivy added, nodding at the bedroom door.

"Maybe it was a sex thing," George said, curling his nose up at the bed. "The scream, I mean."

"Or someone letting off steam?" Ivy turned to face George and leaned on the desk. "That's what they say to do, isn't it? To make yourself feel better. Scream into the void?"

"The delivery driver said it was more of a howl."

"Howl into the void then," she said, walking past him to check out the other bedrooms.

George followed, happy enough to leave the room, and saw that, unlike the first room, each of the other three bedrooms were tidy with beds made, closed drawers, and no demonic drawings on any of the desks or dressers. Only one appeared slept in, however, with softer, flatter bedding and a cup that held the dregs of what smelled like apple tea on the bedside table.

They headed downstairs together, leaving Byrne to rummage through the rest, stepping out into the fresh air, much appreci-ated after the stench of the first bedroom.

"Well," George said, thinking of the prison-like space and turning to Ivy to divulge his thoughts, "it is strange, isn't it? I mean, for one, why was the front door open?"

"Okay let's say someone was screaming and someone did

escape," she answered. "Maybe they were trapped in the house, if not in their room. They ran out the front door and their captor followed them?"

"Maybe." George shook his head. "In which case, we need a search team."

"We don't even know what kind of person we're looking for," Ivy said. "If anyone."

"Odd as it is, Ivy. I, for one, will not be issuing any kind of request for support. I'll call Long. Ask him to put out an alert to local units for anyone who looks– "

"Lost?"

George raised his eyebrows. It was all they had for now.

"Campbell?" he called over to the PC, who was just finishing writing up her notes on Derek McGuinness's statement. The delivery driver had been dismissed and now scurried into his van before George could delay him any further.

Campbell strode over to Ivy and George, brazen and filled with confidence.

"It'll probably amount to nothing, but let's do our due diligence. I want to know who owns this house," he told her and turned away only to turn back again. "And I want to know who lives here," he added, then turned to and fro again. "And if that's the same person."

"Then you'll be the first to know," Campbell assured him as she noted the tasks, then continued closing up the statement.

Through the window, George watched McGuinness start his engine and prepare to leave, offering a friendly beep of his horn as he pulled out of the drive.

"Byrne," George said, catching the attention the PC walking out the house with a look of disgust on his face as though he, too, had discovered the bedroom upstairs. "I want you to talk to the neighbours."

"Me, guv? Door to door? The next house must be– "

"Up the road, yes," George said. "In South Ormsby. There are maybe a dozen houses in the village. Ask them about this house." He turned on the spot. "What number is it?"

"Bluestone Lodge, guv," Bryne said, pointing at an old-fashioned mailbox at the end of the drive. "That's what it's called. All these fancy houses have names, don't they."

"Do they?"

"Well, yeah," he said. "Bluestone Lodge, Chequers." George raised his eyebrows as Byrne struggled to think of another, then remembered one. "Graceland."

"Graceland?"

"Elvis Presley's house," Campbell said, without looking up from her writing but with one ear evidently in their conversation. "In Memphis. I went there once."

"When did you go there?" asked Byrne with the same derisive notion of a younger brother.

Campbell looked up and shrewdly repeated, "Once."

"Graceland," George said, ignoring their spat. "I like it."

Come to think of it, the name of his own house eluded him. He had assumed that the painted smudge on the bins outside had been a three and had just gone with that. After all, there were few houses in Bag Enderby to confuse with his own. For the bits he had ordered online he had just been stating the number three, and in brackets, *the house opposite the church* in the delivery instructions.

"I'll go with Byrne, guv," Campbell said, putting her notebook away and pulling George from his thoughts. "McGuinness is right. There's no signal down here. I'll go to the top of the hill to phone in and find out who owns this place."

"Good," George said and turned to Byrne. "Ask around. Check if anyone has seen anything suspicious. Or heard anything, come to think of it."

"Suspicious?" asked Byrne, and George tried to quell his frustration at being asked to explain such a simple task. "Like what?"

"Like hearing a howl," George said, then turned his attention downward at the drawing he still held in his hands. He stared into the flame-filled eyes of the horned devil that had been scribbled with heavy, erratic lines. "Or, perhaps... "he said, holding the picture up so the sun illuminated the paper, "seeing a demon."

"You think this is connected to the suicide?" Ivy asked.

"I'm not sure. But something doesn't add up here. I don't want to make something of nothing," he said. "But I've come to trust my instinct."

"And what does your instinct tell you?"

"Well, for a start, there's no such thing as demons," he replied. "And secondly, people rarely howl."

CHAPTER EIGHT

From his position in the pulpit, Stephen Cross was able to see the entirety of the congregation. Like all the features of the church, the pulpit was modest. Unlike those larger churches that had six-foot-tall, spiralling pulpits with an ornate, cherub-shaped lectern, they had only a small, wooden box a few steps off the ground. Its lectern was a simple sheet of metal on a silver stand. After all, in a church named after the hermit saint praised for his humility, such grand features would not do in St Leonard's.

He looked up from his sermon and glanced around the room. The old, solid-wood pews were packed. It was busy today, only a few Sundays before Easter. Many of his congregation were keen to attend church at this time of year.

Even so, the vicar knew he was losing them. After all, in twenty-five years of priesthood, he recognised the signs – the glossy eyes, the drooping eyelids, the outright yawning. They were bored. Many of the congregation had turned to stare at the stained-glass windows they'd seen hundreds of times before just to distract themselves from the drone that escaped his own lips.

Although the Sunday 11:00 a.m. service was the most exciting – one might call it – service of the week, it was often full of family members who had been dragged along by their spouses and children who found the rituals long and tiresome, their deeper meaning lost on the young minds.

This week's Gospel was a short reading from John 3 about God sending his only son to save, not judge, the world. It was a passage that spoke for itself, really, and Stephen Cross was struggling to reword it in any better way than John – a poet by all rights – had done so himself.

So, in order to try to recapture the attention of his flock, the vicar turned to an old favourite of his – St Leonard.

"Now, as you all know, we in this parish are blessed under the name of St Leonard, the namesake of this long-standing and historical church."

This change of topic did indeed turn a few heads back his way. They felt connected to the topic of St Leonard. He was their saint, and they could identify his numerous idols around the church, often depicted holding chains or manacles.

"As all of you know, our St Leonard was a simple and holy man who surrendered his worldly goods to live in the forest of Limousin, living only on wild fruits and spring water. It was there he built his monastery, gathering holy men across France to join his natural, impoverished existence in the name of serving our Lord."

He looked around the congregation, noticing the more attentive stares and identifying the ones that were more focused on what was for Sunday lunch when they got home.

"But it wasn't only holy men who were drawn to this saintly man. No, prisoners, too, travelled far and wide to join his way of life and commit their souls to God, knowing that St Leonard would forgive them their sins and release them from their earthly bonds. Let us remember that such miracles are why and how St Leonard became a saint. For when prisoners prayed to St Leonard, they watched the chains that bound them to the cell walls break before their eyes. He teaches us that we do not need earthly possessions that only serve to weigh us down. For without them, we are free to follow the Lord."

Nearing the end of his allocated sermon time, he transitioned to the ending, which concluded, as many great speeches did, with a call to action.

"And so, I urge you to remember, all of you who feel trapped, all of you who feel bound, all of you who feel like prisoners in your own lives, to pray to St Leonard. Pray, as the prisoners of Limousin did, for freedom. Live simple, holy lives, and watch your chains break before your very eyes."

At this, the vicar paused for dramatic effect.

"And in light of this, let us pray together, too, for the poor soul who only last night on this sacred ground lost his life." He took a moment of respectful silence. "May he now be released of his earthly chains and set free to walk in eternity with the Lord."

Of all he had said that day during the service, these were the words that gripped his audience the most effectively. Most of them had heard of the suicide that had occurred there the night before. It was, after all, one of the most exciting things to have happened in South Ormsby for a decade. Nobody knew yet who the man was. But still, these things were always a shock to the community. As well as a brilliant source of gossip.

"Amen," he added.

"Amen," the congregation repeated, more from habit than obligation.

Stephen Cross, glad to have regained the attention of his listeners, went to step down from the pulpit. But before he could take his seat in front of the altar, the church doors blew open. They had been forced by the hand of a single man who pushed dramatically through the entrance. Heads turned for a glimpse of the intruder who stood panting in the doorway, silhouetted by the bright glow of the midday sun. Stephen shielded his eyes. And, as though he had been overcome by the power of the holy spirit, he froze to the spot in awe – or perhaps fear.

Then, to a series of gasps, the stranger stumbled inside the church. He made his way across the back wall towards the aisle. With long, sweat-ridden hair hanging lank across his face, a serious limp, and scars all over his bare limbs that broke through a ripped, sodden T-shirt and grey shorts, he was clearly in need of help. In fact, as the man fell and dragged himself upright again, he did not look dissimilar to Jesus as depicted at the ninth Station of the Cross.

Some parishioners rose to protect their spouses. Others took a step back or turned their noses up at his stench as he passed. There was something fearsome in his eyes that made them stay away. He uttered ugly, animalistic grunts as though each step was a struggle. And in the startled silence, the stranger continued to trip down the aisle, heading straight towards Stephen.

He did not appear to be a threat. His movements were too weak to be dangerous. And the item he carried in his hands was not a weapon of any sort, although they do say the pen is mightier than the sword. For he held against his chest a thick collection of pages bound together as a manuscript.

Still, Stephen Cross prayed for courage as the man approached, who stared at the vicar with intense eyes, black with dilated pupils offering a glimpse into hell. At the end of the aisle, where Stephen had performed so many rituals – announced marriages and deaths, performed baptisms, offered communion, and blessed the sick – the stranger stopped. He stood there swaying for a second and then fell to his knees with a bone-shattering thud.

Stephen rushed forward to help; such was his nature – hesitant perhaps, but ultimately good-willed.

"Please," the man croaked, offering up the manuscript like a sacrifice.

Following only a moment's hesitation, Stephen reached out and accepted the manuscript. It was heavy. Enough so that Stephen was surprised the man in such a weakened state had been able to hold it above his head. It made his own biceps tense beneath his purple robes. And as soon as the papers left his hand, the man sighed as though something deep within his soul had been released.

Then the stranger smiled a smile that the vicar recognised. He had seen it in those who had confessed sins and let go of resentments. It was the smile of freedom.

With that, he fell forward, twisted to his side, and rolled onto his back, issuing a prolonged hiss of rank breath. The slump of his body against the sandstone tiles echoed around the church walls. Only then did the congregation rush forward to catch him. But they were too late.

The stranger lay still, quiet and broken, prostrate before the altar, and Stephen touched his forehead before glancing up at the curious faces around him.

"What's the matter with him?" Geoff Jarvis asked, with one hand holding his wife at bay. "Is he...?"

"He's cold," Stephen replied, holding the man's hand. "Like death."

CHAPTER NINE

George leaned on his car with crossed arms and stared up at the old property. It was what he wanted for his house in Bag Enderby, minus the filthy first bedroom, of course. But the classic features, with the modernised interior, the fresh and the traditional side by side - that was what he wanted. He looked through the summer room window again with envy. He might even treat himself to his own *bureau plat*. Although what kind of story he would write about, he had no idea.

He looked up at the quaint chimney that rose from the centre of the roof and tracked the brickwork down to the white-framed Palladian windows. He could just about make out Ivy's shape in the lefthand one, moving behind the heavy, dark blue drawn curtains. In lieu of much to go on, she had braved another search of the disgusting bedroom, never one to back down from a challenge.

"Guv," said a voice behind him, and George turned to see Campbell walking up the driveway, holding up her phone. "Sorry, it took a while, but I found out who owns this place from the Land Registry. Mr Dean Worthing. He purchased the property three months ago."

"Dean Worthing," repeated George.

"That's right. Bought it from a Mr James Pepper who owned it before him."

"Have you run their names?"

"Of course," she said, and George expected nothing less. "But nothing on either of them."

George *hummed* and frowned at the house. Something was wrong with the scene, the newly occupied, tidy, family-like house with the horrific, devastated bedroom. "Check socials," George said. "Business profiles, bank account, tax info. I want anything you can get on Dean Worthing. Build me a picture."

"I'll need warrants for the financial stuff."

"Well, then get them," he replied, then shook his head by way of an apology. "Do what you need to do, alright?"

"Right, boss," she said, turning to leave and climbing back up the hill for a signal.

But before she left the scene, the crunch of gravel drew her attention to Byrne shrugging onto the driveway from the lane, hands in pockets as though enjoying a casual morning stroll.

"That was quick," she said, in a tone somewhere between shock and scolding.

"There are less than ten houses in the village," he said but still looked somewhat proud of his efficiency.

"And?" George prompted.

"Well, most of them thought this house was empty," Byrne said, coming to a stop opposite George. "They said the owner left about four months ago, a Mr..."He pulled his notebook out of his back pocket and flicked through the bent papers. "Er, God, it was something vegetal, you know, like Plum or– "

"Pepper?" Campbell asked with raised eyebrows.

"Yes," Byrne said, finding the name in his notebook and clicking his fingers at Campbell, at which she rolled her eyes. "James Pepper. That's the one."

George smirked. "Did they say why he left?"

"Family issues, they said," Byrne read from his notes. "He was from the south, somewhere near the coast. Wanted to be closer to his brother."

George waited for more details that were not forthcoming. "That's it?"

"That's it," Byrne said. "He kept to himself," they said. Only told them that he was moving due to family issues because they asked him in the pub one night."

"Who's they?" asked Goerge. "Who exactly did you talk to?"

"Two older couples, one from Louth and the other from Worcestershire originally. A few couples with kids, all primary school age. An old man on his own. Young woman with a dog called... "He flicked through his notes again. "Maisie."

"Alright, alright," George said, holding up his hand.

Byrne got the hint and moved on. "Anyway, they all had the same story. They all thought the house was empty, except one, the old man, who saw a delivery truck dropping off furniture about two months ago. And the woman thought she saw a young man move past the window when she was walking the dog last week, but she wasn't sure. She said the curtains are always closed."

"So, the new owner is not one to socialise down the pub on Friday nights?"

"Doesn't sound like it, guv."

"And nobody's seen anything suspicious?"

"No howling or demons, no, boss," Byrne said. "Like I said, most of them didn't even think anyone was living here."

George sighed and turned once more to face the illusive, grand house. They were at a bit of a dead end. Perhaps Derek McGuinness had heard little more than the howl of the wind after all. He watched Ivy's silhouette move behind the curtains in an upstairs window, leave the room, and then move past the hallway windows, descending the stairs. George could imagine it would indeed be difficult to identify a shape behind that old, thick glass, even if the curtains were open.

"Find anything?" he asked as Ivy stepped out the front door.

In response, she held up a rectangular, white box and shook it like it was a treat for them all to enjoy together. "These," she said, "under the bed."

"What is it?" Byrne said, stepping forward as though they were sweets, of which he wanted his fair share. Campbell stepped up beside him, equally keen.

"Methadone," she told them, reading off the label, then looked up at George. "For detoxing?"

He nodded his head. "Perhaps. It reduces opioid cravings. Would make sense, wouldn't it?" he said, nodding upstairs in reference to the bedroom that could easily have belonged to an addict.

"Could also be for pain relief," said Byrne, stepping up from behind George. "You know, chronic illnesses."

"How do you know that?" George said without thinking. While it is true that Byrne's insight into the specific uses of a medical drug shocked him, he realised too late that it was an unprofessional question to ask. It veered a little too close to ask an employee for details about their health conditions.

The question clearly shook Byrne too, whose ears had turned a bright red. "My er...well, my sister...my sister takes it."

George and Ivy caught each other's eyes and stayed quiet in a moment of awkward silence. Ivy looked down at the box, and George knew what she was thinking. These drugs were a hell of a step up from paracetamol. Campbell looked him up and down with fresh appraisal. It was hard to believe Byrne might have more serious problems in his life than choosing whether or not to shave in the mornings.

"Sorry, lad, I shouldn't have– "

"No, it's fine," Byrne said. "She was in a car accident. Six years ago," he said, finally looking George in the eye. "She has back issues, can't walk or... "He trailed off. "I look after her. Well, me and Mum do, I mean."

George gave Byrne a look that he hoped was reassuring and kind. It was a useful reminder to not assume anything about the private lives of his colleagues and what they faced when they went home at the end of the day. He made a mental note to bear in mind that, having only worked on one investigation so far with Bryne and Campbell, he still had a lot to learn about them both. Then he turned back to the situation in Ivy's hand. "So...pain relief?

"Maybe the guy who lives here is sick and– "

"Dean Worthing," George said, nodding at Campbell. "We found out his name. Bought the house three months ago from a man named James Pepper."

"Alright," Ivy said, continuing her theory. "So, let's say this Dean Worthing is sick."

"There were two bedrooms that seemed, let's say, lived in," George said. "So– "

"Maybe he's being looked after?" Ivy said to which George shrugged maybe.

At this, Byrne spoke up. "I hope so. If someone's in enough pain to take methadone," he said and swallowed. "Then it's pretty bad."

"It fits," George said, nodding at Ivy's theory. "The neighbours have barely seen him, so he must spend all his time inside. They haven't reported any coming or going though, so I'm not sure about a carer. Let's– "

But just as George was about to make a plan going forward, his phone rang in his pocket, and when he saw the name on the screen, he knew it was best to answer promptly. It was their third call in less than twenty-four hours, and each call only seemed to add gas to an already flaming fire. But the dead zone made it impossible to do so. Only when George had speed-walked from the property and hiked halfway up the hill did the call connect.

"Tim," he said. "What is it?"

"George, are you still at the house?"

"Yes, just closing up here though. There's not much to go on, if I'm honest. If someone was being kept here, they're not here anymore. I wanted to ask you to put out an alert for the new owner of the house. A Dean Worthing–"

"Never mind that, George. We had a call from the local vicar, a Stephen Cross. There's been an incident."

George frowned. "What?" The image that came to mind was of the mangled body he had seen only last night, crushed on a car bonnet beneath a gloomy church tower. "Another suicide?" he asked.

"Not exactly," Tim said. "Well, we can't be sure yet. Look, an ambulance is on the scene. Just get to the church as soon as you can, will you?"

"Wait, which one?" George said, a feeling of dread in his stomach, signalling that his body knew the answer before his mind had caught up. "No, don't tell me." After all, the Wolds were too small for three events in less than a day to not be connected. Let alone three events in South Ormsby. "St Leonard's," he said, staring at the building now in his eyeline, just beyond the trees. "The church from last night."

"That's the one," Tim confirmed, although George's statement had not been a question. In fact, the name was already familiar, and he had a feeling he was about to get to know it much better. "I don't know about you, George, but I'd have money on these two incidents being linked."

"And the house?" George asked.

"I don't know. You're the one on the ground. What do you think?"

From where he stood halfway up the hill, George peered down at the remote house.

"What do I think?" he replied. "I think it's a mess, Tim. A terrible, bloody mess."

CHAPTER TEN

In the light of day, St Leonard's Church looked far less sinister than it had the previous night. that eerie sensation that had stirred in George during the previous night now seemed ludicrous, like a child afraid of the dark who can see the next morning that their bedtime monster was nothing but a coat stand. It was just a building, after all, and a rather cute one, George thought. A little haven cosied away in the Wolds' interlocking spurs. Nobody might guess that a man had died there less than twenty-four hours ago. Surely, such a thing could not happen in such a charming place.

But from George's experience, they absolutely did.

Circles of parishioners had gathered in the graveyard, George noticed as he drove along the familiar driveway. Behind him, Campbell followed in her car with Byrne in the passenger seat. The churchgoers huddled, whispering, and stretching their necks to watch a body being pushed on a gurney into the back of a waiting ambulance.

George pulled the car onto the grass before the graveyard, finding the balance between respect for the dead and their resting places while providing room for the ambulance to turn and leave.

He and Ivy quickly climbed from the car to catch the paramedics before they rushed off. He caught sight of the man on the gurney, still and with a head full of wild red hair. But it was his bare feet that caught George's eye. They were black with filth.

"Inspector Larson," he introduced himself to the two paramedics slamming the ambulance doors. "How is he?"

"He's in a stable condition for now, sir," one of them replied briskly. "But he needs hospital care. Excuse me." She pushed past him to climb into the driver's seat.

"Where are you taking him?" George asked before the door closed in his face.

"Lincoln County Hospital," she replied, more focused on the job at hand than being impolite or disrespectful of police procedure. In her role, every second counted, and George understood that well enough.

"Sorry, I don't want to hold you up, but do we have an ID?"

"We've got a pulse," she said. "Nothing else, I'm afraid."

"Thank you," he said, and she nodded before closing the door and speeding off down the church driveway, bringing the red siren to life.

George turned his attention instead to the jumble of congregants. If he knew anything about parishes, it was that they were hubs for local gossip, and that would serve their under-informed investigation very well indeed.

"Ask around," he said to Campbell and Byrne, who had stepped up to George's side. "Find out who that man was." He nodded at the ambulance wailing away in the distance. "Get what you can on him."

"You think he was the one Derek McGuinness heard in the house, guv?" Ivy said.

"Derek McGuinness hears a howling from an empty house, and half an hour later, a dishevelled man stumbles barefoot into the local church and collapses?"

George squinted around the graveyard, looking for the person he was most inclined to speak to. In the crowd of Sunday-best outfits, it was like playing a game of Where's Wally?

"Let's just say, in a village as close-knit as South Ormsby," he answered, "it's hard to believe in coincidences." Then he spotted the man who stood out in black and white amongst the colourful, sun-glowed morning crowd. "Ivy, with me," he said and headed over to the vicar.

The vicar was comforting one of the more distraught parishioners, an older woman crying tearlessly, whom George suspected was rather playing up her reaction to the situation. They were standing directly beneath the church tower, and George wondered if it was the horrific memory the spot held that had stirred the woman's melodrama or whether she was simply traumatised by the disturbance of her Sunday morning service.

"Good morning," George said brightly, and the vicar turned to face George with grave eyes. "I'm Inspector George Larson. This is Sergeant Hart. We hoped we might have a word." He glanced between the vicar and the woman, hoping the vicar would pick up on George's hint for privacy. "Maybe we can speak inside?"

"Yes, I...very well," the vicar said, handing over the woman to a passing parishioner who somewhat reluctantly offered his own shoulder to cry on instead.

"Shall we?" George said, extending his arm to invite the vicar towards the church.

George appraised him as the vicar walked ahead. He was a short man who, like many men, carried a few extra pounds, most noticeably beneath his chin. He had wavy, jet-black hair, a thick growth of stubble, and kind, worrisome eyes. He looked no older than his mid-to-late-thirties, by George's reckoning, and George tried to imagine how it must be to live life as a young vicar, taking on the struggles and joys of an entire community before life had even dealt the man its full hand yet. He mused on the point, likening it to that of an author, deducing that some professions simply required a certain amount of life experience.

When they entered the church, the cold stone offered cool relief from the winter sun glare and muffled the cricket-like whispers of conversations in the graveyard. It was serene and quiet. Much like the exterior, the interior also looked very different in the daylight. There were fewer menacing shadows, and the deep corners were not as dark as they had seemed the night before. George, Ivy, and the vicar fell into a natural slow pacing of the church as though they were being led on a tour of the space. Perhaps it was instinctual to the vicar with new faces, to show them around the church. They began circling the perimeter in silence before George spoke up.

"We just wanted to ask you a few questions..."George said, and he paused, hoping the vicar would announce his name and preferred salutation.

"Stephen," he said. "Please, just call me Stephen."

"Stephen," started George, "do you know the man who walked in here today?"

The vicar shook his head solemnly. "He's not one of my flock," he said.

"So, you don't know him then?" Ivy said, looking for clarity over crypticity.

"No," Stephen said, glancing at Ivy with a frown as though recognising a religious cynic when he saw one. "I don't know him."

"Why not just say that then..."whispered Ivy for only George's ears but dismissing the perfect acoustics of the church that surely allowed Stephen to hear it too.

"Are these Norman windows, Stephen?" George moved on quickly, recognising some Norman features of the church – such as the arches and pillars – and taking a calculated guess.

"No, no, they're Victorian," Stephen said, pointing up at the window. "See the super mullioned tracery. Very Victorian Gothic." At Ivy and George's blank stares, he explained himself. "The perpendicular tracery." To more blank stares, he simplified it further. "The patterns by which the glass is divided, see? At the top of the window."

George nodded slowly. "Ah, yes," he said. "I see."

The vicar looked at George like a teacher who doubted the ability of his student. He continued walking. "Is this really what you wanted to ask me about, Detective? The windows?"

"No," George said, with a shy smile as though he had been caught out. He decided to get to the point. "What exactly happened this morning, Stephen?"

The three of them rounded the corner at the sacristy to begin walking across the altar, and Stephen used their expansive view of the space to tell his story.

"I had just finished my sermon on John 3:14-21. Do you know it?" He looked at them both, and George tried to decipher whether it was taunting or sincerity in his eyes.

To his surprise, Ivy spoke up with little hesitation. "Just as Moses lifted up the snake in the wilderness, so the Son of Man must be lifted up that everyone who believes may have eternal life in him."

She did not look at the vicar as she spoke but like an actor staring at a spot on the wall to remember their lines. Only afterwards did she turn to him with a look of satisfaction.

"That's right," Stephen said, lingering on Ivy before moving on, just as George did himself. "Anyway, that's when the main door opened," he said, pointing to it across the room. "And in walked the man. He was...dishevelled, you know, limping. He walked up the aisle towards me and fell to his knees here," he said, stopping in the centre of the altar. "And then he collapsed. One of the parishioners, Mrs Davies I think, she called an ambulance."

George looked down the aisle, imagining the scene.

"Was he aggressive?" he asked, visualising the ragged-haired man with the blackened feet limping towards him. "Did he have a weapon?"

"No," Stephen said, wincing as though the suggestion was

cruel. "No, he was in need of help. But he was carrying something. A book of sorts. He handed it to me."

"A book?"

"More like a manuscript. Just A4 papers, you know, bound by string."

George looked around the church, from the vicar's empty hands to the empty pews, looking for something out of place. "Do you have it?" asked George. "The manuscript. Is it here?"

"Oh," Stephen said. "It's in the sacristy. Should I go and get it?"

"You put it in the sacristy?" George said.

"Yes, I suppose I did," he said, frowning as though he had not fully considered the significance. "I wanted to keep it safe in all the chaos. It seemed...precious to him. He collapsed as soon as he handed it to me."

"Then yes, please," George said. "I'd like to see it."

Stephen nodded and turned around to walk towards one of the smaller wooden doors off the main area of the church. The man walked at a constant pace, never rushing. Always mindful. It was as though he was continuously crossing an altar. George had never seen someone walk with so much dignity, as though every step he took was on sacred ground. He stopped and turned, wearing a pleasant expression, and George was intrigued.

"Have you always done this?" he said, gesturing at the man's collar and attire. "You know? Be a vicar, I mean."

"If your question is if I'm born again, Inspector, then no. I was destined for this, I believe."

"Religious family?"

"Not really, no," he said. "But I found God. I found peace in him. He called to me."

George nodded, not wishing to cause offence.

"It's one of those jobs," he said. "A rare vocation."

"I'm not much different to you," Stephen replied. "I help people."

"Well, yes, I help people. But that doesn't mean I have to believe in every law. I just have to uphold it."

"Well, I believe in God," Stephen said. "Even when I'm not at work. He's helped me through some very difficult times, and I suppose I couldn't turn my back on him. Not after all he's done for me. He's like... "

"Family?" George suggested, to which Stephen smiled.

"Yes. He's like a brother to me now."

"You're a loyal brother, then," George told him. "Far more loyal than...well, than many brothers I meet in my line of work."

"Brothers should look out for each other."

"Were you an only child, Stephen?"

"Me? No. We were a large family," Stephen said, then saw George's quizzical expression. "I found God when I was young. The others need a little more convincing."

"I admire your faith," George said. "I can't say I share it. But I admire it."

Stephen smiled at the compliment, accepting it with good grace.

"Forgive me, Inspector, but has some sort of crime been committed? The lad was in need of help. That's all."

"Let's hope not," George replied cryptically.

George and Ivy continued walking, again, quite organically, around the perimeter of the church, and organically still, at the foot of a particularly majestic stained-glass window, where they stopped. It showed a man in red robes, holding a golden staff and with silver chains at his feet. Beside him, worshippers were on their knees, crying and praying.

"St Leonard," Ivy said, reading aloud the scroll-like words at the bottom of the window. "Giving freedom to captives."

"Our namesake," Stephen said, who had returned via slow, quiet steps to stand behind them. "St Leonard. Patron saint of prisoners."

George turned to face him. "Is that it?" he said, nodding at the thick bundle of papers that the vicar cradled in his arms.

"Yes," Stephen said, hesitating slightly before handing it over.

George took the manuscript. The pages were hole-punched and bound clumsily with brown string like an old-fashioned present. He glanced down at the front page. *The Unholy Truths*, it read. The text was all in a block typewriter font. But on closer inspection, he saw slight smudges on some of the longer letters. It wasn't a font style at all. He fanned through all the pages of the manuscript. The whole thing had been written with a typewriter, its original ink on the page. George lowered his eyes to the bottom of the page to read the author's name, and he felt himself flinch with surprise.

"Dean Worthing," Ivy said, reading aloud over his shoulder.

George felt he was in the middle of a puzzle being built around him, in the middle of a Jenga tower, unsure as of yet how all the pieces around him slotted together, but knowing that somehow, they must.

"I'd like to keep this," George said to Stephen.

"Well, I..."Stephen mumbled, clearly unwilling to give up the manuscript that he considered a gift, perhaps, from the stranger who had collapsed at his feet. "I mean, he gave it to me– "

"It might serve as evidence," Ivy stepped in. "I'm sure you understand."

"Yes," Stephen said, although he still looked worried. "Yes, of course."

"We want to help him too, Stephen," George said, and he held up the manuscript with one hand. "This might help us understand what happened here."

"By which I assume that you believe this incident to be related to last night's...unfortunate affair," Stephen asked, to which George beamed at him.

"Let's just say we're keeping an open mind, shall we?" he replied.

This seemed to placate the vicar, who sighed as though released of a burden he had been more than willing to carry. "Yes, okay," he said, then added. "In that case, I shall pray for his recovery."

"I'm sure the doctors will be effective enough," mumbled Ivy, which triggered a warning glare from George.

"Stephen," he said to the man who had politely pretended not to hear Ivy's comment, "does the name Dean Worthing mean anything to you?"

The vicar lifted his eyes to the heavens for a few seconds, clearly running through the very long list of local names in his mind that he had collated over the years. "Worthing," he repeated. "No, I'm afraid not. I don't recognise the name."

George sighed, unsure how such an elusive figure could be such a pivotal piece of the puzzle.

"How old is he? This Dean Worthing?" Stephen asked.

George looked at Ivy, who shrugged.

"We're not sure," he admitted. "Why?"

"Well, I moved to South Ormsby ten years ago. If the man is local and older than me or stopped coming to church in the last decade, I might not know him. But I can check our records for the name."

"You have records? What, like a database?" asked Ivy, clearly comparing the vicar's database to their own police database back at the station.

"Of sorts," he replied. "Those who were baptised or married or confirmed or buried here. Subscribers to the newsletter, organisers of local events, and such."

"Then yes, please, Stephen," he said, turning to leave before another thought struck him. "What was the name of the vicar who served here before you?"

"Wassall," he said. "Michael Wassall. Lives out near Louth now, I believe."

George nodded slowly, watching the vicar, still trying to work out the man behind the robes.

"One more thing, Stephen," he started, voicing the one question that had turned around and around in his mind since they'd entered the church. "This man... He walked, half-conscious, up to this church to hand you this manuscript." He held up the papers in his hands, uncertain about their significance. "He didn't hand it to any of the people he passed along the way. No. He wanted only to give it to you."

Stephen paused. "Is there a question, Detective?"

"Why, Stephen? Tell me. Why was it so important for him to give this to *you*?"

"I do not know," he said sincerely.

"Because it's curious, isn't it, Stephen? A man died here last night." At this, Stephen nodded and blessed himself, and beside him, Ivy shuffled uneasily. "And less than twenty-four hours later, a man goes to great efforts to come here, to this very same church."

"Again, Detective, I'm unsure of the question you're asking. It sounds to me like you're keeping more than an open mind."

"What am I missing, Stephen?" George clarified. "What is it about St Leonard's? What is it about this church?"

The vicar sighed and looked down at the manuscript before meeting his stare, and George, more skilled than most men at recognising a lie – though he made a mental note to cross-reference with Ivy later – saw only truth in the vicar's eyes.

"In God's name," he said, "I have no idea."

CHAPTER ELEVEN

"So, what have we got?" asked George, reconvening with Byrne and Campbell in the graveyard.

Many of the parishioners had dissipated, knowing that the height of the drama was over and had turned their attention to their Sunday lunches waiting at home. The morning had spilled over into the afternoon and settled into a calm, sunny day. George wondered how many horrific things could happen at this church before it so quickly returned to a peaceful haven as though nothing had happened at all.

"None of them recognise the man, guv," Byrne spoke up.

"They all just said he stumbled into the church and up the aisle, handed something to the vicar, and then collapsed," Campbell corroborated, though her brisk tone still held that sibling-like desire to provide more information than Byrne.

"Yes," George said, holding up the manuscript. "This."

They both eyed the manuscript with confused expressions.

"So, all the same story?" asked Ivy.

"Yep. Well, except that one guy," Byrne said, turning to Campbell. "Remember? Said he saw in his eyes the...what was it again?"

"The spirit of the devil," Campbell said.

Ivy rolled her eyes. "Very helpful," she muttered. "But it doesn't make sense." She frowned. "If nobody here recognises him, if he doesn't regularly go to church, why did he come *here*? The vicar said the manuscript was precious to him. So why bring it here? Why give it to *him*?"

George shook his head. He had no answers for her.

"And like you said, guv," Byrne added, "you don't believe in coincidences–"

"Well," George said, "it's not that I don't believe in them. It's just that in this job, you learn not to depend on them, that's all."

"Right," Byrne continued, lowering his voice to a conspirative whisper, "but this is the *same church* as the suicide last night."

"That hasn't escaped my notice, Byrne, thank you."

"I just don't think that's a coincidence, boss."

"No," George said, offering the lad a reassuring nod. "I don't think so either."

"Can I?" asked Campbell, pointing to the manuscript that George held, which she had been eyeing since he had brought it to their attention. He handed it over. "*The Unholy Truths,* she read. Then, in a more amazed tone, she read aloud the author. "Dean Worthing. But he's the– "

"Owner of Bluestone Lodge, yes," George said, a plan forming for their next steps. "Makes sense, doesn't it? Alright. Campbell, get back to the station. I want that profile on Dean Worthing. Anything you can find. And you know what, while you're at it, look the previous vicar up. A Michael Wassall. Find me his address. It's somewhere near Louth."

She noted the name in her notebook and then nodded in reply.

"Byrne, go with her. I want an ID on the body the Hawkins found here last night. No doubt he'll be with Doctor Bell by now. Give her a call. I want an ID as soon as she can get me one. And call Katy Southwell, too. Push for her CSI report. I want to know exactly what happened here last night before we arrived."

"Yes, boss," Byrne said.

"What will you do?" asked Campbell, then realised her impertinence. "Just so we know."

"We're heading to Lincoln Hospital," he said with a nod to Ivy. "If nobody here knows who that man is, we'll get an ID from the horse's mouth, as it were." George waved his hands, encouraging them to scatter. "Alright, let's get going. Call me with any updates."

While he and Ivy headed to his car, George watched Byrne and Campbell rush to their own as though in competition as to who could get there first. Their behaviour verged on immature, sure, but in George's eyes, there was nothing wrong with a bit of healthy competition. He'd experienced it himself in his day, with Tim Long when they had both been sergeants. But he made a note to keep an eye that it stayed playful and did not verge into toxic.

George and Ivy, on the other hand, had only ever worked in collaboration with one another. It was one of the few things he liked about the strict hierarchy of the force. There was no need to compete with someone above you, and so they were able to focus only on the job at hand, knowing their respective places and who, in the end, had the last word. The trick was, as the superior, to ensure subordinates' voices were heard and appreciated.

The drive to Lincoln Hospital from the Wolds was a good forty minutes, enough time, by George's count, for Ivy to see and reject four calls from Jamie. Still, they had the expansive Lincolnshire beauty to distract them from their personal lives. They left the Wolds' undulating hills, into the flat, dyke-lined roads of the Fens. It always reminded George of the great plains of America, where he had road-tripped through once with Grace, all the way from Montana to Colorado. That had been back when they had been young and able, but he'd never forgotten the experience. The Fens were the closest thing he had found in England to that broad expanse of rugged wilderness and ever-reaching skies.

"If the man who walked into the church is the same man that Derek McGuinness heard screaming," Ivy said, whose mind had clearly wandered towards her home life and which she was currently lassoing back to the investigation to keep it busy, "then why was he at Dean Worthing's house? Unless– "

"He's Dean Worthing." George grinned at her. "That's what I was thinking."

"I guess he just didn't look like my idea of a homeowner," Ivy said, and George remembered the man's dishevelled appearance in the back of the ambulance, his ragged hair and blackened feet.

George shrugged. "Or maybe it really has been empty the last three months. Just because Dean bought it doesn't mean he's moved in. Maybe he's not Dean. Maybe the house was empty, and this guy found it, and he's been crashing there."

"Makes sense," Ivy said. "Although, he doesn't seem the type to write a book, either, if I'm honest."

"That's very judgemental," George said, pulling onto Greetwell Road, where the hospital was located. "Takes all sorts, doesn't it? I mean, think about Hemingway, Charles Bukowski, even Poe. Not exactly upstanding citizens, were they? Creative, yes, but kind of mad. I mean, there's a thin line between madness and genius. That's what they say, isn't it?"

"I suppose," Ivy said, flicking through the manuscript on her lap. "Guess we can't know until we read it."

"I guess not," George said, pulling into a free parking space outside the hospital and turning off the engine.

He glanced down at the manuscript, held out his hand to take it from Ivy, and in that wordless manner with which parents passed over their children, Ivy handed it to him. George bent down and pushed the manuscript beneath his seat out of view. "Can't be too careful," he explained, then changed tack. "I didn't know you could quote scripture, Ivy," George said, and she huffed in response as though laughing at a joke that she did not find particularly funny. "I always had you down as a religious cynic, if I'm honest."

"Yeah, and for good reason," she said and turned to George to explain. "I was raised religious, guv. My parents were Christian. Church every Sunday, children's liturgy, and all of that. I even studied theology at A Level. We studied John's Gospel," she said with twinkling eyes. "It was a lucky guess, remembering the passage back at the church."

"Still," George said. "That's a good memory you've got. And now?"

"Now what?"

"You said you were raised religious. You're not anymore?"

Ivy shook her head, as though George was asking her questions that she had not considered the answer to in a long time. "I suppose I got disillusioned. All those rules, all the dos and don'ts – and what for? The hypocrisy of it all. I wondered why we make life more difficult than it already is? Then, I started studying criminology. All those case studies, the Steve Wrights, Peter Sutcliffe's, and Mary Ann Cottons. Then, working the job, you know how it is. I guess it's hard to keep faith in anything when you deal with death every day of your life."

George nodded. He knew exactly how it was. What they had witnessed on the job might shake the faith of even the most devout man. If he believed in anything, he supposed it was in the thing Grace had shown him every day of their marriage, the quality in her that he appreciated the most – kindness.

"Unless, of course, you find sanctuary in God. He can help you deal with the type of things we see." He grinned at her. "So I'm told anyway. Each to their own."

Ivy sighed and looked up at the hospital, a symbol of the crueller parts of life that had shaken and ultimately broken her faith. "So, are you going to?" she asked.

"Am I going to what?"

She nodded at the space beneath George's seat. "Read it?"

"Oh, yeah," George said, shoving his door open. He dragged his right leg out of the car, then turned back to her briefly. "The Unholy Truths, I'd like to know what they are. After all, there's nothing like a good mystery, is there?"

CHAPTER TWELVE

Inside the hospital, the path to A&E was a much simpler journey than the one they had made when they had visited Pathology. It was around the corner from the main entrance and opened into a large waiting room. George stepped up to one of the desks and tried to grab the attention of a furiously typing nurse.

"Excuse me," he said. "We're looking for someone."

"Name?" she said without looking up.

"Well, we...we're not sure." At this, she looked up at him and sighed, flustering George with her teacher-like, strict stare. "He has long, kind of ragged hair," he stumbled, remembering the two features he remembered. "And blackened feet?"

"He was brought in less than an hour ago," Ivy stepped in. "He collapsed at St Leonard's Church in South Ormsby."

"Oh! " the nurse said, her face lighting up. "You mean Adrian? Sorry, he doesn't usually have visitors."

"Adrian?" George repeated. "You know him?"

"Of course. We all know Adrian." Her tone oscillated somewhere between pity and impatience.

"Let's just say that he's a regular here, for want of a better word. Has a hard time of it, our Adrian."

"How do you mean?"

She peered at them curiously, and George discreetly flashed his warrant card, to which she mouthed an 'ah-ha'.

"He lives on the streets. In Lincoln, usually." She spoke while flicking through a pile of papers behind the desk, licking her fingers expertly to better search for a single paper. "He comes in every month or so, either from collapsing or getting beaten up. Even a few overdoses. You know how it is."

She seemed sympathetic yet strained, and George imagined it must be hard to repeatedly care for someone who took little care of themselves. Especially considering the state of the NHS, people like Adrian probably pushed their limited time and resources again and again.

"Do you know his last name?" asked Ivy.

"Samson," she said. "Adrian Samson."

George and Ivy met each other's stares. It was not quite the connection they were hoping for. If anything, adding this new name to the mix only complicated the investigation.

"Does he have any emergency contacts? Anyone he comes in with?"

"No one on record," she answered. "But he sometimes comes in with a guy called Freddo."

"Freddo?" George repeated. "Like the 15p chocolate bar?"

"Try 50p," the nurse said distractedly. "But yes. Freddo some-one-or-other. That's all I know. Anyway," the nurse said, standing from the desk, "we're monitoring Adrian in resus, but we'll move him to an acute medical unit soon. He's stable for now but still unconscious. You can see him if you like, but you won't get much from him." She stood from her desk and clicked something on her computer. "I'm heading that way now if you'd care to join me."

"Yes, please," George said, wrapping his head around the new name. Adrian Samson. Not Dean Worthing. He held out his arm. "After you."

They followed her through a set of doors, where they turned

left, passed through an older part of the hospital, and eventually into a large modern space, which George presumed to be the result of the ongoing building works. The nurse's behaviour towards them had changed entirely, as though Adrian was a friend of sorts, and she welcomed any help he could get from the system.

Inwardly, George empathised with her. Getting to know people, perhaps even growing attached to those who she saw at their worst. Then again, perhaps it was not too dissimilar to his own.

The nurse slowed to a stop in the centre of the space beside a central reception desk.

"He's not in trouble, is he?"

"Not that we know of," George said and left it at that. Still, it was enough to create a concerned shadow across the nurse's face.

"It's just that he's a nice bloke. Harmless, if you know what I mean? Deserves better, he does."

"I can assure you, we're only here to help him," George told her, then waited for her to direct him to one of the rooms. She leaned on the central desk and caught the attention of another nurse before speaking quietly.

"Police," she said, her eyes flicking to George and then back to the nurse. "Here to see Adrian."

"Ah," the nurse replied, a redhead, unfazed. "Room one, although we'll be moving him to Hatton Ward as soon as there's a bed ready for him."

She glanced up at George and Ivy in turn, leaving George with little option but to offer an obliging "Thank you."

Room one was in the far corner of the space, and lying on the bed inside, surrounded by a plethora of ceiling-mounted equipment, lay the dishevelled man George recognised from the back of the ambulance. His wild hair had been wetted and pushed back from his face, and his feet were cleaner than they had been before, but it was definitely him.

"Like I said," their obliging nurse said, "he's stable for now.

His collapse was due to respiratory depression, which led to respiratory arrest. We found amounts of opioids in his blood but can rule out heroin. It was more likely– "

"Methadone?" asked Ivy.

"Yes," she said with a frown. "He's been on prescription for a few months now. But it seems, unfortunately, he might have begun abusing the methadone. It can become quite addictive in itself and in some circumstances can produce a high similar to heroin." She turned back to look at Adrian and shook her head slowly. "He just needs a bit of love, that's all."

"Thank you," George said, suggesting that she could leave them if she needed. But the nurse seemed to squirm on the spot as though she was too busy to wait around yet still had something to say. So, George paused in order for her to say what was on her mind.

"He's a nice man, you know," she said, looking between George and Ivy, her eyes wide and somewhat sad. "He just needs caring for, and before you say it, I know what you're thinking. That he should start by helping himself and is probably involved in petty crime to feed his habit, but he's not like that."

"Thank you, Nurse... "

"Wrigley," she said. "Sarah Wrigley."

Neither George nor Ivy replied, but George offered a polite smile, both out of reassurance and as a respectful cue that she could leave, which she did with one last worrisome look at them both. George met Ivy's eye and then stepped inside the room.

It was only when the nurse had left them, that the incessant beeping caught George's attention. It was maddening, relentless, and he wondered how on earth the nurses and doctors could think amidst the din.

Walking over to Adrian, George could see that his ripped t-shirt had been removed in order to attach cardiac monitoring electrodes to his bare chest. Over his mouth and nose was a silicone oxygen mask fed via a tube to a container by the side of the bed.

"Adrian Samson," George said, looking down at the helpless man. "Not Dean Worthing, then."

"True, but the methadone does suggest that he was in Bluestone Lodge," countered Ivy. "I think we can assume he was the one who Derek McGuinness heard screaming. I mean, if he was high, who knows what kind of reality he was in? Could've been screaming at anything."

George analysed Adrian's body as though it was a piece of art. He had lines all over his skin like varying brush strokes, some thin and delicate, others thick and erratic. Some wounds were new and still pink, and George recognised many of them as track marks, red, painful-looking punctures from needles. Others, however, were old. George leaned forward and looked closer at the scars creeping out from Adrian's back and across his chest. They were very old – white and raised, settled into his skin like birthmarks, parts of his very being that had always existed.

"Did you know," George said thoughtfully, bent now to stare at the older scars, "that your cells are constantly ageing, replicating, and renewing, and by the end of every seven years, every cell in your body has replaced itself. So effectively, every seven years, you are a new person. And yet, scars like this," he said, pointing at a particularly deep and ancient-looking scar on Adrian's side, "continue to exist. As though they remain as reminders." He turned to look at Ivy, whose face was close to his own, squinting at the scar in question, whispering now. "Stubborn things, scars, aren't they?"

Ivy frowned in thought for a few seconds. They both followed the longest, deepest scar with their eyes as it journeyed snake-like from somewhere around Adrian's kidney and disappeared behind the curve of his back. It did not look unlike a snake, in fact, or a snake's skin, at least, shed and then ironed onto Adrian's body.

Then George straightened and said, "Come on. Help me turn him over. I want to see his back."

Ivy looked hastily around the room. "Guv. I don't think we– "

"I just want a quick look," George said, slotting his hands beneath Adrian's side. "Come on. Quickly now."

Ivy took a grip beneath his shoulders and they both lifted as one so that they could hold Adrian on his side. He did not react to the movement, not that either of them would have noticed if he had, distracted as they were by the sight before their eyes. Adrian's back was covered in deep, crisscrossing scars. A snake pit. All of the scars were the old, white kind that even collagen and healthy tissue repair could not have repaired. It was all the skin could do to have closed itself off from further harm. But the memories captured on the man's body would last a lifetime.

"My God," Ivy muttered, and then she and George lowered Adrian gently back into his sleeping position. They had seen enough. Ivy took a moment to stare into space before transitioning from sympathetic stranger to detective. "Child abuse?" she asked George.

"Looks like it." He grimaced. "They're old scars, and he can't be older than, what, forty-five?"

It was difficult to tell. Although Adrian did not have a single grey hair, his face was lined with a fair number of wrinkles and worry lines.

"We need to know more about him, what he was doing at Dean Worthing's house, and what connection he has to St Leonard's."

Ivy hesitated, looking between Adrian and George.

"What?" he asked.

"Well, do we, guv? What's the investigation here?" She raised her eyebrows. "I mean, he walked into a church and collapsed. He didn't hurt anyone. What's to investigate?"

"Look at his back, Ivy."

"I know, I saw it," she said and swallowed. "And it's awful, it is.

But that could be from thirty years ago, for all we know. It's not our place– "

"Until we have ruled him out of the apparent suicide, it's our place, Ivy." He took a breath to quell the frustration he was taking out on the wrong person. He knew Ivy thought he was being overly sensitive, overly protective of a stranger who had done little wrong. "Look, something just doesn't feel right. Why did these two events happen within twenty-four hours of each other at some middle-of-nowhere church? It's a hunch," he admitted. "Just indulge me. Just for today, please? If we can prove the two incidents are unrelated, I'll drop it, alright?"

Ivy nodded slowly, understanding. She had experienced enough of her own instincts over the years, knowing that they were usually the most reliable things to follow.

"I'll call Campbell," she said, pulling her phone from her pocket. "I'll ask her to gather whatever she can on Adrian Samson."

But before she could even find Campbell's number to call, a passing visitor spoke up, pointing accusingly at them from the doorway.

"You can't use that in here! "

Ivy turned to face the old, grey-haired, fragile-looking woman. "Excuse me?"

"Those mobile phone thingies muddle with the air, confuse the equipment," the woman said shakily, gesturing at the heart monitor beside Adrian's bed. "What are you trying to do, get them all killed?"

Ivy looked at George incredulously, who only raised his eyebrows accusingly at Ivy and tutted beneath his breath. Their disagreement had gripped the attention of the ward, and the other patients lazily looked over at the entertainment.

"You *can* use a phone in a hospital," Ivy said to the woman. "It's not the forties anymore, love." The old woman clutched her chest dramatically. "It's a myth," Ivy told her, holding up her phone and shaking it, to which the woman reacted as though it was a detonator, throwing her hands to her face. "Oh, for God's– "

But the swing of the door to the ward cut off Ivy's tirade. The sound signalled an authority entering the room to end their disagreement, and like students caught in the throes of a misdemeanor, they all hushed.

"Well, well, well. Inspector Larson, Sergeant Hart," came a familiar but disapproving voice from behind them. The tone was accusatory, and the accent was unmistakably Welsh. Ivy and George tore their attention from the disgruntled busybody to find Pippa Bell with her crossed arms and an infinitely amused expression on her face. "Making friends, are we?"

CHAPTER THIRTEEN

"Pip," Ivy said, "what are you doing here?"

"I work here," she countered. "You're the ones causing trouble. You don't see me coming to your police station and upsetting the criminals now, do you?"

Ivy looked around. "This isn't pathology."

"Well, I was walking past, wasn't I? On my break, I like to get out, surround myself with the living, if that's alright with you." George winced at the morbidity of it. "And then I see you lot starting a fight with one of the patients."

Ivy rolled her eyes. "I wasn't starting a– "

"It's alright, madam," Pip said kindly to the frazzled old woman. "I'll remove this woman from the premises immediately."

"Thank you, dear," she said, narrowing her eyes at Ivy.

"Don't push it, Pip," Ivy muttered as Pip went to grab her arm before leading them towards the door. George, however, found the performance highly amusing. Pip had been quite kind to Ivy the last time they had met on account of Ivy's discomfort around dead bodies, and she was clearly making up for it now.

Ivy shrugged out of her grip as soon as they exited the ward.

"What are you really doing here? Shouldn't you be opening up a chest or something?"

"It's my break," Pip said. "And whether or not you believe it, I do have friends." She nodded at the central desk, from where the redhead gave her a polite wave.

"Well, it's good to see you, Pip," George said, nodding at the pathologist who, in place of her usual scrubs, wore a tight, black t-shirt with the name of some heavy metal band stretched across her chest and baggy, black jeans with fraying ends that were so long, her heavy boots must step on them every time she walked. "I wanted to talk to you, actually."

"Not just here for a catchup then, George?" Pip replied. "No, of course not. Everyone always wants something."

"Ah, you know how it is, Pip."

"Don't tell me," she said, her keen eyes narrowing. "The body from the church?"

George nodded. "That's the one."

"It's out of my hands," she said, holding them up as though to highlight their emptiness. "I've sent the bloodwork off to Katy Southwell. She should have it by now."

"Could you...just have a closer look, will you?" he asked.

Ivy turned to face him. "For what?" she asked. "It was a suicide. I thought we were clear on that."

"Was it?" George said cryptically. "If Sarah Hawkins saw– "

Ivy rolled her eyes. "Sarah Hawkins is seeing what she wants to see, guv. It's a way of processing the trauma. There's no demon running around South Ormsby pushing people off church towers."

"Just get a cause of death for me, Pip," he said, ignoring Ivy. Then he added, "Please."

"I'm pretty sure falling forty feet is a cause of death in itself, George," she said, then softened, seemingly intrigued. "He has significant internal bleeding, a severe brain haemorrhage, and more broken bones than not. But sure. I'll take a closer look. Come and see me tomorrow morning." She checked her watch.

"We'll continue this then. For now," she said, turning to Ivy and nodding at the old woman who continued to glare at Ivy from the confines of her own relative's room, "stay out of trouble, DS Hart."

With a wink at George, Pip strolled towards the central desk as though enjoying the swarm of activity and animation.

"Strange woman, isn't she?" George said, watching her go. "Walking the hallways on her break to remind herself that some people are still alive."

"Hmmm," Ivy said. "Strange is one word." She turned her attention to George. "So, you don't think the guy from last night killed himself?"

"I think we're assuming too many things, Ivy. We need some facts behind us. Speaking of," he said, nodding at her phone. "Let's get on to Campbell."

Ivy hesitated and glanced around the room to make sure they weren't being overheard.

"It either is, or it's not, guv," she said. "And all we've got to suggest it wasn't a suicide is a statement from a traumatised woman claiming she saw a bloody demon."

"Let's go outside, shall we?" He held out his arm. "Just to be safe."

Ivy sighed, clearly unwilling to face any more confrontations, and set off down the corridor.

On their way out, they did not see the nurse who had welcomed them on their arrival, assuming she was preoccupied with other patients, too busy to focus her attention solely on Adrian Samson. Only when they were once again beneath the blue sky in the hospital car park and far away from any hospital equipment did Ivy find Campbell's number on her phone, clearly having internalised the myth herself.

"Campbell," she said when the rings were inevitably answered promptly. "It's Ivy. We need an update on Dean Worthing."

Then she turned the call to loudspeaker. George and Ivy stood around the phone in Ivy's raised hand, watching the slow movements of people on crutches and an old man in a bathrobe savouring a cigarette on one of the benches.

"I've done some digging," came Campbell's voice. "Just the basics for now. But he's local. The first records I found are from Louth Boys Home back in 1979. Then he goes off-grid for a while, but he turned up fifteen years ago having founded Worthing Media, a local video company. There are a few local articles about him, business stuff, profiles, events, donations, and all." George could hear the roll of Campbell's mouse on the other end of the line as she scrolled through her collated information. "Then there's the record of him buying Bluestone Lodge in December. I'm still going through his phone records and bank statements. He's a well-off man, guv. But nothing out of the ordinary."

"Good," George said. "Whoever he is, Dean Worthing seems to be in the middle of everything. Call his company, will you? See if they know where he is. I want to talk to him as soon as possible."

"Yes, guv," Campbell said.

"Anything else?" asked George, but just as he did, his own phone rang in his pocket. He pulled it out and saw an unknown number on the screen and handed it to Ivy. She got the message and took the phone, walking towards one of the free benches off the path to take the call.

"I found Michael Wassell's address," Campbell continued.

"Inspector Larson's phone," George heard Ivy say. "This is DS Hart."

"Good," George replied to Campbell. "Just make a note of it for now. That's a bit further down the list for today."

"Who is he, guv?" Campbell asked. "Can I ask what the relevance is?"

"He's the old vicar at St Leonard's," George explained. "I've got a feeling we might need some more answers from him soon. Oh, and we've identified the man from the church," he updated her. "His name is Adrian Samson. Sounds like he's been sleeping rough in Lincoln for a while now. Find what you can on him, will you? Get Byrne to help."

"Yes, guv. Adrian Samson," she repeated over the subtle scratch of a pen.

"Thanks, Katy," he heard, tuning back into Ivy's voice, which grew louder as she returned. She looked up at him, eyebrows raised. "I'll let him know."

He ignored Campbell's question of, "Anything else, guv?" on the other end of his own phone call and waited expectantly for Ivy's news.

"What is it?" he mouthed.

"That was Katy Southwell," she said. "She was able to identify the body from last night." George felt his eyebrows raise in expectation, but his gut knew exactly what Ivy would say next. "It's him, guv. It's Dean Worthing."

CHAPTER FOURTEEN

"Long day." George sighed and turned off the engine.

After an afternoon of collating what they could on Dean Worthing and Adrian Samson, as well as collecting statements from parishioners at the church and writing up the statements of the Hawkins from the night before, they'd called it a day.

Ivy stared ahead at her own car, which was still parked on his drive. It was heavy and silent, like a moored ship destined for unknown waters.

"So, Dean Worthing kills himself by jumping off the tower at St Leonard's and landing on the car bonnet of Sarah and Richard Hawkins," she dictated. "The next morning, Derek McGuinness hears Adrian Samson screaming inside Dean Worthing's house. Adrian leaves the house while Derek goes to get a phone signal and call the police. He walks or runs to St Leonard's, stumbles inside, hands Stephen Cross a manuscript written by Dean Worthing, and then collapses."

"That's about the gist of it," George said, turning to Ivy. "Questions?"

"Why did Dean Worthing kill himself?" George nodded at

one of the key points so far. "Why was Adrian Samson in Dean Worthing's house? What's the connection there?"

"Why was he screaming?" George added.

"And why did he take Dean's manuscript to the church and give it to Stephen?" Ivy finished.

They sat in silence for a few moments, letting the questions turn over and over in their minds, allowing little tributaries of potential answers to branch off them, offering possibilities. But nothing more than that.

Eventually, Ivy looked at her watch, and, with a defeated sigh, said, "I should get going."

"You're welcome to stay," George said, though he secretly yearned for some alone time with his thoughts. He had planned to pour himself a whisky and do some reading.

"No, I should face the music," she said, then paused. "Thanks for today, guv."

"For what?"

"For our talk," she said. "It made me realise that something's wrong. Seriously wrong. Between me and Jamie, I mean. And it's time we did something to fix it."

"What do you have in mind?"

Ivy let out a heavy breath through her mouth. "I haven't got that far, to be honest." She took a moment to reflect. "Couples therapy?"

But if George was asking her a question, he did not have an answer. Couples therapy had not seemed like a viable option back in his day. He and Grace were of the generation that powered through enduring love and suffering in silence. Not that he and Grace had ever suffered. Although he had watched some family friends and, hell, many suspects and offenders endure miserable marriages for reasons that George now viewed as outdated and unnecessary. While he did not believe in giving up easily, he had learned recently that life was short. Far too short. Too short to sacrifice happiness for old-fashioned values.

Still, he threw Ivy a bone, knowing that right now, she was looking for hope, not pragmatism.

"Yeah," George said, "that's a good idea."

"I think we just need to talk to each other," Ivy said, more to herself than to George. "Like properly talk. Find out what the other really needs."

"Communication is key," he said and inwardly groaned at his tendency to revert to meaningless clichés when it came to offering advice about Ivy's marriage. What could he say? For him, marriage had been more of an instinct, a daily choice to love and care for Grace, one that had been a repeatedly easy choice to make due to her being so very wonderful.

He offered Ivy a smile that he hoped did not look too much like a grimace, which she seemed to accept, reaching for the car handle with a pleasant, "Goodnight, guv."

"Night, Ivy."

Through his windscreen, he watched her walk to her own car. Discreetly, he tugged *The Unholy Truths* from beneath his seat as Ivy reversed. He kept the manuscript out of sight, not wanting to give the impression that he would rather read than be with her. He offered a single wave of his large hand as her car rounded the corner by the church and headed off towards Mablethorpe.

Ivy opening up to him more about Jamie would bring its own load of worries. It had been for that very reason that he had not inflicted his own troubles on her. George still had not revealed to Ivy who his house in Bag Enderby belonged to nor the true state of Grace's condition. Although she must have guessed by now that something was off, he knew that Ivy would not ask him about it until he brought it up. And for that, he was extremely grateful.

George walked through the old front door that reminded him – as it did at least twice a day – that it needed a repaint and a new handle. He wasn't hungry, at least not for food. But a hunger similar to intrigue rumbled in his stomach. So, with a healthy amount of schoolboy glee, George headed straight to his new leather couch and sank into the plush cushions. He rested *The Unholy Truths* on his lap, poured himself his favourite Talisker whisky from the decanter on the table by his elbow, and then settled in for what he hoped would be both informative and enjoyable.

The light from the dimming sunset dipped into view of the living room's casement windows and shone through the glass, lighting and warming George's face. He could see why Grace's parents had positioned their sofa in that spot. It meant that every day, one sat in the glow of the setting sun, and who could pass that up?

George closed his eyes against the soft blaze. It was one of the most ordinary and magnificent feelings he knew – the warm and compelling touch of sunlight on his closed eyelids reminded him of life's small joys. Yet, at the same time, it reminded him that twenty-four hours ago, Dean Worthing had watched the same process of ebbing light before hurling himself or falling from the tower at St Leonard's Church.

With that in mind, George opened his eyes, took a sip of whisky, and turned to the first page of the manuscript. He noticed that the third page was missing, the sheet between the copyright page and Chapter One. It was where the dedication was usually situated, for whomever the book was written. George traced the remnants of torn paper with his thumb.

Indeed, he saw that the page numbers at the bottom jumped from 2 to 4. So, where was page 3? George added it to his and Ivy's list of unanswered questions before turning to the first page of *The Unholy Truths*.

"Talk to me, Dean," he said aloud. "Tell me all about it."

———

Many people's first memories are of building sandcastles or eating ice cream. Or maybe it was their first day of school. But my first memory is quite different. It is of a dark, damp room, the kind of darkness that pene-trates the mind, where only the flutter of eyelashes hints that your eyes are indeed open, and the kind of damp that settles, cold and permanent, in the marrow of one's bones.

The first emotion I remember is fear—fear of the door at the top of the stairs opening, fear of the sound of footsteps on the stone floor, fear of what they might be carrying today—a belt, a pipe, or a scourge.

The first sensation I remember is hunger. Not hunger like a skipped meal. Deeper than that. Far deeper. The kind that protrudes the ribs through one's skin and forces the heart to work twice as hard just to keep itself going. And thirst. A dry scratching of the throat. A weakening of the muscles. Hallucinations of dripping taps and bowls of water that disap-pear like a hand through smoke as soon as you reach out.

In my first memory, it was, as always, James, Samuel, and I hunched together in the corner of the room, taking turns to stay awake so at least one of us would be ready and alert for the next batch of beatings. It was my turn to evade sleep. Their fragile heads rested on my young shoulders. My back ached with the weight of their dreams.

There were other memories, if you can call them that. They were more like fragments. Snippets from a time when I was too young for my mind to fill in the detail. The window was open, and the night was cool. The breeze woke me, but I daren't call out. I have an image in my mind. I was watching him in awe, deserting us, making his escape.

I hope he found peace. I hope his efforts were worthwhile. I hope he knows how our lives changed when they realised, he was gone.

That's when the locks came. That's when any hint of trust they had in us was decimated.

They had given us a single candle. For warmth, they said. It was a kindness, they said, that we did not deserve. I remember watching it flicker away, burning all the way down to its wick, before spluttering on its last breaths. I remember reaching out and relishing the burn on my skin. I remember snuffing the flame out with my fingers, so I did not have to watch it die slowly.

Not long after that, the door opened, bringing with it the icy rush of dread we had come to know.

A set of footsteps grew closer, slowly descending the stairs. It was only one of them this time. I recognised the tap of leather on stone and the occasional clink of a metal buckle. It was a belt this time.

It was at this point that I began to pray, as I had been taught to do. I pulled the boys closer, hoping they remained in the safe ignorance of sleep fortuned for a moment longer. I asked God for forgiveness, although I was unsure what I had done. Whatever it was, I knew I was to be punished for it. I prayed for insight, to understand why I deserved what was about to happen to me.

Yet even now, forty years later, understanding eludes me.

All I can do is remember. And now it is time, finally, finally...to tell my truth. So here it is. This is my story. Of abuse, neglect, cruelty, and punishment. Of a life of downtrodden blues and stone-cold truths.

Of a childhood in South Ormsby.

CHAPTER FIFTEEN

George pulled into the parking spot outside the police station that he had grown accustomed to over the past few weeks. He was a man of habit, and once he found a method or situation that suited him best, he liked to stick to it. As minor as it seemed, habits like that created less choices. Less decisions. Greater focus.

He climbed from the car just as he heard the efficient but short-legged steps he would recognise anywhere, clip-clopping across the station yard.

"Morning, guv," Ivy said, stepping into sync as they walked towards the fire escape doors.

"Ivy," he said cheerfully and pulled out his ID card to scan and let them into the building.

They ascended the concrete stairs with the blue handrail to the first floor. Blue and white was the simple colour scheme that extended through the station, a basic nod to the colours of the force. George, for one, found it a reassuring design choice. It meant every police station he had ever worked in felt rather familiar, and seeing as he and Ivy were new to the Wolds, the colour scheme alone had helped – in its own subtle way – to make them feel at ease in their new surroundings.

"So," he said, embracing their newfound openness, "how did it go last night?"

She paused and when George looked, she was nodding thoughtfully, as a therapist does before delving deeper, despite the question's simplicity.

"It went alright," she said. "We talked. He's going to ask Mum for less help. I'm going to make more of an effort on the weekends, so... Well, I mean, we didn't talk about everything, but we talked about enough for now, and... Yeah, it's okay. It's like we've applied a Band-Aid on a gushing wound, you know?"

From what George had heard yesterday from Ivy, he imagined their marriage required something closer to stitches, a blood transfusion, or even an emergency operation. It sounded a bit like applying a Band-Aid to a severed limb.

"That's great," he answered, choosing only to be supportive.

But Ivy talked no more about it. Instead, she shrewdly changed the subject. "So, did you read it?" she asked, as though knowing George well enough to guess exactly how he spent his evening. *"The Unholy Truths?"*

They pushed through the door to the first-floor corridor and headed towards the incident room.

"Some of it," George admitted, having drifted off around the fifty-page mark. It was not that the book had been boring; it was more that the story was emotionally exhausting. "Dean Worthing had a difficult childhood," he said, then decided difficult was too much of an understatement. "Horrific, actually. Unfathomable."

"Abuse?"

"Abuse, torture," George said. "You could call it either, really."

"So, it's like a memoir?" asked Ivy. "Not fiction?"

The floorboard beneath their feet squeaked loudly, declaring to everyone in the incident room that they were about to enter. On a Monday morning, it was busier than usual with various uniformed officers reporting for duty, although, in such a small police station that covered a low-crime area of natural beauty, the word busy was a bit of a push.

"Yes," George answered, entering the room and weaving between the desks. "It's first-person. It's his life, his story, his childhood."

"Who's childhood?" came a voice from somewhere near George's elbow.

He looked down to see Byrne, wide-eyed and curious, head tilted the way Francis Barraud's dog listened down a gramophone for his master's voice.

"Dean Worthing's," he replied. "Come on. Let's get started. Where's Campbell?"

"Here, guv." She waved from her desk and stood up with a bundle of files in her arms to follow the team to the whiteboard at the back of the room.

George wheeled the whiteboard into position while Campbell and Byrne pulled up chairs. Casually, Ivy took up her position, leaning on the desk in between the Constables and her boss. He waited for them to settle around him like students settling in a lecture hall while the professor waits in front of the blackboard to begin. However, it would not be knowledge that George would be imparting upon them today. It would be questions. Questions to which he desperately needed answers.

"Alright," George said once they were all still and attentive. "Dean Worthing." He wrote the name in the middle of the board, the man seemingly at the centre of their investigation, the sun around which the events of yesterday appeared to revolve. "What have we got?"

Campbell opened the topmost folder on her lap. "Dean Worthing," she repeated by way of introduction. "Lived at Louth Boys Home from 1979 to 1984 before he went into foster care. Then he founded his local media business, Worthing Media, in 2009." She held the file for him to see a few pages bearing the words *Worthing Media* with an oak tree as its logo. "Then he bought Bluestone Lodge in December last year, three months ago."

Byrne frowned at the whiteboard as George jotted down the key facts beside Dean's name. "Why would you bother paying for a house three months before you kill yourself?"

"Maybe he didn't plan it," Ivy said. "About forty per cent of suicides are impulsive."

"Or he bought the house for someone else to live in," George suggested. "Campbell, did he have a will?"

"I haven't looked, guv. I'll add it to my list. I haven't found a next of kin, but there might be somebody out there."

"Good," George said. "Anything else?"

"Well, I've looked at his bank records," she said, her expression attempting to lure George into intrigue. He remained impassive, and she continued of her own volition. "He's a millionaire."

"Jesus," Byrne said.

"Paid for the house outright. Cash, but no noticeable transactions in the months before his death. Barely made any calls, either. Seemed to keep to himself."

"Who took him into foster care?" Ivy asked. "Back in 1984?"

"Confidential. I tried to contact the home, but it's closed now. I can keep trying to track down their records, though."

"It was somewhere in or around South Ormsby," George said. "That should help you find out."

Campbell frowned. "How do you know that?"

"I've been reading his memoir," George said. "*The Unholy Truths*. He says in the first chapter that his childhood took place in South Ormsby."

This information seemed only to trouble Campbell, whose face had contorted into a grimace.

"What?" George pushed.

"Well, just... It's not exactly evidence, is it? A book. We can't depend on it for information."

"Can't we?" Ivy challenged. "I mean, is it any different to a witness testimony?"

"Yes," Campbell said strictly. "It's art. It's subjective. You know what they say, guv? Writers don't let the truth get in the way of a good story."

"So, you think he's lying?" George said.

"I think there's a risk of him elaborating the truth. Names, locations, events might have been changed for the sake of entertainment," Campbell defended herself fervently. "We can't depend on the words of a story."

"It's not a story," George said. "It's a memoir. It's autobiographical."

"So? The stories we tell about ourselves are the most unreliable of all."

"You haven't read it," George replied, feeling strangely protective of Dean Worthing's words. The man had apparently been a powerful writer. George felt connected to him already. "It's not written for entertainment. It's written to reveal the truth. To get it all off his chest."

"Books are written to sell, guv. Diaries are written to get something off our chests."

"The man's dead, Campbell," Ivy spoke up. "I don't think book sales are his priority right now."

"Alright, alright," George said, holding up his hands just as Campbell opened her mouth to snap back. "Look, let's call it a resource. I believe it can be useful. But you're right, Campbell. We'll need to back it up with evidence."

"I might be able to help there," Byrne said, holding up his hand, having watched their debate like an audience member at a tennis game.

"Go ahead, lad," George said, moving the team on.

"Katy Southwell sent over the CSI report after identifying the man who jumped from the church tower as Dean Worthing." He looked around the team and, seeing in their eyes an expectation for answers, he continued. "There were traces of DNA other than his own on his clothing, which heavily suggests– "

"He wasn't pushed," Ivy said. Then she muttered, "There goes Sarah Hawkins's theory."

"A demon wouldn't have human DNA," George said, grinning at her scowl. "Anyway, that doesn't mean nobody else was there. Just because they didn't push him off the tower doesn't mean they couldn't have coaxed him into doing it. Words can be just as powerful a force."

"So, should we ask Katy to collect DNA from the church?" asked Byrne.

"No," George said. "No, there'll be DNA all over the place. Anyway, it's just a theory."

"Guv's right," Ivy agreed. "Until we have a better idea of why Dean might have committed suicide, we shouldn't assume he was alone. Let's not leave anything to faith."

George thought about the first fifty pages of *The Unholy Truths* and how the memories in those first few chapters alone were enough to reason why a man might be traumatised for life enough to want to end it. But he felt Campbell's cynical stare on his face and stayed quiet, turning his attention instead to Byrne, and he urged him to keep going with a wave of his hand.

"Lab results show there were no substances in his system," Byrne said. "He was sober. Other than that, she can't tell us much, guv, to be honest. Dean's time of death was confirmed at between seven and eight p.m. She's running DNA from his body and clothing to get back to us. But in terms of the scene, there was nothing out of the ordinary."

"Except for the dead body on the car bonnet, you mean?" Ivy said.

"Well, yeah," he said as though it were obvious. "She said there were at least three sets of fresh footprints in and out of the church, but that's to be expected. It's always open. Could have been anyone. Hikers, parishioners, even the vicar coming in and out."

"Alright," George said, turning back to the board.

"One more thing, guv," Byrne said, causing George to spin back around. "Katy found a key in Dean's pocket. Proper old, like. Bronze, it was, with like a twirly handle. And on that, she found Dean's fingerprints and some other unidentified DNA."

George stared at Byrne for a few seconds, lost in thought. "An old key?"

"Yes, guv." He shrugged. "Katy said she'd send it over."

"Okay..."All George could do was write *key?* beside Dean's name. He looked at the word for a few seconds before, not unlike the turn of a lock, something clicked. "The church tower," he said. "It was closed when I tried the door. Dean must have had a key to unlock it."

"And he locked it again on the other side?"

"I suppose so. To stop anyone following him maybe?"

"So, he must have been alone. Otherwise, the other person would have needed a key to get out of the tower," Campbell said.

"Unless they had a key, too," added Ivy.

"But why would Dean Worthing have a key to St Leonard's tower?" asked Byrne.

"Yes," George muttered, "why indeed?" He stared at the word *key* for a few seconds more, but when no further clicks followed, he turned away. "Let's move on to Adrian Samson." He turned back to the board and wrote down the name parallel to Dean Worthing's, highlighting his intuition that the two men were related somehow.

"Who's Adrian Samson?" asked Byrne, looking through his notes.

"The man who collapsed in the church," Campbell said, hesitantly pulling out a second file on her lap.

"What have you got for me?" asked George, turning to Campbell with the expectation of efficiency he had come to assume from his most keen-to-please member of the team. But she appeared to shrink with shame. "Well, I... Nothing, really, guv."

He eyed the measly collection of papers in the file. "Nothing?"

"There's an Adrian Sanderson out in Skegness," she said hopefully before the uncertainty returned. "But he's seventy-eight and retired. And the nearest Adrian Samson is in Birmingham, but he's a local headteacher with two kids. Blonde-haired and blue-eyed. Looks nothing like the guy from the church. The other Adrian Samsons are in Lancashire, Cambridge, Glasgow..."She flicked through the papers. "But none of them fit the man from the church. Whoever he is, he's off-grid, to say the least."

"Well, okay," George said, failing to hide his disappointment, which, judging by the frustrated way Campbell slapped her thin file back together, she had noticed well enough. "We've just got the word of the nurse at the hospital then."

"What did they say?" asked Byrne.

"She. Nurse Wrigley."

"Wrigley? Like the gum?"

"Rather dated reference, Byrne," George said. "But yes, fine, like the gum."

"So, what did she say?" Campbell redirected.

"Only that Adrian sleeps rough and gets himself into enough trouble for regular visits to the hospital. But what I want to know... "George said, stepping back from the board to get some perspective, hoping it might all become clear, like a magic eye picture. "Is how Dean and Adrian are connected. Why was Adrian at Dean's house? Why did he have Dean's manuscript? And why did both men turn to St Leonard's church in their moments of need?"

They were rhetorical questions of sorts because none of his team had the answers.

"Byrne," he said, switching to task-allocation mode, "I want you to call Lincoln Hospital and have some of Adrian Samson's blood sent to Katy. Ask her to match his DNA against Dean Worthing's."

"You think they're related, boss?"

George remembered the horrific scars on Adrian's back. "I'll bet you dollars to doughnuts that they're brothers."

"They have different surnames."

"Fine. Half-brothers, then."

"Is he in Dean's book?" asked Campbell, and the thick thread of scepticism that weaved between her words was not lost on George.

"No, actually," he said dryly. He was not lying. There had been no mention of an Adrian in Dean's book. At least not yet. "But why else would he be staying at Dean's house? Adrian clearly has drug problems, probably mental health issues. It would be a big responsibility to take someone like that in. Perhaps Dean was his brother's keeper."

George turned and took another step back, tapped the marker against his palm in thought, and then stepped forward to add a few more names as a list in the top-right corner of the board.

"Derek McGuinness, Stephen Cross, Michael Wassell," Byrne read aloud as George wrote.

"The delivery driver, the vicar, and...who's Michael Wassell?"

"The old vicar at St Leonard's," Ivy explained. "Stephen Cross has only been there ten years.

But maybe Michael Wassell would recognise Dean or Adrian." Then she, too, read the three names, her lips moving silently as she turned them over in her mind. "You think they have something to do with all this, guv?"

"I think that we're relying too much on what they've told us. For example, that Derek McGuinness heard a suspicious noise in an empty house. Or that Stephen Cross doesn't know the man who dragged himself cross country in order to hand him something directly. Should we just believe them?" He turned away from the board, seeing the same doubt on Ivy's face as he felt on his own. "Like you said, Ivy. Let's not leave anything to faith."

CHAPTER SIXTEEN

For the second time in less than twenty-four hours, George and Ivy made the drive from the Wolds through the Fens, headed to Lincoln Hospital in the city. The same snowdrops that had begun to bloom when they had first arrived in the Wolds were still around in patches. They drove past miles of hedgerows and fields before the land began to flatten and stretch into long, straight roads.

"I still don't understand," Ivy said in the passenger seat, "why did both Dean Worthing and Adrian Samson go to St Leonard's Church? They clearly have some connection to it."

"Or do they?" asked George, focused on overtaking a cyclist. They were a common occurrence in the Fens, enjoying the long, straight stretches of tarmac from where they could take in the stunning scenery. "Think about it. Bluestone Lodge is just down the road from the church. It's the most public place within walking distance. That's the whole point of it, right? That the church is a central hub of the community. If Dean Worthing wanted his body to be found, and if Adrian wanted to give the manuscript to someone, it makes sense that they would go to a place nearby that people might visit."

"So, the church itself isn't important?" Ivy asked, a fair amount of uncertainty in her voice.

"I don't know," George said. "But I'd like to find out." He nodded at his phone. "Have we got Stephen Cross's number? Let's give him a call."

Ivy ran the call to Stephen Cross through the car's loud-speaker. It was answered after three rings with a cheerful, carefree voice.

"Hello, St Leonard's Church, Stephen Cross speaking."

So, Stephen had given Ivy the number for the church, George noticed, spying the local code at the beginning of the number on the dashboard. For a moment, George wondered if holy men even had mobile phones. He considered where the church stood on technology, whether it was for or against it, or whether Stephen was old-fashioned and did not own one for his own reasons. It could even have been that the signal on mobile phones was shaky at the church and Stephen had wanted to make sure George could get through to him if he needed. Or perhaps he had simply omitted to offer George his personal number.

"Good morning, Stephen," George said. "This is Inspector Larson." He listened for any sharp inhale or quickening of breath, but the vicar replied with an equal amount of chipperness.

"Inspector Larson, good morning. How can I help?"

"I was hoping you'd had time to look at your records for any sign of a Dean Worthing."

"I did, I did," Stephen replied, and George heard the ruffling of papers as though Stephen was looking at physical records spread across a desk. "But I couldn't find anything, I'm afraid. No Dean Worthing has been baptised, married or buried here. And the name doesn't come up in any of the events, memberships, or newsletter lists. I'm afraid it's a dead end."

George paused, noting the poor choice of words.

"Shame," he said eventually.

"I'm sorry I couldn't be of more help, Detective."

"Perhaps you can still," he said before Stephen could hang up the phone. In his experience, most people wanted to help with an investigation only as much as necessary without muddying their name in its waters. "I hate to trespass on your generosity, Stephen. But can you check for the name Adrian Samson?"

"Adrian Samson," he repeated, and again, George did not detect any shake in his voice or note of recognition.

Instead, he heard typing on the other end of the phone as though Stephen was typing the name into a grander database. Then came the scroll of the mouse, the press of a button, and the click of Stephen's tongue as he searched through the records.

"No," Stephen said eventually. "There's no record of an Adrian Samson here, either." George sighed at the lack of a lead. "That's not to say now," the vicar continued, "that neither of them ever came to St Leonard's. Rather it just suggests that they were not especially a part of the community. Some people prefer to keep themselves to themselves. That's okay with me. We don't judge here."

"Right," George said. "I understand. But you would still recognise their faces, wouldn't you? If they came to services regularly?"

"Of course," Stephen said. "That's my job. But like I said, I've only been here ten years, so perhaps Reverend Wassell before me would remember their names or faces."

"Of course," George said. "Well, thank you for your time."

"May I ask, Detective," Stephen said quickly, this time before George could hang up. He hesitated as though unsure of the line between concern and nosy. "Who are these men?"

George met Ivy's eye before returning his attention to the road. "Dean Worthing," he decided to admit, "is the name of the man who jumped from the tower on Saturday night. And Adrian Samson is the man who walked in on your service yesterday morning."

"I see."

"Stephen, if any of your parishioners come to you with any

information on either of these men, I trust you will pass it on to me?" George phrased the sentence ambiguously, somewhere between a question and a statement. He was interested to know if Stephen would offer an answer or a confirmation.

There was only the slightest of pauses before he replied, "Of course, Detective. Of course."

Leaving the vicar with that promise on his lips, George hung up the phone, and Ivy immediately turned to him. "Do you trust him?"

"I do," George admitted. "It doesn't feel like he's lying. Do you trust him?"

"I think," she said, taking a long pause before phrasing what she had to say next, "that men like Stephen Cross are well-versed in keeping secrets. People reveal all sorts of things to them that they have to keep confidential. I mean, it's like a law, isn't it? That they can't reveal what they learn in confessions? Not in the Catholic world, anyway."

"I suppose it works the same in the evangelical space. Although, the confessions are far less formal," George said, ignorant of the specific religious rules that he had long since foregone. "But St Leonard's is Church of England. It's not as common to go to confession, is it?"

"Yeah, but they're High Anglican, right? Almost Catholics. Still," Ivy said and got her own phone out of her pocket, "I'll look it up."

George focused on the drive for a while, frowning at Lincoln Cathedral which grew ever closer. What had drawn Dean and Adrian to St Leonard's? What was so special about that church? It was a question he struggled to shake from his mind. Something told him he was missing something, an obvious draw that both men had felt for some reason.

"Here it is," Ivy said, reading from her Google search results. "Apparently, the general rule regarding confession in the Anglican world, as you put it, is that all may, some should, but none must."

"Perhaps I'll give it a go then," George quipped.

"And it is an absolute no-no for a priest or a vicar to betray a confessor even if they have confessed to a crime."

George frowned. "Even murder?"

"Yep," Ivy said. "Even murder."

George pulled into a parking space inside Lincoln County Hospital grounds and came to a stop with a sigh.

"So," he said, turning off the engine, "we can trust the vicar only if nobody has confessed anything to him."

"Right," Ivy said, returning her phone to her pocket and reaching for the car door. "Like I said, men like Stephen Cross are used to keeping secrets."

The walk through the corridors inside to pathology was a complex route of sharp turns and general searching for wayfinding signs. But it was a journey that he and Ivy remembered well enough from their previous visit. After a long walk down a sunlit hallway that was adorned with windows on one side, they found themselves standing before the doors. Both of them seemed to need a minute to prepare themselves, knowing that on the other side was a fresh interaction with the infamous Doctor Pippa Bell.

Eventually, George raised his hand to push the buzzer, but the door swung open before he had the chance. He paused, finger poised in the air.

"Ah, it's you two again, is it? Well, come on. Don't just stand there."

Pip looked at Ivy and George incredulously. She was already dressed in her scrubs, which meant that her more defining characteristics – her metal band t-shirt and Welsh dragon tattoo – were hidden from view. Even her bright purple hair was tucked beneath the hood of her smock.

"We were just–"Ivy started.

But George would never know what excuse Ivy had been about to make up because Pip cut her off. "Come on then," she said, re-entering the entrance area. "You know where the scrubs are."

Her reputation as the leading forensic pathologist in the county was second only to her reputation for blowing hot and cold. George didn't mind, really. He could listen to her accent for hours at a time. She had a way of making even the most mundane of sentences sing.

She disappeared into the morgue, leaving the pair alone in the small reception room, bemused. Ivy raised her eyebrows at George but said nothing. They dressed in the provided scrubs, gloves, and facemasks with the same nervous silence of scolded children. He was quickly understanding that Pip's blowing hot and cold changed as frequently as the weather, and clearly, the easy-going, playful Pip from yesterday had been submerged by another personality altogether.

"Ready?" he asked Ivy before entering the morgue.

George was very familiar with Ivy's discomfort with dead bodies, and although Pip had been patient enough last time, her tolerance already seemed to have been tested today.

"Yes," she said convincingly enough.

But as soon as they stepped inside and saw the gurney in the middle of the room, Ivy's footsteps slowed to a groggy and weighty trudge. George walked ahead, leaving Ivy to rest on one of the empty stainless-steel benches.

He walked towards Dean Worthing's body, seeing it clearly for the first time. Dean was still a young man in his mid-forties, with only a few grey hairs in his well-groomed beard, eyebrows, and freshly cut hair. His groomed appearance reminded George of the expensive shoes he had seen on his feet at the church on Saturday night. Although everyone was on equal terms on a gurney in a pathologist's morgue, Dean still exuded a sense of wealth, even though any material signs of it had been removed from his body.

Stepping closer, he noticed a nasty, deep dent in the side of his head, and even though his limbs were beneath a sheet, George could tell that they stood at awkward, unnatural angles and that many had likely all been broken by the forty-foot fall.

"You asked me to look closer at the body," Pip reminded George. "Why, exactly, was that?"

He pulled his eyes from Dean. "We couldn't be sure it was a suicide until you looked closer."

"Well, it has all the hallmarks," Pip said. "Of a suicide, that is."

"Such as?"

"There's no sign of a struggle, George. No DNA beneath his fingernails. No scratches on his arms. No rogue hairs or swelling on the wrists."

"What about scars?" asked Ivy, who had dragged herself to George's side and was clearly compensating for her weakness by asking the direct and objective questions, exercising her mind whilst restraining her nausea.

"Oh, those he has plenty of," Pip said, and she reached across Dean's body, turning him onto his side in a similar fashion to how George and Ivy had with Adrian only the previous day.

Like Adrian, Dean's back was covered in a similar crisscross of old, white, deep scars, the kinds that looked like ironed-on snake skins. George blinked away the image of the child in *The Unholy Truths*, scared and cold in the damp room, desperate, helpless, and vulnerable. He rarely had such emotional reactions to the deaths he investigated. He rarely saw them as fully-formed people even, but more like pieces on a chessboard – cold and wooden. But Dean Worthing had been a warm, breathing body once, alive enough to have written the book that now sat on George's coffee table. His written words had been powerful enough to invoke life or some semblance of it.

"Can you identify them? The scars?"

Pip breathed out. "All kinds. Mostly, your regular fine-line scars from cuts and wounds. Most were deep enough to become hypertrophic. That just means raised." She ran her thumb across one particularly bumpy scar on Dean's shoulder blade as though it were braille. "But some are contracture." At George's blank face, she added, "From burns."

Pip gently lowered Dean down, covering him respectfully once more with the sheet.

"You know, I think some people," Pip began, with a not-so-subtle side eye at George, "assume that my only job is analysing the odd murder victim. And that the rest of my time, I spend, I don't know, twiddling my thumbs? Praying for a call from Katy Southwell at CSI?"

"Pip, I don't– "

"But believe it or not," she continued over George, "when I'm not bending to the whims of local detectives, I'm analysing biopsies, assisting diagnoses, tracking blood-borne illness– "

"You seem tense, Pip," Ivy contributed, clearly not too faint to poke the bear.

Pip glared at her. "You might be tense, too, Sergeant Hart, if you'd been asked to waste time reanalysing a body for no reason."

George resisted a gulp and nodded but asked for just one final confirmation.

"So, there's nothing?" he reiterated. "No sign of anything suspicious, I mean."

"Apart from decades-old scars? No. Nothing. Bugger all, in fact. Now if you don't mind," Pip said, already removing her gloves, as an invitation for them to leave, which Ivy seemed more than happy to do so, "I have enough work to be doing."

George followed her arm out of the door. "Thank you, Pip," he said as earnestly as he could.

"Oh, and George," she said before closing the door. "I'm not often in this position. I try to be courteous and professional, even to the likes of DCI Bloom. But when I give you my professional opinion, I do expect it to be trusted."

"I was merely asking you to double-check, Pip. There's no evidence that I can see that his death was a suicide or otherwise. It's my job to determine which it was."

"And it's my job to give you the facts," she replied, her voice low and brooding. "So, if you want to prove me wrong, Inspector Larson, be my guest." She glanced at them both, lingering on George for a moment longer. "I'll email my report. You can see yourselves out."

"Perhaps I will," George told her, then winced at his reaction.

"Perhaps you will what? See yourself out?"

"No," he told her. "No, perhaps I'll prove you wrong. Good day to you, Doctor Bell."

CHAPTER SEVENTEEN

"So," Ivy said, thankful for the fresh air outside the hospital. She breathed it in like a fish in water. "Feel better for that, do you?"

"Not really," he said, still reeling from the interaction.

"I guess we should confirm Dean's death as a suicide."

George pushed his hands into his coat pocket and looked gloomily around the hospital gardens. "Pip obviously seems to think so."

"But you're still not sure." Ivy turned to him. "Even now, you're resisting calling it a suicide, guv. Why?" He took a moment to reply, and this moment, Ivy filled with her own assumption. "Oh God, don't tell me it's because of Sarah Hawkins' demon. Guv, she was– "

"No, that's not why," George said. "It's the note."

"What note?"

"Dean's suicide note."

Ivy frowned. "There wasn't a suicide note, guv."

George turned to her and raised his eyebrows. "Exactly."

Then he set off across the gardens with his typical long strides that Ivy always struggled to match.

"Not everyone leaves a note, guv," she said, taking two steps for one of his, incredulous that this alone was the reason for his doubt. "Only thirty per cent."

She reeled off the statistic, remembering it from her studies, even now, ten years later. Some statistics, the more shocking ones, just stuck with her – 30% leave a note, 40% are not planned, 66% are men. Dean Worthing's circumstances were far from unusual.

"It just doesn't match," George said. "Think about it. Dean's death specifically. Forget the statistics. Forget the percentages. Think about the type of man Dean Worthing might be. Because if this was a suicide, Ivy, then it was quite... "

"Quite what?"

George found the word. "Theatrical."

"Theatrical?"

"I'm sure Dean Worthing looked down before he jumped, don't you think?"

"Sure," Ivy said, "but what does that– "

"So, he would've seen the Hawkins's car. Hell, he probably heard it pulling up to the church."

"So?"

"So why jump onto it? Why not take a few steps to the right? Why not wait for them to leave?" Ivy's thoughts turned over one another, but she had no coherent answers. "Because he wanted an audience," George answered for her. "He wanted a show. And a man like that Ivy, a writer, a man who had just exposed his entire life story in a manuscript, that man would've written a note."

Ivy had no counterargument to offer, and so lost was she in her thoughts that she only just realised what route they were taking through the hospital. It was still familiar to her from the day before.

"And there's one other reason," admitted George, as though making his own confession to Ivy. "The stories he tells in that book... "When Ivy looked at George, who had slowed as though simply the memory of reading weighed him down, his face sombre, his eyes tearful. "How a boy could survive that, I don't know, let alone how he could learn to live with those memories as a man. And if he has lived with those memories for the last forty years, then why give up now? What made him suddenly unable to bear being alive? After surviving so many years with strength?"

Ivy shook her head. Although she understood George's reasoning, it was emotional, not logical. It was the type of reasoning that one got from a book – from emotive language and a first-person perspective. There was a reason why detectives resisted taking the diaries of their victims as fact. It was biased. It was illogical. It was subjective truth.

"Our reactions to terrible events don't happen linearly," Ivy said. "Trauma can manifest years later, decades even. Repressed memories can resurface. It can quite suddenly become unbearable. Or maybe he was just tired, guv. Tired of pretending to be strong. I'm not sure people ever get over childhoods that cause those types of scars."

They stopped at the doors to Hatton Ward, and George pushed the buzzer to gain entry. It took a few moments for a nurse to buzz them in, and once they had shown their warrant cards, the friendly nurse steered them to a bay of twelve beds, six on either side. She didn't even need to point him out. He was a broken-looking man who lay staring at the world outside with blank eyes. Ivy smiled a thank you to the nurse, who left them to it, her trainers squeaking on the smooth floor.

"Perhaps you're right. But until we can be sure, I'm not ruling anything, or anyone, out," George said, and he stepped closer to Samson.

Ivy followed him, eyeing the other patients, who each shared a moment of hope that the visitors might be for them, which was followed closely by disappointment.

It was hard not to pick up on the other patients' sense of abandonment. In fact, the entire hospital unsettled Ivy. From the bodies in Pip's morgue to the hollow stares of the living and to the sick kids whose lives were far harder than they deserved. It was a building that reeked of death and suffering, and how anyone could bear to work there, she could not understand.

Although she imagined people might say the same about her job. But Ivy would take a raving madman with a gun over a lifeless body on a gurney any day. At least the worst days of her job reminded her she was alive.

"Adrian," George said gently, approaching the bed as a zookeeper might approach a sedated tiger. "My name's George." It did not escape Ivy's notice that he omitted his police title. "How are you feeling?"

Adrian Samson turned his blank eyes from the window to whip between Ivy and George. They were wide, bloodshot, and scared. "Been better," he croaked.

"We just wanted to ask you some questions, Adrian. Is that okay?"

Instead of answering, Adrian simply turned back to face the window, though Ivy could not be sure that what he saw on the other side of the glass was the same flight of birds and passing clouds that she saw.

"We wanted to talk to you about Bluestone Lodge," George began, to which Adrian did not reply but did offer a shadow of a nod. "You've been staying there. With Dean Worthing. Is that right?" Again, Adrian didn't reply. "Do you know Dean, Adrian? Are you friends?"

At this, Adrian only released a long, shaky breath. George retreated a little as though playing a particularly tentative game of Jenga. Ivy understood why George might be vague on the subject. Unless the nurses knew and had told him, Adrian might not yet know that Dean was dead. However, how important this was to Adrian or what kind of reaction it would provoke, only time would tell.

"We saw the manuscript that you gave to Stephen Cross," George began, and the mention of the manuscript invoked an immediate reaction. He whipped his gaze from the window.

"You've seen it?"

"I'm reading it," George replied. "It's long. It'll take a while."

"You have it?"

"I do," George said.

Adrian went to sit up, but Ivy placed a gently discouraging hand on his shoulder, feeling his arms tremble from the exertion.

"It's safe?" he asked with wide eyes.

His voice was higher than Ivy had imagined from his appearance. It seemed to be perpetually stuck in that awkward phase of a teenage boy's during the process of breaking.

"I'm looking after it, Adrian," George said softly. "I promise."

"Why did you have it, Adrian?" asked Ivy. "Did Dean give it to you?"

The man's eyes moved to Ivy. They were permanently wet and red, as though perpetually saturated in tears.

"He told me it was important. That it held the truth. And I should make sure it got into safe hands." His voice faltered and spluttered like an old car. "If he didn't make it home one night. If anything,...if anything happened to...to Dean...."

Ivy and George met each other's glance, wondering the same thing. Ivy was the one to ask it, knowing it was an important piece of information to confirm before they could move forward.

"Do you know, Dean?" she asked in the same soft voice George had heard her use with her own children when they were upset. "Do you know what's happened to him?"

He looked at Ivy, and his large, wet eyes might well have held the same childlike stares of Theo or Hattie, full of fear and fright. And when he spoke, his voice was a coarse whisper.

"He's dead, isn't he?"

For a few seconds, nobody spoke, and only Adrian's ragged breaths filled the silence. But then, eventually, George said, "That's right. He's dead."

It started off slowly, Adrian's breakdown. First, he lay down flat, staring at the ceiling in despair. But soon enough, whatever misery he was bottling began to escape.

"No. No, no, no, no," he said over and over again, smashing his head back against his pillow.

"Adrian, I really don't think–" George started, but Adrian's emotions were in full flow. He flung his head back and forth, shaking it violently as though hoping to shake the memories and hurt from his own mind. "Adrian?" George said. "Adrian, this is important. I need to know where you were on Saturday night. I need to know when you saw Dean last."

But Adrian only writhed harder, flailing his limbs as though gripped by a seizure. George cursed himself for telling him about Dean so soon. He tried desperately to throw in key questions, all the while keeping an eye out for the nurse who was sure to come and investigate the disruption.

But it was too late. Adrian was in a state of full denial.

"Why did you take the manuscript to St Leonard's Church, Adrian?" George pressed, hoping to pull him from whatever terrors, memories, or fears had gripped him.

Adrian issued a scream. It was quiet at first, like an old kettle beginning to boil.

"Why give it to Stephen Cross? Is he safe hands, Adrian? The hands of a vicar?"

But Adrian wasn't listening. His screams intensified to a high-pitched shriek, and his body convulsed. And for the first time, George truly understood the noise that Derek McGuinness had tried to describe. It was a horrific combination of scream and howl, a genderless, animalistic cry. It was all Ivy and George could do to look on helplessly.

Then, in one swift, painful movement, Adrian ripped the IV from his forearm, causing blood to spurt from the wound. He tried to pull himself from the bed, covering his ears against the equipment's shrill alarms.

Suddenly, Ivy reached forward and, for a second, George thought she was going to be foolish enough to try and restrain Adrian, the same foolishness he would judge of someone putting their arm into the cage of a wild beast. But instead, she grabbed a hanging red button by the bed and pushed it with the palm of her hand.

It did not take long before the nurse rushed into the ward, closely followed by two of her colleagues. They pushed Ivy and George aside.

"What happened?" The first asked.

"We were just asking him a few questions," `George started.

"I need to ask you to leave, please," the nurse told him as her colleagues manhandled Adrian back into bed.

"I'm sure this is all just a misunderstanding-."

"I said, get out," she said briskly, snatching at the curtains around his bed and pulling them into place.

They stood helplessly and watched as the nurses struggled against Adrian. One of them adjusted the drip, which George guessed contained a sedative.

"Are you still here?" she cried again when she saw them. "Don't you think you've done enough?" Ivy opened her mouth to argue their cause, but George pulled on her sleeve, knowing that their chance to question Adrian Samson was over.

"We'll be back," George told her as they backed off. "He knows something. He knows why a man died, for crying out loud. This is a murder investigation."

The final statement was powerful enough for the lead nurse to venture out from behind the curtain. She glanced at the enthralled patients in the other beds and walked quietly towards George.

"Is my patient under arrest, Inspector?" she said, her voice low and discreet.

"No," George explained, pleased for the tension to have eased. "No, but he's a key witness. We need to speak to him."

She gave the comment some thought, licked her teeth, and then pursed her lips.

"I can't have this again," she said.

'Understood," George replied, to which she nodded regretfully.

"There's very little we can do for him," she said. "He'll be out in a day or two. If you want my advice, you'll find yourself another witness."

CHAPTER EIGHTEEN

As George and Ivy walked through Lincoln, it felt like they were back in uniform, patrolling the streets on a Monday afternoon. When George was a young lad starting out in the force, people respected police officers. He and Tim would receive nods and good mornings as they patrolled, and of course, there was the odd troublemaker, the occasional yell of pig or a rogue lump of phlegm landing in their path. But for the most part, they were respected. In contrast, most of the looks officers received nowadays, he knew from his team's anecdotes, were less than friendly. Thankfully, he and Ivy were no longer bound to uniforms and so could enjoy the old city undisturbed.

"What did she say his name was again?"

"Freddo," George reminded Ivy. "Like the chocolate."

"Where do we even start?" Ivy asked. "If he lives on the streets, he could be anywhere."

"We're just going to have to ask around," George said. "We need more on Adrian Samson, and clearly, he is in no state to give us answers."

"Clearly," Ivy agreed, and George recalled Adrian's breakdown and winced at the affair. "So, hopefully, this chap, Freddo, has answers for us?"

George nodded. "Hopefully."

They began their search around Castle Hill, at the top of Lincoln's Steep Hill. But after just twenty minutes, George came to the conclusion they were looking in the wrong place. They headed south towards the newer end of the city, home to more fast-food restaurants and convenience stores, with the idea that somebody sleeping rough would stay close to a food source. Just like the skin on Dean Worthing's back, the city bore its own scars. Empty shops caused by a failing economy gave home to a number of men and women, all of whom appeared hopeful when George and Ivy approached but clammed up when they realised there was no money being offered. The street was a tough place, and information was a currency. However, George knew all too well how far a hungry individual might stretch that information, and he wasn't about to hand out pound notes to anybody with a winning smile.

"What now?" he said as they peered over a railing into the water. They had exhausted any potential sources of information, and the only people in sight appeared to be tourists or locals out enjoying the shops on the high street.

"I'll ask that girl," Ivy said, heading towards a young woman in a North Face jacket sitting on the kerbside beside a large, red backpack.

"She's not homeless," George said.

"How do you know?"

"Well, look at her. Nice jacket, nice bag. She's probably just travelling."

"What's she supposed to look like, guv?"

"Ah, come on, Ivy," George said. "Don't do that. I know not every homeless person is a druggie criminal who just needs a start in life, but... "

"But?" Ivy said, backing off on her way to speak to the girl.

George had no reply. He just watched as Ivy walked over to the girl and crouched down beside her. They exchanged a few words, the girl gestured to the right, and she and Ivy seemed to share a pleasant goodbye before Ivy headed back to George with a smug smile on her face.

"This way," she said without slowing, and it was George who was forced to play catch up for a change.

They walked along the water, heading east until they arrived at a footbridge, beneath which, sheltering from the elements, were several individuals. Some of them were making use of old and tatty sleeping bags, while others had made a bed of flattened cardboard boxes and had wrapped themselves in warm jackets. Among them were three women and two men, and each of them raised their head as George and Ivy closed in.

"Afternoon," George said. "How's everybody doing?"

He had intended for the statement to break the ice, to demonstrate they meant no harm.

"Oh aye," one of the men said in a thick Northern Irish accent. "We're grand. Ain't that right?" he glanced across at his companions. "We're all tickety-boo."

"That's right," one of the women added in an equally heavy Belfast accent. "Tickety-boo, we are."

The sarcasm wasn't lost on George, and he regretted his approach, choosing instead to lay his cards on the table.

"We're looking for someone," George said. "I was hoping you could help?"

"Help?" the first man said. "What do you think we are? The bloody A-Team?"

The comment raised a few yellow-toothed grins and phlegm-filled guffaws, one of which escalated into a cough, a hawk, and finally, the offending article was spat onto the ground a few feet away.

"His name is Freddo," George said. "I just need to know if you know him, and if so, perhaps where he might be."

"Freddo?" another man said, pulling himself out of his sleeping bag. "Like the wee chocolate bar?"

"That's right," George told him. "Do you know him?"

The man shoved a grubby finger into his ear, rummaged around for a moment, and then inspected the digit before looking across to his friends.

"Can't say I recognise the name," he grumbled.

"Na, me neither," the first man added, and he made a show of not making eye contact. "There's a Frankie. Maybe you mean Frankie?"

"No, it's definitely Freddo."

"Like the wee chocolate bar?"

"Like the chocolate bar, yes," George replied, to which they shook their heads in turn.

"It's not like they call a register, you know? We're not part of a club. Is that what you think? That we all meet up and discuss the weather?"

"No, of course not-"

"Or maybe you think we're all pals?"

"Of course not, no-"

"So why would we know this fella? What do you want with him anyway?"

"We're friends, that's all."

"Friends?" he said, beaming at the word. "Well, ain't that sweet."

"Bless," the woman said.

"Well, I'm a friend of a friend of a friend, really."

"And what is it you want with our man Freddo?"

"Listen, if you can't help, then you can't help," George said, nudging Ivy to move away. "Thanks for your time. I'll let you get back to..."He paused, and the Irishman cocked his head expectantly.

"Get back to what?"

"Well, whatever it was you were doing," George said.

"Ah, I see. You hear that?" he asked his friends. "We can all go about our business now."

"Thank God for that," one of them said as he nestled back into his sleeping bag.

But the first man wasn't quite finished. George was mid-turn when he called out.

"Out of interest," he said, his keen eyes meeting George's with a hard stare. "What is it exactly you think we do all day, eh?"

"Well, I have no idea-"

"Drugs?" the man said.

"That's none of my business."

"How about a wee bit of pilfering?"

George stiffened at the implied accusation, and the man rose to his feet. He was gaunt but strong. Wirey, Grace would have called him.

"It's not like begging works much these days. Nobody's got money, have they?"

"Listen, how you spend your days is none of my business. I'm merely trying to help a friend. If you can't help. If you don't know Freddo, then I'll ask elsewhere."

"Persistent bastard, ain't ya?" he replied as George began to turn away again. He stopped once more, the comment striking a nerve somewhere in his already agitated mind.

"I'm sorry?"

"I said, you're a persistent bastard, ain't ya?"

"Come on, guv," Ivy said, tugging on his sleeve.

"Guv?" the man said. "Guv? You're coppers?"

The remaining individuals raised their heads, and for the first time, George felt an injection of adrenaline. They were the pride of lions, and he and Ivy were the forlorn fawns who had stumbled into their path. He backed away with Ivy by his side and immediately heard the man's heavy footsteps running to catch up.

"Got a nerve, ain't ya?" he said when he had caught up with them. George and Ivy quickened their steps, but the man kept pace. "Come to us for help, eh? In your cheap trousers and shirt. What about us? What about the help we need, eh? Quick to move us on when we're asking for help, aren't you? When we're polluting the high street. But when it's you who needs help, it's different, ain't it? The rules are different." He ran ahead and turned to face them, taking large backward strides so he could look each of them in the eye. "You're all the same, you lot. First sign of trouble, and you pick on the downtrodden."

"I'd appreciate it if you moved out of our way," George said.

"Well, what is it? What do you need Freddo for, eh?"

"I'm done talking with you, sir. I suggest you return to your friends so we can all go about our days."

"What's he done? Or should I be asking what it is you're going to pin on him?" the man asked, still walking backwards. "Don't tell me, shoplifting. It's always shoplifting. What is it? Need to get the statistics up, do you? The top man having a wee crackdown, is he? Must be election time. That's what happens, isn't it? The top brass wants to be re-elected, so he sends you lot out to have a clean-up. We're off the streets, the public are happy, and what do you know? He keeps his six-figure salary and corner office. Everyone's a winner, eh? Everyone but us-"

George had heard enough. He reached out and grabbed onto the man's filthy jacket and, hooking a leg behind his, knocked him off-balance so that he fell backwards. His descent was slowed by George, who held him against the ground and dared to bring his face closer.

The man silenced, his eyes wide. Not with fear but surprise, and that was enough. It was a move that had worked twenty years ago and would work for as long as people read him wrong.

"Listen to me, you filthy little beggar," he said. "I've nothing to gain from nicking you or your mates, but I will if I have to." The man opened his mouth to argue, but George silenced him with a hard shake. "If you must know, I'm on your side. The side of the downtrodden, as you put it. I'm helping someone in your position. A man who is, as we speak, lying in a hospital bed with a drip in his arm." George let the statement sink in before continuing. "I asked for help. I asked if you knew anybody named Freddo, not because I want to pin some minor crime on him, but because that's the only name we have of anybody that might know Adrian Samson. Our mutual friend. So, if you can't help or won't help, then I suggest you bugger off back to your sleeping bag. And as for what you do when you get there, I really couldn't give two hoots. Do I make myself clear? If I see you again, I *will* nick you, and even if it means you get a roof over your head for a night or two, I'll do my damndest to make your life harder than it already is."

He let go of the man's jacket, easing him to the ground, then stood up and straightened his own attire. He looked up at a wide-eyed Ivy and shook his head to tell her that any attempt at humour would not be appreciated.

"Let's go," he said and stepped over the man, entering into a brisk pace. "Let's get back to the car. I want to see how the other two are getting on."

They were barely twenty yards away when the man called out. George ignored him at first, expecting some kind of verbal abuse or antagonisation.

"You should have just said in the first place," the man said, his voice cracked and dry. "There's no need for violence."

"Walk on, Ivy," George said. "Don't look at him."

"I can take you to him," he said, and George slowed. "To Freddo, I mean. I know where he sleeps." George sought an opinion from Ivy's expression and found the confirmation he was looking for. So, he turned to face the man who was up on his knees, carefree and grinning from ear to ear. "But it'll cost ya."

"But I know Freddo," he said. George turned on the spot, looking for sincerity in his eyes, whose poker face again revealed nothing that George could read into. "I can take you to him."

CHAPTER NINETEEN

"Guv?" Ivy said, her hands deep in her jacket pockets, where George knew she kept a small bottle of pepper spray, "I'm not sure about this."

On receipt of a large coffee and an almond croissant, the man who had eventually introduced himself as Paddy had led them out of the city centre and into the industrial area. They walked beside the river where abandoned, red brick warehouses provided shelter and privacy. They trod on broken glass and bricks, keeping a keen eye on Paddy as he navigated the little pathways, stopping infrequently to ensure they were following.

"You coming, or what?" he called out. "Not far now, so it is."

"Come on, Ivy," George said playfully, though his eyes kept busy, keeping track of his environment, remembering the route back and vigilant for any sudden movements. "I thought we weren't supposed to generalise?"

"There's a difference," she hushed, "between not generalising and following a desperate man down dark alleyways."

George remained silent, as the only reply he could offer was admitting that she was quite right. Still, they had wanted to get somewhere, and they were achieving that, at least.

Outside a particularly ruined factory, which George assumed to be Victorian, they stopped. Its four walls were still intact, but the tall windows had long since been put through, and bricks from surrounding buildings lay scattered across the concrete like a garden of terracotta wildflowers. Paddy tugged hard on a large, steel-panelled door that creaked open in his hand.

"After you," he said, gesturing for Ivy and George to enter the dark warehouse first.

Ivy hit George with her most disconcerting stare, but he took a long stride forward into the darkness, and, of course, despite her body screaming with reservations, she followed close behind.

Inside was surprisingly sheltered. A peppering of daylight from holes in the roof barely touched the deep shadows, but caused a handful of puddles on the expanse of concrete floor, and contributed to the collection of pigeons that fluttered high in the exposed steel rafters. The original machinery had been stripped away. What was left was a large, empty space and a wide steel stairway that had split under its own weight, making the mezzanine inaccessible.

Their footsteps echoed, spooking the pigeons high above. Ivy always found it rather unsettling to find herself in a setting that was no longer used for its original purpose. Like the building itself had lost its soul.

"Paddy?" George said. "Where the hell are you taking us?"

"To John," he said, then grinned back at George. "A.KA Freddo."

"Freddo was the name we were given," George explained. "You're sure it's the same man?"

"Certain," Paddy replied. "Everyone knows John."

A smattering of trash marked the spots where groups of homeless people had once set up camp, and the air was filled, among other things, with that pungent stench of ammonia.

"Paddy, if this is some kind of trap, I can assure you-"

"It's not a trap," Paddy said, his words almost a song.

"So, Freddo is actually called John? Or is John called Freddo? Which way round is it?"

George kept his voice low but felt it carry into the farthest corners.

"You can ask him yourself," Paddy said.

"Is that common?" asked Ivy, joining the conversation to distract her troubled mind more than anything else. "To use a fake name?"

"It's not uncommon," he replied. "What would you do if you were running from something, eh?"

"Use a nickname?" George suggested.

"It's more like a pseudonym," Paddy challenged, and his glare at George highlighted the difference between the playfulness of a nickname and the seriousness of a pseudonym. "It protects us."

"From what?"

"From people like you lot," he said. "Police, politicians, doctors. The system."

"Oh, you mean the people trying to help you?" George said.

Ivy groaned inwardly at his provocation.

Paddy scoffed. "Help us? You lot got us into this in the first place. Anyway, these days, anonymity is a superpower that most people don't have. Let's face it. It's our only advantage. It keeps us safe."

"And I suppose Paddy is little more than a cliché, is it?"

"Ah," he replied. "That's a conversation for another day."

"And another breakfast, I presume?"

Paddy grinned, revealing vile and yellowed teeth.

"Fast learner, ain't ya?"

George left the debate there, and together, they followed him to the other side of the building and through a doorless frame into what might have once been a meeting room or a canteen. Broken chairs remained scattered around the walls, now used as makeshift bedside tables for the old mattresses beside them. For an abandoned building, it was actually quite an

appealing space, with solid walls and high ceilings. George imagined that the summer sun would light the place fairly well as it
shone through the bank of broken windows along the west side
of the building.

Most of the makeshift beds were occupied with lounging
bodies or people perched on the ends, clinging to a bottle of
something. Paddy headed straight to the mattress closest to the
door, where an attractive, blonde man lay reading *Walden* by
Henry Thoreau. He looked like an aged nineties heartthrob, with
tanned skin, floppy, thick hair in a stylish centre parting and a
colourful shirt, open at the collar, more shabby chic than shabby.
Up close, George realised he was closer to thirty than forty, and
when he spoke, he did so with a strong Midlands accent. More
black country than Birmingham.

"Y'alright, Paddy?" he said, looking up and snapping his book
closed. He stood to greet the man who had led them there.

"Who're ya mates?"

"Some visitors for ya," Paddy grunted. "Want to talk to you
about Adrian, so they do."

"I thought you didn't know Adrian?" George challenged, but
Paddy only smirked in reply, breaking the poker face he had maintained throughout the journey over.

"S'that right?" Freddo asked, looking over George's shoulder as
though he might be hiding something. "Haven't seen him in a few
weeks now. Who's asking, anyway?"

"He's at Lincoln Hospital," George said, getting straight to the
point.

"Hospital?" said Freddo, the colour draining from his tanned
face. "That your doing, is it?"

"He's okay," Ivy stepped in, clearly noticing the concerned
panic in his eyes. "We saw him this morning. He's awake and
stable."

Freddo seemed unconvinced.

"What d'ya do to him?"

Ivy hesitated, then said, "The doctors think he overdosed on Methadone."

Freddo sighed and ran a practised hand through his hair as though he was used to worrying about Adrian. "The idiot..."he mumbled, but not without a hint of affection.

"We want to help him," George said. "But he's not exactly talking right now. So, we hoped to ask you some questions, Mr...?"

It was a common way for detectives to naturally pull a last name from someone. But Freddo was not one to fall for it. He smiled charmingly. "Freddo is fine," he said. "What are you, some kind of charity or something?"

"They're coppers," Paddy clarified in a final warning to Freddo before he skulked off to the back of the room with the other men to greet some more of his acquaintances.

"I should have guessed," Freddo said with a grin, looking George and Ivy up and down. He lingered on Ivy a moment too long. "Though, in my defence, the standards are improving."

"Freddo," George started, the name rolling around his mouth like an unsavoury boiled sweet. "When was the last time you saw Adrian?"

"Like I said, a few weeks ago," he replied. "Listen, as much as I'd like to sit and chat." He raised his book for them to see. "I've got a lot on."

"We're trying to help your friend, Freddo. We're not out to nick any of you. He's in trouble, and yours is the only name we can find. I do understand that yours is a hard world, but you'll forgive me if I thought that friendship might rank somewhere above saving your own face." Freddo eyed him as if he was unused to being spoken to in such a tone. "Yes, I'm a copper. But you know what? That doesn't mean I'm bent or out to get you. But if you can't speak to me because you're afraid the rest of them will turn their backs, then that's fine. But I don't think Adrian will appreciate it. Right now, that lad needs all the help he can bloody well get."

The closing statement reverberated around the room both audibly and visibly, in the form of turned heads and wide eyes that seemed to glow in the dim light. Eventually, Freddo nodded.

"He's been living here with us for a couple of years now. He's had a hard time of it, that boy has. I helped him."

"We've heard," George said. "Addiction issues?"

"To start with," Freddo said, running another hand through his surprisingly springy hair. "He has... freakouts. Breakdowns. Don't much like being confined. He'll wake up feeling like the walls are closing in, freak out, and just run off for a few days. But he always comes back, tail between his legs. Usually when he's hungry or has scrounged enough for a fix."

"But not this time?"

"No," Freddo said. "Not this time. Went off with some woman, didn't he," Freddo said, and George noted a hint of jealousy in his voice, although what kind of jealousy, he could not be sure.

"What woman?" asked George. "Who was she?"

Freddo shrugged. "No idea. Some posh tart in a suit. She came looking for him, just like you two. Must've followed him here. She talked to him for a bit, gave him an address, and the next day, he was gone." Freddo picked at a piece of loose skin by his cuticle and added, "Didn't even say goodbye." He glanced up at George. "There's gratitude for ya, eh?"

"What did she look like, Freddo? This woman?"

He held his hands behind his head and looked up to the pigeons that had gathered on the rafters, his eyes closed in thought. "Blonde," he said. "Slim, tall, black trouser suit. You know? The type they like to wear to be taken seriously. George felt Ivy stiffen at the sexist remark but said nothing, allowing Freddo to continue. "Cute little heels, long legs. You know the type." He rubbed his thumb and forefinger together. "Plenty of the good stuff."

"I'm afraid I'm unfamiliar with *the type*. You'll have to enlighten me," George said.

"Businesswoman. You don't get much of her type around here. She parked up on the main road."

"You saw her car?"

"I did," Freddo said. "Little, red sports car. Surprised she left here with her windows intact, if I'm honest."

"What did they talk about?" George asked. "Her and Adrian?"

"None of my business," he insisted. "And none of yours neither, is it? Adrian's a big boy. Doesn't need me looking over his shoulder all the time."

"But you were, weren't you?" Ivy said. "Looking out for him, I mean?"

Freddo met her in the eye and let down some of his mask of carelessness. He took a deep breath and closed his eyes again, remembering. "Something about a guy. Dean Someone."

George and Ivy made eye contact. "Dean Worthing?" he asked.

Freddo shrugged. "Maybe. Honestly can't remember, mate."

"Could it have been his brother?" George asked. "Does Adrian have a brother?"

"No idea."

George frowned. "I thought you knew Adrian for years?"

Freddo looked between George and Ivy as though they were tourists in a foreign land, and as Virgil was to Dante, he was their guide through this harsh and unforgiving world.

"Everyone has a story. Everyone's here for a reason." He gestured around the room, and Ivy looked at the mix of people, young and old, of various nationalities, some light-skinned, some dark. "But if they don't want to share their story with me, I'm not going to force them."

"And Adrian?" asked George. "He never shared his story with you?"

"Bits," Freddo said with a fair amount of pride.

"So why was he here?" asked Ivy. "What happened to Adrian?"

"It's not my story to tell," Freddo said, his eyes glistening, not with mischief or rebellion, but simply with integrity.

"We're trying to help him, Freddo," George said. "We're trying to understand."

Freddo looked around the room as though considering the stories of all the men and women in it, the parts of their lives he knew all about, and the parts they had omitted, perhaps even from themselves.

"I'll tell you one thing," he said, his face thoughtful and a hundred times more expressive than Paddy's had been. "People don't choose this life. It's inflicted upon them. They lose their job, or their spouses leave them. By courts not letting them see their kids, by society rejecting them, by politicians pretending they don't exist. But Adrian... "

"He chose this?" asked George.

Freddo nodded. "He liked living on the streets. He said it made him feel free. Said he'd sleep beneath the stars every night if he could."

Ivy watched Freddo's face soften with some indication of compassion for his friend. He seemed like a gentle soul who had been forced to toughen up a little, though his sensitivity lay just below the surface. Ivy looked at George. They had heard enough.

"Thank you, Freddo," George said, and he looked across the room to Paddy and nodded at the man who had led them there. "I just have one more question."

"Go ahead," Freddo said, though he had moved back to his bed.

George paused as though trapped between respect and curiosity. "What's *your* story?"

Freddo laughed to himself, lay down on the bed, and picked up his book in a silent gesture that he had told them more than enough. "My story?" He opened his book at the dog-eared page. "You wouldn't believe me if I told you."

CHAPTER TWENTY

George and Ivy retraced their steps along the River Witham, through the city centre, and up Steep Hill towards the car park. The colourful shop fronts inviting customers to update their wardrobes and their living rooms for twenty-five per cent off provided a harsh contrast to the dank and dingy world from whence they had emerged somewhat enlightened. It made George's skin crawl to witness so harshly these two lifestyles side by side, only a bridge-crossing apart. But it was not his job to close the chasm of fortunes. He would leave that to the politicians and the activists, though he wouldn't hold his breath for a result.

No, right now, it was his job to solve the mystery that had only continued to surround Dean Worthing and Adrian Samson, expanding with every inquiry he made, like feeding flour and water to a sourdough starter. They had a forty-five-minute drive back to the Wolds in which to dissect the scant information that Freddo had imparted, and they did so against the backdrop of the lush, green fields.

"Do we know anything more about him?" asked Ivy, never one to allow her thoughts to go unheard.

"Adrian hasn't been seen in a few weeks," George reminded her. "That's something. And that he was approached by a woman just before he went missing, who spoke to him about Dean Worthing. It's a connection. That's something."

"And that Adrian had a fear of enclosed spaces, as well as mental health and addiction issues," Ivy continued, remembering Adrian's panic-fuelled freakout at the hospital. "Not that we didn't figure that one out already."

"So, who is the mystery woman?" George started.

"Someone who knows Adrian?" Ivy suggested. "A sister? An ex-lover?"

"Freddo said she was in a suit," George said. "Maybe she was there on business."

"What business could that be? I don't wish to sound judgmental, but he's hardly employee of the month material, is he?"

"Prefixing a statement with, I do not wish to sound judgmental, Ivy does not give you a clean slate on which to generalise. Besides, Freddo said she gave him an address. Maybe he applied for a job. Plenty of businesses like to give people like Adrian a new start in life, you know? Or at least, they enjoy *being seen* to be giving people like Adrian a new start in life. Whether or not their presence is entirely appreciated, we'll never know. The fact remains that he was approached by a woman driving a red sports car. She gave him an address. And then he went missing. That, my friend, is the sum total of our discoveries."

The statement only served to prevent Ivy from venturing down a hypothetical rabbit hole.

"I doubt very much any CCTV will still have the video of her car, will they?" she said, to which George chuckled. He let his silence confirm her suspicion, so she changed tack.

"If we were to take the scars on both of their backs, then we can assume that Dean and Adrian are acquainted, right?"

"Stands to reason," he agreed.

"And we at least know that, even if it's only been for a few weeks, Adrian and the woman were acquainted."

"Right," he said, following along with one eye on the road.

"So, was Dean acquainted with her?"

"You mean, did Dean put her onto him?"

"No, I mean, did she approach Dean in the same way she approached Adrian. Out of the blue, like."

"Ah," George replied, falling in with her direction. "You're wondering if she's behind it all."

"No," she said, then faltered. "I don't know. It's just odd, isn't it? Dean dies, and Adrian nearly dies. What would she have to gain? What would motivate her to get rid of them both? I mean, you could almost understand her offing Dean if his death meant she was in line to receive something. But Adrian? What on earth could she gain from him dying?"

"You're overthinking it," George told her.

"I'm throwing ideas out there..." Ivy countered. "She's a beautiful, put-together woman. Adrian is a vulnerable mess. Easy to manipulate, easy to control."

"So?"

"So, what if she was there behind Dean's back?" Ivy said, the theory developing only as she spoke it aloud. It was part of their process, hers and George's, to talk through all possibilities, however wild or ungrounded they seemed in the moment. "What if she was bringing him into something? Offering him an opportunity?"

"What kind of opportunity?" George said, not challenging Ivy's theory but rather pushing her to develop it.

"I don't know. To get off the streets. To get clean, maybe? I mean, that room in the house looked like the perfect place to go cold turkey, didn't it?"

"Sounds to me like you're forcing what little information we do have into a theory, Ivy."

"Maybe they worked together," she said, ignoring him. "This

woman and Dean. It's a bit convenient, isn't it? That a stranger enters Adrian's life, and a few weeks later, the man whose house he's been holed up in is found dead."

"What are you suggesting?"

"If this woman could manipulate Adrian, maybe she manipulated him to murder Dean. Once he'd done that, maybe she gave him a little too much methadone? He sleeps rough. Nobody reported him missing. He's the perfect scapegoat. All she had to do was make sure she was somewhere else, entirely."

"Why on earth would she do all of that?"

"I don't know. Maybe she's a woman scorned? Or maybe something more practical, more financially motivated, like... "

George side-eyed her and smirked.

"Look, it's a theory. I just think it's worth bearing in mind that Adrian is a vulnerable man, a wild card. We don't know what he's capable of. And we don't know if this woman's intentions were entirely honest."

"Fair enough," George said and then nodded at his phone in the car's centre console. "Get onto the team. I want to know if we can track down this woman; find out who she is."

Ivy found Campbell's number in George's phone as he drove across the Fens. George wasn't a man to put his foot down, especially when his mind was awash with ideas. He was far more restrained in his actions, a behaviour that Ivy imagined accompanied maturity. In contrast, Campbell answered the phone with a clatter, as though she had knocked the phone off the receiver in haste to pick it up.

"Campbell?" she answered.

"Campbell, it's Hart," Ivy said. "We're looking for someone we think is connected to Dean Worthing."

"We don't know that for sure," George said, announcing his presence.

"She came to speak to Adrian Samson a few weeks ago," Ivy

continued. "We think maybe she was Dean Worthing's ex, or an old employee or something."

"We think nothing of the sort," George said. "It's just an idea, that's all."

"Alright," Campbell said, and Ivy heard the scroll of a mouse on the other end of the line.

"As it happens, I've been compiling a list of his employees. Do you have a name?"

"No," Ivy said.

"A description?"

"That we do have," Ivy said. "Blonde, slim, and..."She omitted long-legged and replaced it with, "tall. Witness says she was wearing a suit and drove a little, red sports car."

"Not much to go on," Campbell said. "He's got dozens of employees, guv. At least half of them are women."

"Have a look on LinkedIn," Ivy said.

"On what?" George asked.

"LinkedIn. It's like Facebook for businesses," she explained, then turned her attention back to Campbell. "Find the company. You should see a list of employees on there with profile pictures. You can cross-reference any females that match the description with your own list.

There was a silence as Campbell scrolled through the database, perhaps hoping one of the young, blonde women jumped out at her. But rarely were they ever that fortunate.

"What are you doing?" asked Byrne, his voice distant.

"It's DS Hart," she explained.

Over the line, they heard a chair scrape across the incident room floor, presumably as Byrne joined Campbell at her desk.

"Wait, wait, wait," Campbell said excitedly, clicking furiously as though switching between tabs on her computer. "I think I've got someone. A Juliet Shaw. His PA."

"Juliet Shaw?" Byrne said. "I know that name." The sound of him flicking through paperwork followed, and then a swish as he whipped an individual sheet from the pile. "Here it is," he explained. "I did a deeper dive into Dean Worthing's bank accounts. Found a few recurring monthly payments. One was to an individual's account, a Juliet Shaw."

"There she is," came Campbell's voice, and she gave a low whistle. "And boy, is she a looker."

"So, she's linked to Dean Worthing," George called out. "Check her vehicle registration on the DVLA database."

"We're looking for a small, red sports car," Ivy reminded her.

At this, George, who had been listening to their discussion, suddenly slapped the wheel with the palm of his hand. Ivy looked up urgently but saw nothing dangerous occurring on the road. The road was as long, straight, and near-empty as before. She studied his expression, struggling to interpret what she saw.

"What?" she asked.

"I saw a red convertible," he said slowly. "On Saturday night, when I was driving back from the church. It passed me on Ormsby Road. It was a Mazda. An MX-5."

"Nice," Byrne said. "If you're going to enjoy the Wolds, there's nothing better than a little sports car."

"Exactly," George said, "That's why I remembered it."

"Didn't remember the number plate too, did you, guv?"

"I'm not Rain Man, Byrne."

"Juliet Shaw," came Campbell's voice, staccato, as though reading from a screen. "Mazda. Red. R-S-19-K-V-B."

"Good," George said. "Finally, a lead! Get me a phone number, address, anything you can on her. It's time she answered a few questions."

"Yes, boss," Campbell said. Then, before Ivy could hang up, Byrne called out.

"Guv, I've got a bit more on Dean Worthing."

"Go on," George said.

"So, he founded Worthing Media in 2009, but he hasn't been

CEO since 2015. He owns the company but isn't particularly involved, by the looks of it."

"Alright, so what does he do? Day to day, I mean."

"Well, I wasn't sure," Byrne continued, although Ivy got the impression that he was laying the groundwork before building up to a reveal. "But according to his accounts, he had a tri-monthly income from a small publishing company."

"Royalties?" George asked.

"Nothing huge, but enough for someone with his bank balance to get by on. I looked the publishing firm up, and it turns out they're a small business specialising in romance."

"What, like smut?" asked Ivy. "Well-thumbed pages, that kind of thing?"

"Smut might be a bit strong," Byrne said. "Sex is more acceptable these days, isn't it? Besides, they're all queer romance, you know, gay and lesbian stories."

"It's a popular niche," Campbell added.

"Alright, so?" George pushed on. "I'm not making a connection here."

"Alright, so I had to do some digging because Dean's name came up, but only as a writer about to release a book. The blurb reads as follows: Dean is currently working on his tell-all memoir about his childhood in a remote Lincolnshire village. He enjoys long walks and is one of the few authors to still work with a traditional typewriter, claiming that some elements of history are best forgotten, while others should be clung to and never let go."

"A little pretentious," Ivy muttered.

"Okay," George said. "So, if he hasn't published anything yet, where's the money coming from?"

"I honestly don't know," Byrne admitted.

"Here we go," Campbell said. "I've just looked up a few mucky romance books, at the previews of the first few pages, you know," she continued, "and from what I can see, one author's books includes a business logo on its copyright page."

"Campbell, we're driving. We can't see what you can see, and as much as I enjoy hearing your voice, I'm not a fan of suspense."

A silence followed.

"He means, just get on with it," Ivy explained and eyeballed him.

"It's Worthing Media's logo. I recognised it, an oak tree. I think it's Dean Worthing; meaning he writes under a–"

"Pseudonym," George said, making eye contact with Ivy. "Seems to be a common practice these days."

"Exactly."

"What's the pseudonym?" asked Ivy.

"Nothing familiar," Campbell said. "Baxter Steele."

Each of them took a second to run the name through their mind, hoping it might shed light on their investigation. But it was Byrne who spoke up before anyone else could react.

"You're joking?!"

"What?" asked Campbell.

"Baxter Steele?" Byrne's voice was high and fast with excitement. "Are you serious?"

"You know him?" Ivy said.

"I read his books all the time. They're incredible! "

"Byrne," George said, shuffling in his seat, readying himself for clarification. "You read gay romance books written by the man whose death we're investigating?"

"Yes," he said, without, Ivy noticed admiringly, an ounce of shame in his voice. "I mean, I'm not gay, not that it matters, I just...well, I like the stories. They're always about disobedience and defiance through love and relationships. Set during different times in history, so you always learn something too. It's very interesting. He's a brilliant writer."

There was a pause during which the rest of the team processed this latest reveal about Byrne's personal life. With his new, surprising hobby, the boy was becoming harder and harder to fit into a box the more they got to know him.

"I know," he said eventually, "my friends say it's weird."

"I don't think it's weird," Campbell said, and for the first time, Ivy could not trace any sarcasm or dismissiveness in her tone against Byrne. "Gay people watch and read and listen to stories about straight people all the time. Why shouldn't straight people do the same with gay stories?"

"I agree," he said firmly.

A pause followed, during which Ivy imagined the two warring PCs to have found a rare instant of mutual agreement.

"Well then," George said slowly, breaking the moment between the young PCs, "I guess we know how Dean spends his time."

"He had that old-fashioned writing bureau in his house," Ivy said. "So, if he's been writing these books while his business takes care of itself, that makes sense."

George slowed to take a left turn, heading back towards the Wolds. "Right. But we still need more, both on Dean and Adrian. And this woman seems like the link. Campbell, Byrne, both or either of you, I don't care how you do it," he said. "Just find me Juliet Shaw."

CHAPTER TWENTY-ONE

After a non-stop day of driving from the Wolds to Lincoln County Hospital, then gallivanting around the city centre and climbing up the forty-five-degree Steep Hill before driving forty-five minutes back towards Horncastle, George was looking forward to sitting down with a coffee.

However, that was not to be the case.

As always in his job, as soon as he and Ivy walked through the fire escape doors and climbed the stairs to the first floor, it became clear that a moment's break was entirely off the table.

"George, Ivy?" DCI Tim Long had an uncanny ability to be walking along the corridor at exactly the same time as them, usually wanting an inconveniently timed update for which George was usually unprepared.

"How's the St Leonard's investigation going?"

Tim strode towards them from his office at the other end of the corridor, stopping between them and the incident room, perhaps as a way of blocking their path.

"It's going well," George lied. "Things are...coming together."

"I have to admit I'm a little confused, George. The death at the church on Saturday night was a suicide, was it not? Unless, of course, Doctor Bell has advised you otherwise?"

"Not exactly," George said. "We're following up on a few leads. There are other factors at play."

"The man who entered the church on Sunday morning?"

"Exactly. We think the two incidents are connected."

Tim frowned, still clearly far from understanding. "But nobody was hurt? What exactly– "

"We might be looking at a case of child abuse too," George cut in, defending their investigation, albeit a little abruptly and with more than a little circumstance. He was well aware they should have more to go on by now. But claims of child abuse always seemed to argue a case of urgency to those higher-up.

"Child abuse?" Tim said. He looked between George and Ivy, whose expression George hoped was convincingly sincere. He was not sure though, seeing as the next question Tim asked was the very question that George had hoped he would not. "A recent case?"

George licked his lips.

"No," he admitted. "An old case. But we can't know if it was closed. Not yet."

"An old case," Tim repeated slowly. "How old?"

George hesitated, but there was no way around the truth. "About forty years ago."

Tim threw his hands up incredulously, energetically too, as though he had been waiting for the opportunity to do so. "Christ, George, forty years ago?"

"It's relevant to what happened this weekend."

"I don't know, George," Tim said, seeming to wobble somewhere between trust in the instincts of his old colleague and putting his foot down. "It doesn't seem like the best use of your time."

George felt the tension in his head and stomach – which would have been eased by a sit-down and a cup of coffee – escalate to breaking point. "Look, if somebody did push Dean Worthing off St Leonard's Church on Saturday night, then we have a murderer on the loose. I don't want their freedom hanging over my head, Tim. Do you?"

George felt Ivy's eyes on the side of his face, but he continued only to meet Tim's stare, stressing their power play without wanting to bend it too far. Tim, too, seemed unwilling to break their alliance, although he must have bristled at George's impertinence.

"Two days," he said eventually. "You've got two more days to work this out, George, and then I want your team elsewhere. We don't have the time or resources to have our only two detectives and two officers on a forty-year-old child abuse claim and an innocuous suicide. Do you hear me?"

"Yes, Tim," George said. "I hear you. That's all we need."

Again, Tim looked between George and Ivy as though trying to work out their intentions, as if those intentions were not, in fact, in the best interests of the station or the force. It was a suspicion that George had noticed growing just in the few weeks since they had moved to the Wolds.

"Have you spoken to Sergeant Wilkins," Tim said, referring to the lazy, moody-faced officer on the front desk downstairs.

"No, we came in through the fire escape," George explained. "Why?"

"He was looking for you a while ago. Apparently, you have some guests downstairs who are keen to talk to you."

George turned to Ivy and motioned for her to accompany him. She offered a "Thanks, guv," to Long before they left, which was a far friendlier goodbye than George's curt nod.

Together, they left the way they had just come, through the fire escape doors and down the stairs, and then they buzzed through into the reception. Inside, they met Sergeant Wilkins at the front desk, a seasoned officer with rosy cheeks, who welcomed them with a grunt and nodded towards a couple in the corner. The couple in question rose from their plastic blue seats at seeing the gesture.

"Inspector Larson," Richard Hawkins said, and he closed the gap between them. "Sergeant Hart, wasn't it?" He shook each of their hands vigorously. "You remember my wife, Sarah?" He motioned to the woman beside him, who seemed much taller than the last time they had met. She smiled warmly at them both with wide, watery eyes.

"Of course," George said. "How can we help you?"

"We, erm, well, we wanted to speak to you." Richard Hawkins seemed a little nervous. He put an arm around Sarah Hawkins' shoulders as though used to protecting his wife in times of duress. "About our statements, that is. About what happened on Saturday night."

"Very well," George said, and he gestured towards the door off the waiting room that led to the cells and the interview rooms. "This way, please. We'll be more comfortable in one of the interview rooms."

It was a turn of phrase. In fact, the interview rooms boasted the same uncomfortable, blue plastic chairs as the waiting room. But George found that witnesses were more willing to take their statements seriously in private, across a table where a long line of criminals had sat before them. It served as a subtle reminder of the stakes.

Sergeant Wilkins buzzed them into the corridor from the front desk, and Sarah and Richard Hawkins followed George and Ivy into Interview Room Two, where they all took seats around the table.

"So," George started, linking his fingers, "what is it you'd like to add, Mr Hawkins?"

He glanced at Sarah before answering, who gave a minute nod of her head in response. "My wife and I, we've had time to reflect on what we saw on Saturday night. See, we were rather flustered at the time, as I'm sure you understand. And, well, we've thought of something."

At this, Ivy opened her notebook and clicked her pen. George remained silent as she wrote the date and time and then looked up at the Hawkins, pen poised.

"Go ahead," George said.

"The face I saw," Sarah Hawkins stepped in. "I remember it. I mean, I remember it clearly now."

"The *demon*?" asked Ivy, her voice as dry as a desert.

"I was being melodramatic," Sarah said, nodding her head humbly. "I realise that now. It was a man. A youngish man. In his thirties or forties, I think."

"Do you have a description?" George asked.

"He had wild, unkempt hair. It was dark and slightly curly, or at least knotted. I couldn't tell. And his arms were wet."

"Wet?"

"They were shining."

"Shining?" George said, failing to hide the doubt in his voice. "Was he tall or short?"

"Five-eight," Sarah said promptly, then shuffled in her seat. "Give or take."

"That's quite specific, Mrs Hawkins," George said, and he tapped Ivy's hand for her to stop writing. "I'm sure you'll appreciate that I'm wondering why you failed to tell us all this at the time?"

"I was in shock," she said, looking George in the eye, unblinking. "I needed a few days to process it all. To reflect on what I saw."

"And now you're sure, are you?" asked George.

"As sure as I can be."

George glanced at Ivy, who continued to stare at Sarah Hawkins as though she was a piece of artwork that Ivy failed to comprehend. She was fascinated but baffled by its meaning.

"I do have one question, Mrs Hawkins," Ivy said, to which the elder of the ladies glanced across at her. "Where were you on Sunday lunchtime?"

"Sunday lunchtime?"

"Yes. From eleven a.m. to one p.m.?"

"At the garage," Richard spoke up. "Checking up on our car. Your lot sent it over to a garage in Louth once they were done inspecting it. Will take a few days yet. Needs a new bonnet and windscreen. As you can imagine, it was quite the..." Richard ended his rambling when he caught Ivy's inpatient stare. He pulled his phone out of his pocket. "I have a confirmation email from the garage if you want to see it?"

"That won't be– "

But Ivy cut George off with a brisk, "Yes, please," and held out her hand.

Richard took half a minute to find the email on his phone and then handed it to Ivy. A quick scan of the screen clearly showed an appointment had been made for Sunday morning at 11 a.m., and a follow-up email that outlined the work that needed to be done on the car suggested well enough that they had indeed made their appointment.

Ivy handed back the phone dismissively. "Very well," was all she said.

George waited a few moments for Richard Hawkins to pocket his phone and to let the tension of the moment pass. Ivy's mistrust had electrified the air in the interview room like a storm cloud.

"I'll have to ask you to amend your original statement," George said eventually. "Are you willing to do that for us?"

"Yes, of course," Sarah said. "Anything to help."

"And you, Mr Hawkins? Is there anything you would like to tell us?"

"Ah, my eyesight has never been the same since I got sand in it on Skegness beach twenty years ago," he said with a nostalgic chuckle. At George's stoic expression, he continued, "I can't say I saw anything, no."

"Alright, Mr– "

"But I'll tell you one thing, Inspector Larson," Richard Hawkins interrupted. "I trust my wife with my life. If Sarah says she saw a man of that description, then she did." He tapped the table with an index finger as though the words in Ivy's notebook were spread out on the surface of it like Scrabble tiles. "Trust me," he said with a wink aimed at George. "The woman is always right."

Sarah squeezed his arm affectionately.

"Very well," George said, pushing his chair back. "I'll send an officer down to take your new statement, Mrs Hawkins. If you could just wait in here for now."

He stood from the table, and Ivy followed his movements, flipping her notebook closed with a snap. But before he could leave, Sarah Hawkins reached across the table and grabbed his wrist. Her grip was surprisingly strong.

"I was wrong to say he was a demon," she said. "He was a man, like any other."

George snatched his wrist from her hands and glared at her.

"Like you said," he added. "You were emotionally charged, shall we say?"

"We all have our demons, Inspector. And this man's demons were strong. The strongest I've ever seen." Then she leaned forward and whispered, as her husband watched on with concern, "He had the devil in his eyes."

CHAPTER TWENTY-TWO

"How'd it go?" asked Ivy to Byrne, who walked through the incident room and over to the whiteboard around which Campbell, George, and Ivy were concentrating their efforts.

"I've updated Sarah Hawkins' statement like you asked." Byrne slumped down at his desk at the back of the room. "She says she saw a man, gaunt, scruffy, with messy, long hair, about five-foot-eight, and thirty to forty years old–"

"Devil in his eyes?"

"Yeah," Byrne said, shuffling uncomfortably. "She did mention that too."

"Not sure how that'll hold up in court," Campbell chipped in.

"I'd be embarrassed to submit it to the CPS," Ivy said. "Anyway, a jury will want to know why she changed her statement."

"For God's sake, she needed time to process it," George said. "It's not unusual for witnesses to remember details a few days later after the event."

"Sure, it's not unusual," Ivy said. "But it's also unreliable. I mean, there's the misinformation effect. She's probably talked it over with her husband and added the details to her own version of events in which case, it's likely to be dismissed as evidence."

"Her husband told us he didn't see anything," George said. "I doubt he influenced her memory if he didn't even see the man."

Ivy paused before answering and looked at George for a few seconds, trying to work out his intentions. When she could not, she asked him outright, "Why are you defending her?"

George pushed off the desk on which he was leaning in order to pace in front of the whiteboard. "I'm not defending her, Ivy. But she's a witness, and we should at least consider her testimony, even if we don't believe it. Christ, I've had enough arguments for one day. If I'm honest, I was glad to get out of there on good terms."

"Guv, come on. We can't take her seriously."

"I think you're allowing your religious bias to blind you, Ivy," he said in that frustratingly stoic manner of his. "If we do take Sarah Hawkins seriously, then we have a suspect lead for the first time in this investigation."

"A man with the devil in his eyes? Hardly something to go on, guv."

"Sarah Hawkins uses religious language where we might not, but the meaning is the same. It's a matter of linguistics, not reliability. Imagine a witness told us that a suspect had a dark stare or a wild look in his eyes; would you take them seriously?"

"I..." Ivy faltered.

She had heard witnesses use that exact phrase more times than she could count. But something about Sarah Hawkins' demeanour had unsettled her. How could they trust the word of a woman who fervently believed in things that could not be seen? Who lived her life according to what she had faith in rather than what she could prove? To follow the testimony of such a woman would be to rely on someone whose way of life directly opposed the goals of a police investigation – to find facts, not faith.

"Wild, dark, unkempt hair?" George continued, taking Ivy's silence as an answer. "Shiny arms? That's who Sarah described. Sound like someone familiar?"

"Shiny arms?"

"Scars," George said. "They're smooth. They shine."

Ivy sighed, defeated. "Adrian Samson."

"Adrian Samson," George confirmed, circling the man's name on the board.

"Speaking of," Campbell said, looking through the file of notes she always seemed to keep in a neat pile on her lap. "We got a call from Katy. Lab work shows no relation between Dean Worthing and Adrian Samson."

George turned to face her, a visible expression of shock on his face. "None?"

"Nada," Campbell confirmed.

"So, they're not brothers?" George confirmed.

"No, guv."

"Just because they're not related, doesn't mean they're not brothers," Byrne said with surprising wisdom. "I mean, didn't you say Dean was fostered?"

"True," Ivy said, raising her eyebrows with respect to Byrne's insight. "Maybe they grew up together?"

But she could see on George's face that he did not buy it. He frowned and twitched his head in a subtle shake as though confirming to himself that was not the case.

"You said Adrian's not in the book, right, guv?" she said. "Dean's memoir?"

""No, he's not," George said. "Not yet, anyway."

"So, they could've met later? Lived in the same house as teenagers?"

"Why are we assuming they didn't meet each other as adults?" Campbell added, and the look on her face made it clear she was eager to move on from accepting stories from a book as truth in an investigation. "I mean, there are infinite ways they might have met. Through work, through friends." She paused as though a thought had only just struck her. "Through dating."

This theory gripped the group's attention.

"They were lovers?" asked Ivy.

"Maybe," Campbell said. "I'm just saying, just because they weren't related, doesn't mean they didn't care about each other. Dean might have been looking out for Adrian for any number of reasons."

"Well, we're assuming still," Ivy said, "that Dean was actually looking out for Adrian. Derek McGuinness seemed to think someone was trapped in Dean's house. Maybe he was right. Maybe Dean was keeping Adrian there without his consent."

"Dean's scars, remember?" George inputted. "The same scars as Adrian's. That's their connection. That's why we think they grew up together."

"But we can't be sure, guv?"

"No," he conceded. "We can't. Look, we're throwing around a lot of maybes," George said.

"Let's get back to the facts. Campbell, anything else from the lab?"

"Yes," she replied, with a glint in her eye as though saving the more interesting revelation for last. She paused for a moment of drama and then said, "We sent Katy Southwell some of the soiled clothing from the house."

"Right, so?"

"There's a match to the traces of DNA they found on the coat Dean was wearing when he died."

"Adrian Samson?" George said. "Next time you withhold any nuggets of information like that, I want to know, alright?"

"Boss," she replied, still pleased with her efforts.

Ivy, however, shrugged at the news. "Well, that makes sense. If they were living in the same house, their DNA would have crossover."

"Sure," Byrne said. "It would also make sense if Adrian pushed Dean off the tower."

"Yes," George replied, but he looked only at Ivy. "Yes, it would."

It was Byrne who broke the thoughtful silence that followed.

"So?" he said, looking between George and Ivy. "That's it? We arrest Adrian Samson?"

"No," Ivy said before George could answer, and she avoided the sharp stare he sent her way.

"We don't have enough to go on. We don't have a motive for one thing. What are we going to do, drag an addict from his hospital bed and expect him to come clean? Come on."

"We have his DNA on the victim and a witness testimony that places a man of his description at the scene of the crime," George replied. "It's enough to bring him in for questioning, Ivy."

"Well, wait," Campbell said. "Speaking of the whole misinformation effect, what if the Hawkins were at the church on Sunday morning? What if Sarah saw Adrian Samson there and combined that event with her memory of Saturday night?"

George looked at Ivy for an answer, and she once more admitted defeat with a sigh.

"No," Ivy said, "I thought the same. I asked the Hawkins where they were on Sunday morning, and they could prove they were at a garage in Louth to get an update on the car that was damaged by Dean Worthing's body."

"What proof?"

"An email," Ivy said. "A confirmation of their appointment and a follow-up email later that day."

"Well, I could call the garage if you like?" Campbell said. "Get a confirmation that they definitely were there?"

This time, it was Ivy who looked to George, whose turn it was to sigh with defeat. "Alright," he said. "Let's confirm that the Hawkins definitely didn't see Adrian at the church on Sunday and, therefore, didn't let his image taint their memory of the night before."

He was clearly trying to find the right balance between allowing his team to voice their opinions and progressing the investigation, but his patience was wearing thin.

"And then we bring Adrian in?" Byrne said, his voice somewhere between excitement at the action and nervousness at the memory of the last time he had been required to arrest a suspect. In that case, he had ended up with a bleeding nose and a bruised ego.

"Yes," George said firmly. "But first, there's one more person I want to talk to."

He turned to Campbell, who, as she so often seemed to be, was one step ahead and already writing an address on a pad of paper, which she ripped off. "Thirteen Tetford Hill," she said, handing George the slip of paper and sitting back in her seat. "Home address of one Juliet Shaw."

CHAPTER TWENTY-THREE

Juliet Shaw's house was a perfectly symmetrical, white cottage tucked away off Tetford Hill with a triangular porch, two downstairs windows, and two upstairs windows each with dormers that gave the impression of a raised-eye, browed smiley face. The two identical chimneys on either side of the roof added ears to the image.

George pulled onto the driveway and stopped the car just behind the red Mazda convertible he recognised from the previous Saturday night. Its front bumper was low to the ground, and once more, George wondered how it managed to navigate the sharp bends, countryside debris, and the Wolds' often flooded dips.

The springtime sun was beginning to set, and just as he had the previous evening, George thought about Dean Worthing and the sunset he must have witnessed on top of St Leonard's Church before his untimely death. Following the ebbing shadows of light up the driveway, George and Ivy came to stand outside Juliet Shaw's ornate, wooden front door, where he knocked twice.

After a few seconds, they heard footsteps and the door was opened by a tall, slim, blonde woman, approximately thirty years old, with bright, blue eyes. George imagined that by day, her slight panda eyes and puffy cheeks would be well-hidden and contoured by expertly applied makeup. But she looked settled for the evening. Her blonde hair was tied into a messy bun on top of her head, and she wore grey joggers with cosy, oversized socks and a faded Nottingham University t-shirt. Completing the modern woman's look of domestic leisure was the brimming glass of red wine in her hand.

"Can I help you?" she said, as cautiously as a woman living alone greets two strangers on her doorstep.

"Good evening," George said. "I'm Inspector Larson, and this is my colleague, Sergeant Hart. Are you Juliet Shaw?

"I am?" she replied, with evidence suspicion.

"We were hoping for a quick word?" George explained. "It won't take long."

"Oh," Juliet said, relaxing in the face of authority. "Of course, come in."

She opened the door and stepped to one side, inviting them to follow. Inside was well-ordered and neat, which might have been the result of an interior designer. Either that or many an hour spent in Dunelm.

She led them to a spotless living room with a carpet so soft it could have been fur. Everything seemed to have a place, from the perfectly positioned cushions on the sofa to the labelled photo albums on the sideboard shelves. On one wall was a chic neon sign that glowed with the words *This Is My Happy Place*.

"Can I get you anything?" she asked, taking a seat on a shell-shaped, purple chair and glancing self-consciously at the wine in her hand. "Tea?"

"No, thank you," George said as he and Ivy settled on the yellow sofa. "We won't keep you long. We just wanted to talk to you about your boss– "

"Dean?" she said, her face lighting up. "Is he alright?"

George and Ivy shared a glance. It was both of their least

favourite part of the job, telling someone that a loved one, even a colleague or neighbour, had died, or possibly been killed. In order to avoid the awkward situation of neither George nor Ivy knowing who should break the news, it was Ivy who usually stepped in at this point.

"Miss Shaw," she started, leaning forward to subconsciously prepare the woman for a serious moment. "I'm sorry to tell you that Dean Worthing's body was discovered on Saturday night."

Juliet did not react at first. She simply stared at Ivy's face in shock until she whispered, ever so quietly, "What?"

"He was found outside St Leonard's Church in South Ormsby," she said, and George searched Juliet's face for any recognition of the place but found only a continuation of shock.

"It appears he...fell from the church tower."

Juliet shook her head, a reaction George had seen hundreds of times to the news of death. "I don't...I don't understand...He... *Dean?*"

"I'm afraid so."

Juliet no longer seemed to be self-conscious of the wine in her hand. Indeed, she clutched it like a security blanket before taking a huge swig that emptied half the glass.

"Juliet," George continued, trying to bring her out of the shell into which she was about to hide and close shut, "you work for Dean. Is that right? What's your job role?"

"I'm his...erm, his PA," she said, stumbling over her words, her eyes darting back and forth across the floor as though still processing the news.

"And what does that entail exactly?" George said, playing to his old-man mannerisms. "Forgive me. I've been a police officer my whole life. I'm not well-versed in the day-to-day of business workings."

"I'm his personal assistant. I do administrative tasks, organise his schedule, make calls on his behalf, book meetings, that kind of thing."

"For his business? Worthing Media?"

"Sometimes," she said. "But it's mostly his personal life. Like, I helped when he moved house a few months ago. And I help organise his writing schedule, notifying him of deadlines, communicating with the publisher, that kind of thing. So, he can just focus on writing."

"He writes romance fiction, is that right?"

"Yes," Juliet said, nodding. "Gay romance mostly. He's written a few series."

She was answering but still retreating, her skin pale. So, George switched tact.

"I see," George said. "And tell me, does the name Adrian Samson mean anything to you?"

The sound of Adrian's name pulled Juliet Shaw from her shell, and she turned to face George with wet eyes. "Adrian?"

"Samson. Yes."

"Yes, I...I know Adrian."

"He's a friend of Dean's?"

She frowned as though it was the first question to genuinely stump her. "I don't know really how they know each other."

"How do *you* know Adrian, Juliet?"

"Dean asked me to track him down," she said simply. "A few weeks ago. He gave me his name − Adrian Samson − and it was my job to find him. He didn't say why." She took another large sip of red wine. "And it wasn't easy, I can tell you. There was no record of him. I had to traipse around half of Lincoln before anyone even recognised the name. The dumps I went to, you wouldn't believe."

"Dumps like what?" asked George.

She puffed a breath out through her mouth. "Dodgy areas, you know? Places you wouldn't walk through at night. Bridges, random houses, car parks. Found him eventually in an abandoned warehouse down by the river."

"And is that part of your job description, Miss Shaw?" asked Ivy. "Tracking down a homeless man throughout Lincoln?"

"I do what Dean asks me to do," Juliet answered. "Asked..."
She stifled a sob but spoke through it. "That's my job. Being there
for him, whatever he needs."

"Did he say why? Why did he want you to find Adrian?"

She shrugged. "No, I don't know. He didn't say why. He just
told me to find him and say that Dean wanted to help. He told me
to invite Adrian to stay with him at his new house."

"His new house?" asked George, feigning ignorance.

"Yeah," she said, sniffing back her emotions, which were
settling now. "He bought it a few months ago. It's down in South
Ormsby. Bluestone Lodge."

"Why did Dean need a new house?"

"He didn't need it. He had an apartment in Lincoln. Nice
place at the top of Steep Hill. But he said he needed somewhere
quieter to write from." She frowned at her soft, furry carpet as
though the image of Dean's apartment stirred specific memories.

"I'll be honest with you, Miss Shaw," George said, wanting to
bring Juliet back into the room and the reality of her situation as
harshly as possible. "I saw your car by the church on Saturday
night, only half an hour after Dean died." Juliet's mouth formed a
perfect *O,* but she didn't rush to deny it. "What were you doing in
the area?"

Soon enough, her expression developed from shock into fury.
"You cannot possibly be suggesting– "

"Do you know how police investigations work, Miss Shaw?"
asked George calmly.

"I...you...yes, of course I do."

"First, we must eliminate those closest to the victim as
suspects. To do this, we must establish where those people were
at the time of the victim's death. It's purely routine, I can assure
you."

"Right," she said.

"So, if you can provide an explanation for where you were at the time of Dean's death, we can rule you out of the investigation."

"Provided, of course," added Ivy, "that it can be backed up by an alibi or evidence."

"Of course," George said and then turned back to Juliet Shaw, allowing her the chance to fill the silence that followed.

"I went to Dean's house," she said through gritted teeth. "To Bluestone Lodge."

"Why?"

"He'd asked me to do something. But when I got there, he wasn't there."

"Miss Shaw," Ivy said, leaning forward, "Inspector Larson has just explained how important it is to rule you out of our investigation, so if you would so kind as to offer us some *details* in your explanation– "

"He wanted to give me the manuscript he'd been working on," she spat at Ivy. "He told me to meet him at the house so he could hand it to me. But I was running late, okay? I was busy. I practically manage the whole bloody company at this point, and I'm at his beck and call. I was only thirty minutes late, but he'd already left, I guess, to..."She rubbed her face aggressively. "God only knows why he was in such a rush, why he couldn't have waited another thirty minutes to kill himself, for Christ's sake. It's not like he was on a deadline."

She went to take another desperate sip of wine but realised her glass was empty, and she threw her hand up in despair as though the glass was useless to her in its current state.

"What time were you supposed to meet Dean at his house?"

"Six-thirty," she said. "But I got there at seven."

"And does Dean often hand you his manuscripts?"

"Yes," Juliet said, quieter now as though having exhausted herself. "He writes everything on his typewriter. It's like a ritual to him, something therapeutic about the sound, I don't know.

Anyway, there's always the risk of any digital manuscript being pirated. And this one especially, he said, had to be protected."

"And the publisher is alright with that, are they?"

"They're used to it," Juliet said. "It's his little eccentricity, Dean's typewriter-written manuscripts. Let's just say they put up with it. Dean's books are good enough to make it worth it for them."

"Was anybody at the house?" asked Ivy. "When you arrived at, what?" She looked at George for confirmation. "Seven p.m. on Saturday?" He nodded. "Was Adrian home?"

Juliet laughed. "You haven't met Adrian, have you?"

George and Ivy didn't reply.

"He's not exactly reliable. Look, I knocked. I looked through the windows. Even if he was home, he wouldn't have answered the door. But I don't know; he might have been there. He might have been whacked out on God knows what. He might have just been ignoring me. I waited for at least an hour on the drive in case Dean came home."

"Then you left?"

"Yes," Juliet said, her voice thick with regret. "I figured I'd see Dean today anyway and get it from him then."

"And do you have anyone to corroborate this, Miss Shaw?" asked Ivy.

She waved an arm around the living room. "I live alone. No, okay? If Adrian was home, he would have heard me knocking. You can ask him."

"We will," George said, standing. "Thank you, Miss Shaw."

Ivy stood beside him and offered a curt nod to Juliet on the way out. But before they could leave, Juliet spoke up, clearly with more to say.

"Inspector?" she said, her big, wet eyes suddenly focused like a laser through water. "If you go to the house, please let me know. Let me take the manuscript. It was important to Dean. It cannot fall into the wrong hands."

"The wrong hands?" Ivy said. "It's a book."

"Dean has written many books, Miss Shaw," George said, rephrasing Ivy's comment more gently. "Why was this one so special?"

"I don't know. It's his life story, I guess?" She sighed. "Look, I know, I don't really get it either. But it was important to him. The way he talked about it, like it was a ticking time bomb or something. I didn't understand how important it was to him. Making sure it was published. But if what you say is true, then it was his dying wish. I see that now."

"He trusted you with it?" George said. "More than anyone else?"

"Yes."

"More than Adrian?"

Juliet laughed. "God, yes." She stepped forward. "You will let me know if you find it, won't you?"

George was not a man who enjoyed lying, and he did not plan to do so. Instead, he simply looked into Juliet's eyes and offered a nod to Ivy that it was time to leave, then said, "We'll be in touch, Miss Shaw,' he said. "If I were you, I wouldn't plan any trips away."

CHAPTER TWENTY-FOUR

"Don't you think it's a little convenient, guv," Ivy said, as soon as they climbed into George's car, "that Juliet's only alibi on the night Dean died is Adrian? The junkie who can't say two words before having a meltdown?"

"Maybe," George said.

"Maybe?"

"I saw her too, remember?" George said. "A good half-an-hour after Dean died. If she did somehow push him off the tower, what was she doing for the next half an hour? Driving around?"

Ivy processed the logic and offered only a quiet, "Hmmm."

They sat watching the house for a few seconds until a curtain in the living room twitched as though Juliet was anxious as to why they hadn't left. George had no desire to torture the girl. He might not one hundred per cent trust her, but there was little yet to point to her as a suspect. Turning the engine on, he reversed out of the drive and back onto Tetford Hill, turning left back towards the station.

"Something she did say stuck with me, though," George said. "About Dean being on a deadline."

"What do you mean?"

"Well, she's right. Why didn't he just wait half an hour? If Juliet was running late on Saturday night to meet him, why didn't he just wait and hand her the manuscript, if it was so important to him, at seven p.m. instead of six-thirty?"

Ivy paused, pondering the question.

"When I was studying, I took a sociology class on suicide." She looked at George's raised eyebrows. "Dark, I know, but it was kind of fascinating, about strain theory, anti-suicide laws, all that. Anyway, in some of the case studies, survivors talked about planning it for weeks, months even. They planned their last meals, saying goodbye to loved ones, where and, when and why, down to the last detail. Many suicides are spontaneous, sure. But some are *meticulously* planned. If Dean had decided to commit suicide at seven-thirty p.m. on Saturday, then that exact time and date might have seemed immovable. Maybe he thought that if he didn't do it then, the moment would pass, and he might change his mind."

It was George's turn to stay quiet, thinking.

"That's awful," he said eventually.

"Yes," Ivy said, looking out of the window at the stunning beauty of the Wolds. "It is."

"So, you believe her?" asked George.

"Well," Ivy said with a grin, "I wouldn't go that far."

The sun set quickly behind the thick clouds, turning the sky a low, dimming purple, casting a lilac glow over the meandering dips of the Wolds, turning the dips of the road to tenebrious holes and chocolate-box houses to shadowy outlines. The day was coming to a close.

George leaned forward to tap a name on the car's phone console so that it rang through the speaker. "Let's give the kids an early night, shall we?" he muttered.

The call rang five times before Byrne's somewhat laissez-faire voice answered. "PC Byrne?" he said as though it was a question.

"Hello, PC Byrne, it's DI Larson."

George could hear a scuffle over the line as though Byrne was making an effort to sit up straight. "Alright, guv?" he said. "How'd it go with Juliet Shaw?"

"It went alright, thank you. How's it going with you?" asked George, copying Byrne's casual language playfully.

"Just typing up Sarah Hawkins' new statement, guv, and Campbell's working on Adrian's file."

"Well," George said, "finish up, then take yourselves home. We'll reconvene in the morning."

"Really, guv?" Byrne said, sounding like a little kid who'd been told he could leave for playtime earlier than usual.

George had been pushing them hard recently, he realised. He doubted they had worked many weekends in their small police station on the edge of the Wolds, but since he had come to town, he had asked his team to work two in one month and to zero complaints.

"Yes, Byrne. Get an early night. Bright and early tomorrow."

"I'll pass on the message to Campbell."

"You do that."

"Goodnight, guv."

George hesitated. He wondered if he realised how boyish he sounded in moments like these or if he was simply shameless. "Goodnight, Byrne."

"Nighty-night, Byrne," called Ivy over the phone. But this time, Byrne only replied with an embarrassed-sounding mumble and hung up rather quickly. "That boy," Ivy said, shaking her head. "I know he's entertaining, but seriously... Are you still sure about him, guv?"

George took the turning onto Tetford Road towards the station.

"I am," George said, at least less hesitantly than since the last time Ivy had asked him that question a couple of weeks ago. "He's stepping up, don't you think?"

"He's doing fine," she said. "He hasn't screwed up, at least. But he lacks…" She struggled to find the right word. "Maturity. Self-confidence. The ability to use initiative, enough steam to just work on something without needing to be asked."

"That comes from experience, Ivy, you know that."

"Exactly." She paused as though unwilling to dismiss any member of the little team that they had gathered here in this new place. "I just wonder if there isn't anyone else in the Wolds who might be better suited to investigations. We haven't even spoken to any of the other officers, let alone vetted them. What if there's another Campbell at the station whose talents we aren't using?"

George grimaced. He had to admit that she was right. His decision to bring Byrne onto the team had been a hunch at the most. He supposed he'd rather someone inexperienced and malleable than experienced and arrogant. Over forty years on the force, he'd worked with plenty of the latter and was in no rush to do so again.

"Let's give him a chance," George said. "See how he goes."

"Alright, guv," Ivy said. "I like the lad; you know I do. It's just…
"

"I get it," he said. "He's got some proving himself to do, I agree. Let's just see."

They left it at that as George swung into the police station car park and parked, not in his favourite spot, but right next to Ivy's car, saving her the walk across the pot-holed tarmac. He turned off the engine, letting it groan into silence.

"Heading home?" he asked, as though double-checking.

"Yeah," Ivy said. "Hattie's got this big piano recital on Wednesday. I said I'd help her practice."

George laughed. "I didn't know you played piano?"

She shrugged. "I did when I was younger. Now I can play it as well as a seven-year-old. You've really just got to stay one lesson ahead of the kid, guv."

He laughed. "Good tactic."

"Yeah, well, she really just wants me to watch her anyway. Give her some attention." She paused. "I guess I haven't been doing much of that recently."

George wasn't sure what to say. He thought it was better to just stay quiet and listen rather than throw out another clichéd response. He and Grace had never had kids. Parenthood was one part of a marriage about which he could offer little advice anyway.

"What about you, guv?" Ivy said, seeming willing to change the subject. "What will you do tonight?"

George pretended to think about it. He supposed he could take at least the evening off work, give his mind a break from the investigation, and continue his development of the house. Perhaps start on the kitchen? But deep down, he knew that the book on his coffee table would be too hard to resist.

He smiled heavily and decided to be as honest as Ivy had been.

"I've got some reading to do."

CHAPTER TWENTY-FIVE

As the tangerine glow of the fading day stretched across his living room walls, George savoured the moment he sat back in his plush, leather sofa and rubbed his eyes until little, colourful dots akin to fireflies on a night sky took flight across his retina. He had barely caught a break all day. It had been one thing after the next, each seeming to bring its own puzzles to the mystery. Surely, they were collecting more questions than answers. But now, at last, he was home.

Home, he repeated in his mind. He thought that was the first time he had called it such, even to himself, rather than the Bag Enderby house or Grace's parents' house. *Home* would take some getting used to, but getting used to it, he clearly was.

He continued to press his palms against his eyelids, enjoying the dreamy display of dancing dots that were beginning to form faces like a pointillism painting − of Freddo, of Paddy, and of Juliet, as though they too had merely been tricks of light. He opened his eyes, unsure who to trust. At least one of them knew more than they were willing to share or were, perhaps, sharing information that he should take with a pinch of salt. After forty-odd years on the job, George thought he should probably know how to spot deceit by now, but unfortunately, it was no easy task; even veterans had lapses of judgment.

He reached for the crystal whisky decanter at his elbow and poured himself a generous measure of the Talisker. Taking a long sip, he closed his eyes to savour the burn, an enjoyable pain similar, he supposed, to the pain people experience when getting tattoos. There was a reason he was faithful to this specific whisky. He and Grace had travelled to the sea-soaked, white-housed distillery on the Isle of Skye one cold, blue September weekend. The taste alone reminded George of his wife's red cheeks, her chin tucked beneath a burnt-orange scarf, and the view from that distillery window of foggy, jagged spurs, so breathtaking it seemed as though the gods themselves had carved the mountains with a loving, skillful hand. Soon enough, Grace's face formed amongst the colourful dots on the blackness, laughing, her dying spark merging with the other mysteries in his life until George had to force his eyes open in order to flee the memories swarming his mind.

Then George did what so many people do when they crave an escape; he turned to the book at his side and placed it onto his lap, opening the page from which he had left off.

But this was no work of fiction or bedtime story.

He felt like he was getting to know the man with each turned page – his life, his trauma, his childhood. And it was a far from easy read.

———

It was not that every day in South Ormsby was filled with fear, cruelty, and punishment. It was simply that any day could have been. The best days were when we could go to school. Our teachers were kind. Not kind enough to look closer at the bruises that protruded from our shirt sleeves and shorts. But still, kind enough not to make them worse. At school, we could run and jump and play in the playground. We could do normal schoolboy things as though we were indeed normal schoolboys. We could be like everyone else for a short while.

But we kept to ourselves. After all, we had learned from an early age that anyone outside of our family was not to be trusted. Of course, we missed many days of school - lost days spent in the stone-walled cellar. Sometimes just one of us, sometimes all three. But on one rare Tuesday summer morning, all of us were allowed to go to school, so long, of course, as we did not misbehave.

Even though there were only a few years between us, Samuel was by far the smallest of us three boys. James was the biggest. I was awaiting a growth spurt, but when it came, I would surpass even James in height and become the tallest boy in my class. But Samuel, his slender wrists never did seem to grow, not since he was a toddler. I remember, so many times, grabbing one of those wrists in moments of fear or action, and every single time I did, I'd be afraid that it would snap in my hands. For someone as delicate as a porcelain doll, I have no idea how he lasted so long.

On one particular Tuesday, James, Samuel, and I were playing marbles in our favourite corner of the schoolyard, shaded beneath a tree, far away from the other boys who took up most of the yard with their football game, when Billy Jones walked over. Billy Jones... How could one describe Billy Jones? He was one of those tall, wide kids with the characteristics of a cartoon bully – a thick head, large, boisterous limbs, and small eyes that resembled two raisins pressed into a piece of dough.

In a flash, he grabbed Samuel's oh-so-delicate wrist and shook him back and forth as though it was a rag doll, forcing the marbles from his hand and into Billy's palm. I remember it now, the glare of the sunlight on the Neptune-blue marble, falling through the sky like a crashing planet. I, of course, was the first to stand. But not to defend Samuel, you see – to flee. That was my well-developed coping mechanism: to run at the first chance of trouble, remove myself from a situation, and escape.No, it was James who stood slowly and purposefully, widening his stance, planting his feet, ready. He was the fighter. He always had been. Just as Samuel had always been the freezer, the deer in headlights, the one hoping that if he stood still long enough, everyone would just forget that he was there at all.

And with a single well-placed right hook, James punched Billy Jones in the face. He fell to the ground like a sack of Maris Pipers, where he writhed in pain, clutching his nose. It was far too powerful a punch for a child. But after all, James was used to defending himself against much stronger adults.

The incident meant that James got in trouble with the teachers. Of course, he did. Five licks of the paddle. But it was nothing compared to the trouble he endured when he was sent home with a note. He was suspended for two weeks, and I cannot imagine a more horrific punishment than to spend two whole weeks alone outside the safety of school. Samuel and I were punished, too, though not nearly to the same extent as James. We were all kept in the cellar that night, without food, without water, but in the morning, when that fateful door at the top of the stairs opened, Samuel and I could leave. James remained, cowering in the corner for the next two weeks. I didn't want to leave him. Of course, I didn't. But to this day, I cannot resist an open door, a way out, if it is offered to me.

That morning, they brought chains to punish James, and as they walked downstairs, they swung them like thuribles, like we would see at church, back and forth, back and forth, while chanting. It's hard to know how many voices constitute a chant. Maybe they were just speaking, but it sounded like a chant to me. That day, it was the verse from Proverbs:

"My son, do not despise the Lord's discipline, and do not resent his rebuke, because the Lord disciplines those he loves, as a father the son he delights in."

Their movements were synchronised, as were their words, and I remember feeling sick at the thought that they might have rehearsed before giving this performance, putting on a show only for James, only to heighten his fear before the inevitable.

Those were the longest two weeks of my life..

After that day, James was never the same. At the end of the two weeks, we found the door to the cellar open, but he was still huddled in the corner, shaking and wet like a half-drowned dog. The lashes had torn the shirt from his back, and it hung in tatters around his trembling shoulders.

It feels obvious to me now why they were so hard on him. James had shown an ability to fight back. He had displayed strength against bullying. He had performed an act of resistance. We were growing fast, at that point, developing before their eyes, from boys into men. In a few short years, we would be their size, meeting them eye to eye, able to defend ourselves. But the punishment was effective. James never fought back again. Instead, he retreated into himself, preoccupied, from then on, with only the strength to fight his own demons.

As for me, I continued fleeing. And Samuel, well, he would soon become frozen in time.

CHAPTER TWENTY-SIX

George was often preoccupied with the tasks of the day during his morning drive. Which of his team would be best suited to which task? Which of the tasks were most important to him? And conversely, which were the most important to Tim?

It was a process of creating to-do lists on the blank canvas of his mind. But today, his thoughts were far less practical, and the canvas was far from blank. It contained a myriad of images, colourful and clear, as though life, like light, was being filtered through a prism. Something about the way Dean Worthing expressed himself in his memoir had filtered through into George's perception of the world. The blue-hued edges of the clouds reminded him of the glare on the marble that had been shaken from Samuel's hand. The smooth, black tarmac of the road contrasted the rugged sandstone walls of the cellar. And the long grass that he drove beside reminded him of the freedom Dean expressed in the few-and-far-between days when Dean, James, and Samuel had played in the long, grassy fields outside their house.

George wasn't one to read literary fiction. He preferred historical memoirs and biographies, mostly concerning the twentieth-century wars, the division of Europe, the rise of fascism, and the forces that held it at bay. They were often logical, date-heavy, and objective texts, not dissimilar to a police report. Dean's memoir was one of the few creative pieces of writing he had read since he attended school, and he was surprised to find how the prose had stuck with him in a way that other books did not.

Therefore, when George pulled into the police station car park, entered the building, walked up the fire escape stairs to the first-floor corridor, and stepped over the squeaky floorboard into the incident room, he strode straight over to the whiteboard before he'd even set his bag down, and in the top right-hand corner, he wrote two names.

"James and Samuel?" Byrne read aloud. "Who are they?"

The team had arrived before him and had already settled into their usual positions, Byrne and Campbell at their desks with notebooks open and ready, and Ivy with her arms crossed leaning on a desk in between the two PCs and George's spot at the whiteboard.

"That's what we're going to find out," George said, avoiding Campbell's narrowing eyes. He clicked the lid back on the pen to signify that the names were the day's focus. "Boys from Dean's childhood."

"How do you know–" Byrne started.

"I read about them in Dean Worthing's memoir," he stated, looking up to meet Campbell's stare. "There's another. He mentions him early on, but there's no name. I get the impression it's an older boy."

"What happened to him?"

"He got away," George said. "Unlike Dean and these two."

"So, they're book characters," she said.

"No, they're his brothers."

"Guv–"she started.

"These were significant people in Dean Worthing's life," George said, tapping their names with his pen far harder than he had meant to and causing some nearby officers to startle at their desks. "If they're still alive," he said, blinking away the image of James, shaking, traumatised, and beaten, like a – how had Dean described it? – like a half-drowned dog. "And that's a big *if*. Then there's no way Dean would have left them with nothing. We need to find them," George insisted. "They can shed more light on all of this."

Only then did he look to Ivy for her reaction. Although he saw the small ridge of a frown between her eyes, she nodded slowly in support. She looked tired, he noticed. The rings around her eyes were becoming deeper every day, more and more like a panda's. Despite her insistence that she and Jamie were communicating, George could only imagine that their relationship had bled through the Band-Aid by now and that it hung uselessly by failing glue.

"So, what else have we got?" asked George, turning to the team as one.

Putting their differences aside, Campbell spoke up. "The lab has been in touch overnight," she said. "In addition to Adrian's DNA being on Dean Worthing's coat, his DNA was also present on his body."

"Saliva?"

"Seems to be," she said. "Could have just been spittle, I suppose. If they were arguing, I mean. That happens, right?"

"It does," George agreed. "But the amount would be miniscule. Anything else?"

"The hospital report came through," Byrne said. "It confirms that Adrian had a significant amount of Methadone in his system. More than his prescribed dosage."

George had expected some kind of bickering between the two as each of them fought for the limelight. But the seamless takeover from Campbell's point without rebuttal was a pleasant surprise.

"Alright," he said. "That's all well and good. But it's nothing we didn't know already."

"I also called the garage, guv," Campbell said and turned to look at Ivy, who had been the one insistent on following up on where the Hawkins were on Sunday morning. "They were there. From 11:00 a.m. to 1:00 p.m., sorting out the car. There's no way they could have seen Adrian at the church that morning."

George watched Ivy's mouth contort into a grimace, but she gave a small nod in acceptance.

"So, the Hawkins didn't see Adrian at the church on Sunday morning, and therefore, he couldn't have influenced the change of their statements," George said, outlining what everybody knew.

"And there was no press?" Ivy tried. "No one posted a video that might have reached the Hawkins?"

"No press, guv," confirmed Campbell. "No one picked up the story. We could check socials, but it's a long shot that the Hawkins would have seen somebody post it on Instagram. I mean, they're practically prehistoric."

Ivy paused, clearly not appreciative of the sarcasm, but eventually, she gave another silent nod in defeat.

"Does that mean..."started Byrne.

"Yes," George confirmed before he could finish. "It means we're bringing Adrian Samson in." The team was silent for a moment, allowing this course of action to sink in. "Campbell, call the hospital. See if he's in a fit state to be discharged, will you?"

"He's in Hatton Ward," Ivy added, and George nodded a thanks.

She nodded once and set to work, looking up the phone number. In the meantime, George turned to Byrne. "Any update on the last will and testament?" he asked.

"Dean's?" he said, which triggered a snort from Ivy.

"No, Byrne, the Queen's. I hear it's being released to the public any day now," she said.

"Yes," Byrne said, flustered, turning back a few pages in his notebook. "As we guessed, the house has been left to Adrian. And his shares in the business..."He looked up. "Left to Juliet Shaw."

George hesitated. "Anyone else?"

"No, guv," Byrne said, killing George's hope and reading between the lines. "Nothing about a James or a Samuel, sorry."

"Right." George turned once more to face the whiteboard and added Juliet's name in a prominent space, outlining it with a large, red circle. "Tell me, Byrne," he said without turning around. "How many CEOs do you think leave their entire business to their personal assistant?"

"Like, a percentage? I'm not sure there's a statistic, guv."

Again, Ivy laughed and shook her head.

"Take a wild guess for me," George said.

"Well...not many, guv."

"No," George said. "Not many. In fact, I'd be inclined to say none at all."

It was Campbell's voice that caused George to spin around. She had the phone pressed to her collarbone as though she was still on the line. "He's still at the hospital, guv, but about to be discharged."

"Good. Tell them to hang tight and ask Sergeant Robson if he can send a couple of uniformed officers to bring him in."

"I'll go," Ivy said, standing up and muttering something about the need to stretch her legs. George watched her leave the room, unsure of her motivation for accepting such a menial task.

Campbell finished her call with the hospital and strode over to the whiteboard, absorbing the latest addition.

"How did you get on with Juliet Shaw?" she asked. "Anything we should know?"

"We did," George said, and as he relayed their conversation from the day before, he added the main points to the board around her name. *Dean's PA. Spotted around eight-fifteen p.m. Was supposed to collect the manuscript.*

"Do you trust her, guv?" Byrne said pointedly, and George

glanced over his shoulder at the young officer. "I mean, how did she seem?"

George thought about it. He remembered the tears rolling down her cheeks and falling into her wine glass. "Devastated," he said.

"But that doesn't really tell us anything, does it?"

"It tells us she's either truly devastated or she's a fantastic actress," George said. "But at the moment, it could be either. The jury is out, as they say." Once more, George was drawn to the two names in the corner of the board, like a strong tide pulling at his limbs. It felt somewhat strange to see the two names he had read so many times in *The Unholy Truths* written on the board, as if they were coming to life.

"Any updates from the boy's home?" he asked.

"Absolutely nothing, guv," Campbell said with disappointment in her voice. "These paper files are damn near impossible to track down. Nothing was digitised. You know what it was like back then."

"I do, do I?" George said, turning to her with raised eyebrows.

Her cheeks flushed, and she started to sputter before recognising the humour in George's eyes. "Oh, you know what I mean."

Once more, George looked to the whiteboard for answers, resisting the two names in the corner. He couldn't very well ask Byrne and Ivy to search for two relatively common names in a sea of people. He pushed against the tide to stare, instead, at the largest circled name in the middle of the board. *Adrian Samson.*

"Put everything we have on Adrian in a file," George said, turning his back on the two magnetised names, ready to leave the incident room before he changed his mind. "And meet me in interview room one. I'll be downstairs."

CHAPTER TWENTY-SEVEN

When George pushed open the doors to the custody suite, Ivy was still there leaning on the desk, speaking with Sergeant Robson, who also leaned on the desk, his dark, curly hair flopping over his eyes. The man must have been at least thirty-five, George seethed, old enough to get a haircut. When he heard the squeak of the door and footsteps, he looked up to see George over Ivy's shoulder and stood up straight. Ivy turned and too adopted a more professional position.

"Guv," she said, and George noticed a tinge of surprise in her tone. "We were–"

"Have you sent somebody to pick up Adrian Samson?"

"I have, yes," said Robson through a grin, his green eyes sparkling. He was a charmer, some might say, but to George, the man lacked the professionalism to go much further. They all had ways to cope with the gravity of their jobs – tricks of the mind, humour, dissociation, even hobbies. Robson seemed to rely on flippancy, like one of those annoying individuals who cracked poor jokes when under stress. "They shouldn't be too long."

"Good. I want a cell and interview room one ready."

"All done, guv," he said, leaning his elbows on the counter once more. "Ready for guests."

George stared at the man's elbows in the same manner his father had stared at his elbows when he'd placed them on the table during Sunday dinner. "Maybe you should double-check, Sergeant."

Even Robson recognised the undertones in George's voice. The grin on his face dissipated, and he pushed off the counter. He nodded once at George and offered a shadow of a wink at Ivy before walking through the door towards the corridor of cells and interview rooms. To George's disappointment, he witnessed a schoolgirl flush spreading across Ivy's cheeks that faded as fast as it had emerged.

By the time she turned to face him, the usual shameless, hard-faced expression had returned, reminding George of a stubborn teenager when they know they've been caught.

"We need to prepare Samson's interview," he said coldly. "It's not going to be an easy one. There's a fine line to tread here between garnering information and pressurising a vulnerable individual."

"He'll need a duty solicitor," she replied as if the little interaction she had shared with Robson had never happened.

"Maybe an appropriate adult, too," George added. "The last thing I want is to lose the statement on a human rights technicality."

"We're all human, guv," she replied flatly.

He wasn't sure where his disappointment in her was rooted. He supposed he didn't like the idea of her keeping something from him, even a harmless flirt with the custody officer. But he knew that he had no leg to stand on, having been lying to her about the situation with Grace for weeks now. He was a man stuck in his ways, and despite the state of their marriage, Ivy still had a husband at home and two small children. It was inappropriate, he told himself; that's what it was. Yet he couldn't help but feel some kind of fatherly protection for her.

"Everything okay, guv?" she asked, leaning into his line of sight, breaking his stare.

"How are things with Jamie?" he asked, clearing his throat with a quick cough.

"Rubbish," she said, unblinking. "Difficult, uphill, pointless. Want me to go on?"

"What about the Band-Aid?"

Ivy didn't even bother to extend the metaphor. She merely scoffed.

"Are you separating?" he asked.

"No," she mumbled, shuffling her feet and adding. "Though I'm sure that would make him feel better."

"What do you mean?"

"Well, God only knows what he's up to when he says he's working late. Or who."

"Ivy, come on. It's Jamie, he wouldn't–"

She turned on him. "How do you know?" she said softly. "I don't even know. He doesn't talk to me, guv. He doesn't tell me anything. How would I know what he's up to?"

"And what are *you* up to, Ivy?" George said, nodding at the door through which Sergeant Robson had walked. It came out of his mouth before he knew it, and he immediately regretted the accusation that had caused Ivy's expression to slide.

If Ivy had been entirely innocent, however, she wouldn't have allowed the silence to linger; she would have stormed out of the room at the insinuation. But instead, she stayed, glaring at George and gaping wordlessly. It was in that state that Campbell found them – staring each other out – when she burst through the doors to the custody suite with Adrian Samson's file in her hand.

Reading the room, she slowed and practically tiptoed up to George, holding out the file. "Everything on Adrian Samson, guv."

George kept his eyes fixed on Ivy's, which were starting to water. He held out his hand, and Campbell placed the file in it.

"What have we got?" he said, an open question to the two women.

"Visual ID from the witnesses Sarah and Richard Hawkins, who saw somebody fitting Adrian Samson fleeing the scene of the crime," Campbell said.

Finally, Ivy broke her eye contact with George, only to roll her eyes at the mention of the Hawkins' and their changed witness statement.

"Good," George replied, looking down at the job in hand, the file in his grip.

"DNA found on Dean Worthing's person and coat belonging to Adrian Samson," Campbell continued.

"Adrian Samson living in Dean Worthing's house." Ivy sighed, relenting to also return to the job. "And being in possession of Dean Worthing's manuscript."

"And a witness heard screaming the morning following Dean Worthing's death–"

"Ah," George said, cutting her off. "We don't know that was Adrian."

"But all signs point to–"

"We can't build a case on signs, Campbell," George said. "We need facts." He flicked through the papers in his hand, seeing the glaring mistakes, the missing pieces. "Get on to CSI. Send them to Bluestone Lodge. I want *proof* that Adrian was there–"

"We've got proof," Ivy said. "We sent the clothing if you remember–"

"We've got proof he was there. What I want is proof that he was *staying* there, and if we can prove it, then how long has been staying there? Does the timeline fit what Juliet Shaw told us?"

Campbell looked to Ivy for support and received a curt nod in response.

"We've also got the scream, guv," Campbell said.

"The howl, you mean?" George replied. "Tell me, Campbell. How would we prove that the delivery driver actually heard a howl, or a scream, or whatever it was? Is Derek McGuinness a reliable witness? Does he have previous?"

"You're not suggesting he could be part of all this?" Ivy said.

"No, I'm suggesting that, if he indeed has a criminal record, or if he's reported crimes in the past, then any defence lawyer would find it out and convince the jury he's not fit to stand trial."

"I see," Ivy replied and issued another nod at Campbell.

"I'll keep you posted," Campbell said, and with one final glance, as though hoping to read between the tension of George and Ivy, she left the room.

"Guv," began Ivy, and George expected her to close off their disagreement, apologise or defend herself to settle the matter. But instead, she stuck only to the job at hand. "The person Derek McGuinness heard screaming. If that wasn't Adrian, then who the hell was it?"

CHAPTER TWENTY-EIGHT

Ivy stared at the man across the interview room table. He reminded her of a wild man from an old children's fable, one she'd seen illustrated long ago in a book, along with wicked witches, wiley wolves, and wondrous elves. Adrian Samson's long, scraggly hair had become so matted it was verging on dreadlocks. He had at least changed from his hospital gown into his dingy t-shirt and shorts, which gave off a musty stench akin to a garbage heap on a summer's day. He sat in the chair, wound as a coiled spring, body tensed as though primed to launch into an attack or to defend himself if need be.

But the most capturing element of Adrian Samson were his wide and savage eyes. His stare darted between George and Ivy, laser-focused, but never resting for longer than a second or two. She hated to admit it, but she could see now, close up, how a religious woman might describe them as Sarah Hawkins had.

To his right, the duty solicitor, a snooty-looking man, peered over his frameless glasses at George and then down at his watch, his fountain pen never once seeming to cease his incessant scribbles.

To his left sat a far more endearing character. Jane May felt no obligation to take notes. She sat as if waiting for a train, her hands folded on her lap, her handbag by her feet. She wore a smart blouse with a tiny floral print. A heart-shaped locket hung from her neck, and her hair had been pulled into a no-fuss ponytail that rested on one shoulder. She was one of those women who despite being well into her middle-age, somehow managed to retain an element of youth. She wore a slight smile, the type borne from a life of innocence, and so she should, Ivy thought. As an appropriate adult, her role was merely to ensure Samson's vulnerability wasn't exploited.

It had been a shrewd move on George's behalf. Having initiated the request as the lead detective, any questions regarding his morality and ethical practice that might crop up during a potential trial could be well and truly snuffed before they took root in the jury's opinion.

Ivy flicked the switch to begin the recording, waited for the introductory buzz to complete, and then nodded at George, who cleared his throat, then commenced.

"This interview is being recorded and may be given in evidence should this case be brought to trial," he started, before relaying their location, the date, and time. "I am Detective Inspector George Larson. The other police officer present is Detective Sergeant Hart." He looked over at Adrian. "Please state your full name."

Adrian didn't reply. Not because he was belligerent or playing the silent game. He was frightened. Pure and simple.

"Okay then. For the benefit of the recording, we are interviewing Adrian Samson," George said and then paused, giving his full attention to the man across the table before glancing across to the duty solicitor expectantly.

"Morris," he began. "James Morris. Duty Solicitor."

"Thank you," George told him, laying a blanket of good manners on which even the testiest of solicitors would find difficult to find fault in.

"Jane May. Appropriate adult from the Hearts and Minds Foundation," May added.

"Thank you for coming on such short notice," George told her. "Now then, Adrian," he said softly, treating his words as though they were movements, nothing quick or shocking, only small, manageable steps that even Samson could follow. "We need to talk to you about Dean Worthing. For the benefit of the recording, we have informed Mr. Samson of Mr Worthing's death. However, under the circumstances, we felt that further questioning at a time when he was in a hospital bed himself was wholly inappropriate." He left a pause that Ivy recognised as a little window of opportunity for Samson to react somehow. A micro expression, perhaps. But Samson bowed his head and fiddled with his grubby fingers. "Mr Samson, I'd like to begin by understanding your relationship with Dean Worthing."

But Adrian remained silent. He raised his head and stared between the two detectives as though the language was alien to him, as though he was from another world, trying to translate this entirely arbitrary interaction.

"We understand you have been staying with Dean at his house. The Bluestone Lodge?" The house name triggered a shudder through Adrian's shoulders, though Ivy could not be sure that it wasn't from the lack of insulation his holey t-shirt offered. "Were you roommates with Dean?"

Again, he didn't reply. He stared as a cornered dog might, with his head turned away and his hyper-vigilant eyes buried deep in the corner of their sockets.

"You were quite upset, weren't you, Adrian?" George started, and Ivy sensed that he was indeed trying to provoke the man into a reaction. "To hear of Dean's death? You were close, no? Good friends, maybe?"

But it seemed Adrian had exhausted his grief at the hospital, for his response was little more than his suspicious stare.

"Adrian, we're not here to hurt you, okay? We're not here to do anything other than find out why Dean died. Surely you want that, too?" He paused again, and Samson's eyes slid to the floor. "So come on, Adrian. Tell me. How did you know Dean?" George asked again. "Were you friends? Brothers? Lovers?" George reeled through the options like a so-called mind reader might, watching for any twitch that suggested recognition.

But Adrian Samson was either in his own wild, little world behind his eyes, or he had the best poker face Ivy had ever seen. It was not quite a poker face, though; it was more the look of a hyper-intelligent creature, an animal that understands but doesn't indulge in the futilities of human beings and whose instincts allowed it to comprehend behaviour far greater than Ivy or George.

"We found Methadone in your room, Adrian. Do you take Methadone?"

Adrian didn't reply.

"Do you take other drugs, Adrian?"

Adrian didn't reply.

"I would suggest that my client's personal affairs have no real pertinence to Mr Worthing's death, Inspector," Morris said.

"And I would argue that it has every pertinence," George countered, glancing across at Miss May. "Are you happy for us to continue, Miss May?"

Morris rolled his eyes and shook his head, realising he'd been outplayed in the first innings.

"So far, so good," she said, her voice as warm and soft as duck down.

"George smiled his thanks, then leaned down, hoping to draw Samson's gaze from the floor.

"We talked to Nurse Wrigley at the hospital, Adrian. She knows you. She says you're a regular there. How often do you go to the hospital, Adrian?"

Adrian didn't reply.

"We spoke to your friend Freddo, too." Ivy noticed George's

voice adapt as though talking to a child. But it made no difference. "How do you know Freddo, Adrian?"

Again, Adrian didn't reply.

George opened the file and took out two of the erratically pencilled sketches he had found on the desk in the disgusting bedroom in the Bluestone Lodge. "Are these yours, Adrian?" he asked, pushing the papers towards him. "Did you draw these?"

Adrian looked down at the devilish creatures and monstrous forms drawn with heavy, messy lines on the paper, but he did not reply.

The interview continued as such, with George asking questions and Adrian not so much refusing to answer as merely ignoring them, seemingly unaware of how such questions pertained to his problems. More than once, George asked if Adrian understood, and without any response, they could not be sure that he did. It was almost like speaking to a deaf man.

"Okay, okay," George said. "Listen. I know you can hear me, Adrian. And I know you're scared. But, I feel I must remind you that you have been arrested on suspicion of murder. Murder, Adrian. Murder. Currently, you have two choices. You can remain silent. I will continue to ask my questions, and at the end of it all, my team and I will have no reason to consider your innocence. You'll be held on remand, and given your...condition, that will likely be in a secure hospital. Somewhere, you'll be safe. A date for the trial will be set, and you'll be forced to attend. But unless you can provide answers to my questions, a jury too will find it difficult to believe you innocent."

"That's conjecture, don't you think?" Morris said, peering over his spectacles, pen poised.

"You call in conjecture, Mr Morris. I call it reality," George said, his eyes never once leaving Samson's. "We have an eyewitness who claims to have seen your client at the crime scene. We have your client's DNA on Dean Worthing's body and in his home. Add to that the fact that your client has yet to provide a single explanation as to his whereabouts or his relationship with Mr Worthing, then I would suggest that there is little room for you or anybody else to provide a defence." Scorned, Morris scribbled a series of notes, then sat back, his nostrils flaring. George, however, retained his composure. "Adrian, for the last time, where were you on Saturday night?"

It was one thing to sit through a no-comment interview, but even George was beginning to grow tired of the monologue. Mostly, the silent types broke eventually, if the right buttons were pressed and the right questions asked. They caved. People want to talk. They want to tell their story. But this was different. Adrian seemed to have little desire to speak at all, as though his story had been lost – to time, to drugs, perhaps even to himself.

"Adrian, Dean Worthing died on Saturday night. We need to know where you were. Otherwise, you will be charged for his murder. Do you understand?"

Adrian didn't reply.

"That would mean life in prison, Adrian. Whether that is in prison or in a secure hospital, it will be a life behind bars."

At this, Adrian did shuffle in his seat, which was the most reaction they had garnered so far. George ran with it.

"You wouldn't like that, would you, Adrian? To be locked up?" Adrian looked up, his eyes red and moist. "To stop that from happening, we need to know where you were on Saturday night." Give me something to work with. Anything."

Adrian, of course, didn't reply.

"Do you know what an MMO is, Adrian?" George asked, to, of course, no reply. "It is a method we use to help us determine if a suspect is guilty. It stands for means, motive, and opportunity, and if someone has all three, we build a case around them. You have all three, Adrian. You have the means in that you had the ability to push Dean from the tower that night. You have the motive of Dean leaving you his house in his will-"

"That is subjective," Morris countered, but George spoke over him.

"And you had the opportunity. Two witnesses claim to have seen you at the church that evening, only minutes after Dean Worthing died."

George leaned across the table.

"Help us out, Adrian. Give us your alibi, at least. Tell us why you *didn't* kill Dean, that it can't have been you, and then we can let you go."

It was Ivy's turn to squirm a little in her seat. She eyed the recording. They were swerving a little too close to empty promises for her liking. But she knew what George was doing. He was probing for a trickle. A trickle of words, which would lead to a stream, and then onward to a flood. It was human nature. But it wasn't working. The moment had passed. Even the tinge of fear at the threat of imprisonment had faded from his face.

George sat back, visibly exasperated. He turned to Ivy, who met his eye in reassurance but could offer little help. Her observations of Adrian throughout the interview told her nothing. He was an empty book. Or, more likely, a book written in white text against a white page, with a hidden story like a code, unreadable except to those who knew the key.

George leaned forward with one last question.

"Michael Wassall," he said. Something flashed behind Adrian's eyes, something quick and spectral – a memory perhaps? Or a ghost? "The old vicar at St Leonard's Church. Do you know him?"

Adrian didn't reply. But his eyes were even more intense than before, holding a depth to his stare. Perhaps that was the only kind of communication of which he was capable – varying intensities of eye contact.

"Dean died at St Leonard's Church. You took Dean's manuscript to St Leonard's church. What is it about that church, Adrian? Why did you go there?"

Adrian didn't reply.

"How do you know Michael Wassall?"

Again, that flash behind the eyes came like an involuntary twitch that Adrian tried to blink away.

"We can help you, Adrian. If you just talk to us. We can find justice for Dean. You see, I don't believe that you did it. I believe you were there. Our witnesses are reliable. But I don't believe you had anything to do with Dean's death."

Adrian's blank stare had returned. It was almost as if when he did show a reaction, he then retreated into himself ten-fold.

George sat back and turned to Ivy as if he was open to suggestions. But Ivy had nothing.

"Miss May," she said. "Are you happy that our line of questioning has been fair, given Mr Samson's medical condition?"

"I am," she said. "I think Inspector Larson showed great restraint and compassion."

"In that case, the interview is paused," Ivy said, checking her watch, "at eleven-twenty."

She jabbed at the pause button and slapped her notebook closed.

Wearily, George rubbed his face, and Ivy rose and strolled around the table to Adrian. Gently, she took his arm and pulled the man upwards.

"I was under the impression you would be charging my client," Morris said, and Ivy halted, seeking confirmation from George.

"Given the circumstances," he said. "I'd like to give Mr Samson another chance. Maybe once he's had a taste of incarceration, he'll feel compelled to help our investigation."

Ivy tugged gently on Samson's arm, and he followed the movement obediently enough, like a dog on a leash. She led him out of the interview room towards the cells, the foul odour from his clothes warming the back of her throat.

Samson's steps became heavier as they neared the cell, as though traversing deeper and deeper through thick mud until he stopped entirely, his feet rooted to the floor. By this point,

Robson had joined them. He stepped up to Samson's cell door, unlocked and shoved it open, stepping to one side to allow the prisoner to enter. But Adrian refused to move another step. It was only with Robson's help that the two of them pushed him through the cell doorway, where he stopped in the middle of the small room and began to whimper. Pathetic, small cries of "No, no, no, please," rebounded off the blue-painted walls, and by the time they had closed the door, his cries had escalated to an outright scream that seemed to vibrate throughout the pipes of the entire building.

George joined them in the corridor as Ivy and Robson stood transfixed by the cell door, the noise radiating from inside.

"My God," he said, his voice barely audible above the raucous.

Mixed within the howls, Samson began to speak, breathlessly and quietly at first, but louder with each rendition of the repeated sentence.

The two men screwed their faces, trying to understand what he was saying.

"It's a prayer," Ivy said.

George leaned forward to peer through the security hatch.

"Like the vast distance of your heavens to earth, your mercy is immeasurable!" Samson shouted. "Therefore, I humbly ask for your forgiveness as I strive to become an obedient child to you and your heavenly kingdom! Like the vast... "

He continued the same prayer over and over again.

"Do you hear that?" Ivy said. "He's praying."

"No," George said, turning his back to the door and closing his eyes. "He's not praying. He's repenting."

CHAPTER TWENTY-NINE

"How did it go?" asked Campbell as George and Ivy trudged back into the incident room. It was a question George could have done without having to answer.

He felt as if he and Ivy were on the losing side of a football match, slouching into the changing room at halftime with zero points on the scoreboard and nothing to show for their hard work.

"Well, he didn't say much," Ivy said.

"Didn't say anything, actually," added George, standing beside Campbell's desk for once, looking at the whiteboard from further away as though he might see something he missed before. "Campbell, where's the address for Michael Wassall? I think it's time to pay him a visit."

"Why did Adrian suggest he could help?" asked Byrne.

"Adrian said nothing," George reiterated.

"So, he's guilty then?" Byrne said. "Surely? Why else wouldn't he say anything?"

"There's every chance he's guilty," George admitted. "And every chance he's innocent. And as long as there's a chance of his innocence, then it's our job to prove it one way or another."

"But if he didn't say anything—"

"Not every form of communication is verbal," George said. "We'll just have to read into what micro expressions he did offer involuntarily."

"You mean twitches and the like?"

"The CPS might not accept them, but that doesn't mean we should ignore them. He twitched when I mentioned Michael Wassall. And given his stoic approach up until that point, I'll take that as a direct hit, thank you very much."

"Here you go, guv," Campbell said, ripping a slip of paper from her pad and passing it to George. "Wassall's address out in Louth."

"Good," George said. "Are CSI paying a visit to Bluestone Lodge?"

"Yes, guv, they're on their way there now."

"Good. Good..." he said distractedly, still trying to interpret Samson's silence. He had expected some kind of reaction, be that erratic and unpredictable, a reaction at least. What he hadn't expected was to stare at what he could only describe as a gormless halfwit for the entirety of the interview.

He took the piece of paper from Campbell.

"Ivy, I'll do this one alone. Get on to CSI, will you? Make sure Katy fast-tracks any DNA found at the house. If Samson isn't going to prove his innocence, then it's down to us."

"But, guv—"

"And to do that, we need cold, hard facts."

She looked mildly disappointed, either because she believed Samson to be guilty or that she wouldn't be joining him on the drive to Louth. The truth was that the tension that had ignited in the custody suite still sizzled between them, and George would not relish the uneasy car ride. Supposedly, she felt the same. Sometimes, air and distance proved a worthy cure for a fractious mood.

"And us, guv?" asked Byrne. "What do you want us to do?"

The truth was that they had reached somewhat of a dead end, but George knew as well as anyone, in this job, there was always work to be done. "Continue building evidence on Samson," he said. "Let's put some meat on the bone, so to speak."

"You want us to fail," Ivy said, and he grinned. "You want us to fail so we can all sing from the same song sheet." George performed a sharp turn and strode towards the door, choosing to ignore her powers of deduction. "And keep working on the boys home," he called out, stopping at the door. "I want to know who fostered Dean Worthing. Also, Byrne," he added with a click of his fingers, "forward me a photo of that key found in Dean Worthing's pocket." He shoved the door open, threw his coat onto his back, and before the door closed behind him, he gave them a warning. "I'll be back soon, and I want some answers."

It felt strange to be leaving without Ivy, but the space would be good for them. Maybe George had assumed too much. Maybe, with her frequent stays at his place, he had considered them friends more so than she did. But when he considered the truths he was hiding from her and the truths she was hiding from him, it seemed their friendship would always harbour a shadow or two.

The drive through the Wolds towards Louth was becoming a familiar journey. He opted for the slightly longer route that took him through South Ormsby, and he slowed before he reached the village. Spying St Leonard's through the trees, he wondered for the hundredth time what it was about that beautiful old church that had captured the attention of both Dean Worthing and Adrian Samson. If Samson wouldn't tell them what it was—and Dean was unable to— then George would have to find some other source of information.

Michael Wassall lived on the edge of Louth in a small, sixties-style bungalow appropriate for a retired single man. George pondered how lonely the man's life might be out here in the middle of nowhere, with no companion. Then, a pang of hypocrisy struck him, and the likeness to his own looming retirement revealed itself. Indeed, it was yet another reason to resist retirement, despite the days creeping by, day by day.

He had left friends behind in Mablethorpe, yet for many of them, their company he had only really enjoyed in the presence of Grace. With a stab of guilt, he realised the closest thing he had to a friend in the Wolds was Ivy, and with a second jolt, he realised that the other people whose company he most enjoyed were Campbell and – God help him – Byrne.

He pulled up on the grass verge and shook his head from his thoughts.

"Head in the game, old boy," he muttered.

The garden was, as George might have predicted, well-kept. Spring bulbs were in full flow, and those that had gone over had been dead-headed.

The door was answered by a grey-haired yet lithe-looking man wearing corduroy trousers and a knitted Aran jumper.

"Michael Wassall?" George asked as pleasantly as he could.

"That's me," the man replied, his smile jovial. "How can I help?"

He had a personable quality, a friendliness that George felt in an instant, and one imagined had been curated during his years as a reliable reverend.

"Inspector George Larson," George said, holding out his warrant card, although Wassall didn't give it a second glance, as though he had been trained to trust people upfront. "I'm investigating an incident that took place last Saturday night. I wondered if you could give me a few moments of your time."

"An incident," the old reverend exclaimed. Then his face stiffened. "The church, you mean?"

"I'm afraid so."

"Suicide, wasn't it?"

"May I?" George asked, hoping for a chance to sit and discuss the matter inside.

"Who was he?" Wassall asked, clearly adept at maintaining control of a conversation.

"Dean Worthing," George said. Lived down the road from the church in South Ormsby. Do you mind if I come in?"

"Dean Worthing," Wassall repeated, and there was only the hint of a question mark at the end of the name, as though the man was unsure where to place him in his memories. "Ah, where are my manners? But of course," he said, opening the door wider for George to enter the house.

When George entered the house, it was not as he had expected. There were no religious symbols, ornaments, or otherwise anywhere to be seen. He had expected to find at least one embroidered psalm hanging on a wall or perhaps a wooden cross somewhere. But the house was minimally decorated and adorned only with the occasional framed photo or painting of a local scene which piqued George's interest. But none of them were Grace's. He could spot those from a mile off.

In George's experience, people decorated their homes according to the image that best expressed themselves, that retold their story of self, and expressed it as such to visitors. But this house told very little about Michael Wassall, let alone his life as a vicar. It was a stark contrast, for example, to Juliet Shaw's house, whose personality shone in vivid, neon lights as soon as you stepped into the living room.

"Tea?" asked Wassall, who had followed George through the house.

"Why not?" George replied, not so much to quench his thirst but because he knew people appreciated having something to do in the presence of a police officer. It made them feel useful. And innocent. "This is a lovely house you have."

The icebreaker fell flat, and Wassall seemed lost in thought.

"May I ask?" he said, his calm belied by his shaking hands as he pulled two mugs from the kitchen cupboard. "How did he die?"

It was a curious question for a man who had already heard of there being an incident.

"He fell," George said, watching closely for a reaction. "From the tower."

As it turned out, George didn't need to watch closely at all. Wassall was unable to hide his reaction, which was to let the two cups slip from his grip and smash loudly against the kitchen tiles.

"Damn and blast," Wassall said in surprise; whether at the information or the smashed cups, George was unsure. Wassall stooped to gather up the shards of ceramic. But as George knelt to help, Wassall seemed to lose energy in the task, sitting back on his haunches instead so that the two men faced each other, eye to eye.

"Was it?" he asked George quietly. "Suicide, I mean?"

"We're not able to say just yet," he answered, matching Wassall's voice level. The man's eyes were sad and dropped with exhaustion. "You knew him."

"I did," Wassall said flatly. "I knew him when he was a boy."

"We're trying to find his parents. To inform them of Dean's death," George said, bending the truth a little. "Do you know them? How might we find them?"

Wassall hesitated, and then, in a blatant lie, he said, "No. No, I didn't know Dean's parents. He always came to church alone."

"Reverend Wassall," George said, "I find that hard to believe–"

"Don't," Wassall said. "Don't call me that. I'm not a vicar. Not anymore."

"Right, but you were," George said. "You were the vicar at St Leonard's Church before Stephen Cross, is that right?"

"I was," he said, wiping a rogue tear from his cheek.

"And why did you leave?"

"Because we move on, Inspector," Wassall said. "It's a rotating system. You go where you're needed. I was needed here, in Louth."

"I see," George said, rising to his feet with a collection of broken cup in his hands, which he placed on the counter. Wassall followed and restarted the tea-making process from scratch, taking two more cups from the cupboard. "Forgive me, but I can't help noticing something... "

Wassall sighed, filling the kettle and putting it on to boil. "And what is it that you notice, Inspector?"

"Well, you see, my grandmother was deeply religious. She had imagery all over the house, you know. She had a Saint Christopher pendant to guide her in her travels. She had a statue of Saint Anthony in the kitchen because that was where she was most likely to lose things. Even a prayer of St Francis above the dog's bed."

"People express their faith in various ways," Wassall said.

"Of course. But I can't see a *single* thing in this house that might suggest you're a religious man. No statues, no Bible quotes, no symbols at all. You were a vicar for, what, forty years?"

"Fifteen years," he said, offering George the information for which he was digging. "I quit the church when I moved to Louth."

"You lost your faith?" asked George, taking the cup of tea that Wassall handed him.

Wassall laughed, cradling his own tea in his hands for comfort, George assumed.

"Lose my faith," he said, chuckling as though sharing his own private joke. "I always found it a strange turn of phrase, don't you? To lose one's faith, as though it's somewhere down the back of the sofa. No, it's not that I forgot where I put it, Inspector. I did not *lose* my faith. It lost me." He stared George in the eye knowingly, the way an old man might stare at his grandson mid-anecdote. "I turned my back on it."

"Can I ask why?"

His answer was simple. "People do horrendous things in the name of religion."

George paused to absorb this information. "So, you stopped being a vicar once you left South Ormsby?" Wassall nodded and took a sip of tea. "So, we might assume," George continued, "that something happened in South Ormsby to cause you to lose – sorry – turn your back on your faith."

"You can assume anything you like. It is, after all, your prerogative."

"But you won't tell me?"

"I'm sure you understand that there are the rules of the faith that outrule even the highest of man's laws."

"Confidentiality?"

"For one," he said, looking George in the eye.

"And you stand by that rule, even now?"

"Even if I am not a vicar now, I *was* one. Those…secrets are as much a part of me as they are the people who disclosed them to me. They did so in the name of a God that I no longer speak to. But they do. And I will never break that trust in a faith that belongs only to them."

George stared at the man, unsure whether to consider his answer as honourable, naive, or simply unjust. Either way, their conversation ended with the slide of the kitchen doors to the garden. George turned to see a pretty, small, old lady enter the kitchen carrying a handful of weeds in her gloved hands and bearing muddy patches on the knees of her slacks. Her grey hair still retained shades of its original red, and her full-cheeked smile matched its rosy glow.

"My wife," Wassall said, "Fran. Fran, this is Inspector Larson."

"Oh," George said, failing to disguise his surprise. "I thought…
"

"You thought he was a bachelor, did you?" she said, dumping the weeds into the kitchen bin with a grin. "No luck I'm afraid. I tied him down a long time ago."

"It's the Catholics, Inspector… "

"Larson," George reminded her.

"Right. It's the Catholics who aren't allowed to marry," she said.

"That's good to know," he replied.

Her husband retrieved George's half-empty cup and placed it in the sink before joining his wife. The display of unity was an obvious introduction for George to take his leave.

"Well," he said, "I'll be off then. It was a pleasure to meet you, Fran." But as he moved towards the front door, George turned, one unspoken thought remaining. "One more thing, if you will."

"Yes?" Wassall said curtly.

"You said he came alone. To church, I mean. Did the church ever take in children?"

"Take in children?"

"Yes. Those who needed homes. Those who were orphaned, perhaps, or abused or neglected. Those who needed to be fostered, let's say."

It took Wassall a few seconds to respond, and in those seconds, he took a deep breath in and out. "It is the responsibility of the church to care for all of God's creatures where it can. But no, Inspector, it is not the church's responsibility to foster them. I have never heard of such a thing. Certainly," he said, his eyes as sharp as his voice. "At least, not in South Ormsby, anyway."

CHAPTER THIRTY

As always, the door to St. Leonard's was unlocked. George pushed through into the outer porch and then through the heavier wooden door into the church. He welcomed the cold chill and felt the rush of calm that was becoming familiar to him now, the feeling of leaving the rest of the world behind. Or perhaps it wasn't so much that he was leaving his world behind but moving into another. His family had been religious, but that particular gene must have passed him by. Yet, he could well understand why people found reassurance in the faith. Every man needed a haven, after all.

His drive across the Wolds from Michael Wassall's house in Louth had been somewhat frantic, a metaphor to his mind. He was tiring of half-truths and perhaps felt somewhat belied by Wassall. The image of truth and certainty was tainted somehow. It wasn't what the man had said but rather what he hadn't said that had fanned the flames of fantasy, allowing his imagination to run free, blurring the lines between fact and fiction.

He took slow steps through the church towards somebody he had come to trust during the last few days. Stephen Cross was lighting candles with a long brass instrument. On one end was a lighter, and on the other, a bell-shaped snuffer. The candles were positioned high up on the walls, out of reach, and as Stephen made his way towards the altar, George stepped forward into the light.

"Inspector Larson," Stephen said without turning. "To what do I owe the pleasure?" He glanced over his shoulder and saw the look on George's face. "Forgive me," he said. "I had a sense you'd be back."

George had never considered himself to be predictable before, but he supposed a man like Stephen Cross was used to reading people, perhaps even more so than a detective.

"I was just passing by," he explained. "I hoped I could have a word."

George imagined this exact sentence to have been said to Stephen Cross many times over the years. But George wasn't there for condolence or forgiveness.

"A word?" Stephen replied. "That sounds ominous."

"Well, it's more of a favour actually," George added.

"Ah," Stephen replied knowingly.

"I'd like to see the tower."

Stephen released the lighter switch, and the flame vanished, casting his face in shadow. "The tower is kept locked, I'm afraid."

"But you have a key, don't you?" George said. "You must do; you're the custodian of the church, are you not?"

"The tower is very old, detective. That's why we keep it locked. It's not very safe, you see, a dark, tight space with uneven steps."

"And if I promised to be careful?" George persisted, and when Stephen still didn't move, George held out his hand expectedly. Power dynamics were difficult between a man in George's position and a man in Stephen's. One held earthly authority; the other held authority with God. "I just need to see where Dean Worthing...well, you know."

"Of course," said Stephen, and he eyed George with suspicion before making his way towards the sacristy.

He was gone for a good few minutes, and George amused himself with a stroll around the church. But just as it had that first night, nothing appeared to be out of place. It was orderly, and that pleased him.

"I'm surprised you left it this long, if I'm honest," Stephen called out, the echoes of his voice singing from the vaulted ceiling.

"Well, we hadn't the need before now," George called out, gazing up at one of the stained glass windows.

"How so?" Stephen said quietly, and George startled, finding him standing a few feet behind. It took a moment for George to regain his composure.

"Is that it?" he asked, gesturing at the large brass key in the reverend's hand.

It looked like a prop - like the kind of key you might see in an adventure film - Indiana Jones, maybe. An ancient artefact in its own right, and as old, George considered, as the church itself. Stephen held it up proudly, a bronze work of art with a design on the end similar to the fleur-de-lis.

He removed his phone from his pocket, navigated to his emails, and opened the image that Byrne had sent him. Stephen Cross looked confused but stood still.

"Everything alright?" Stephen asked, and George roused himself from the comparison he was making.

"Dandy," he replied and extended his arm, inviting Stephen to lead the way. "Shall we?"

He followed the vicar to the locked wooden door bolted into the tower's stone walls of the church tower, and watched curiously as Stephen placed the three-pronged key into the lock. He turned it once, having to jiggle it back and forth a few times until, finally, there was a click.

"Bingo," Stephen said, struggling to retract the key from the lock. Eventually, the door creaked open to reveal a narrow, winding staircase that reminded George of his visit to Notre Dame with Grace. So tight was the spiral when Stephen opened a second door that barely a scrap of light graced the stone floor at its base. It was only when George clicked on the little pen torch on his keyring that the little space was illuminated.

"Shall I go up first?" Stephen asked.

"Wait," George replied, as a sense of déjà vu stilled his frantic mind. He stepped inside, running his hand across the stone walls. "It's exactly as he wrote," he whispered to himself.

"What's that?" Stephen asked from the first step. But George was captivated. The walls were the same. The dark, dank corners were the same. Dean's words swam amongst his senses. *A dark, damp room, the kind of darkness that penetrates the mind, where only the flutter of eyelashes reminds one whether one's eyes are open or closed, and the kind of damp that settles, cold and permanent, in the marrow of one's bones.*

"Inspector Larson?" Stephen said gently. "Are you okay?"

He could see them. He could feel the claustrophobia. The thick doors, the stone walls, and that dampness that would get into a person's bones.

"Yes," he replied, although rather distantly. "Yes, I was just admiring the stonework."

Stephen smiled disbelievingly. "This way, if you will."

George pulled himself away from the nightmarish cellar that had preoccupied his evening reading for the last few days.

"After you, Stephen," he said, turning his back on the space, and slowly, step by step, they ascended the old stone staircase.

The steps were uneven, but smooth, sometimes offering little in the way of purchase for his brogues, and with every step he considered those poor boys, trapped below.

It didn't take long to reach the top. George had climbed many church staircases in his time on holidays with Grace – up the shell-like Sagrada Familia in Barcelona and to the top of Cologne

Cathedral. St Leonard's Church was nowhere near that kind of climb. Another small door blocked the exit onto the turret of the church tower, but this door had no key lock, only a stiff, sliding bolt.

After the dark, claustrophobic staircase, the bright, expansive view offered a picture of the Wolds. The daylight blinded George for a few seconds and he shaded his eyes against the afternoon sun so that he could better appreciate the image before him. From the top, Ketsby could be seen at the bottom of the hill, and the village of South Ormsby even closer. He could even pinpoint the Bluestone Lodge between the trees. The fields beyond were a patchwork of greens and yellows as carefully stitched as a family heirloom. Hovering kites harnessed the wind as captivatingly as their namesakes, and trees lined the interlocking spurs like ancient protectors of the land. The view grew misty in the distance, adding an ethereal beauty to the scene.

Yes, he thought, he understood Dean's choice. He could think of worse places to die.

However, as stunning a view as it was, from a detective's perspective, there was nothing to be seen. No blood, footprints or discarded pieces of clothing that might have nudged him towards an understanding of what happened during Dean Worthing's final moments. But there was nothing.

He turned to face Stephen, who seemed similarly captivated by the view as though it was as fresh to him as it was to George.

"It's a shame it's not open to the public," the vicar mused.

"Maybe that's for the best," George said darkly remembering what happened to the last member of the public to have stood here. "Stephen, who else has one of these keys to the tower?"

"Only me," he said confidently. "I was given it when I took over the church. Part of the inventory."

"Then tell me why," George said, "Dean Worthing had the exact same key in his coat pocket when he died."

Stephen took a moment to pull himself from the landscape.

"I have no idea," he answered, frowning. "I was given only one key. I thought there was only one key. I mean, I can double-check."

George leaned heavily on the parapet wall so that these small stones indented the skin of his elbows through his thin, white shirt.

"I've been to see Michael Wassall," he explained conversationally, watching Stephen in his peripheral for reaction. "Did you know he lost his faith?"

The change of tack gave the vicar pause for thought.

"Yes, I did hear something about that. It happens. A tragedy, but it happens."

"He lost it soon after he left South Ormsby. Something happened, perhaps?"

Stephen too leaned on the wall, casually, as though they were two men simply enjoying a view. "That's what he said, is it?"

"Not in so many words," George said. "But in my line of work, you get used to reading between the lines."

"In my line of work, too," Stephen said. "Everything is open to interpretation."

"And yet you have such rigid rules based on those interpretations, as you say."

"As I'm sure so do you, Inspector."

"Not so much. I work with facts," George said. "I gather evidence and develop a case based on logic and the truth."

"Truth?" Stephen laughed. "But it's just another story, no? You're telling a story of what happened based on the limited knowledge you have and based on the stories of others who were there. Or not, as the case may be. At the end of the day, it all comes down to the credibility of the witness, surely? The credibility of the individual telling the story." Something in his voice told George that Stephen had more to say. Like he was teasing at something or offering a thread on which George could pull. "Everything we think we know is really nothing more than a story,

Inspector," he continued. "That's where faith comes in. Faith allows us to believe in something, even in the absence of facts."

George turned to him. "What are you trying to say, Stephen?" But the vicar continued to stare forward, his dark hair flapping slightly in the breeze. "Do you know why Michael Wassall lost his faith? About what happened in South Ormsby twenty years ago?"

Finally, Stephen turned away from the view to look George in the eye.

"I don't know anything, detective," he said, "It's all a story, remember?"

CHAPTER THIRTY-ONE

George waited until he was around the corner from the entrance to the church and amongst the wonky headstones before pulling his phone from his pocket. As always, Campbell answered promptly.

"Campbell, it's me," he said before she could speak. "Gather the team. We need a debrief."

"Sit tight," she replied, and George heard the muffled sound of her palm covering the headset. "Byrne." He heard her distant voice as though it was through a wall in the next room. "Guv wants us." George failed to decipher the muffle that followed. "All of us," she hissed, and a deeper, muffled voice replied. "Well, where is she?" George heard Campbell ask in reply. Then the atmospheric noises of the incident room came back over the call, along with a deep breath from Campbell, followed by, "Byrne and I are here, guv. Sergeant Hart has just stepped out."

"Stepped out where?"

"I saw her head downstairs, guv," came Byrne's voice clearly he'd been listening in. "Think she's in the custody suite."

George bristled at the idea of the two of them.

"Fine," he said. "We'll just have to do this without her. I need you to look into a series of abuse allegations made against churches across East Lincolnshire in the mid-eighties. Find out if any of them mention St Leonard's."

"Bloody hell, guv!"

"Sorry?"

"I mean..." Byrne started. "That's a mammoth task, that's all. We can do it. It's just...it might take a while."

"Have you made plans?" George asked.

"Well, no-"

"So, what's the problem?"

"Well, there isn't one, I guess. Sorry, it just caught me off-guard."

"Right," George said, letting his tone do most of the heavy lifting. "I want to know if Michael Wassall was involved."

"The old vicar?"

"That's right. I went to see him today. He left the church soon after being transferred from St Leonard's. He said something about people doing terrible things in the name of religion."

"Eh?"

"I don't know. It didn't make sense, and he clearly wasn't prepared to go into detail. Hence, your mammoth task."

"And that's why he left the church?"

"Could have been disillusioned?" Campbell suggested. "Or he could have caught wind of something."

"Maybe a colleague was up to no good?" Byrne suggested.

"Or maybe he was up to no good," added Campbell, voicing George's train of thought. "It's not unusual for ex-abusers or addicts or those in recovery to refer to themselves in the third person, to distance themselves from the person they used to be."

"Either way," George said. "There's something in what he said, and I want to know what it is. If he's not willing to tell us what it is, we'll have to find out for ourselves."

"But he told you this? About the allegations against the church?"

"No," George explained. "The current vicar did. Stephen Cross. He said they were just stories, but even he heard about the rumours before he moved to South Ormsby."

"Well, it's not exactly the wildest allegation, is it?" Byrne said.

"No," George said. "Unfortunately, it's not. So look into it, will you?"

"On it, guv," Byrne said, then paused. "What's your plan? Are you heading back?"

"Not yet," George said. "I want to know who else knows about these stories. Do you have the address of where the Hawkins are staying in Ketsby?"

"Give me a second," Byrne said, and George heard the familiar flicking of pages being turned.

George put his phone on loudspeaker and asked Byrne to repeat the address, typing it into Google Maps on his phone.

"It's a five-minute drive away," he said. "I'm going to pay them a visit."

"Do you think they know something?" asked Campbell.

"I'm not sure about knowing," George said, "but if they lived in the area. Maybe they heard the same stories as Stephen, and maybe they're not as bound to secrecy as he is."

"So you don't want us to write up Adrian Samson?" asked Campbell.

"Not yet," George said. "It doesn't feel right to me. There are too many moving pieces still. How long have we got him for?"

"Until ten a.m. tomorrow, guv. He hasn't let up, though. He's still screaming. You can hear him from the stairwell."

"Well, let him tire himself out," George said, again imagining himself as a father allowing a baby to cry themselves to sleep. "If he hates the cell so much, maybe being free will motivate him to start talking."

George walked around the church, past where Dean had fallen, and back to the church entrance. He looked up at the tower with its black and gold Roman numerals. That gave them about twenty-one hours to convince Samson to talk.

"Stephen Cross insists he was only given one key to the tower," George said, half to himself and half to the PCs on the other end of the line.

"Maybe Dean stole it?" Byrne said.

"Impossible," George replied. "I just saw it. Just now. In Stephen's hand. He unlocked the door, and we went up to the top of the tower."

"And Katy sent over the key found in Dean's pocket," Campbell said. "I'm looking at it right now on my desk."

"Maybe Dean made a copy?" Byrne tried again.

"I don't think it's exactly the kind of key you can take down Timpson's," George said.

"So there were always two keys," Campbell said slowly.

"Not according to Stephen Cross. He's adamant the inventory only listed one."

"Well, how did Dean have one, then?" Campbell asked.

"Maybe he was given it," Byrne said.

"By who?"

"That, Campbell," George said, turning away from the tower, away from the church, away from the graveyard, and bee-lining towards his car, "is exactly what I plan to find out."

CHAPTER THIRTY-TWO

Ivy took slow steps towards the closed cell door as if she were sneaking up on a lion's cage. Behind it, Adrian Samson howled like a wild animal – contained, frightened, and desperate. Over the years, she had visited many prisoners in their cells. They usually greeted her with wolf whistles designed to intimidate her, sneers to make themselves feel better or feigned indifference. Often, they'd pick at their cuticles or roll onto their side with their back to her, pretending the whole experience was little more than a mild inconvenience.

Adrian Samson, on the other hand, seemed very bothered indeed.

"Are you sure about this?" asked Robson, pulling the cell keys from his belt. "He hasn't stopped screaming for two hours."

"I'm sure," Ivy said, her eyes focused on the door.

"If you wait a few minutes, I can get someone to be on hand."

"No," she said flatly.

"Well, me, then," he said. "I can just stand in the corner. You won't even know I'm here."

"No," Ivy said. "It's better that it's just the two of us. We'll be fine."

She knew he was trying to help, to protect her, but she didn't need protecting, not by him, not by Jamie, not by George. She knew what she was doing. She only wished they had as much trust in her as she did in herself.

"Your call," he said, choosing the key to cell one.

Only when Robson slotted the key inside and turned the lock did the howling stop. The loud clunk of the mechanism broke through the continuous groans, and she pictured Samson, head turned towards the noise, like a deer in tall grass.

Robson glanced through the security flap to make sure Samson wasn't waiting to jump them, then pulled the door open for Ivy to enter the cell.

"Call out if you need to," he said, to which she gave a slight nod of her head, with no intention of doing anything of the sort, and Robson clearly had no intention of leaving her. He took a step back but made a point of being close.

Samson was sitting huddled in the corner of the bunk, his knees drawn up to his chest. His wild hair stuck out at angles as though he'd been tugging at it, and the grease held it firmly in place. Groups of four parallel red lines crisscrossed his forearms and his neck, and even from the far side of the cell, Ivy recognised the traces of blood beneath his fingernails. The brown, standard-issue blanket remained folded on the sticky blue mattress, untouched. Ivy was suddenly reminded of the filth in the bedroom in Dean Worthing's house, how the covers had been pulled from the bed and bundled in the corner.

And the stains.

And the smell.

"Hello, Adrian," she said.

He didn't turn. Instead, he just stared that same savage stare, darting between Ivy and Robson in the doorway, and when Ivy nodded again at her colleague, inviting him to leave, he did so with a disappointed shake of his head.

She felt the full weight of Adrian's suspicious stare as she stepped inside, and she started when the door closed behind her.

But this was not the time to show fear, and not the time to demonstrate power. She needed to reach him somehow.

Ivy perched on the blue mattress, and its synthetic cover squeaked under her weight. She had never had to sleep on one herself, but it reminded her of those thin, inflatable beds she took camping along the coast, north of Mablethorpe, with Jamie and the kids. She winced and fleetingly wondered why everything she did, every small movement, even the squeak of a slippery mattress, reminded her of her family. They were always on her mind.

"Is there anything I can get you, Adrian?" she asked, to which, after a few long seconds, he shook his head. It was the most response they had gleaned from him so far if you discounted the incident in the hospital. "Water? A sandwich, maybe?"

He studied her lips and her eyes, perhaps marrying the meaning of what she said to the intent in her eyes.

He shook his head and pulled his knees closer to his chest.

"Do you know how many people I've seen in this place?" she asked, and he surrendered a shake of his head almost freely. "No, me neither," she admitted. "But it's a lot, I can tell you that much. Most of them were guilty, too. You just know sometimes." She spoke as she might speak to George. Relaxed and slow, her gaze fixed on the door so as not to intimidate him. "But every now and then, we get somebody like you. Somebody who was just in the wrong place at the wrong time." She held her hands up in defence. "We have procedures to follow. We have to treat everybody the same. Innocent until proven guilty."

Just as he had in the interview room, Adrian exercised his silence, and she gave a heavy sigh.

"Listen," she said. "I know you don't like being in here. But prison is a lot worse, believe me. Imagine it, Adrian. How long has it been so far? A few hours? You could spend the next fifteen to twenty years in a cell like this." His eyes widened, and his gullet rose and fell. "Unless we find the person responsible for Dean's death."

A flash of fear crossed Adrian's face. Ivy sat back against the cell wall and rested her head. In direct contrast to Adrian, she found it rather soothing, to be closed off from the rest of the world. She wouldn't mind being locked away from her responsibilities, from work, from family, from the constant pressure of having to make a decision about her marriage. Just for a while. Like a retreat. She closed her eyes. She could just stay here, listening to Adrian's ragged breathing as though it were white noise.

"To tell the truth, I don't know why I'm even here," she said and looked over at her cellmate. "You're not going to talk, are you, Adrian?" He neither nodded nor shook his head. "Then, do you mind if I do?"

Again she took his lack of reaction as an affirmative.

"I get why you hate it here," she said, staring around at the grimy walls. "I mean, it's cold and depressing. But then again, listen..." She stayed quiet for a few seconds and saw Adrian's ear turn up slightly, like a dog listening for the pull-up of a car on a driveway. "Silence," she whispered. "Absolute silence. It's actually rather peaceful, don't you think?"

She leaned back again as though she was relaxing watching a sunset with a friend.

"But it's different, isn't it? When you don't have a choice? Sure, I could walk out of here right now if I wanted. But I know what it's like to be trapped, Adrian. To feel like there's no way out." She paused. She thought only for a second about the morals of what she was about to say, but it felt right. After all, they say the best listeners are those who don't try to offer advice. "You see, I'm trapped, too." She rolled her head around to watch his expression, but it didn't alter. "I'm trapped in my marriage. I don't want to be a wife. Sometimes..." She picked at her cuticles. "Sometimes, I don't even want to be a mother, or a police officer. Sometimes I yearn to be somewhere else." At this, she laughed again, startled by her own brutal honesty. "That's why I like coming down here and talking to Sergeant Robson. He's a good listener. Not as good as you, but still. He cheers me up. He makes me laugh. God, you wouldn't believe how long it's been since someone properly made me laugh. Cry, yes. But laugh? No. Not for a long time."

At this, Adrian looked up as though he had indeed been listening. Perhaps she had struck a chord. She couldn't imagine him laughing or see any joy on his face.

"Laughing and crying sound so similar, don't they? Perhaps at some point, our laughs become cries. Or vice versa. I almost believed I couldn't do it anymore like I had forgotten a language I used to speak fluently. But of course, that's all it is with Sergeant Robson – laughs and flirtations, nothing serious. He's asked me out a few times. Can you believe that? Only for a drink - for coffee - and I always said no. That's not what I want right now. Of course, it's not." She exhaled shakily. "I could never do that to my husband anyway. Could never do it to the kids. You know, I envy them sometimes. Do you ever wish you were a child again, Adrian? Back in the days when all you had to worry about was where to ride your bike that afternoon, or what time to be called home for lunch, or who was around you could play with. They don't know how good they have it. When you grow up, things become infinitely more complicated. Normal things you always thought that you wanted, you get, and all they do is close you in a little box until you can't even escape yourself anymore. And you can't complain because you told yourself growing up that this was all you ever wanted. I wish I could do it. I wish I could go back in time. Do you ever wish that, Adrian? Do you ever wish you were a child again?"

She laughed to herself, and, mirroring his position, hugged her knees to her chest.

"I hated being a child," he said quietly. The words were so fleeting that Ivy thought she had imagined them. She had been staring at an obscenity scratched into the cell wall, lost in her own thoughts. But when she shifted her eyes to Adrian, she found attentive, intelligent eyes. "I hated it," he whispered. "You have no control over your life. No control of your...destiny. You just have someone telling you what to do and who to be. I can't think of anything worse than living that way again." He looked at Ivy with something like pity. "Don't you think you have a choice? At least your cell door is open. Unlike mine."

"Not all childhoods are like that, Adrian," Ivy said cautiously, ignoring his advice and focusing on the information he had offered.

"*My* childhood was," he said quickly. He looked around at the four walls of the cell room. "I'd rather die than live like that again."

"Then tell us what you know. Help us help you, Adrian. For God's sake."

But the talk of childhood had clearly triggered something in Adrian. He had started to rock back and forth once more, and that intelligence in his eyes was slowly fading away.

"Adrian," Ivy said, leaning forward. "Adrian, talk to me."

"It was her," he said, rocking back and forth. "I know it was. I saw her."

"Who, Adrian?" Ivy said urgently. "Who did you see?"

"She was at the window," he said. "She was real. I know she was. She was there at the window."

"Who was there, Adrian?" But he regressed to whimpering. "At what window? Where were you?"

"Dean's house. Bluestone Lodge," he said. But the effort seemed to sap the last of his energy. Ivy had the impression she was losing grasp of the man with whom she had almost held a full conversation.

"There was a woman at Bluestone Lodge?" Ivy repeated. "Looking through the window?"

"Yes," he said, as though it was painful now to speak.

"When?" Ivy said. "When was she there? Who was it?"

But Adrian had begun to scratch his arms, reopening wounds with his short, dirty fingernails. It was only a matter of time before he started screaming again.

"Was she there on Saturday, Adrian? Did you see someone on Saturday night before Dean died?"

"Dean," he said and threw his arms around his body, hugging himself. "Dean, Dean, Dean," he repeated. "My Dean!" And at the final mention of the name, his voice developed into a howl, and he began banging his head against the wall.

Ivy scrambled up from the mattress. It was a wild, disturbing sight. But she rushed forward to crouch in front of him, trying to shake the man back to reality. "Adrian," she said. "Adrian, *stop.*"

But he looked up sharply and screamed in her face. He launched himself from the bunk, hissing and clawing at her like a cornered cat.

Ivy backed off and put some distance between them, wondering if Robson had been true to his word and was waiting outside. If he was, then he was taking his sweet time about stepping in. She banged on the closed cell door as Adrian began to rise from the corner, his head cocked to one side.

"Dan!" she said, hoping he would hear the urgency in her voice. "Dan, open up." The irony of being trapped after all she had just told him was not lost on her. Samson approached, his eyes black and soulless. "I just want to help," she told him. "I meant no harm."

He strode up to her, stopping just out of reach.

"You tricked me," he hissed, his eyes wild and accusing. "You tricked me."

His body tensed as if summoning his strength, and just as he was about to hurl himself at her, the door burst open, and Ivy sank to the floor. In a blur, Robson lunged at Samson, twisting his arm and forcing him up against the wall. He pulled the handcuffs from his belt and Ivy heard the reassuring click of the mechanism, before Robson pulled him to the floor, then dragged Ivy through the door. She stumbled into the corridor, and Robson slammed the door closed behind them as the familiar tune of Samson's wailing resumed.

With a firm, strong arm under her arms, Robson led Ivy down the corridor and back into the custody suite, where the external door muffled most of Samson's cries.

"Are you all right?" he said, spinning to place both his hands on Ivy's shoulders. "Ivy," he said, giving her a little shake. "What happened in there?"

"I'm fine, I'm fine," she said, her voice sounding stronger than she expected. She hung her head, processing what had just happened – from the trance-like state she had gone into when monologuing to Samson - to hearing him speak and seeing his descent into animalistic madness. "I'm fine," she repeated, quieter this time. She wondered how many times someone must repeat that they are fine until the other person fails to believe them.

Gently, Robson raised her chin, and stared into her eyes, said, "You're not fine, Ivy." He tucked a loose lock of hair behind her ear.

"Don't. Don't do that," she said, reaching up and grabbing his hand. He had soft, caring eyes. She saw that now. "Please. Just don't."

"Ivy, come on," he said.

"Just..." she started, then pushed past him to the door, where she stopped, closed her eyes and took a breath. "I'm sorry, I just can't."

CHAPTER THIRTY-THREE

Richard and Sarah Hawkins had opted for a guest suite in an old, converted barn in the grounds of a large house outside of Ketsby. George imagined the owners made a mint from the Airbnb, especially during the summer when tourists flocked to the Wolds for its rolling fields, secret valleys, and idyllic villages. He drove up the long, gravel driveway, stopping to ask a man wearing a waxed jacket and Wellington boots and with a very well-trained cocker spaniel for the direction of the guest suite. A few minutes later, George parked up outside, climbed out of the car, and knocked twice on the red stable door, the first to rouse the occupants' attention. The second to confirm they hadn't misheard the first. Any more would be superfluous.

Richard Hawkins answered, and as the door opened, George spied a spacious, open-planned living space. Richard's wife was lounging on a weathered Chesterfield sofa smoking, to George's surprise, a cigarette. As soon as she saw George in the doorway, she stubbed it out in a glass ashtray.

"Inspector Larson," Richard said, clearly as surprised to see him as his wife was. "To what do we owe the pleasure?"

"I don't wish to intrude," George said. "I just have a few more questions, if that's alright?"

"Of course, of course, come in," Richard said, stepping back to welcome George into the large, oak-floored, beamed-ceiling studio. "Apologies for the mess; we weren't expecting visitors."

The mess that Richard alluded to constituted only a few empty bottles of locally brewed beer, a full ashtray on the coffee table, and a few unwashed cups in the sink. Sarah Hawkins rose from the sofa to meet George.

"Good to see you again, Inspector Larson. How is your investigation going? Have you any leads to follow?" she asked.

"Sarah watches too many crime shows," Richard explained, to which George smiled as pleasantly as he could. Everyone watched too many crime shows. If real life was as the TV depicted it, there wouldn't be an issue with the growing population. Half the country would have been murdered.

"One," George lied, omitting the other various open-ended pathways they had not yet concluded. "Which is what I'd like to speak to you about."

"Please, please, sit," Richard said, taking up a seat beside his wife on the sofa and offering George the matching Chesterfield armchair. The pair appeared quite at home and relaxed in light of their recent experience, which George suspected was a result of their surroundings.

"How's your car doing?" he asked politely and out of curiosity. "I hope you won't be stuck out here in the Wolds without transport for much longer."

"Oh no," Sarah said with a high, shrill laugh. "It's been lovely, hasn't it, Richie? We've been taking walks, enjoying the scenery, reminiscing about the old days." She leaned forwards, and George got a whiff of her tobacco-laced breath. "There are worse places to be trapped, you know, than in the middle of the Lincolnshire Wolds."

"Very true," George said. "Very true indeed."

"It should be ready for us the day after tomorrow," Richard said. "Until then, we'll just have to continue enjoying the country-side on foot. We considered getting a rental to tide us over." He raised his hands to present the place. "But why on earth would we drive with so many good walks on our doorstep?"

"Best way to enjoy the place, I say," George said, finding it surprisingly easy to settle into conversation with them. Maybe it was a generation thing. They were the kind of couple he and Grace might have once befriended in Mablethorpe and perhaps enjoyed long walks in their company along the wild beaches.

"So," Richard said, rubbing his hands together. "What can we help you with, Inspector?"

"Oh, sorry," George replied. I was just taking in the place. I love what they've done here, although I must say, I'm not usually one for open-planned living. I like a nice warm room with a fire-place. But this," he puffed out his cheeks. "I wouldn't turn this place down."

"Inspector?"

"Michael Wassall," he said, hoping the sudden mention of the name might inspire a reaction. He was right to think so. Both Sarah and Richard winced in synchronisation as though they had encountered a bad smell. "You know him," George said. It wasn't a question. The look on their faces was answer enough.

Richard coughed and leaned forward with his elbows on his knees. "Michael was the vicar at St Leonard's when we lived here." This much George already knew, so he stayed silent, allowing Richard room to expand on his knowledge. "And he was, well... How would you describe Michael, darling?"

"He was friendly enough. A little too friendly, if you ask me," she replied.

"How so?"

"Well, between you and me, Inspector, I'd go as far as to say he was intrusive," Sarah said. "Liked to stick his nose in where it wasn't wanted, if you know what I mean."

"Not really," George said.

"There were rumours," she continued. "From parents in the local area. Some of his colleagues had been accused of...you know?"

"No, not really."

She made a show of checking behind her, then lowered her voice to a hiss. "You know? The kids. The boys."

"Oh my," George said, to which she nodded emphatically.

"He had known about it, too. Even covered it up. I mean, God knows what else he was up to."

"God does know," Richard said, taking his wife's hand and nodding. "And it will be he who Michael has to answer to, when the time comes."

Without wanting to encourage the Hawkins to continue down a path of religious sentiments, George probed further. "Could you be more specific," he said, "about these allegations?"

"Abuse," Sarah answered, then lowered her voice. "*Sexual* abuse. Of young boys."

"Bloody awful business," Richard said next to her.

"Disgusting," Sarah said sharply, as though disagreeing with him. "*Ungodly* is what it is."

"And did you ever get that impression from him? That he might be involved?"

"Well, you never know, do you?" Richard said. "You know how it is. Even if he wasn't involved himself, he covered for others. They all watch each other's backs–"

"I don't think we should generalise," George said.

"Puts the church to shame, it does, that type of thing."

"You said you heard the rumours from parents in the area," George said, pleased to have coaxed them into speaking but not entirely content their opinions were wholly fair or just. "Were these parents your own children's friends, perhaps?"

"Children? God no," Sarah said, looking at her husband as though they were sharing an inside joke. "No, we never had any of our own, did we, Richard?"

"No, it wasn't in the stars for us," Richard said. "Slow swimmers," he added, with a wink at George that earned him a playful slap on the arm from Sarah.

"And did you go to church often?" George moved on. "At Saint Leonard's?"

"Every Sunday," Richard said. "And, of course, we were married there. I mean, we got to know Michael quite well. We admired him, really. Until, well, you know... Once the rumours came out, he left to live somewhere near Louth, last time I heard. And we moved to Norfolk soon after, too."

"And are you still in touch with anyone from the parish? Any of the parents?"

"Oh, no, no," Richard said. "It's been twenty years since we even lived here, detective. Some of them will be dead by now. Some of them will have moved on to other places. Doubt anyone will remember us."

"So, to be clear, you never *saw* anything yourselves? Regarding the rumours, that is."

Richard thought for a second, giving weight to his answer as though he wanted it only to include the truth. "No," he said. "If we had, believe me, we would have stopped it. But he was that type. Very touchy-feely, if you know what I mean."

George sat back in the armchair. He had been a policeman since the eighties. He knew how it was back then. Rumours spread around about the odd dirty old man. Hell, even Jimmy Saville, a famous man in the public eye, had got away with it for decades. Allegations were just that – allegations. They weren't taken half as seriously as they were today.

"Very well," George said, and he stood up from the armchair to button his coat. "Well, give my best wishes to your car. In the meantime, I'm sure you'll have a pleasant enough stay."

"I'm sure we will. Thank you, Inspector," Richard said, chuckling and rising to shake his hand. "Drive safe, now."

"Oh, I'm always careful, Mr Hawkins," George said with a parting smile. "You never know what's around the corner, do you?"

CHAPTER THIRTY-FOUR

"Now then," Ivy said, approaching the whiteboard and taking up the marker pen in George's absence. She pointed to a name in the middle, encircled to make it even more pronounced. "Juliet Shaw," she said. "What do we have?"

Campbell and Byrne had both scuttled from their desks towards the whiteboard when they saw Ivy strut into the incident room, focused as a laser beam.

"What about Samson?" Byrne said, looking through his notebook as though he had missed a major event. "I thought we were sure-."

"Samson is a deeply troubled and traumatised man," Ivy told him. "But that doesn't make him a killer."

"Yeah, but I thought-"

"And so did I," she said. "But the boss doesn't think so, and if I'm honest, I'm beginning to wonder myself. Besides, every shred of evidence we have is open to dispute. None of it is irrefutable."

"No," Campbell said. "But the MMO speaks for itself, surely? He was seen at the scene of the crime, he was living in Dean's house, and he was set to inherit generously when Dean died. Not to mention his DNA was found on Dean's body."

"All disputable," Ivy dismissed.

"How is it disputable? He was living at his Dean Worthing's house-"

"Like you said, PC Campbell," Ivy said in a subtle reminder of rank. "Samson was living with Dean. DNA crossover is to be expected."

Campbell hesitated. "Did you speak to him? Downstairs?"

"I did," Ivy said.

"*Alone?*" asked Byrne. "What about the boss?"

"The boss isn't here, Byrne, in case you haven't noticed."

Campbell and Byrne exchanged confused glances.

"Well, what did he say?" Campbell asked.

"Samson isn't a man of many words," Ivy replied. "But he is more vulnerable than we thought. A man like him is easily manipulated. He's been manipulated his whole life. He's used to it."

"So you think Juliet Shaw manipulated Samson into killing Dean Worthing?"

Ivy sighed. "Look, Samson said he saw a woman at the Bluestone Lodge before Dean died. It would be nice if we could put a name to that statement before the boss gets back."

"Sarge?"

"What is it, Campbell?" Ivy said, mulling over the limited information on the board.

"It's just..." Campbell started. "I mean, he's hardly a reliable witness; he's..." She struggled to find the right word, which Byrne found for her.

"A nutcase?" he said.

In Ivy's mind flashed the image of Adrian Samson, his eyes wild and animalistic as though there was no intelligent life behind them, only carnal instinct.

"Let's try and rephrase that into something a little more politically correct, shall we?" Campbell added, to which Byrne shrugged. "But yes, that is what I mean."

"Look, Juliet Shaw is an unexplored avenue," Ivy said. "That's all I'm saying. She has an MMO, just like Samson. So let's explore it, shall we?"

Both Campbell and Byrne did not look especially convinced, but they settled down as though ready to listen.

"So," Ivy said, once more holding up the pen, "what do we have?"

"She was seen heading towards the crime scene half an hour after Dean Worthing died," Campbell said. "It doesn't matter which direction she was heading. She was in the area. That's opportunity."

"Good," Ivy said, writing down *car at scene of crime* on the board. "What else?"

"She's in the will," Byrne said. "Set to inherit the business. That gives her a motive."

"Good," Ivy said, writing down *inherits the business.*

"If we're going down the manipulation route," Campbell said, "then she was seen speaking to Samson just two weeks ago, and we only have her word that Dean sent her there in the first place. For all we know, Dean knew nothing about it until he arrived at the house."

"Yes," Ivy said, adding *seen with Samson* and stepping back to admire the whiteboard. "But it's not enough. We need to back this up with some facts. Campbell, have we requested a warrant to search her financials?"

"Came through while you downstairs, sarge," she replied.

"Good. Look into her accounts, would you? See if there's any urgent financial motivation. We're looking for overdue debts, credit cards, and loan sharks. Run a credit check if you have to. You know the drill." She turned to Byrne. "You can look into ANPR. Track where her car has been in the last two weeks since meeting Adrian. I want to see where she goes, what she does, what her routine is. Gather the evidence and get me an outline."

It was a big task and one that, from the look on Byrne's face, was rather daunting. But he swallowed any protests and took a deep breath.

"Yes, Sarge," he replied.

"Gather what you can, and let's meet back here in an hour or so. Remember, we only have Samson for another..." She checked her watch. "Eighteen hours. I want to eliminate Shaw from the investigation so we can focus on building a solid case for the CPS."

With satisfaction, she watched Byrne and Campbell scuttle off to fulfil their duties, and felt a tinge of accomplishment. Leading a team had been a long-term career goal for as long as she could remember. Yet, to attain that goal would mean George's retirement, rendering the achievement little more than bittersweet. Although it seemed he wasn't going to retire anytime soon. Not that she wanted him to. She loved working with George. In fact, she wasn't sure she would even enjoy the job without his company. But still, it was fun to take the reins every now and again.

She glanced at her watch again. He'd been gone for over two hours now. No phone call, no updates. Just radio silence. She checked her phone, hoping to find a missed call, but there was nothing.

She stared at the board once more, and her eyes were drawn to Samson's name. She pictured him in the cell, as he had been, so wild and unpredictable, yet tame and timid and able to hold a conversation.

"You're an enigma, aren't you?" she said aloud. "Is this all a game, Adrian? Is that what this is? A game?" her eyes wandered to the top right, where George had penned the names from Dean Worthing's memoirs. "And if it is a game, then where do they fit into this?"

"James and Samuel?" a voice read from behind her. "Last names would be helpful."

"Sorry, Robson, but I don't have time for this right now."

"I just wanted to apologise-"

"No need," she said curtly, refusing to turn to face him. He stepped up beside and touched her shoulder, but she pulled away. "I said no," she told him, then caught a flash of pain in his eyes.

He made a show of putting his hands in his pockets.

"If you want to talk," he said.

"I don't."

"But if you do," he pressed. "No pressure. No expectations. Just good company. Friendly company."

"I'll bear that in mind," she said, hoping some good manners might convince him to leave. And it was that thought that shone a light on her behaviour. "Look, I'm...I'm in the middle of something right now."

"John and Samuel?" he said. "Want me to grab a phone book? We could call them all up."

"Not this," she said, waving a hand at the investigation and failing to hide her amusement. She looked up at him apologetically. "When I'm ready. When I'm not..."

"In the middle of something?"

"Yeah," she said. "Then I'll let you know, alright."

He smiled one of those smiles that belied his truest thoughts and then turned on his heels.

"Dan?" she said, hoping not to draw the attention of the other officers in the room. He turned again, eyebrows raised. "Cheers, yeah? I don't know how long it'll take. The..."

"The something?" he replied and seemed to take a second or two to admire her features. "Take your time."

CHAPTER THIRTY-FIVE

It was only after the hour was up, and Ivy had called for Campbell and Byrne to once more gather around the whiteboard that George finally showed up. He ambled through the incident room, lost in his thoughts as if he were in a meadow with the sun on his face. He made his way to the back of the room without saying a word.

"Alright, guv?" she said.

"Hmm?" he replied as if she had startled him from his musings. He glanced between Ivy and the board. "What's this?" His tone was not harsh or accusatory. That was not George's style. But evidently, he was a little taken aback.

"Guv," Ivy said, answering with her own subtle allegation. "Been anywhere nice?"

"I've been driving all over the Wolds, it seems," he said, letting his coat slide from his arms and placing it over the back of a chair, which he then perched on. He seemed content for Ivy to lead the briefing. Either that or he was keen to give her a chance to explain. She followed his gaze and realised the name she had circled perplexed him. "Has there been a development?"

"I just wanted to rule her out, guv," Ivy defended. "Before we interview Samson again."

"I thought we had ruled her out," he replied. "Given that I saw her thirty minutes after Dean Worthing died, heading towards the crime scene, I might add."

"Well, yeah, but that doesn't mean she couldn't have circled back."

"Agreed," he said. "But I thought I asked you to build a case against Samson." He glanced at Byrne and Campbell. "And I asked you to look into records of child abuse. Have we completed these tasks? If so, then I congratulate you all and wholeheartedly support any efforts to progress the remaining leads." He waited for an answer. "Byrne? Anything to add? Were there any reports of misconduct within the local church community pertaining to Michael Wassall?"

"Well, not that I've come across so far-"

"Campbell?"

"Guv?"

"I asked you to request warrants for the financial records. How's that going?"

"They came through a while back, guv."

"And have you made any progress?"

"Well, I was going to..."

"That's a no then, is it?" he said.

"It's my fault, guv. I didn't realise," Ivy said.

"And what have you busied yourself with?" he asked. "You were downstairs with Sergeant Robson when I called, and now I find you're looking into a suspect with an alibi. And I am that alibi, I might add."

"It's not exactly a solid alibi," she replied. "You said it yourself."

"I know, but when I left here, you were dead set on charging Samson. I half expected to find you tying a noose and ready to string him up."

"I know, but..." she said.

"But what?"

She sighed.

"I went to see him. I went to see Samson, not Sergeant Robson."

He narrowed his eyes and bit down on his lower lip.

"I see," he said. "Alone?"

"Yes," she said, not wanting to mention that Robson had been on the other side of the door.

"Well, that was a poor move," he said.

"It was a calculated risk."

"I see. Well, did your calculations add up to anything?" George asked. "Were you able to lull him from whatever daydream he was in?"

This time, his curiosity outweighed his concern.

"He did, actually."

"Sorry?"

"He talked. Only briefly," she added, seeing the intrigue in George's raised eyebrows. "He told me about his childhood, how he hated being a kid, that he didn't find it freeing but trapping."

"You got him to open up?"

"Like I said, it was a calculated risk."

"Well, that shines a new light on the subject," he said. "What else did he have to say? Did you ask about John and Samuel?"

She winced a little.

"I didn't get that far," she said. "He just said that he had a rough childhood."

"Well, that makes sense," George said. "The scars on his back could have told us that much. Anything else?"

"There was something. He said he saw a woman's face at the window of Bluestone Lodge the night Dean died."

"Definitely a woman?"

"That's what he said."

"I see," he replied, eyeing Juliet's name on the board as though it now made more sense. "Out of interest, how exactly did you get him to talk?"

Ivy hesitated. "I just spoke to him, guv."

"You spoke to him?"

"Yes. He was, well, he was mostly listening, and something I said, I guess, touched a nerve and opened him up." She wanted to distance herself from what exactly she had talked to Adrian about. It had been a vulnerable monologue. One she had not shared with anyone, not George, not a therapist, and barely even with herself. Only with Adrian Samson. "But then it was like he changed. Something in his eyes changed. There was an intelligence there. He could hold a conversation with me. But I think I pushed him too far. He regressed again."

"Regressed?"

"Yeah, he..." she glanced up at Campbell and Byrne and then back at George, hoping he might see fit to discuss the matter in private. But he waited patiently. "Well, he came at me, guv."

"He came at you? Jesus, Ivy-"

"I know, I know-"

"What were you thinking? You shouldn't have been in there alone."

"I was thinking that maybe he would open up one-on-one, without the formality of an interview room, and I was right. He's vulnerable, guv. I think he's more vulnerable than he is dangerous."

George let this observation settle for a minute, and then he seemed to make a decision, crossing his legs as though happy for Ivy to start the show.

"Hence your decision to look into Shaw?"

"I think you're right," she said. "While everything points to him right now, I think there's a chance he's been played."

"Well, as disappointed as I am that my instructions have not been followed and that you chose to break protocol, putting your own life in danger," he said, "I have to confess, I am mildly impressed."

"Guv?"

"Why don't we set Samson to one side for now? Flip the board over, will you? Let's try looking at this from a different angle. Namely Michael Wassall. See what we've got on him." He rested his notepad on his knee and began noting something down. Ivy didn't move. She left the whiteboard as it was, with Juliet Shaw's name in prominent lettering. Eventually, he looked up, glanced at the board, and then at Ivy.

"Did you hear what I said?" he began. "I want to start this over. I want to focus on Michael Wassall, at least hypothetically. Let's see where it leads us, shall we?"

"That was decades ago, guv,". she said. "Even if Wassall was involved in these abuse allegations, we already know that Dean Worthing was abused. Like you said, the scars on his back tell us that much."

"Whatever happened all those years ago, Ivy," George said patiently, "connects to this case now."

"We don't know that–"

"*I* know it does."

Ivy held his stare, stubborn. It had been exactly the same with their previous investigation, George obsessing over the past, thinking he could solve two cases at once. But life was not always so neat. Investigations did not always connect. Life was not a story in a book.

"And you think that because of the memoir?"

"Yes," George said, rising to her challenge. "I do. Why would Dean finish his memoir and then kill himself? Think about it. More likely, he finished his memoir, and someone didn't want it to be released to the world, so they killed him. If we find out *who* exactly abused Dean Worthing forty years ago, then we have a lead on who might have killed him a few days ago."

"Campbell's right," Ivy said. "We can't rely on a book to help us with this investigation."

At this, Campbell shuffled uncomfortably in her seat as though not wanting to be used as a pawn in their power play. "It is not a book," George said calmly, for what felt like the hundredth time. "It's a memoir. If it was a murder mystery or a romance novel, then fine. But it's not, Ivy. It's his story. It's the truth."

Ivy threw her hands up. "It's a *sellable* story."

"Ivy," George said, literally putting his foot down and leaning on his knees with his elbows. "We're looking into Michael Wassall. Juliet Shaw can wait."

It was a clear order. Ivy had clearly pushed her luck enough for one day. Even a relationship as familiar as hers and George's had its limits. At the end of the day, he was her boss, and even though he rarely reminded her of it, he was above Ivy in the hierarchy.

"Yes, guv."

Ivy flipped the whiteboard, removed the pen lid, and in the middle of the board, pressing heavily to outlet her frustration, she wrote a single name – *Michael Wassall.*

She turned to face him, waiting for the next request, like the woman from Countdown.

"Right then," he said, clearing his throat the way he often did as a means to reset himself. She had to admit, he demonstrated great control over his emotions. "I want to know everything about the man, and when I say everything, I mean *everything.*"

CHAPTER THIRTY-SIX

"Here we go," Byrne said excitedly. "It's not much, but..." He turned his laptop for the others to see.

"What is it?" George asked, squinting to see the text from a good eight feet away.

"It looks like there was a series of allegations against churches across East Lincolnshire. Wassall's name comes up. Quite a few times, actually, but from what I can tell, it wasn't as someone who was being accused but someone who defended others who were accused. He gave a number of statements to the local press and was quoted as dismissing the allegations as a lynch mob against the church."

"Right," George said, feeling that same flame of disgust that he always did when confronted with such stories.

"It's not bad enough that they did it," Byrne said. "But they had to go out of their way to make sure no one found out. That's just as bad, isn't it?"

"Not just as bad," Ivy said. "But still pretty terrible."

"So, this is why Wassall left the church?" Byrne asked George. "Because he..." The lad looked back in his notebook for the exact phrasing George had used. "He knew people who did terrible things in the name of religion?"

"Seems so," George said. "Although he wasn't quite so specific."

"But we can't rule him out," Campbell said. "Just because he was never accused doesn't mean he wasn't involved. If he was so committed to covering up other people's abuse, he could well have been abusing boys too and covering his own tracks."

"I agree," George said, then muttered. "All signs point to Wassall."

"*All* signs?" asked Ivy. "What other signs are there?"

George sighed and looked up at one of the two people in the room who would be sure to scoff at his next words. "The stone walls," he said.

"The stone walls," Ivy repeated, monotone.

"In the memoir," George said, holding her gaze, unashamed of the hold Dean's words had on his thoughts. They were the closest thing they had to a witness report from the dead man, and he was unwilling to dismiss them as fiction. "Every time the boys were punished, they were taken to a cellar with stone walls. When I was in St Leonard's, I noticed the tower walls were stone, and at the bottom of the tower was a space just like the one Dean describes. I believe that's where the boys were taken. That's where they were punished. That's where the events of Dean's story happened, his childhood of abuse."

In the silence that followed, George could practically hear the cynicism stirring in both Ivy and Campbell's minds. While Ivy had been willing, at first, to support George's investment in the memoir, it seemed that her focus on Juliet Shaw had swayed her patience.

As though not wanting to merely repeat the same criticisms that they had expressed during the last few days, both women stayed silent, and it was Byrne who spoke up.

"If that's where Dean had been abused," he said, "that doesn't necessarily mean that it was Michael Wassall who did it. I mean, that church is open twenty-four-seven, isn't it? That's the point. It's a...what do you call it?" He clicked. "A sanctuary."

"Right, but the door to that tower is always locked. Stephen needed a key to get in."

"The same key that was in Dean Worthing's pocket?" Byrne said.

"Exactly."

"So, how many keys are there?" Ivy finally spoke up.

"Only one, according to Stephen Cross. The one he was given when he took over the church which was passed on by Michael Wassall. But now we know there must be two. Maybe more."

"Maybe Wassall kept one?" Byrne said.

"Maybe," George said.

"Then how did Dean get it?" asked Campbell.

George stayed silent, for he did not have an answer to the very same question that had been swarming his mind all afternoon,

"You said signs, guv," Ivy said quietly and slowly. "Plural. What other signs are there in the memoir that Wassall is our man?"

"The religious imagery during the punishment scene is intense," George said. "This wasn't just child abuse; this was religiously motivated child abuse. Punishments were made while reciting Bible verses, chanting, and performing religious rituals. These were God-fearing people."

"People?" Byrne said. "There was more than one abuser."

"Well..." George hesitated. "Dean was vague about that."

"Christ," Campbell muttered under her breath.

"What was that, PC Campbell?" George said, in a rare display of authority, the same way a parent might use a child's full name only when they were in deep trouble.

"Guv, come on," she pushed. "If Dean's memoir was meant to be a tell-all about his childhood of abuse, then why didn't he name his abusers? Why doesn't he describe them? Why does he keep it *vague*, as you say?"

"It's a literary technique," George said faltering, "to symbolise the abusers as the high and mighty characters that Dean saw them as when he was a child."

"Guv," Ivy said slowly and surely, in a manner that he had heard her speak to her children. "We can't build an investigation on literary techniques."

"Thank you, Ivy," George said. "I am aware of that. That is why I'm trying to build a case based on evidence. And if you hadn't noticed, we have a series of well-documented abuse allegations that happened in the area where Dean lived and against young boys Dean's age. Give me some credit, would you? This isn't some shot in the dark."

"Those allegations have been settled, guv. It was forty years ago."

"I know when the eighties were, Ivy. So?"

"So, I think you're losing focus on the actual investigation here."

"Which is?"

"Dean's death!" Ivy said, throwing her hands up in despair. "His suicide, likely."

"What are you saying, Sergeant Hart?" George couldn't remember ever using Ivy's title before, but for the first time, it felt fitting. A tight ball of frustration was growing in his chest.

"I'm saying, is it possible that this all could have been a wild goose chase for four days while we investigated a troubled man's suicide?"

"These allegations," George said, standing to slap the whiteboard with the palm of his hand, "muddy the waters of whether it *was* a suicide. Dean had just written a memoir about his childhood of abuse, and then someone who didn't want that information to come to light might have killed Dean and made it look like a suicide. Can't you see that? Or do you not think things are worth being brought to justice just because they didn't take place last week?"

"That's not what I'm saying."

"Then what are you saying, Ivy?"

"That–"

"That we shouldn't bother looking into past allegations against religious abuse because they're so common at this point?" George interrupted the tirade and yet was surprised at the calmness of his own voice.

"No, I–"

"That the potential murder of one man, just because he falls in the category of a suicide victim, should not be investigated?"

They were face to face now while Byrne and Campbell looked on like worried teens watching their parents fight.

"*No*, guv," Ivy said. "I would never–"

"Then what are you saying?"

"That this is about *you,* guv, not Dean," she blurted out when she got the chance. "I'm saying that you have a tendency to live in the past."

The comment was far more personal than anyone in the room could have known, considering their recent conversations about George's marriage, his romanticisation of his memories of Grace, and his inability to remember a time with his wife that was anything less than perfect.

They stared at each other in silence.

Something about the move from Mablethorpe to the Wolds had brought their relationship into the spotlight in a way they had never experienced before. Never once had they spoken harshly to each other. They had never even talked over each other. Indeed, they had worked in something akin to harmony for the past five years. And yet, only a month into their transfer, they had shared more tense conversations than they ever had previously. Perhaps the secrets and troubles of their personal lives, stirred by the move, were blocking their ability to work together.

The two PCs were wise enough to keep quiet, and it was only the shrill ring of Campbell's desk phone that disturbed the stand-off. For a moment, George thought she might let it ring out, but of course, she was unable to leave a phone unanswered. She rose slowly, as though not wanting to spook anyone, and went to answer it.

George was the first to break eye contact by rubbing the bridge of his nose.

"We're bringing in Michael Wassall," he said, leaving no space for interpretation. "We're going to question him about abuse allegations in the eighties and find out what he knows about the abuse of Dean Worthing. Whatever unanswered questions remain in this investigation, Wassall has the answers."

"Yes, guv," Byrne said, without his usual pep but still loyal to the task.

"Whatever you say," muttered Ivy.

They heard Campbell hang up the phone with a polite "Thank you" and she stepped back over to the whiteboard.

"We're bringing in Michael Wassall," George repeated to her. "Please talk to Sergeant Robson. Ask him if we can use two of his team, will you?"

"We can't, guv," she said

"What?" George said, more exasperated than challenging.

"We can't bring in Michael Wassall."

"Why not?"

"Well…" she started, then took a deep breath. "Because his body has just been discovered. He's dead, guv."

CHAPTER THIRTY-SEVEN

"Give me a minute, will you?" George muttered and dropped back into his seat. Each of them collected their notes and laptops in silence and headed towards the door. "Not you."

Ivy stopped, and from the corner of his eye, he saw her nod to the other two in a 'Go on, I'll catch you up' fashion.

"Remember what I said," George called after the two PCs. "I want everything we can get on Wassall."

"Guv," Byrne replied by way of confirmation.

Ivy idled back to him and dropped into the seat opposite his.

"Listen," she said quietly. "I'm sorry-"

"No," he said, stopping her before she committed. "No, it's me who should be sorry. And I am." He looked up at her. "I taught you to question my instructions. Therefore, I have no right to reprimand you for doing so. Especially not in front of the team."

"The team?" she said, clearly aiming at humour. "Byrne and Campbell?"

"They're better than you give them credit for," he replied.

"Campbell, maybe-"

"Byrne, too," he said. "He's twice the copper he was a few months ago."

"Right, but what we need is for him to be on point *now*, surely?"

"I disagree," he said. "What we need is somebody we can mould."

"We can mould? *You*, you mean."

"No, I mean we. Us. We can mould him." There was a compliment in there, but he had neither the energy nor the gumption to explain it. "Anyway," he said with a sigh. "Michael Wassall."

"You're sure, are you?"

"No," he replied. "But I'm sure Samson isn't as guilty as his predicament suggests. What else have we got?"

"Well, there's always Shaw?"

He sat up straight, laying his hands flat on his thighs.

"Tell you what. If Wassall is a dead end, we go after Shaw," he said. "And you can lead it."

She nodded slowly but countered his offer.

"If Wassall is a dead end, if you excuse the pun, then we'll see where we're at, and I get to call the direction," she said. "Who knows what else we might've dragged up by then."

"Deal," he replied, then dropped back into a slouch. "Christ, Ivy. I was talking to the man not two hours ago."

"I'd be ready for some backlash," Ivy muttered, which was enough for George to raise his head. "The uniform who attended the scene didn't call in to let us know what Wassall had done. He called in to warn us that she's ready to make a complaint."

"Ah, brilliant," he said, or rather, the words escaped.

"Did you lean on him?"

"I did nothing of the sort. In fact, if I'd had my way, I would have stayed and asked more questions. I would have pressed harder."

"So why didn't you?" she asked.

"We're not ready," he told her. "Not ready to put him in the limelight, anyway. I just wanted to get a feel for who he is...or was."

"And?" she asked. "What feeling did you get?"

He shoved himself from his seat, walked to the board, and then turned, his hands firmly in his pockets.

"Something isn't right," he said. "The wife-"

"Francesca?"

"Right. Fran. She's quite protective. It was obvious I wasn't going to get much more from either of them. I think he knew I'd caught the scent and saw little room to manoeuvre."

"We'll never really know, will we?" Ivy said. "But I don't think you can blame yourself. Not if you're sure you erred on the side of caution."

"Are they sure it was a suicide?" he asked.

"His wife found him hanging from the curtain rail in his study. Aside from you, nobody had been in or out of the house. She said his behaviour had been off."

"Since my visit?"

"No. No, for the past few days."

"Since Dean Worthing's death?"

"Possibly," she replied, then mirrored his posture. "Listen, if Fran Wassall does make a complaint, investigating him for a crime will be harder. We're likely to have Long on our cases, blocking any progress for fear of creating a media storm."

"In which case, we need to gather what we can now before the roads are blocked."

"I'm just being pragmatic, guv."

He sighed heavily. She was right. Or at least, she was potentially right.

"What do you suggest?"

"There's a few things we can do," she said, as if she had already contemplated their next moves. "First of all, let's get Wassall's DNA over to Katy Southwell. Have her run it against the samples taken from the crime scene and from the house."

He nodded.

"That's a start."

"That's the easy one," she replied and stared across at him in warning.

"You want to interview his wife?"

She winced. "Interview is such a formal word," she said with an accompanying wink. "A chat would be more appropriate. You know? Maybe myself or Campbell could pay her a visit. A friendly female-."

"Out of the question," he told her. "Absolutely out of the question."

"Guv, we're running out of leads. We've got a lunatic in custody, a woman with a questionable alibi, and a man who was embroiled in scandal who, only a few hours ago, strung himself up. Unless you want to investigate Stephen Cross, we've got nothing to go on." He opened his mouth to speak, but she cut him off. "And I draw the line at Cross," she said, to which he nodded.

"Agreed," he said. "But we're not talking to Wassall's wife. "Her threatening to complain could very well have been down to her emotions. Her husband has just died, after all. The last thing I want to do is to kick a hornet's nest."

"Then what do you suggest?" she asked. "Where do we go from here?"

"We do what we're paid to do," he said. "Leave those two to look into Wassall. Have Katy Southwell analyse his DNA. Meanwhile, I suggest we close off any other avenues."

"Other avenues?"

"Shaw," he said and smiled an apology. "Eliminate her from the investigation. Even if we do manage to posthumously find Wassall guilty, you can be sure the defence team his wife pulls together will raise the idea of her being responsible."

"Reasonable doubt?"

"They don't have to prove his innocence, remember?"

"Right," she said. "We need to prove his guilt-"

"And if there's a remote chance that Dean Worthing's death could have been down to somebody else, he'll walk."

"Walk?"

"Hypothetically," he said.

"What about you?" she asked. "What are you going to do?"

He slid his coat onto his shoulders.

"I think I need some time alone," he said. "I need to come to terms with it all."

"You're going home to read that manuscript, aren't you?"

"Have a look at registered births, will you?" he said, distracted by the promise of those alluring pages. "See if there's any record of a Samuel or a James being born that fits our timeline."

"You didn't answer my question, guv," she said.

"Dean Worthing knew Michael Wassall, Ivy. As did Samuel and James, whoever they are." He collected his bag and tapped his pockets for his keys. "And now I find that I'd like to know him, too. Or at least, I would have liked to have known him. We are, after all, running out of people who can help us."

CHAPTER THIRTY-EIGHT

The first time I really met Reverend Wassall, I found myself opening up to him. He was good like that. Easy to talk to. He seemed to get as much from those moments of privacy as I did.

Of course, I had met him before, at services every Sunday morning. But he held a kind of celebrity status during those times, as the man at the front of the room, the messenger from God, relaying his wisdom to everyone. No, I had never spoken to him one-on-one, not until that day.

We were all encouraged to speak to him. Catholics might have called it a confession. It felt more like cleansing to me. It was a kindness, to cleanse our filthy souls. At the end of the day, I just wanted somebody to talk to.

It was a Sunday after the service had finished. I stayed behind, and he welcomed me. I remember it being a chilly, foggy morning sometime during winter; the sun struggled to break through the clouds. Inside the church was just as cold as the outside, its stone walls offering little insulation. I waited on the hard, wooden pew for the vicar to finish his after-service duties, and when he finally approached me, he seemed curious.

"Dean?" he asked. "Is there something wrong?"

I felt so small, peering up at him.

"I've something to say," I said shyly. "Something I should tell you."

I was always shy around adults, unsure what their triggers were, *what words I could or could not use around them, and what specific behaviours and antics might set them off.*

"Is there something you'd like to get off your chest?" he asked, to which I nodded. "Something you've done, perhaps?"

Again, I nodded, and he sat beside me, staring up at the stained glass windows.

"Did you enjoy the service this morning?" he asked, and of course, I was obliged to nod. Yet, somehow, he saw through the gesture. "Did you listen to every word?"

I hesitated, and he smiled.

"I try," I explained. "I do try to follow."

"Do you recall the prayer of preparation?"

Again, I hesitated, and shame crimsoned my cheeks.

"It's okay," he assured me, and he placed his arm around my shoulder for comfort.

"Almighty God, unto whom all hearts be open, all desires known, and from whom no secrets are hidden. Cleanse the thoughts from our hearts by the inspiration of thy Holy Spirit that we may perfectly love thee, and worthily magnify thy holy name..."

"Through Christ our Lord, Amen?" I said, fearful I had exposed my ignorance.

But he nodded.

"Do you know why we say that at the beginning of each service?" he asked. "Do you understand why we must all say it?"

I shrugged.

"I just say it," I told him. "Because I have to. Because everyone does."

He squeezed my shoulder and crossed his legs to get comfortable.

"We say it to cleanse us," he explained. "So we may enter into the communion fresh and clean, as it were. In peace." I gazed up at him. His voice was alluring, and, on reflection, seemed to resonate throughout the old church. "My boy, whatever it is you've done, you have no cause for shame." He raised his hand to present the old vaulted ceiling and beyond. "God understands. God forgives."

He took my hand in his and held it palm-facing up. Then, one by one, he closed each of my fingers until I held a fist, which he squeezed tight in his own.

"Keep it," he said. "God has heard you." He leaned forward and placed his hand against my chest. "He's in you. He's in all of us. You know that, don't you? There's nothing you could do that He wouldn't forgive. But you must want to. You must yearn for forgiveness. Does that make sense?"

I shrugged. "I guess."

"Well, that's the important thing," said Michael. "Now, come with me," he said, placing his hands on his knees and standing from the pew with far more energy than he had ever displayed before.

"Where?" I asked. "Where are we going?"

He strode down the aisle, his footsteps seeming to hang in the air.

"I want to show you something," he said, coming to a stop at the back of the church. "My special place."

"But...how do I know He's heard me? How do I know He's forgiven me?"

"You have to trust Him," he said, putting two gentle hands on my shoulders and forcing me to look into his deep, kind eyes, "You have to believe. You must exercise faith."

From his pocket, he withdrew a large brass key that looked far older than any kind I had ever seen. He pushed the key into the old tower door, glanced at me, and then winked as he shoved the door open. I had never seen it open before. I thought it was one of those places that were out of bounds. But open, it did, to reveal another door leading to a narrow, winding staircase.

"Follow me," he said, his words somehow distant.

He stepped through the doorway and beckoned me inside, where the shadows had engulfed him and his kindness, leaving only an ethereal outline in its wake - featureless and foreboding.

Until he reached for me. A hand from the darkness coaxed me inside with a firm grip on my arm. We descended two steps into a dank space that time had long since forgotten, and light had long since warmed.

"Do you still feel the need to repent?" he asked, his voice stunted and his words succinct.

"I'm not sure," I replied, and I turned to leave, but he held me tight, and I could feel his breath on my face.

"Have faith," he whispered, and he took my hand, and he led me into the light. Out of the shadows, we climbed. I counted forty steps on the way up, though I stumbled once or twice, trembling with fear, until at last, we broke out of the staircase and into the sunlight, where he beamed with joy, raising his arms to the heavens.

I could see for miles in every direction. I gazed east, towards the coast, and west towards the Fens. I could even see our house – and it looked tiny and insignificant.

"This is my favourite place," he said.

"In the church?"

"Maybe even the world," he explained. "Whenever the world feels dark and hopeless, as it often does. I climb up here to be as close to the sky as I can get. It gives me perspective. It offers me beauty. And I can see the world as it really is – large and vast and full of opportunity," he said, and he drew my attention to rays of sunshine spilling through the clouds and grinned. "There is always hope, Dean. You are never alone when you have God by your side."

I remember my eyes welling at this point, unsure, even now, if it was because of the inference of hope I'd never been encouraged to feel or whether it was from the emerging sun dazzling my young eyes.

"I think I understand," I told him.

"Because God is by your side," he said. "And if ever you can't feel him. If ever you need that reassurance, Dean, you can always come here. If you need to feel hope. When the world feels dark and dangerous. Reach out to him."

"How...how can I come here?" I asked, laughing nervously. "The door is always locked."

"My boy," he said, and he held the large brass key up. His smile radiated a kindness that I had never experienced in all my short life. "All you have to do is ask."

CHAPTER THIRTY-NINE

Somehow, the sentiment in Dean Worthing's words had carried through to George's morning. He leaned against his car and watched while she parked.

"Forgive me. I was wrong," he said immediately, by way of a greeting.

"Is that right?" she said, appearing perplexed. She locked her car and strode over cautiously before accepting the coffee he had bought her.

"I was wrong about Wassall. You were right. We should be considering more recent events. We should be looking forward."

Ivy took the peace offering and savoured her first sip of coffee. "If we're confessing and begging forgiveness," she said slowly, "I should never have said that about you living in the past."

"Ah, it's okay," he said. "You're probably right about that, too. The truth is, I *have* been living in the past. It's time to look to the future, or present day, at least."

The statement covered the investigation and beyond, and Ivy tapped her coffee against his as though toasting to moving forward in their lives.

"So why the change of heart?" she said.

George took a big breath, unsure whether what he was about to say would unravel any of their recent coming together. "Dean's memoir," he admitted. "Wassall was kind to him. He was the only kind adult in his life. He offered him sanctuary. A place to go during times of darkness."

"Guv, abuse victims often have a complex relationship with their abuser. He might have been kind to him one day and cruel the next. He might even have claimed that the abuse was a kindness. He—"

"It wasn't him, Ivy," he said. "I know it wasn't."

That, it seemed, was all she needed on the theory, George's insistence.

"Well, that figures."

"How so? I thought you'd be relishing in my misgivings."

"I had a call from Katy Southwell this morning," she began. "She ran Wassall's DNA against every sample they have, including Dean Worthing's body, his house, the lot. There's absolutely nothing to suggest he was involved."

"But he was still culpable. One way or another, he's involved."

"Guv?"

"He knew," George said, opening his car door.

She strode briskly to the passenger door, opened it and climbed inside, automatically reaching for the seat belt.

"He knew what?"

"He knew that Dean was...troubled. That something was going on."

"What makes you say that?"

"Because he offered the lad sanctuary, Ivy. He told Dean that... " George struggled to articulate the sentiment of the prose. "Why else would he take the time to give the lad a place to go in times of darkness?"

"In times of darkness?"

"His words, not mine," George said as he started the car and moved out of the car park.

"And you still think we should follow him up?" she added.

"For the time being," he replied. "Campbell and Byrne are on it. I'd be interested to see exactly how much he knew."

"Guv, you're not making sense. We're jumping from suspect to suspect. First it was Samson, then Shaw, then Wassall, and then it wasn't Wassall, and now you're saying he was involved."

"Welcome to the world inside my head, Ivy," he said, hoping his grin would ease her concerns.

"Where are we going?" she asked, giving her a sideways stare. "Oh no. Not Francesca Wassall?"

"The key, Ivy," he said cryptically. "The key."

"Guv-"

"How did Dean get the key to the tower?" George said. "In the book, Wassall holds it out in front of him. He says that whenever he needs to use it, he can."

"So that damp little space beneath the tower is his sanctuary?"

"No, the sanctuary *is* the tower," he told her. "It's the wide open space. It's the heavens above. It's the connection to God."

"Christ, you missed your calling, guv."

"He didn't give him the key," George said. "He just gave him access to it. The question is, did Wassall still have access to it all these years later?"

"So, you think that's how Dean got the key? He simply asked Wassall, and Wassall gave it to him?" she said, to which George nodded. "That would mean-"

"There are two keys," George finished. "I mean, think about it. What lock maker creates only one key for a lock? Michael Wassall gave only one key over to Stephen Cross when he took over the church. The other one, he must have kept for himself. After all, if you had a key to your favourite place in the world, would you give it up?"

The mid-morning roads were devoid of traffic, and even the tractors seemed to be having a day off. The drive through the Wolds went by in a flash of imagination and possibilities, broken

THE HARDER THEY FALL

only by Ivy's infrequent attempts at small talk. But she knew well enough when he was and was not open to distraction.

It was only when they pulled up outside the 1970s-style bungalow that George relinquished the spaghetti junction in his mind, hoping that whatever they learned from Fran Wassall would help to create a road through the centre of it.

Once more, he was reminded of how lonely life could be. The remote house, and now a woman forced to endure her remaining days alone. And for what purpose?

When Fran Wassall opened the door, her eyes were bloodshot, vacant, and soulless, like those of someone who had been up drinking all night. Perhaps she had.

But when she spoke, her words were clear, albeit frail, and the youthful, reddish glow that had shone through in her hair and cheeks the day before had faded.

"Hello, Mrs Wassall," George said. "I'm so, so sorry to hear the news."

It wasn't a lie; although Ivy squirmed uncomfortably beside him, George meant every word. If Wassall had been aware of abuse, they should also consider that he had also been the man to offer the suffering boy a slither of hope and kindness. Anyway, Wassall wasn't there. His heartbroken wife, however, was, and George would do what he could to comfort her.

"You'll want to come in, of course," she said, pushing the door open, and George and Ivy followed Fran down the hallway and into the kitchen in the same manner as George had done on his previous visit. "Can I get you some tea?"

"I'm okay," George said, not wanting to add to her burdens. "Ivy?"

"I've just had a coffee." She smiled kindly at the offer. "Thank you, though. Perhaps I can make you one?"

"It's no bother," Fran said. "It does me good to keep busy. Keeps my mind..." Her words trailed off, and she gazed at his photo on the sideboard.

"Is there somebody who can look after you?" George asked, to which she glared accusingly at him. "I mean, somebody who can sit with you. Keep you company. That sort of thing."

She shook her head and pursed her lips.

"There's nobody," she muttered, and she gazed through the window, perhaps remembering her husband tending the gardens or perhaps wondering who would tend them now.

"I was actually hoping, Fran," George said, for fear of having his arm twisted, "that we could see..." He hesitated. "Your husband's study?"

Fran winced only slightly but then relented.

"Of course, of course," she replied, her voice monotone, as though it was, in fact, the very last place in the house she wanted to go. "You'll understand if-"

"We'll find it," he told her. "You just rest up."

Unlike the other doors, the door to the study was closed. He took a deep breath before entering, forcing himself to see past the image of Michael Wassall hanging by his neck. He needed a clear mind for what he was about to do.

It was a study like any other. Just like in the rest of the house, there were no religious symbols on the walls and very few things that belied Michael Wassall's personality. The furniture comprised a bookcase and a single desk with a computer that even George knew to be ancient. The bookcase, which took up the entirety of one wall, hadn't been organised for what looked like decades. The sun's morning glow streamed through the east-facing window, and George's attention was drawn to where the curtains had, until yesterday, hung. They had been removed, along with the rope and Wassall's body. But where the flock wallpaper was old and faded around most of the room, where the curtains had hung, the wallpaper, with its raised fleur-de-lis pattern, appeared almost new, protected from the light for years.

"He was a troubled man," Fran said quietly from the doorway, and both George and Ivy turned to face her.

"Mrs Wassall-"

"No, it's okay. It needs saying," she said, and George eyed Ivy's obvious unease. She might appear as hard as nails, but there was a heart in there somewhere. "He'd been...struggling," Fran continued. "For a while now, if I'm honest. Ever since he left the church, really. It was everything to him, you know? Imagine it? Imagine everything you believe in and live for being ripped from you."

"It must have been a terrible time," George said.

"All those lies," she said, her voice low and grumbling. Bitter. "His faith was his anchor, you know? Without that, Michael was lost. He became depressed. Existential. I should have known he would... I should have helped..."

She covered her face with her hands, and Ivy rushed forward to place a comforting hand on the old woman's arm. "Everyone has a tendency to blame themselves in these situations. But it's never anyone's fault." Fran looked up at Ivy with wet, desperate eyes. "It is not your fault," she reiterated.

Fran collected herself, pulling a tissue from her sleeve. She smiled her gratitude, but it faded like the sun disappearing behind the clouds.

George returned to the job at hand, clearing his throat to preempt a difficult topic.

"The reason I came to see Michael yesterday..."

"Yes?" she said.

"The rumours."

She hesitated, then stiffened like a true Brit.

"Go on."

"Does the name Dean Worthing mean anything to you, Fran?"

"Dean Worthing," she repeated, blowing her nose. "Not until recently. This is about that whole church tower business. Michael told me about it. He was rather upset, he..." She stared, shocked, at the empty curtain rail once more. "You don't think that Michael...That wasn't part of the reason..."

"No," George said firmly. "Your husband was ill, Fran." Fran gulped and nodded. "And you didn't know Dean before...before this week?"

"Well, *I* couldn't really remember the boy, but Michael said he attended St Leonard's during his time there. I suppose I must have met him at some point. But I met so many people. I don't remember them all. Not really."

"From what I understand," George said, "Michael was somewhat of a mentor to Dean."

"That sounds like Michael," she said fondly.

"He was kind to him at a time when no other adult in his life was."

She smiled. "He was sensitive. Maybe too sensitive," she said, glancing back at the window, perhaps recalling what she'd found. But this time, when her eyes passed over it, she frowned.

"What is it?" George asked.

"Sorry?" she replied, distracted, and George leaned forward to look through the window. There was nothing out there but fields and trees.

"It looked like you saw something," he said.

"Me? No. No, just my imagination," she said.

An awkward silence followed, and she refused to look either of them in the eye. Ivy stepped forward, intrigued as to what was through the window.

"It's nothing," Fran said, though with very little conviction in her voice.

Ivy stopped, her focus fixed on a single spot. She moved closer to the window, her head cocked to catch whatever it was she had seen in a different light. She came to a stop on one side of the old sash window, in that space between the window and where the curtain once hung.

"Ivy?" George said quietly, and Fran turned away, seemingly unable to watch. But Ivy was transfixed. She reached out and ran her hand down the wall, then snatched it away with a hiss. "What is it?"

She leaned forward, examining the wall a little more carefully this time.

"It's a nail," she said, her finger tracing a faint outline on the paper. "Something was hanging here. The wallpaper hasn't faded; it's just lying behind where the curtains were."

"A picture, maybe?" George suggested, and they looked to Fran for an answer. But her back was turned, and she carefully lowered herself into the chair at the desk.

"Would have to have been a small picture—"

"It was a key," Fran said, and both George and Ivy silenced.

"A what?" George asked, and Ivy's eyes flashed brilliant and excited.

"A key," Fran repeated.

"What kind of key?" he asked. "Can you describe it?"

"It's just an old brass key," she said, shaking her head. "I don't know what it's for. I doubt it even opened anything. He just... liked it, I suppose."

"Fran?" George said, hoping his tone was enough to warn her that he was no fool. "Fran, what was the significance of the key? Is there a chance that it was removed with the curtains when they... when the curtains were removed?"

She turned to look George in the eye. "He said it symbolised hope," she told him.

"Hope? Fran, when did you last see the key?"

"I don't know," she said. "You know how it is. You see things often enough, and then one day, you don't see them."

"Fran, I'm sorry to add to your burdens, but a large brass key was discovered in Dean Worthing's pocket." He took a step to one side to enter into her line of sight. "Is there a chance that was the key that was hanging there?"

She sighed and dabbed at her nose with her tissue.

"Mrs Wassall," Ivy said, adding incremental weight to the pressure George was imposing.

"He must have given it to *him*," she said.

"Sorry?" George said. "He must have given what to whom? The key?" He dropped to a crouch beside her. "Fran, who did he give it to? This is important."

"When he came by to see Michael," she replied. "He must have given it to him then."

George could almost feel the surprise on his face.

"Dean Worthing?" he said. "Dean came to see Michael? When was this, Fran?"

"I thought he might have mentioned it," she replied, her tone innocent.

"No," George said. "No, he didn't."

"I wonder," she said.

"Fran, I realise you're grieving-"

"It makes perfect sense," she muttered, more to herself than to them.

"What? What makes sense, Fran?" George pressed, and behind her back, Ivy tapped her temple, then made a circle with her finger.

"He felt responsible."

"Fran, you're not making sense, love," he said, and he gave her a gentle squeeze.

She dabbed at her eye and resumed that stoic expression before taking a deep breath.

"Dean Worthing was here," she said. "He was in this very room, in fact. I suppose Michael must have given it to him. For hope, I suppose."

"Are you sure it was him?"

"It was Friday afternoon," she said, nodding. "He came by the house to speak to Michael."

"He stopped by to speak to a retired vicar? Why not go to the current vicar? Is that usual?"

"It's not unusual," she said. "As I said, I didn't recognise him. But Michael explained how they knew each other. He seemed like a lovely boy, handsome, well-dressed, and even had a nice car. You would never have thought that only a day later..." She trailed off. "Well, you never know, do you?" she said, glancing once more at the window.

"And what did they talk about?" asked George, his mind still whirring with this new piece of information.

"I have no idea," Fran said. "I made them a cup of tea, and they came in here."

"And is that the last time you saw the key?"

"I think it must have been. I remember seeing it last week. I'd just washed the curtains, see? We discussed reorganising the room, but Michael liked it this way," she said, nodding at the messy bookcase.

"Wait," Ivy said. "Wait, Dean didn't have a car. There's no record of one, anyway, and there wasn't one at the house or the church."

"What?" George said, confused at why this was her focus.

"Dean didn't have a car," she repeated. "He used a company car but returned it a few months ago. Presumably, when he began writing full time."

"So?" George said, amazed at how she was missing the impact of the key.

Don't you see?" she said. "Fran, you said that Dean had a nice car."

"Oh," she said, brushing Ivy's comment off with a wave of her hand. "Well, it must have belonged to his wife or his girlfriend."

George twisted to face Fran, finally understanding Ivy's intrigue. "He was single," he said. "As far as we know, anyway."

"She came with him in the car and we chatted for a bit while the men were up here," Fran said, with a look of motherly disapproval on her face. "Blonde, she was. Long legs. They arrived together in a little red sports car."

CHAPTER FORTY

In a momentary lapse of reason, George pressed down on the accelerator hard enough that Ivy had to hold onto the grab handle above her passenger's seat. She was busy finding Campbell's number on her phone, and when the call finally went through, Campbell took a whole five rings to answer.

"Hello?" came a voice, but it was too jovial and low-pitched to be Campbell.

"Byrne," Ivy said

"Sarge?" he said, sounding unconvinced.

Ivy rolled her eyes at George. "Byrne, I'm with DI Larson. What are you doing answering Campbell's phone?"

"She's just getting coffee," he said. "I thought it might be important."

"Well, it is," Ivy said. "We need you to put together everything we have on Juliet Shaw. We're going to her house now. We want to bring her in."

"Juliet Shaw?" he said. "I thought you were going for Michael Wassall?"

"We were wrong," George said simply.

"Wrong?" he repeated, and Ivy closed her eyes impatiently.

"We took Wassall's death as an admission of guilt," Ivy told him. "But we shouldn't have. His suicide *was* out of guilt but only because he gave Dean the key to the tower where Dean died."

"Why would he do that?" asked Byrne.

"Because he told Dean as a child," George said, "that whenever he needed the key to the tower in a time of need, all he had to do was ask."

"How on earth do you know–"

"The memoir," George said. "I read it in the memoir."

"How did Wassall even have a key to the tower?" asked Byrne. "I thought he'd retired."

"There must have been two keys all along, and he kept one when he left St Leonard's."

"But why?"

George understood that Byrne and Campbell lacked the new information that he and Ivy had gathered that morning, but his patience was wearing thin. He needed the headspace to deal with Fran Wassall's revelation.

"If you had a key to your favourite place in the world, Byrne, would you give it up?"

Byrne paused for a few seconds as though the question was a genuine philosophical thought experiment. George couldn't help but wonder where Byrne was imagining. "No," he said. "I guess I wouldn't."

"Exactly."

"But why are we going after Juliet, guv? What's she done?"

"She lied," Ivy said. "Well, she omitted important information. She went with Dean to Michael Wassall's house the day before he died so that Dean could ask Wassall for the key."

"She must have had some idea what he was doing," added George. "Even if she didn't know exactly why he went there, she must have known something. She should have told us this information, but she didn't, and I want to know why."

"So she's hiding something?" Byrne said.

"Yes, Byrne," George said. "She's hiding something."

"Alright," he said, sounding more confident now he was up to date. "I know Campbell has been working on collating Juliet Shaw's file, like you asked, guv."

"*I* didn't ask for it–" George corrected him.

"He means me," cut in Ivy. "Just have it ready when we bring her in. Thank you." She reached forward to end the call, recognising the upcoming turn towards Juliet Shaw's house.

"Wait, wait. What about Adrian?" Byrne said. "We've only got him for another hour."

"Christ, I'd forgotten about him."

"We can't let him go, guv. Aside from being implicated, the bloke's unstable," Ivy said. "Can't we get an extension?"

"In an hour? I doubt the judge would have even looked at his emails, let alone received his roll of red tape from his top drawer." He pondered the possibilities and drew the only conclusion. "Let him go," George said.

"You don't want to keep him for the last hour?" Byrne asked.

"No," George said and repeated. "Let him go."

Ivy ended the call before Byrne could ask another question, and George swung round the corner towards Tetford Hill.

"Not like you to put your foot down, guv," Ivy said.

"Is that reference metaphorical, Ivy?"

"No, I was referring to your actual driving. But now you say it."

He caught her wry smile and relaxed a little.

"Tim Long wants this one wrapped up today. If we start dragging it out any longer, he'll start pulling our resources."

"Great, maybe he can take Byrne off our hands."

"I'll ignore that," he replied as he pulled the car up to the kerb.

"Damn it," he muttered.

"Where's her car?"

The house looked lifeless; the windows were closed and the curtains drawn.

Still, he and Ivy climbed from the car and rushed to the door anyway, banging three times today. It was a three-knock kind of situation, George felt.

"Juliet!" George called. "Juliet Shaw, this is Inspector Larson. I need you to open the door, please."

He nodded for Ivy to check the rear of the house, and after completing a full circle, she came up the alley on the other side. "Empty. She's not here, guv," she said.

"Damn it," George said, but despite the frustration in his chest, he heard the calmness in his voice. It was as though he had lost a queen in a game of chess. But the game was far from over. He'd just have to do what he could with inferior pieces.

"What now?" Ivy said. "We could go to Worthing Media? See if she's there?"

"No, we don't have time for a goose chase. Put an ANPR out on her car," George said. "I want to know where she's heading and what her game is."

When Ivy called Campbell this time, it was answered after only two rings.

"Campbell," she answered, her tone abrupt but professional.

"It's me," Ivy said quickly. "I need you to put out an ANPR on Juliet Shaw's car. The details are in the file. She's not at home, and we need to speak to her sooner rather than later."

"Juliet Shaw?" she said calmly. "I can tell you exactly where she is."

Ivy turned to look at George and caught his eye, putting the call on loudspeaker. "Say that again, Campbell."

"I know where Juliet Shaw is. She's downstairs right now. I just saw her car through the canteen window."

"What's she doing?" Ivy said, and then her voice trailed away with recognition. "She's–"

"She's there to collect Adrian," George finished for her, and he stared at Ivy as if to say, 'we should have bloody known'. "He must have asked her to pick him up."

"It's not like he has anybody else to call, is it?" Ivy added, and she waited for George to make his move.

On the other end of the call, Campbell listened to the interaction, patiently waiting for an order and it came in the form of two simple, imperative words.

"Follow them," George said.

"Follow them?" Campbell said. "Guv, can we do that?"

"This is a murder investigation, PC Campbell," George told her. "And the only two people alive and with motives are about to drive off into the sunset. Follow them."

CHAPTER FORTY-ONE

Campbell and Byrne were represented by a little grey circle within the maps app on Ivy's phone. She called out their progress as George drove, along with the subsequent turns they would have to make to either catch up with Shaw and Samson or head them off.

"It's left here, guv," she said.

"Left?"

She studied the map again.

"Yeah, it should bring us out on Harden's Lane-"

"I know where it brings us out, Ivy," George said.

"We'll be ahead of them, so we should be able to stop them-."

"I don't think that'll be necessary," he said, holding his hand and relaxing for the first time on the journey. "Well, at least we know they're not doing a runner. I'm telling you, if I called Tim Long now and asked him to start closing roads off, he'd be signing my retirement papers before you could say Jack Rabbit."

"I'm not following," Ivy said, and George eyed her to see if she was being genuine or if the geography of the Wolds had yet to embed itself onto her fertile mind.

"Three days," George said. "Three days of going around in circles."

"We couldn't have known, guv-"

"Do you know what I'm looking forward to when I retire?" he asked, glancing her way, saying nothing. "No more lies. That's what I'm looking forward to." He jabbed at the air with an index finger to emphasise his point. "Where will I go? The team rooms in Alford. What's it called?" he clicked his fingers, trying to recall the name of the little place with wingback armchairs and cake to die for.

"Willow?" she said. "Willow Tea Rooms."

"Right," he said. "There. I'll go there for my breakfast. Nobody is going to hand me a pack of lies in there, are they?"

"Suppose not," she said.

"I might spend some time perusing the antique places in Horncastle."

"Ah," Ivy cut in. "Now, you might get the odd tall tale in one of them."

"Tall tales I can handle, Ivy. Besides, it's not like I'm in the market for a Georgian dresser or an Edwardian dining table. But I do like to browse." George said. "No, it's barefaced lies that really get my goat."

"That surprises me," Ivy said.

"Why? Did you think that because I've spent my entire working life being lied to, that somehow I might miss it in my well-earned retirement?"

"No, I just thought you might like a nice old desk. You know, like Dean Worthing's. Only nicer. Fancier."

"Ah," he replied as he pulled onto the driveway and noted Campbell's car parked behind Shaw's little Mazda. "To write my own memoirs, you mean?" he tugged the handbrake on and switched the engine off. "The problem I'd have is working out which of the barefaced liars I've had the pleasure of knowing in my career is worthy of chapter one."

"It doesn't have to be a copper, guv," she said. "You could start off with us. Or maybe someone you used to work with. An old boss or something."

He laughed at the notion and shoved the door open. "Those were some of the most prolific liars of the lot, Ivy. Come on, let's get this done."

The house was admirable, enclosed by trees with its glassy writing room and the old, solid brickwork that had stood the test of time, and no doubt would still be standing for decades to come.

It took just a couple of clicks of George's fingers to send the two uniformed officers that Campbell had arranged to venture to the rear of the property. George waited a few seconds to give them time, then gave two loud knocks on the door.

Campbell and Byrne waited at the foot of the steps, alert and waiting for an instruction. In the few short months he had known them, they had come on in leaps and bounds. As PCs, they were still in uniform, but it wouldn't be long. One day, he hoped, Ivy would lead the team. The question he was pondering when the door was opened, was which of them would be her Sergeant. The ever-reliable Campbell, who rarely deviated from protocol, or Byrne, who seemed to live by the seat of his pants. Both traits had their virtues.

"Inspector Larson," Shaw said, eying an additional three cars and then counting the four officers. Astute as she was, she would have guessed there was nowhere to run.

"Miss Shaw..." George said, finding a smile from somewhere within. "May I have a few words with you?"

She eyed Ivy and then reluctantly welcomed them into Dean Worthing's house by turning from the door with a sigh and strolling back inside, her hips brimming with confidence.

The house was a mess. Boxes of Dean Worthing's belongings had been upturned, their contents strewn across the floor. The scattered furniture had been upturned. Cushions had been pulled from the sofas and armchairs, their zips opened, leaving the foam contents exposed like organs in the victim of a knife fight. Cupboards had been emptied with little care for the items inside, as if somebody had swiped the contents from the shelves and trodden the broken shards into the floor.

Juliet Shaw stood in the centre of her destruction, defiant.

Each of the officers was familiar with the scene. It was akin to the aftermath of a robbery.

"Do I need to ask?" George said, gesturing at the mess.

"I was..." Juliet hesitated. "I was looking for something."

"Looking for something?" repeated Ivy.

"It looks like a bloody tornado has blown through here," George said. "And unless I'm mistaken, the weather report didn't mention one."

Shaw's expression remained neutral. Her eyes were clear and intelligent. "You said you wanted to speak to me," she said. "As you can see, I'm quite busy."

"Is there a reason you're going through Dean Worthing's belongings?" he asked in reply.

"He would have wanted me to sort through everything," she said, her voice suddenly fragile. "That was my job, to organise his life."

"And this is what?" George said, picking up a broken lampshade and setting it on the upturned coffee table. "This is organisation, is it?"

"I'm sorting through his affairs," she insisted. "I was all he had."

"You weren't though, were you?" Ivy said.

The comment seemed to break Shaw's concrete exterior.

"Sorry?"

"You weren't, were you?" Ivy said again. "You weren't all he had. If you were all he had, you would have got the house."

"What?"

"What's this place worth, anyway?" Ivy said, looking back at George. "Nice bit of land out the back. Five or six bedrooms."

"Plenty of potential," George said, to which Ivy made a show of agreeing.

"Nine hundred thousand?"

"A nice round million to the right person," George added, and Ivy nodded her agreement.

"But he didn't leave it to you, did he, Juliet? He left it to Adrian." At this, Shaw opened her mouth to reply, but no words came out, and she gaped soundlessly. "Where is he, anyway?"

"I..." Juliet said, trailing off.

"You picked him up from the station," Ivy said, and George heard the concern in her voice as though the two had bonded over whatever they had talked about in the cell the day before. "Where is he, Miss Shaw?" The tone in Ivy's voice was not open to interpretation, and Juliet pointed to the ceiling. "Upstairs?"

"He's in his room," Shaw said quietly.

With a nod from George, Ivy rushed back into the hallway.

"I'll be honest with you, Miss Shaw," George said, earning her attention as Ivy exited the room. "I came here with every intention of arresting you."

"What?"

"You omitted important information that could have furthered our investigation," George said, and he stepped over a pile of papers onto a bare patch of carpet. "I want to know why."

"And what might that information be, Inspector?"

"You knew that Dean went to visit Michael Wassall the day before his death. Why didn't you tell us?"

She laughed, scoffing, as though George only knew half of a story to which she was privileged. "I'm supposed to let you know everyone Dean saw before he died, am I?"

"That would be helpful, yes."

"I had just learned of his death, for God's sake. Do you have any idea how close we were? How much I..." She trailed off once more. "I was upset, okay? I couldn't think straight. But I have nothing to hide. Yes, yes, we went to Michael Wassall's house the day before Dean died. I had a cup of tea with his wife. We chatted about the weather. She was excited to plant her tomatoes. Exactly how much information would you like me to share, Inspector?"

"I want to know what they spoke about," George said, to which Shaw threw her arms into the air.

"How would I know?" she said, pronouncing every syllable of the sentence with her teeth bared. "I drove him there. I did what he asked me to do. That doesn't mean he disclosed every part of his day to me. We weren't bloody well married, you know?"

At this, George heard Ivy's steps coming down the stairs, the tempo of her rubber soles faster than before. She stepped straight up to Shaw with scant regard to where she trod.

"What did you give him?"

"Sorry?"

"I said, what did you give him? Adrian. What have you done?"

"I..."

"What did you give him, Miss Shaw?" Ivy repeated, her tone bordering the point at which George might need to step in. Ivy was not a particularly tall woman, but he could easily imagine being on the other end of that sharp stare beneath her long fringe.

"I didn't *give* him anything," she insisted, backing away from Ivy's fiery face. "He asked for it."

Ivy raised her voice. "What? What was it? What did you give him?"

"Methadone," she said quickly. "It's just methadone. He's passed out. He's high. He's used to it. He needs it."

Ivy sucked her teeth and turned away from Shaw as though unwilling to spend another second looking at her face lest it bend her patience too far.

"He's a junkie," Shaw said, defending herself.

"He's vulnerable," Ivy snapped. "He doesn't need you stockpiling him with drugs."

"You're the one who kept him in a cell for twenty-four hours. If you think he's so vulnerable, why did you do that? If you haven't noticed, he doesn't exactly thrive in tight spaces."

"So, what?" Ivy spat back. "You locked him up here instead?"

"*He* called *me*," she threw back. "*He* asked *me* to pick him up. He *trusts* me. He trusts Dean's trust in me. I'll do what he asks me to do, and the last time I checked, that wasn't against the law."

Shaw folded her arms and looked around the room, tapping her foot and biting down on her lower lip as though their presence was proving to be more than a mild inconvenience.

"So?" she said. "Are you going to arrest me or not? Because if not, I have things to do."

George almost laughed out loud at how brazen she was. She was clearly a woman used to getting what she wanted. "I *will* arrest you, Miss Shaw, yes. Unless you start answering some very important questions."

"What questions?" she said, staccato, as though talking to a machine over the phone.

"See it from our perspective, Juliet. You are one of the last people to have seen Dean, and then he dies. You are one of the last people to have seen Michael Wassall, and then he dies. It's quite the pattern you're developing."

At this, Juliet's head snapped up. "The old man died?"

George studied her face, taken by her surprise. He said nothing, and she gasped.

"How?" she said softly.

"We're not in a position to go into details," Ivy said bluntly.

"Shame," Juliet said sadly. "He was a nice man."

"Dean left the business to you," George said suddenly, watching for a reaction. "Did you know that?"

"What?"

"Dean left Worthing Media to you," George said. "His personal assistant. Why?"

She shook her head and shrugged.

"He trusted me, I suppose," she said. "We were close. He knew what I'm capable of, that it would give me the chance to prove myself."

"What it gives you, Miss Shaw, is a motive," George said sternly.

"A...what?"

"A motive. To kill Dean. With him dead, you get the business." She vehemently tried to voice her objection, but George spoke over her. "You had opportunity too. By your own admission, you were in South Ormsby at the time Dean died."

"I was here," she said. "I wasn't at the church. I was waiting for Dean."

"And who can confirm that?"

She scoffed, then threw up a long, pointed finger. "*You*," she said. "You said you saw my car."

"*After* Dean died," George said. "But I don't know where you'd been beforehand."

"Adrian then." She lunged forward as though reaching desperately for her own alibi. "He was here; I'm sure he was."

"Adrian did see you, yes," Ivy said. "He told me. He saw you looking through the window. He was rather upset by it. He didn't give me a time, though. He could have been having one of his episodes, I suppose."

"What? Upset? Adrian *knows* me. Why would I upset him?"

Ivy shrugged. "You tell me."

Shaw rubbed the bridge of her nose, seeming to hold her breath. And then, finally, she broke.

"Look, I told you why I was here. To see Dean. To get the manuscript. How was I to know that he wouldn't wait for me? It was a simple mistake. That's all." Her voice began to break. "And I *failed*, okay. The door was locked. I couldn't get in. So I left. And now..." She looked around the room tearfully, her lower lip shaking. "And now it's gone! I've been looking for it for days." She stared up at George, her eyes glistening and crisscrossed with red.

"I don't know where it is. I don't know where..." She just about managed another "I don't know," before slowly folding to the ground like a concertina and breaking into a series of rib-racking sobs.

Campbell, who had been silent until then, stepped forward, and from her belt, she withdrew a pair of handcuffs. She looked across at George, waiting for his nod. From the floor, Shaw raised her head, her eyes wide.

Slowly, George raised a hand.

"Not yet," he said, and he dragged an old pine chair from beneath the little four-seater table and then dropped down wearily. He met Shaw's pleading stare, trying to read something in the darkness of her eyes. "I'm nowhere near finished with her yet."

CHAPTER FORTY-TWO

To Ivy, the woman on the floor seemed vastly different to the woman they had met only a few days ago, enjoying a glass of wine after work in her spotless house. She was broken, not with grief, but fatigue. It was the type of broken formed from sleepless nights. Accusing her of murder in this state would yield little results. She was hurting. She could see that now. She was in deep emotional pain. They needed to understand her. But understanding somebody like Shaw involved setting opinions and judgements to one side, and Ivy was struggling with that concept.

"You're a smart woman, Miss Shaw," George said gently. "You know full well that Dean's visit to Michael Wassall was important. You know that we should have heard that from you."

"No," she pleaded. "I was upset. I-"

"That little omission bought you a few days," George said. "A few days for what?"

"I'm telling the truth," she said. She was on her knees, her feet splayed, and her hair hanging over her face.

"Why didn't you just tell us? When we asked you when you saw him last, you could have told us then." George said. "Be honest, Juliet. That's all I ask. "Be honest with me, and I'll do everything I can to make you as comfortable as possible."

She gazed up at him with exhaustion in her eyes, and something in her expression cracked like a thin sheet of ice beneath a soft footstep.

"He told me not to tell anyone," she whispered.

"Who?"

"Dean. He told me not to tell anyone that we had been to see Michael." George could practically hear the ice breaking, its cracks spreading, unveiling the lake that was Juliet Shaw. "He was planning something. It was about his book. But he didn't say what it was–"

"What do you mean planning something?"

She sighed and summoned the last of waning strength. "He gave me a series of tasks in the last few months. They were specific but also a little mysterious. Usually, I know why he's asked me to do something. But this time, he didn't explain anything."

"Like what, Juliet?" George said. "What did Dean ask you to do?"

She sighed, refocusing her attention, tuning into business mode, and setting aside her emotions in the same way George and Ivy had to do every single day.

"First, I had to find Adrian. That's what he asked me to do a month or so ago. Like I told you, it wasn't easy. It took me a few weeks, but I did it. I brought him here, to this place. I set up his bedroom, painted it, and bought new furniture. Not that it matters now. You've seen the state it's in," she said to Ivy, unaware that the entire team had been privy to it. "I didn't understand why or who he was. I didn't know why Dean wanted some junkie living in his house. But like I said–"

"You just did what he told you to do?" Ivy said, to which Shaw nodded.

"Okay," George said slowly. There was no new information,

but at least the conversation was moving in the right direction. "So what else did he ask you to do?"

"There was a letter," she said.

"What letter?"

"He gave me a letter to deliver. It was already sealed before you ask."

"And the address?"

"The address was already written on it. He just didn't have time to go to the post office. He didn't like leaving the house, you see. Not when he was writing and working to a deadline."

"So you posted it for him?"

"Yes," Shaw said. Why wouldn't I?"

"What was the address?" asked George.

"How the hell do I know?"

"Well, you must have looked at it," Ivy said. "You must have looked at the address before you posted it?"

She closed her eyes. I don't remember. I didn't write it." She squinted. "Somewhere beginning with *N*, maybe?"

"This isn't eye-spy," Ivy said.

"Well, I don't know," Shaw said, and George gestured for Ivy to ease off, then nodded for Shaw to continue. "Maybe it was Nottingham or Norwich, something like that?"

"Is there someone that Dean knows in either of those places? A colleague or a member of his family?"

Shaw shook her head in despair. "Dean didn't know anyone. I knew him for ten years. I never met any of his friends or family. Once he started pulling away from the business, he became a hermit. A recluse. He just wanted to stay inside and write. Especially for the last few years."

"And what else?" George said. "What else did he ask you to do?"

Juliet shook her head, whether at her own blind sightedness or at Dean's behaviour, Ivy couldn't be sure. "He asked me to sort out his will," she said thickly. "To talk to a lawyer and arrange a meeting at the house."

"Do you remember the lawyer?"

"His details will be in here somewhere," she said, gesturing at the mess of papers around them. "I figured he was just, I dunno, being safe, now that he had the new house and everything. But I swear to God, I didn't know he was leaving the business to me. I didn't know he was leaving the house to Adrian. He didn't tell me anything. And even if I had known, I would never... I *loved* him," she said, the admission as much of a surprise to her as it was to them. "I loved him."

While Shaw buried her face in her hands, George gave Ivy a look she recognised. It wasn't an act. She really was devastated by Dean's death.

"Miss Shaw, I'm sorry to ask. But were you and Dean in a relationship?" asked Ivy. "Romantically, I mean."

"No..." She shook her head, tears streaming down her face. "No, he didn't see me like that. I wasn't his type if you know what I mean."

"Dean was gay?" asked George.

"I think so. I don't know. He could have been asexual for all I know," she said. "It's not like he ever had any romantic partners. He never showed an interest in anyone." She paused, seemingly processing it all at once in her emotionally-shattered, sleep-deprived state. "I could have asked what was wrong. What he was planning. But he didn't want me to know. I always thought I knew when and when not to ask. Where the boundaries were, you know? And *now*..." She let a sob escape her throat, unable to hold it back. "Now I know it was his own bloody suicide!"

"Was he depressed, Juliet?" George asked, and she peered up at him. "I'm sorry, I'm just finding it difficult to understand why a man as successful as Dean was, would go to such lengths."

"I don't know. I don't know what was going on in his mind."

"How did he seem?"

"I don't know," she repeated. "He could have had a number of reasons. Why does anyone do that?"

"Guilt," Ivy suggested. "Shame, self-loathing, pain, loneliness." She maintained her hard stare, waiting for a crack in Shaw's exterior to appear. "To name a few. Could it have been guilt, perhaps?"

"Guilt? What on earth could he be guilty of?" Shaw said. "And even if he was guilty of something, I would never betray him."

"So even in death," George said. "You're loyal to him?"

"Always," she whispered. "Always. Don't you get it? He was genuine and kind, and God, he was so beautiful. Do you have *any* idea," she said, straining with the pain of it all, "how hard it is to find a man like that?"

She looked to Ivy then as though she might relate to her question. But Ivy could not relate. She had a genuine and kind and beautiful man at home, and for some reason beyond her own comprehension, he still wasn't enough for her.

Then Shaw turned to George for answers.

"I don't understand why. Why wouldn't he tell me? About Michael, about the key? Why would he keep all this from me?"

George cleared his throat and rocked his jaw back and forth. It was a move Ivy recognised as him preparing to deliver a truth.

"Because he was trying to protect you."

"What?" she whispered.

"He knew you loved him, Juliet," George said. "Maybe he even loved you too, in his own way." She scoffed at the prospect but continued to listen. He took a few steps, venturing further into the mess. "Maybe not in the same way, but I think he did love you. I think that if you *had* asked him about the key, he would have had to lie to you about what it opened. Because if he told you the truth, and if you knew that he was planning to climb St Leonard's tower at twilight on Saturday night, you might have guessed why. And you might have tried to stop him. In fact, he knew that you would have tried to stop him."

"Of course, I would have," Shaw said with a quiet determination. "I'd have done whatever it took."

"Exactly. He couldn't take that chance," George said. "He didn't want to lie to you, and he didn't want you to stop him. So he kept secrets from you instead. Because secrets aren't quite lying, are they, Juliet? They're just omissions of the truth."

George stood up straight from his crouched position with only a slight groan, as though not wanting to downplay his authority but also acknowledging the ache in his joints.

"You should go home, Juliet. There's nothing you can do for Dean now." He looked down on the woman who could well, in another life, have been the same age as his daughter. He passed on what Ivy guessed was his attempt at fatherly advice. "Go home and rest. Look after Dean's business. Live your life. Don't waste your time looking for answers that aren't there." George looked around at the chaos caused by a desperation to find something in his own possession. However convincing his solemn guidance had been, Ivy imagined that when they left, Shaw would continue her search. "There's nothing left here for you."

At this final comment, Shaw's expression settled like sand falling through fingers as realisation spread across her features. "*You've* got it," she whispered. "You have it, don't you?"

George didn't reply. He just nodded at Ivy, Byrne, and Campbell, saying that it was time to leave. They had all the information they needed. Shaw was many things – loyal, lovesick, laborious – but she did not murder Dean Worthing.

As they turned to leave, she scrambled to her feet and blocked the doorway, her fingers digging into the architrave.

"Miss Shaw–"

"Where?" she said, her eyes wide and sore looking. "Where is it?"

George waited, and Ivy noted the rise and fall of Shaw's chest.

"It's in safe hands," he replied.

"No," she said, shaking her head back and forth. "No, you

have no idea how important it is. Dean left it only to me. He said no one else could know about it. Not until it was published."

"But someone else did know about it, Juliet," Ivy said. "See, Dean had a backup plan, just in case you failed that night."

"What?" She shook her head, this time in disbelief. "You?"

"No, not us," Ivy said, stepping forward and she glanced up at the ceiling.

"Adrian?" she said, putting the pieces together, just as Ivy and George had. "So Adrian knew how precious the manuscript was to Dean. So when he didn't come home the next morning, he took it to the safest place he could think of. The church at the top of the road. Dean told Adrian about the manuscript," she repeated to herself.

"He must have," George said, softer now. "So Adrian gave it to a man he could trust. A man of the church."

"And the vicar gave it to you?"

George nodded. "That's right."

"So where is it?" she said, looking behind him as though George might be holding it behind his back. "Do you have it here?"

"It's evidence, Juliet. For now, at least."

"*Evidence?*" she spat. "Evidence? It's Dean's story, his life. It's not evidence. It's more precious than that. It's art." Somewhere behind Ivy, she heard Campbell shuffle, perhaps in a small movement of triumph at hearing someone else express the words that she had expressed all along. "He was a writer. He didn't know how to tell his story to anyone except through the written word. It was his dying wish for that book to be published. To be shared with the world. Not locked away in some damn evidence locker!"

George said nothing, as though tired of her manic tirades, or, more likely, thought Ivy, to hide the nerve that her words touched, causing a flash of concern across his face. He pushed past Juliet, and she made no effort to stop him.

"Like I said," he called over his shoulder. "It's in safe hands."

Shaw watched them leave, devoid of fight or, defence, or energy. From the hallway, Ivy looked back. She hoped Shaw would move on from Dean's death. She honestly did. She had seen the effects of grief ruin too many people, and it had already almost ruined Juliet Shaw, who leaned heavily against the doorframe.

"You should listen to what he said," Ivy said. She looked around the house, wondering if one man could live in such a family-sized home without spiralling into loneliness. "Move on."

But Juliet ignored her, eyes fixed only on George and his receding back as he walked away.

"You have to publish it, DI Larson!" she cried through the open front door as they left the Bluestone Lodge. And then she added in a whisper that was quickly lost to the wind, "You have to."

Ivy climbed into the passenger seat and watched George staring up at the old house.

"So?"

"So what?" he asked.

"So, we're done. Worthing did kill himself." George stared across at her, his expression impassive. "Tim Long will be happy you hit your deadline."

"Is that right?" George asked, his voice as distant as his eyes. In front of them, Campbell, Byrne, and the other two uniformed officers were preparing to leave.

"Guv, come on. We've exhausted every possible angle. We have a plausible explanation," she said. "Dean Worthing got the key from Wassall and launched himself off the tower."

"And Wassall? Why did he kill himself? Why would a man who had seemingly put everything behind him do what he did?"

"Guilt?" Ivy said. "Christ, can you imagine how bad he must have felt?"

"Guilt? For what, giving him the key, or because he had protected whoever had been abusing Dean, James, Samuel, and God knows who else? There's a cover-up here. He wouldn't have killed himself because he gave him the key to the tower, Ivy. No, this is bigger. There's more to it than that."

"Oh, come on," Ivy said. "Guv, it's over. Whatever happened is over. Everyone involved is dead."

"Right," George said, starting his car. "They're dead. They died."

"Right," she replied.

"It's plausible, I'll give you that. Worthing and Wassall could quite easily have killed themselves. But..." he said, nudging the car into gear. "This is far from over, Ivy."

CHAPTER FORTY-THREE

The incident room was bustling. Phones rang incessantly, fingers tapped on keyboards, and printers whirred endlessly as the team confirmed everything Juliet Shaw had told them.

George sat at the desk that he hardly ever used. Beside him, Ivy was signing off statements and reports, gathering everything about the investigation into neat, disclosable files. He sipped his coffee and winced. It was the third cup he had let go cold already in all the fuss.

"Guv," Campbell said, bringing over a print-out of an image from an old, black-and-white CCTV camera.

'Where did you get this?"

"What's that, guv?" Ivy asked.

He stared at Campbell, impressed.

"It's an image of Juliet Shaw," he said, and Ivy stood to have a nose. "Campbell?"

"I made some enquiries when we got back, guv. I figured she would have had to post it somewhere. Who carries stamps these days?"

"So? Juliet Shaw was seen two weeks ago posting a letter at the

Post Office in Alford," Ivy said. "She's already told us she posted a letter."

"Who sent you this? The postmaster?" George asked, to which Campbell nodded. "Call them. Find out if there's any way of finding out if it was recorded delivery, will you?"

Campbell returned to her seat, and Ivy slumped in hers.

"I don't see what that's going to achieve, guv," she said.

"Neither do I," George said. "But it's an open end, and it needs closing." He looked across at Byrne. "What else have we got?"

Byrne made a show of finishing what he was typing, then grabbed a handful of paper from his tray.

"I talked to Dean Worthing's publisher, finally," he said as he placed another print-out before George. "A month ago, they confirmed a new arrangement that all of Worthing's royalties would go towards the SCA. And look at this," he said, pointing to a line in the agreement. "For all existing books and yet-to-be-published manuscripts."

At the bottom of the page was Worthing's signature. George felt oddly drawn to it. Dean's hand had moved across that page only a month ago, knowing that soon enough, he would never write again.

"The SCA," repeated George. "What is that?"

"Stop Child Abuse, guv. It's a charity."

Some of the darker images inspired by Worthing's memoir flashed before George's eyes. He couldn't imagine a more appropriate place for the money from such a story to be sent.

"Good," George said, nodding to the whiteboard. "Add it to the timeline."

They had wiped Michael Wassall's side of the board to create a timeline of the last three months of Dean Worthing's existence since he had bought the Bluestone Lodge and the tasks he had ticked off before taking his own life. Just before his death, they had included the deadline,

Finish The Unholy Truths. Then, just beneath that, *Give to Juliet for publishing.*

George had every intention, once he had finished reading the memoir, to pass it on to the publisher, both to get the story out there and now to ensure that the proceeds did indeed go to the SCA. However, he was two-thirds through the book now and Dean's abusers still had not been named. He wasn't sure that they would be. They were consistently portrayed as the shadowy, scary, elusive figures he had experienced as a child. Figures that must have haunted his mind until he took his dying breath.

George lowered himself into his chair. He was of the age now that plopping down was likely to cause an injury.

"Why did Dean consider that his memoir would be a tell-all story, enough that he was so careful to stop the manuscript from falling into the wrong hands that he had instructed Juliet to pick it up only an hour before his death?"

"What are you saying?" Ivy asked, distracted by her own work.

"Well, if it was designed to name and shame, then surely he would have named them by now."

He left the question hanging there. But it was when Ivy collected her files, tapped them into a neat pile and slid them across to him that the end was and should have been in sight. All he had to do was pick them up and walk them into Long's office.

"Conclusion?" he said, knowing the answer already.

"Dean committed suicide. He had been organising it for months, she said. "He bought a house with a beautiful writing room in which to write his memoir. He had found a man from his past – although they still didn't know *who* exactly Adrian was to Dean – and given him somewhere to stay. Given him a future. He informed Juliet Shaw to perform a series of tasks to bring his affairs into order. It couldn't be neater."

"It could be a lot neater," George said. "For a start, who did Sarah Hawkins see? If it was Samson, then why was he there?"

"Was he there, though? Was anybody there? She's already

changed her statement once. Can we really keep this investigation open because of the word of an unreliable witness?"

"True," he said.

"Guv, the only demon, was the one that a devoutly religious woman might have expected to see after witnessing a young man's death in a creepy, old graveyard. It was not unusual for the mind to fill in the blanks with an explanation, however far-fetched."

"Are you lecturing me, Ivy?"

"No, I'm just trying to find some reasonable way through this."

"And I'm closing off loose ends," he said.

"You're looking for loose ends," she said.

"Who abused Dean Worthing? Who were Samuel and James? Who did he send a letter to? Aren't you keen to get to the bottom of this, Ivy?"

"I'm keen to move on, guv," she said, to which George sat back in his chair and pondered. Was it that she was young with a life ahead of her that she could think so little of two preventable deaths? Or was it that he was old, and the value of life was marring his mind?

"Guv," Byrne said, walking over to his desk hesitantly, as though not wanting to disturb his meditative state. "I found something."

George took a sheet of paper from his hand and held it up to the light.

"What's this?"

"I don't know if it's relevant, but just after he bought the house, Dean Worthing got in touch with the LPA about planning permission."

"Okay," George said, narrowing his eyes at the whiteboard, trying to spot the missing piece. "That's not unusual for a new home. I've thought about extending my house on numerous occasions. Was permission granted?"

"They wrote back saying they needed to see the proposed plans."

"But what was it?" George said, turning to the lad, struggling to remember any major building work inside the house. "What was he planning?"

"I asked, but they said they needed to look at the records. They said they'd call me back."

"Alright," George said, turning back to the whiteboard distractedly. "Thanks, Byrne." He watched Byrne return to his desk and then eyed Ivy. "Another loose end."

"It's not a loose end, guv. "It's...admin. That's what it is."

"Right. How long has Dean Worthing owned the house?"

Ivy shrugged.

"A few months."

"Right," George said. "And when did he begin to plan his suicide?"

Her head cocked to one side, and her eyes narrowed. But the conversation ground to a halt as the incident room door opened, and a familiar voice called out.

"George," Tim said, standing in the doorway. "A word, if you will."

CHAPTER FORTY-FOUR

"Time's up," Tim Long announced, getting straight to the point. George didn't need to be invited to sit. He dragged the guest chair across the room, eased himself in, folded his legs, and then took a deep breath. "I need you and DS Hart over in North Kesteven first thing in the morning. You'll report to Chief Super-intendent Granger for a few days while they deal with a resourcing issue. I'm hoping that by the time you return, you'll have reset your priorities, George."

"North Kesteven?" George replied.

"That's right," Tim said. "It's not too far."

"I know where it is," George replied. "I'm just wondering why an area with a team of two detectives-"

"Four," Tim added.

"Two detectives," George reiterated. "Accompanied by two uniformed constables, would send those two detectives halfway across the county to help another station out."

"Like I said, it's not far."

"Why didn't they ask Lincoln HQ? It's only up the road. They must have a dozen officers who could have helped out."

"Because I volunteered *you*," Tim said. "And for the record, only twenty-five per cent of the local team will be going."

"Twenty-five..." George started, then fell in. "I'm going alone, am I? You're keeping Ivy here."

"Like you said. Why would I send the entire major crimes team? I fought hard enough to have one in the first place."

"This is a dirty move, Tim," George told him. "And I'll credit you with my belief that it was not instigated by you. You might not have done much to stop it, but you didn't instigate it, did you?"

Despite his bitterness, George recognised that, unlike so many who had sat in his seat, Tim had not let his career taint his personality. He wasn't a bad man. If anything, he was one of the few individuals George could count on if push came to shove. This was political. This was a passive-aggressive move designed to avoid any direct conflict.

"So, I'll need the Worthing investigation wrapped up," Tim said. "Before you go, that is."

George stretched his arms out above him, and the previous few days clung to his muscles as if there were barbed hooks on the end of each memory.

"Ivy's doing it now," he said calmly, which seemed to ease Tim's anxiety. "You were right. Dean Worthing's death was suicide." He spoke the words aloud for the first time, then swallowed the bitter aftertaste.

Tim shook his head and leaned forward, studying George's forlorn expression.

"What's all this been for?" he asked. "We could have had this wrapped up days ago."

George simply shrugged. "Just doing my job, Tim."

"So that's it?" Tim said. "All of this was for nothing?"

"They were highly suspicious circumstances," George argued. "We had a witness statement claiming that a man was seen at the scene of the crime, a man who we now know was living at the victim's house. We had to follow up on that. We had to eliminate foul play. Come on, you know how it is."

"A witness statement?" Tim said. "That was all this was based on?"

"Not just–" started George.

"We don't base an investigation solely on witness statements, George. They cannot be relied upon." He tilted his head patronisingly. "You know that."

"I do know that, Tim, yes, and that specific witness statement has indeed been dismissed. But there were other factors."

"What other factors?"

"For one, Dean Worthing had been abused as a child. He was writing a memoir about that abuse, likely naming his abusers. That gave us an extremely solid motive for anyone wanting to kill Dean Worthing on Saturday night before he could publish it."

"Stories," Tim said incredulously. "Your whole investigation was based on stories?" He took a deep breath, which George mirrored.

"You know what the job's like, Tim. It takes time to develop leads, and most of them are dead-ends.

"Where is this manuscript?" Tim asked, and George hesitated. "George?"

"It's safe," he said. "I've been reading it at home."

"At home? You took it home?"

"I could hardly find myself a nice recliner in the incident room and put my feet up, could I?" George told him. "I thought there might be information in there we could use. A lead," he added.

"But there isn't?"

"There was, as it happens," George defended. "We worked out *how* Dean Worthing gained access to the church tower using information from his manuscript."

"So that he could commit suicide?"

"Yes."

Tim looked long and hard at George. "Is there any identification of his abusers in this memoir?"

"No," George said. "It doesn't seem so."

"Then bring it to me," Tim said sternly. "Let's bundle it up as evidence and pass it on to a team that knows what they're doing."

"I know what I'm doing, Tim."

"I meant a team specialising in cases of abuse, George. It wasn't a dig at your competence. If what you say is correct, then it might go some way for me to explain why my only two detectives spent *four whole days* on it. Write up a report and make it clear how exactly you spent your time so that I can explain it if I need to."

George matched Tim's long, hard stare.

"No, Tim," he said eventually. "I can't."

"I'm sorry?"

"I can't," George said.

"Detective Inspector Larson," Tim began. Just as George had with Ivy, Tim was reverting to titles to put his foot down, and just as it had been with George, it was a desperate, misaimed step. "Would you care to reevaluate-"

"What's this really about, Tim?"

"Excuse me?"

"You know the job, Tim. You know *me*. You know I wasn't wasting time here. So what's the problem? Really?"

"My problem, *George*, is that we are low on resources." He swung his arm down the small, empty corridor. "In case you haven't noticed. I spent six months waiting for *you* to be transferred here while your old station was being decommissioned, and I can't afford to spend time and money on wild goose chases. It puts my neck on the line, too. Those officers in Lincoln HQ? I could have had one of them, couldn't I? Maybe I should have?"

George leaned forward and shoved his desk phone towards him.

"Go on, then. Make the call. Get one. Get somebody young," he said. "Somebody who'll spend more time filling in forms and handing in case files so you can put a tick on your quota. So you can secure your funding."

"Is that what you think of me, George?"

"No. I think it's more than that," George said, allowing the storm in his chest to inspire his unwise words. "Are you threatened by me? Is that it? Do you think I'm here for this?" He waved a hand around the small office, feeling a sneer spread across his face.

"How dare–"

"I don't want your job, Tim," George said, exasperated. "I just want to be allowed to do mine." At this, Tim merely stared, open-mouthed at George's audacity. Either that or George had touched a nerve. Either way, he used the silence to continue. "That manuscript has to be published," George said. "It was Dean Worthing's dying wish. It was what he spent the last three months of his life working on. He poured his heart out into that book. Likely reliving horrors that you or I couldn't even imagine. And what? You want to tuck it away in a neat little file so it can be forgotten?"

"That's not what I said," Tim said, slowly finding his voice. "I said we should pass it on to the relevant team."

"Where it'll sit in a pile until one day the leading officer decides that it's all a dead end. That there is no Samuel or James, and that two of the primary individuals are dead." George's heart slammed into his chest, and he clenched his throat, securing the emotions within. "That's when it'll go to the archives, Tim. It might not be now. It might take a year. But that's where it'll go. You know it, and I know it."

"We know nothing of the sort–"

George bristled. "We have a responsibility. It's the same responsibility we have to follow up on will readings. Surely you understand that? Where is the line? Where is the line between common bloody decency and legal procedure?"

"You know what, George? I don't understand why you are obsessed over this. I don't understand why you spent four days on this when I could have gone down there on Saturday night and ruled this a suicide in the first place."

"I was looking into the *abuse* allegations against Dean Worthing, for which there is no record."

"Which you also didn't accomplish!" Tim said, his voice louder now, and George could just imagine the silence in the incident room next door as every officer's ears, including those of his own team, were tuned in.

Tim shook his head, out of something between disappointment and disbelief, or both, George thought more likely.

"Look, you and Ivy are the only detectives in this station. We have other things for you to be working on. Do you understand?"

"Tim," George said, hearing the tinge of desperation in his own voice. "Just give me one more day. I can find out who it was. I can find out who abused Dean Worthing. Then, we won't need to hand the manuscript to some other team. One day."

"No, George," Tim said. "This is over." He laughed. "Christ, it wasn't even anything to begin with. Let it go." His face softened as though Tim, too, could remember the days back when they were both sergeants, equal and unthreatening. But his next words revealed that times had changed, and despite the level playing field George enjoyed, Tim was prepared to use the ace up his sleeve. "I want that manuscript and the files on my desk when I come into work tomorrow morning."

He stood from his seat, snatched his jacket from the hook, and pulled it on, straightening his collars in the reflection of his glass-fronted bookcase.

"Or?" George said.

He felt immature and boyish, like a frustrated teenager finding no other way to express his frustration. Tim, on the other hand, didn't even turn around to face George man to man. He spoke through the reflection.

"Or I'll be forced to reconsider my options, George," he said. "Don't make me do that. For both our sakes."

CHAPTER FORTY-FIVE

Ivy closed her laptop and shoved it to one side. She dragged the files on Juliet Shaw, Adrian Sampson, Michael Wassall, and Dean Worthing in front of her, and after a few heartless flicks through the summary pages, she closed them in turn and stacked them ready for George to sign off.

It was that time of day when the incident room began to thin out. Only a handful of CID officers remained, including Ivy, Byrne, and Campbell. She leaned back in her chair, staring at the ordered pile of papers and wondering how it was that the turbulent events of the last four days concerning four people's lives could be organised so neatly yet amount to nothing. They were meaningless. A waste of paper and resources.

"Are we done, sarge?" Byrne asked as he ambled up to Ivy's desk, smoothing his hair.

"I couldn't have put it better myself," she said, to which Byrne appeared perplexed. "Yes, we're done, Byrne. Go home."

Campbell, who had been listening in, took the affirmation and closed down her computer with a few sharp clicks of the mouse. She stood to button her coat, a navy duffle with surprisingly whimsical, chequered toggles.

"Well then," she said, staring at the lives of four individuals neatly bundled up into pointless packages, "this has been..."

"Messy?" Ivy suggested. "A wild goose chase? A waste of time?"

"A man died, for God's sake," Byrne said as he closed down his own laptop. He caught the expression on Ivy's face, then backtracked. "Sorry, but we can't be sure that it was a suicide. I know that's what we have to do, but..."

"It's not perfect, is it?" Ivy said. "It's not like we can tie a neat little bow around those files and walk away content that we've done our jobs."

"But I suppose that's the job, isn't it?' Byrne said. "To come to a conclusion. Even if it's not the conclusion we were looking for or if we feel like there's more. We have to move on. We have to draw a line in the sand."

"Yes, I suppose," Ivy said. "That's one way of looking at it, anyway."

There were certainly times when Byrne proved to be insightful, thoughtful. Mature, even. He had a kind, optimistic spirit that in unsatisfying moments such as these shone the world in a new light.

"Any plans for tonight, Byrne?" Ivy asked, playing on his positive attitude.

"Pub quiz," he said, as though it was as regular an occurrence as having dinner. "Down the Wig and Mitre tonight." He rubbed his hands together theatrically. "Fifty quid prize money."

Ivy grinned. "Part of a team? Or do you go alone?"

"Oh, a team," Byrne said, sneering. "Lot of use they are, though. I'm the brains in our little quintet."

Campbell laughed as she packed up her bag. "No offence, but I find that bit hard to believe."

"Believe it," Byrne said, holding his lapels like a proud landowner. "My team is in eighth place. Getting closer to first place by the week."

Ivy raised her eyebrows. "*Every* week?"

"There's a league," Campbell explained with a grin.

"Yup," Byrne said proudly. "Some stiff competition, I tell you."

"I bet there is for that money," Ivy muttered. "That's some serious business."

Campbell's bag was packed by now, but she crossed her arms and leaned on the desk, clearly staying for the conversation. "How did you get into pub quizzes anyway, Byrne?" she asked. "No offence, but you're not exactly..." She trailed off.

"Yes?" he encouraged. "Not exactly what?"

"Not exactly a walking encyclopedia, are you."

"Well, *no offence*," he said to Campbell, "but we didn't all go to some posh school and study at some big university. Everything I know, I learned the hard way. University of Life." He tapped his chest with an index finger. "Graduate with honours."

Over Byrne's sincere look, Ivy and Campbell met eyes and then burst out laughing.

"What?" he said.

"The university of life?" Ivy repeated.

"Look, I don't know how," he said, his cheeks now burning crimson, "but things just stick in my head, you know? I've got a good memory." He tapped his head hard enough that Ivy heard the thud of skull bone.

"Well, good for you," she said, her laugh simmering. "I hope you win."

Campbell coughed away the last of her laugh, too. "Yeah, Byrne. Good luck. What will you spend your fifty quid on?"

"Well, ten quid," Byrne said quietly. "Once I've split it between the team..." At this, Ivy and Campbell refused to meet each other's eyes. "And I dunno. Probably something for my sister. She likes plants. Maybe I'll get her an aloe?"

"That's nice," Campbell said, her face softening. "She deserves a treat, eh? Having to live with you, I mean," she said, smiling to show she was joking.

"Yeah, good luck, Byrne."

"Thank you," he said, pretending to tip his hat.

"What about you, Campbell? What are you up to tonight?"

Ivy was enjoying learning about the hobbies of her team. There was so little time during the day to actually get to know each other. All she could do was grasp the nuances of their work behaviours, like Campbell's attention to detail and Byrne's inability to recognise the subtleties of a joke.

"Football tonight," she answered, pushing off the table as though unwilling to be left in the spotlight. Where Byrne was an open book – and if anything, too oversharing – Campbell preferred to retain a shield of mystery.

"Oh, who's playing?"

"I am," she said, as if the answer was obvious. She nodded a goodbye and walked towards the door, and when she walked past Byrne, she leaned in close to him and muttered loud enough for Ivy to hear, "We're *third* in the league."

And with a final grin for Ivy, she walked out the door.

"Well, I'm happy you both have such blooming social lives," Ivy said. "I wish I could say the same for myself."

The comment seemed to resonate with Byrne. He hesitated by the door.

"Well, it's important, isn't it?" Byrne said. "Especially in this line of work. Keeps things light, doesn't it? Reminds us of life on the outside."

"Yeah," Ivy said, admiring his insight again. "I suppose it does." She stood from her desk, and in the same manner she often used to push her family out of the door, she said, "Come on. You don't want to be late for your quiz."

"Are you coming, sarge?" he asked, noticing her coat still on the back of her chair and her belongings still scattered on her desk.

"I've just got a few things to finish up," she lied, with no desire to return home before she absolutely must. She had planned to just meet Jamie at Hattie's piano recital rather than going through the awkward ritual of getting ready at home, awkwardly ignoring each other between the wardrobe, the bathroom, and the mirror.

"What about you?" he said, as though hesitant to leave before returning the question. "Any plans for tonight?"

"It's my daughter's piano recital," she said. "Just a small thing at school."

"Well, good luck to her," Byrne said. "Tell her to break a leg."

Ivy smiled. "I'll pass on the message."

"Alright, goodnight, sarge," he said.

"You too, Byrne. Break a leg at your quiz."

He turned awkwardly. "Oh, we...erm, we don't really say that," he said sincerely.

"Oh?"

"Yeah, I prefer *go forth and conquer*."

"Well then, go forth and conquer," Ivy said, failing to repress her smirk.

Byrne's face broke into a smile. "Thank you," he said and then bounced after Campbell.

Ivy watched him go, deeming him more and more difficult to read. The man swung like a metronome from insightful and knowledgeable to useless and borderline immature. But George was right. He had potential. How to fully unlock it, however, was still open to interpretation.

The final officer left the room. A man whom Ivy had yet to speak to in the few short months she had been there. Maybe one day she'd meet them all. But officers came and went. They moved on and up and sideways. A polite nod sufficed.

The door closed behind him, and she looked around the silent incident room, enjoying a similar peace and quiet to the one she had experienced in Adrian's cell only a day earlier. She stood up and stretched her legs. Once, what felt like a lifetime ago, she had taken a yoga class and had even made a few friends through it. These days, she could barely touch her toes. Maybe that was something she could kick start once more. Maybe she could be a woman who had hobbies again.

She turned to face the whiteboard, if not for anything else than for something to look at. Just like their investigation, it was a mess. There were four main names on the board, some with a complete, albeit questionable MMO. But in the top-right corner were two names she had barely registered. *James and Samuel*.

She remembered George writing them on the board and explaining that they were characters in Dean Worthing's memoir. But they hadn't come again, not in any of the statements or evidence they had found. How could they have spent four days investigating one man's life and not come across two names that were seemingly extremely important to his childhood?

Reluctantly, she picked up the rag from the little tray beneath the board, then with a final glance, as if to take a snapshot in her mind, she wiped it clean.

As the last justifiable task for her to do, Ivy was out of reasons to delay the drive home. She switched off the lights and was walking towards the door when one more reason presented itself.

A desk phone rang.

She glanced around the room, her eyes drawn to a green glow on Byrne's desk. She rushed across the room, dumped her bag on his desk, and hit the button to speak on loudspeaker.

"DS Hart," she said.

"Oh..." somebody said. A man, middle-aged.

"Who is this please?" Ivy asked.

"Hi, I'm looking for PC Byrne."

"I'm afraid you've just missed him. Can I take a message?"

"Oh, erm. Yes. I suppose. My name's Joe Kemp. He called me earlier regarding a request for planning permission at...Bluestone Lodge in South Ormsby."

"Oh," Ivy said. "Okay. We weren't actually expecting you to call back so soon."

"Well, you see, he asked for more details surrounding the request. It was made by a Mister Worthing. A Dean Worthing."

"That's right," Ivy said. "He was the registered owner."

"Was?"

"Is," Ivy said. "It's his name on the land registry."

"Well, you see, I found out what Mr Worthing was hoping to do with the place."

"Go on," she said, closing and rubbing her eyes, ready for a long, unnecessarily technical explanation about property laws and permissions. But what Joe Kemp explained was very simple, and when he spoke, she sat up straight, fumbling for her notepad.

"I'm sorry," she said slowly, her heart racing. "Say that again?"

CHAPTER FORTY-SIX

George settled into the exact same position he had for the last three nights, on his leather sofa, in the glowing embers of the dying sun. He had left the station just after his talk with Tim, too thwarted to continue with the paperwork. Ivy could handle it. His presence would have been superfluous.

And so he sat with *The Unholy Truths* on his lap, only this time, he omitted his usual glass of Talisker, thinking it might be to blame for his inability to read more than a hundred or so pages at a time. If Tim wanted Dean's manuscript on his desk by the morning, that still gave George the entire night to finish it. It was not a Talisker night.

But George was struggling to focus. His phone dinged every few seconds with emails confirming inquiries he had sent out about Dean, from Dean's publisher, Katy Southwell, and Worthing Media. But none of them presented any new information. Unless Dean Worthing rose from the dead to call George and tell him that his death had *not* been a suicide, then George was not expecting an important call. He set his phone on silent and settled into the final one hundred pages of the book.

———

Until that fateful night in the middle of March, the abuse inflicted upon us could be covered up. We would wear long sleeves or button our shirts to the collar, or wear long trousers even during the summer. But even we were not aware of their true capabilities, not until that day.

And only then did we realise that everything they had done to us up until then had been restrained. If you can imagine that. They had been holding back. A form of kindness in the sickest sense of the word.

It was a dark, wet evening, during which the rain fell in buckets, saturating the land around our house, which, later that night, would come in useful, for James, at least. We had gone to bed early, straight after dinner, which was always a treat. It meant they were tired, too tired to punish us for anything we had or had not done. Instead, they turned the TV on loud and smoked and drank the evening away.

James and I played cards cross-legged on the floor in the dark. We had to squint to see the numbers, sometimes aided by a rogue flash of lightning. We had never been taught how to play anything, so we'd made our own games, something between snap and rummy. To this day, I still remember the rules.

"Samuel," I remember saying, calling over to the shivering pile of blankets in the old, lopsided bed the three of us shared. "Come play with us."

But I received only a whimper in reply. If there was anything Samuel was more scared of than the dark, it was a storm, and with the next loud crack of thunder, he whimpered so loud that I had to remind him not to disturb them downstairs. I didn't love the storms either, but I preferred to distract myself. James, on the other hand, loved a good storm. They made him feel like the wilderness was right there, just outside his window, and I would even catch him some nights with his head outside, letting the rain dampen his long, matted hair while he worshipped the fierce forces of nature.

A few times, the wind blew so ferociously, it caused the tree branches to tap against the glass like slapping palms, which only served to heighten

Samuel's fear. But eventually, after one too many cracks of thunder, a strong smell of ammonia wafted through the room.

We knew what it was. James and I.

I got up, leaving James to admire the storm through the window, and walked over. We were often dehydrated. It wasn't that we were denied water; more that we feared venturing downstairs to get it. And as a result, our urine was a dark brandy colour and pungent with it.

Hopeful that I was wrong, I felt the blankets and closed my eyes in horror of what was to come.

"No, Samuel," I groaned, knowing this was grounds for punishment. The TV blared downstairs, audible even over the storm. We were safe, for now. "We need to clean this up," I told him. "Before they notice."

I tried to move him, but Samuel wouldn't budge, as if he was frozen in time, and cold to the touch. So unreactive was he to my efforts, the only thing that proved he was alive at all was the violent trembling of his body and lower lip.

"Samuel, please," I said. "Come on. Let's get you cleaned up, or you'll get in trouble."

But he wouldn't budge. He had curled into a tight, immovable ball, his head and limbs tucked in like an armadillo unwilling to unravel itself.

"James," I hissed, turning my attention instead to pulling the blankets off the bed, planning to wash them in the bath. "Help me, would you?"

James was stronger than me-stronger than both of us. He was able to pull Samuel straight, where he stretched him out and began removing his pyjamas, so they too could be washed before anyone found out.

I should have known then how it looked. How much more trouble we would be in if they found us like this than if they had found Samuel had wet the bed again. But all I could think about was getting him clean so we could have one night – just one night – of peace.

After all, we'd all heard the rumours about the allegations against local churches, from whispers between the pews during Sunday service. They had even asked us boys, James, Samuel, and I if Reverend Wassall had ever touched us inappropriately as though he was the one to be feared. Not that he ever had or ever would. See, it disgusted them, the idea of sexual abuse.

Physical abuse, pain-induced torture against us, that was fine. That was a well-taught lesson. But sexual abuse - that was a sin. That was ungodly.

And so, when they did climb the stairs and enter our bedroom, they saw Samuel like that, half-naked on the bed, with James and me tearing at his clothes. It was only natural for them to jump to their own sick conclusions. They were obsessed with the idea of it. Repulsed. And they assumed in us a darkness where there had only been brotherly love.

"What on God's Holy earth are you doing?" one of them whispered.

"Sinners!" the other yelled.

And together, they rushed at us.

If I hadn't been a runner, if Samuel hadn't frozen with fear, perhaps things would have turned out differently.

They held nothing back. They attacked him with punch after punch, on his face, his stomach, his genitals, hammering him with drunken and unrelenting fury.

We were powerless. James and I.

Samuel lay there, taking the blows, absorbing them.

James and I huddled in the corner of the room until he could bear it no longer. I tried to stop him, but James, being James, had to try.

He was backhanded to the floor before he had taken five steps, sending him sprawling. They returned their attention to Samuel, dragging him up from the bed for the other to beat. His limbs flailed like a rag-doll until they didn't. Until he was beat.

Where they had once kicked Samuel, they now stamped on him. Where they had once slapped him, they pummelled him. Where they had once bruised his bones, they broke them. And I heard them - like the crack of thunder.

I considered jumping out the window and running across the field to the church, to the tower, where I might climb to the roof. Where I might call for help from God.

But God couldn't save Samuel now.

I don't remember him even making a sound. It was as though he had resigned himself to his fate. Welcomed it, even.

James was the only one to fight it. With his final attempt to save

Samuel, he rushed in, reached under Samuel's arms, and dragged him towards the door.

A single blow knocked James to his knees, but in a last attempt to save his brother, he threw Samuel towards the landing, to freedom.

But despite James' larger frame, even he lacked the strength.

Samuel's limp, bleeding body crashed against the doorframe, and his head smashed into the rusty, old lock set into the wood. The crack was louder than any thunderclap they'd heard that evening. A streak of dark crimson streamed from his forehead, and he gazed into some far-off world. A world where, I hoped, and to this day I still do, there is peace.

A terrible silence followed, filled only with ragged, drunken breaths, strained from physical exertion.

"James," one of them hissed. "James, what have you done?"

I watched my brother stare at Samuel, his chest heaving with despair, then look between them in shock, his face almost unrecognisable, such was the miserable burden in his features. Then he looked my way. It was all I could do to meet him eye to eye. I was in shock. I was lost in time and space. I wanted to run. And at my hopeless expression, James screamed. He screamed for what seemed like an eternity. It was beyond human. Animalistic. A wild and desperate howl that, to this day, still haunts me.

CHAPTER FORTY-SEVEN

George pulled himself out of the pages like a free diver, pulling himself up from the depths of the ocean and taking a lungful of air. He stared for a while into the barren fireplace, only just realising the depths of the darkness. He rubbed at his eyes and pinched the bridge of his nose. The sunset had long gone, and when he looked at the manuscript, he realised he only had a few pages left.

This changed everything.

Throughout the book, there had been no mention of a home. The rooms had been described as a frightened child might recall them; damp, dark, and miserable. Only the cellar had been described in full. Never a bedroom, never the landing, or a window, nor that their abusers were sometimes just downstairs watching TV, drinking and smoking.

"It doesn't make sense," he said to himself. "Was the home a church? The vicar's home, maybe? The vicar from a neighbouring parish, perhaps?"

The urge to open his laptop and continue where Byrne had left off was overshadowed by the alluring final pages on his lap. He held onto the thought. A local vicar. Somebody Wassall had been protecting for the sake of the church. That's where the boys must have stayed. A vicarage.

But now Dean's custodians were not only abusers; they were murderers. It may have been James' actions that had caused Samuel's death in the end, but there was little doubt in George's mind where the blame lay.

The thought sickened him. After all these years, they'd walked free. They'd got away with their crimes.

No, thought George. This was beyond crime. They'd got away with their evil behaviour.

George knew he had to read on, desperate for signs of identification. Desperate to know who these people were. Desperate to discover how he might track them down and bring them to justice. He poured all his trust into Dean's words, took a deep breath, and once more delved into Dean's manuscript.

———

"You've killed him," one of them hissed when James' screams had faded, like Samuel's final breath. He was on the floor, rocking back and forth, knees drawn up to his chest. I was eyeing the door, considering my escape. But where would I go? I was a witness. Who would believe me? How far could I get? To the church? And then what?

"They'll lock you up and throw away the key, boy. You know that, don't you?"

"Look what you did."

"You killed him. You did this."

"Your own brother."

I could see their words penetrating James' mind, his eyes welling as he absorbed them as truth. I watched my brother spiral into a cavern of guilty despair, a depth from which he would never arise, and neither would I.

"I saw you. I saw you attack him," one of them said, standing and

rubbing Samuel's congealing blood from his forearms. "I saw you kill him. With your bare hands."

"I saw it too. I saw what you did, and if you think you're going to get away with it, you've another thing coming."

"I saw what happened," I heard myself say, to which they both glared at me, daring me to voice what I had seen. But I'd started, and something inside me, some strength I had yet to discover, rose. "It's not fair. It's not fair on James, it's not fair on me, and..." I peered down at Samuel. So weak in his miserable life, yet so free in death. "And it's not fair on Samuel."

They left the room, stepping over Samuel, one of them stopped and glanced down at Samuel's body, then between James and me.

"There are spades in the shed."

We sat in silence. James and I. We sat for long enough that the worst of the storm passed. I stared at a single stain on the wall until I could write a poem about it; such was my attention to its detail – its colour, its curve, its uneven texture. We didn't speak. Not a single word. In fact, for the rest of the time I would know him, he would barely utter a single word again.

Of course, I wanted to tell him that it wasn't his fault. Of course, it wasn't. For all we knew, Samuel was dead before James had tried to save him; such was the horror of their beating. But I couldn't. I couldn't find the words. My throat was thick, like it was caked in mud or as if it was bound by a rope. I could barely breathe through it, let alone express my thoughts.

I instigated what had to be done. Me. The runner. The one who was neither strong enough to fight back nor too weak to cower. James simply followed suit. Though it wasn't James. Not any more. James was a ghost, and his mortal remains belied his vacant stare. We carried our brother's body downstairs, past the blare and shadows of the TV, and into the garden. They didn't help. They were hiding somewhere, we thought. Yet I know now they were planning their escape. They would run, just as I would have, given the chance.

We moved like spirits burdened with chains and manacles. The house sat on a few acres of land, so we carried our brother far away until we reached the oak tree under which he liked to sit on our more peaceful, *punishment-free days. I looked only upwards, never down, never into Samuel's dead eyes. I could not bear to meet his lifeless gaze.*

The large oak had thick, muscly roots that weaved an impenetrable mesh beneath our feet, that I hoped might cradle Samuel, like strong, sinewy arms. The dense canopy above would offer him shade, and the thick trunk blocked the view of the church. God would have no part in this.

James dug the hole. I tried to help, but he pushed me away. He owned that task, and in some way, I hoped that in completing it, his mind might take up his body once more. Sadly, it wasn't to be.

So I just stood there and watched, his heavy beads of sweat glistening like dewdrops in the moonlight. By the time the hole was waist-deep, his shirt was soaked through. But even when we had dragged our brother's remains inside, James did not stop. Not until he covered Samuel up with the dirt, without a break, without ritual, without ceremony-just spades full of soil and streams of tears.

When the task was done, he stopped. And we prayed. Not aloud, but we prayed. Then we lay beneath the ink-black sky for the last time. Three brothers, the lonely moon, surrounded by miles of open farmland, yet incarcerated by the truth.

Soon after, in the days that followed, we found ourselves alone. There were no goodbyes. There were no tears. Only a period of peace. A time when we should have rejoiced, James and I. A time when we feared their return and for the beatings to resume.

But that day never came.

We were free. But the price of our freedom was our souls, our childhood, our future, our hearts, and finally...my guilt, my shame, and my reprehensible mind. I should have stayed with James. I should have helped him. I should have been his brother.

But I didn't.

I'm a runner.

And runners run.

This is where my story ends, where my brother's life ended, where James' life ended, where my life ended.

It has taken a lifetime to unravel the truth of what happened from the evil I was led to believe.

So here it is. The Unholy Truth, by Dean Worthing.

For Samuel. For James. For myself. Brothers. I hope that my final work brings peace to us all.

For our parents, our guardians, and our custodians, whom I have named in the dedication of this book, I hope it brings you justice. And if, by chance, it fails, then my remaining hopes lie in God's judgement.

May you rot in hell.

Amen.

CHAPTER FORTY-EIGHT

Heart racing, George slammed the manuscript closed. He licked his finger, flicked over to the title page and the copyright page, and...

"It's missing," he whispered aloud. He scanned through the contents page and foreword and then back to the missing page. "There's no dedication."

Once more, as he had four whole days ago, George thumbed the torn paper ridge where the page had been ripped from the spine, only now realising its significance.

But who had taken it? Who would have torn it from the manuscript?

He snatched up his phone to call Ivy, but found the screen filled with notifications: seven missed calls, and reels of messages, all of which were from Ivy.

'Guv, call me back.' *'Where are you? Call me back!'* *'URGENT. CALL ME BACK'.*

She answered almost immediately, but for a while, all he heard were the sounds of scraping chairs, mutters of apologies, and distant, clunky piano music in the background.

"Ivy?" he said. "Are you there?"

"I'm here, guv," she whispered. "One sec." Then came the whoosh of wind and street noise as though she had stepped outside. "Sorry," she said, breathless. "I'm at Hattie's recital. Had to get out of the building." She took a breath as though refocusing her thoughts and then blurted, "Where the hell have you been?"

"Finishing Dean's memoir," he said. "Listen, I know what happened. It's worse than we thought. He wasn't abused in a church. It was a home. His home, where he lived with James and Samuel and whoever was supposed to be caring for them."

"Guv?" Ivy said, but George was unloading.

"I need you to pick up where Byrne left off. I need the list of vicars that Wassall was protecting. I need details of any allegations against them, and we need to somehow marry those profiles up with what Dean says in his memoir. He refers to one of them as *her,* which means it's a man *and* a woman, so we can eliminate any that were unmarried at the time."

"Guv!" Ivy said a little more forcefully this time.

George stopped, blinked, and then spoke.

"What is it?"

"I heard from the planning authority that Byrne contacted."

"Okay..." George said, not seeing the significance considering the gravity of what he'd just explained.

"Guv, Dean wanted planning permission to tear down Bluestone Lodge. He wanted to rebuild it from the ground up."

"Ivy, I don't think you're understanding–"

"...from the *cellar* to the attic, guv. His words, not mine."

George sat up. "What? There isn't a–"

"There is," Ivy said. "The bloke I spoke to went there. Dean wanted to knock the house down, fill the cellar in with concrete and then rebuild it."

George let his head fall back onto the chair.

"Oh, God. The house. The bloody house. There were boxes piled against the walls, remember? Unpacked appliances." He closed his eyes, straining to remember. "He hadn't not unpacked because of time. He was hiding behind the door. He didn't want to look at it."

"What's it built from, guv?" Ivy said as if he needed any further convincing.

"Spilsby sandstone," George muttered.

"Same as the church," Ivy said. "Do you remember what Byrne asked? Right at the beginning. He asked why Dean would buy a house and then kill himself three months later. He asks a lot of questions," Ivy said. "I ignore him half the time."

"But this time, he was onto something. We thought it was probably spontaneous suicide. But we know now that it wasn't spontaneous. Dean planned everything. Including buying a house. But not just any house, *that* house, the Bluestone Lodge, because–"

"That's where he grew up," Ivy said. "That's where it all happened."

"Ivy, whoever abused Dean, they used to live in that house. They were his parents. That's what he calls them, at the end, our parents. We need to find out who they were."

"Well, we know, guv. That guy, remember? God, what was his name? The one who owned the house before Dean. Byrne got his name from the neighbours."

"Pepper!" remembered George. "Someone Pepper. You're right. I need to call Campbell. Get her to find out who he is, where he lives, and anything else we can get." For a second, in the momentum, he had almost forgotten about the manuscript lying heavily on his lap, like a stone blocking a flowing stream. "Ivy," he said, slowing down their conversation. "There's more."

"What do you mean?"

"I mean..." he paused. "This went beyond abuse."

"What's worse than that?" she asked, then her breath rasped across the microphone. "Murder?"

"One of them died from their injuries."

Ivy paused.

"Who?" she said softly. "Which one?"

"Samuel," George said. "He was the youngest. They killed him. They made Dean and James bury his body in the garden."

"I'm sorry, guv," she said, as though Samuel was someone George had known personally.

"Ivy, I don't care if this happened almost forty years ago," George said. "I'm not letting this go. I want to find out who killed Samuel. I want to find out who abused them all. And I want to find out tonight."

"What are you going to do?"

"I'm going to the house," George said. "If Tim wants evidence, I'll give him bloody evidence."

Ivy didn't reply. Perhaps she knew what George was planning to do. Perhaps she didn't want to question it. Perhaps she just didn't want all the disturbing details.

"Guv, are you sure about this? I mean, surely this is enough to convince Tim to give us a few more days?"

"There's something else," he said. "I think I know who James is. I just can't prove it, and I doubt he'd admit to it."

"Right?" Ivy said after a pause for thought. "So what do we do?"

"I need to go into Lincoln," George said. "I need to...I don't know. Split myself in two."

Over the phone, George heard Ivy rub at her mouth the way she did when she was indecisive or at a loss. "I can't go, guv. I'm sorry. But if I leave Hattie's recital now, Jamie would never... I'd be loading his gun with ammunition."

"It's okay, Ivy," George said. "That's why we've got a team, remember?"

"Send Byrne," she said, her voice hopeful. "He's in town. He's at the Wig and Mitre doing some quiz thing."

"The Wig and Mitre," George noted. "Right."

George took a few deep breaths, wishing that he could have Ivy by his side during all of this.

"Good luck, guv," she said.

"Yes," he replied softly. "Yes, you too."

George ended the call, debated his priorities and clicked the most pressing name on his recent contacts.

"Campbell?" he said when she answered the phone out of breath.

"Guv," she gasped.

"Why are you..." George started. "Are you okay?"

He thought he heard a whistle in the distance.

"I'm fine, guv. I'm just at football practice."

"I'm sorry to do this, but I need your help. I need you to look into the man who sold the house to Dean Worthing. Pepper something or other. I think it was you who found his name in the land registry."

"I thought this was closed, guv," she said.

"Well, I just reopened it," he said, then quietened. "Listen, one of the lads died. Ivy and I...That is, Sergeant Hart and I have reason to believe it all happened at Bluestone Lodge. That's where he was living. That's where it happened. The abuse. The murder."

"The murder-"

"The what?"

"One of them died, Campbell. They're buried on the grounds."

"Jesus-"

"I hate to ask, but-"

"No, no, it's fine," she said.

"I've got a feeling this Pepper, whoever he is, is responsible. If he's a retired vicar, I'm going to drag him from his bed myself."

"Okay," she said, still breathless, not from the exercise but the new information, perhaps.

"I'm on it, guv," she said. "I'll call you as soon as I have something."

The call ended abruptly, and George flicked just one contact down and then clicked on Byrne's name. Unlike Campbell, George thought the call was about to run out before he answered.

"Guv?" he yelled through the speaker, loud enough that George had to pull the phone away from his ear. The noise on the other end was deafening. The unmistakable atmospheric sounds of a pub came through clearly. "*Can you hear me?*"

"Yes, Byrne, I can hear you. Step outside, would you?"

"I can't hear you," Byrne said. "I'll go outside."

George closed his eyes, feeling that nauseating yet addictive tightness growing in his chest. He was close.

Then came the much quieter sounds of a cold night on Lincoln High Street.

"Sorry, guv," Byrne said, his voice still too loud. "I'm at the Wig and Mitre in town doing a pub quiz. Everything alright?"

"I need you, Byrne," he said. "I need you to do something for me. It's very important."

"Okay..." the lad said, the uncertainty in his voice shining through. George imagined him looking between the street and the closed pub door, no doubt wondering if it would take so long that he couldn't make it back in time for the next round of questions. "What is it?"

"Listen up," George began. "I need you to find someone for me. A man named Freddo."

CHAPTER FORTY-NINE

The ribbon of roads that wound between George's house in Bag Enderby and Bluestone Lodge passed by in a blur. A lonely blur, so quiet were the roads. He glanced at the two objects he had brought with him that now lay on the passenger seat, one a symbol of wit, the other a symbol of brute strength – the manuscript and a spade.

In the depths of darkness and under a cloud of historical horrors, Bluestone Lodge held a menacing quality that George had yet to see. He had always thought the house magnificent, a family-like home with its beautiful writing room and sturdy construction. But he saw it now for what it was. A dungeon. A house of torture and horror. The opposite of a home. He drew his car up to the side of the house and turned his headlights to full beam to illuminate what, to the uninformed, was a picturesque scene of innocent beauty.

But the scene was far from innocent.

The idea of being there alone set his nerves alight. He twitched at every flit of a bat or hoot of an owl. But he had no other choice. He needed answers, and the answers were and always had been, right there.

George grabbed the manuscript and flicked on the interior light. He flipped through to the final pages to where Dean had described where they had buried Samuel's body. The words were meant to be savoured, to inspire shock and disgust, not to be dissected and analysed like a treasure map. But George read them again as though they were a legend, turning the symbols on the page into meaningful directions, instructing him how he could find what he was searching for.

There were many trees on the property, but the one George was looking for was prominent. A large oak standing alone, like the logo of a renowned publishing house.

Or a media company.

George smiled at the symbolism. How many eyes had seen Worthing Media's logo yet had not understood the significance?

He set down the manuscript on the passenger seat, grabbed the spade, and reassuring himself that it could be used as a weapon, he climbed from the car.

The house loomed above him, and he was drawn to one of the windows, black and lifeless in the dark night.

At the front door, he knocked twice, then stepped back to peer up at that window.

There was no answer, and part of him was grateful. Perhaps Adrian would be better off in a comatose state, than having to relive that awful night.

Quietly, he stepped away and edged round to the side of the house, where his headlights lit the paddock before him, casting the landscape in an eerie glow.

He had never been particularly afraid of the dark, and the tremble in his legs belied his confidence. But then, he had never before done what he was about to do.

He knew what he was here to find, and while a part of him longed to find it, another part of him dreaded the moment that he did.

The clues had all been there in the manuscript. He stood

where James had stood, spade in hand, under the night sky, the stars, and the moonlight. The thick tree trunk blocking his view of the church. He placed his phone on the ground, angling it so the torch could light his way.

And he dug.

Unlike that stormy night, the ground had not seen rain for a few days, and before long, George was removing his coat with the exertion of breaking through the crusty soil. But just as James had, he persevered. He owed the lad that much.

While he dug, George felt himself enacting his own penance. He felt responsible, somehow. For Dean's death. For Samuel's. It was all of their responsibilities, really, as a society. To keep children safe from evil. Unquestionably, they had all failed. George had been a police officer in the eighties. He had been part of the force already. A system designed to enact justice. And it had failed to protect those boys.

Michael Wassall had known. George could see that now. That was the root of his kindness to Dean. But still, he had not stopped it from happening. Perhaps he had felt like he couldn't stop what happened at home. Perhaps he had feared being held responsible. Or perhaps he had been bound by the laws of the church. Maybe *that* was the terrible thing in the name of religion he had been so unable to live with that he had turned his back on his lifelong faith.

And so George's guilt fuelled his digging, bearing the weight of a system at large and venting his frustration on the spade, stamping it down and heaving it up, the soil spilling from the tool like blood from a blade. Over and over, on and on, he dug. Over and over, on and on, his guilt gained momentum. He dug so deep that he had to drop to his knees to reach the bottom, dragging the soil from the hole like water from a sinking dinghy.

And then he struck something hard.

George stopped, breathless and lightheaded.

He heard Grace's voice in his mind as his eyes swam with

little, white dots. *You're a sixty-six-year-old man, George. Take it easy, love. You don't have time for a heart attack.*

He tapped the spade again and heard a definite *clunk*. Not a thud, as if he'd hit a root. A *clunk*.

He lay on the ground and reached to dig with his bare hands, the rough stones opening fresh wounds on his knuckles as he groped for...for...he felt something. Something hard, smooth, and alien.

He snatched his arm back, staring into the hole in horror, and sat back on his knees. A gasp escaped his throat. His eyes filled unexpectedly with tears, and though he wanted nothing more than to call it in, to call Tim Long and berate him for his obstinance, he couldn't.

He reached in once more, slowly this time.

And he felt it. Unmistakably smooth, small enough for his fingers to encircle, yet large and long enough to identify.

The light buzzing of his phone beside him roused him from his stare into the depths of that terrible grave. But when George's grubby fingers hit the button to answer the call, he couldn't speak, such was the lump in his throat.

Eventually, Byrne spoke.

"Guv?" he said. "Guv, you there?"

George cleared his throat and breathed for what felt like the first time in minutes.

"I am," he said. "I am. Go on."

"He doesn't believe me, guv."

"What?" George croaked.

"I'm with him now," Byrne said. "Freddo. But he doesn't believe that you sent me."

George couldn't believe it. Byrne had actually followed his directions. He'd actually found him. "You're at the warehouse?" he asked.

"Yes, guv. I'm with Freddo now. But he won't talk to me."

"Byrne," George said, finding his voice. "Put me on loud-speaker."

George thought the line had gone dead for a second, but then a whole atmosphere of sounds filled the call. He couldn't quite believe his situation, kneeling in the dirt, above a decades-old body, chatting to Byrne on the phone.

"Freddo?" he said. "It's me, George Larson. We met the other day."

"Inspector Larson," came Freddo's unmistakable Birmingham accent. George recognised too the echo of the old warehouse. "Who's this you've sent me then?" George thought he heard Fred-do's voice grow quieter as though Byrne had backed away a little.

"He's one of mine," George said. "I promise you that."

"He's asking questions, Georgie. About Adrian," Freddo said. "I told you. It's not my story to tell."

"Freddo," George said, "I promise you, I wouldn't be asking unless it was important."

"Even so—"

"I know who he is," George continued.

"Oh yeah?" Freddo repeated.

"Listen, the truth is about to come out about his childhood. There are people who don't want that to happen. If you know Adrian's story, Freddo, if you know what happened to him, then you know how bad it is."

The silence that followed told George all he needed to know.

"You know what these people are capable of, Freddo. I need to stop them." George paused, hoping his message was sinking in. "But to do that, I need you to confirm something. I need you to work with me."

Freddo was silent. George took this as a positive sign. He wasn't trying to talk his way out of anything, which, as a man of wit, seemed to be his usual tactic. No, silence showed that he was mid-thought. He was doubting himself.

"He's James, isn't he?" George said. "That's his real name.

Adrian is a pseudonym, isn't it? Just like yours, Freddo. A fake name to keep you safe. To distance you from who you used to be."

George paused, and Freddo eventually replied.

"He's in danger, you say?"

"I believe so," George said. "But I can't protect him unless I know for sure. I need to be sure that Adrian's real name is James. I promise you," he said, looking down at the femur before him. "I wouldn't be asking if it wasn't a matter of life and death."

George heard the same thoughtful silence. Then Freddo sighed audibly, in exasperation, as though deciding whether or not to betray his friend.

"It's James," he said clearly and confidently. "His name is James Samson."

"James Adrian Samson," George pressed, and Freddo relented.

"That's it."

George let out a long, shaky breath. In his mind, the two men merged, the James he had read about and imagined and the Adrian he had met and gotten to know, however briefly. They had the same wild eyes, the same ragged hair, and tragic backstory.

"Thank you, Freddo," George said. "Thank you."

"Don't make me regret telling you that," Freddo replied.

"I won't. You've done a good thing, Freddo."

"I'll walk your mate back to the river," Freddo said, choosing not to acknowledge the gratitude, perhaps preferring to pretend that he had not betrayed his friend at all. "Some of the lads are eyeing up his fancy jacket."

Even in the darkness that surrounded him, George couldn't help but chuckle. He imagined Byrne pulling his coat around him self-consciously.

"Thank you."

George's phone buzzed once in his hand to alert him of another incoming call.

"George," Freddo said before George could answer the new call. "Let me know, will you? I want to know he's alright."

"I will," George promised, and with that, he ended the call and answered the next.

"Campbell," he said. "What have you got?"

"Guv?" she started, her voice thick and heavy, with urgency. "John Pepper. His name is John Pepper. He owned the house from the fifties right up until he sold it to Dean Worthing a few months ago."

"Don't tell me. He's a retired man of the cloth," George said. "And his name is one of those in the child abuse allegations Michael Wassall was covering up."

"No," she said. "None of that." George closed his eyes to the world around him and listened. He's a retired school teacher living in Yorkshire," she continued, "where he's lived since nineteen-sixty-four."

"Sixty-four?"

"No previous criminal record. No mention of a Pepper in Byrne's research."

"So-" George started.

"It was his family home. He couldn't bear to sell it, but he made a life in Yorkshire, so he rented it out."

"He rented it out?" George said. "Who to, and where the bloody hell have they been hiding?"

"He doesn't know," she said. "An agency dealt with it for him. I looked the firm up, but they went out of business years ago."

"A dead end? They cared for orphans and poor kids. Surely there's some kind of paper trail? Surely they had to be registered with some kind of authority."

"There were laws, guv. But it was the seventies and eighties. These things were, by all accounts, far less...controlled."

"And he has no records of who it was?"

"Nothing," she replied. "He said he met them when they moved in. A nice couple, but he can't remember their names. He can't even remember what they looked like."

"Because they blend in," George mused aloud.

"I can look into him a bit more. If the agency was still going, we might stand a better chance. I suppose I could get onto the electricity provider. They might have records going back that far, but..." The sound of breaking glass echoed through the night, and George tore the phone from his ear and followed the noise to his car. "What was that?"

"Shh," he hissed, his head cocked, listening to the night.

"Guv?" he heard her say, but the sound of a car door slamming rang out through the darkness. "Guv, are you still there?

His car door. He would know that sound anywhere.

"I'm at Dean Worthing's house," he whispered into the phone. "Get onto the station. I need backup."

"What's happened? What's wrong?"

"Just..." he said, zeroing in on his car in the distance. "Just send it, and for God's sake, make it quick."

CHAPTER FIFTY

He ran as fast as he could, ignoring his wife's voice telling him he was too old for this nonsense, too old to be sprinting across an uneven field in the middle of the night.

The scene before him played out like one of those old theatre shows where the cast were little more than silhouettes behind a screen. A black, human form against the glare of the headlights, staring directly at George.

He slowed to a walk, not eighty yards from the form.

"Adrian? Adrian, is that you?" he called out, his heart thumping an easy allegro and his hand held up as a shield against the headlights. But he said nothing. "Adrian. We need to talk."

The figure froze for a second or two, as if deliberating. But from afar, George's power of persuasion proved ineffective, and the dark shape slipped into the shadows.

"Stop there," George called, then set off after them. Never in the history of policing had anybody actually paid heed to such a command. Yet, in light of the situation, there was little else he could have said.

By the time he reached the limits of the paddock, where a flower bed marked the division between grass and gravel, a car door slammed. And by the time he reached the front of the house, a car was reversing out of the drive onto the quiet country lane. He ran forward a few more steps, hoping to catch a glimpse of the number plate, but he was slow, too late, and exhausted.

Blood thumped in his ears like a drum circle, round and round, ebbing and flowing. He placed his hands on his knees and leaned forward, retching for breath, his chest burning. Then he stood straight, gasping, and watched the car's tail lights winding down the lane and into the night.

His own car lights were still on. The headlights lit the paddock, the tree, and the spade jutting from the ground, marking Samuel's grave.

The rear lights, however, cast a red glow across the gravel, turning the tiny stones to rubies.

Slowly, he ambled across the driveway to inspect the damage. The ground on the passenger side sparkled like a diamond mine. Tiny shards of safety glass were strewn across the ground.

"Oh, for Christ's sake," he muttered, and he peered through the broken window. "Ah, I don't bloody believe it..." he turned away, grabbed onto his hair, then turned again and kicked the door. "Damn it."

He took a breath, calmed himself, then tore the door open to check in the footwell. But it was empty. He knew it would be.

Once more, he was on his toes, sprinting as fast as a sixty-year-old man might, towards the house and the front door. It was ajar, and light spilt onto the steps from inside.

"Bloody useless junkie," he muttered as he barged his way inside, tore up the stairs, and then came to a stop outside Adrian's room, preparing himself for what he might find inside.

Gently, he nudged the door, and slowly it swung open to reveal what he could describe as devastation, The room stank of sweat and God knows what else. Carefully, he dragged the duvet from the bed and dropped it in a heap.

Behind the door, an old duffle bag sat open with its contents spilt onto the floor.He kicked clothes and the bedding from where the items had been heaped but could find no shoes and no coat. A man like Adrian Samson, who had spent a large portion of his miserable life on the street, would struggle to leave possessions of any kind in another room.

A vibration in his hand stirred him back to the now, and the glow from his phone's screen lit the scene like a horror movie.

"Guv?" Campbell said when he answered.

"I'm here," he said as he backed out of the room.

"I've got a unit on its way. What the bloody hell is going on?"

"Samson is gone," he said quietly.

"Gone? What, as in gone from the house, or...or dead, guv?"

"Gone from the house," he said, irritated at having to explain himself.

"So what, is he on foot? Has he recovered? Should we alert anybody?"

"I don't know. I need to think," he said. "I saw him at my car."

"It was definitely him?"

George hesitated. There was no way he could put his hand on his heart and say it was Samson he had seen.

"Who else would want the manuscript?"

"He's got the manuscript?"

"Yes," George said, admitting defeat. "I thought it was just kids at first. He smashed my bloody window."

"Guv, you're not making sense-"

"He took the manuscript," he said. "He took it and did a runner. Without him and without the manuscript, we've got nothing. Zero."

He checked each of the upstairs rooms as he spoke, then descended the stairs.

"Can't you go after him? He can't have got far-"

"He took my keys," he said, resigning himself to a world of ridicule. "I stupidly left them in the ignition so I could use the headlights to see where I was digging."

"Digging?"

He paused again. That explanation required far more than an off-the-cuff statement over the phone with adrenaline coursing through his body.

"I think we're going about this the wrong way," George said. "I think we've known the answer to this all along."

"What are you saying?"

"He's the last one," he replied. "He's the only one who can testify to what happened all those years ago. The manuscript implicates him."

"Implicates him? For what?"

"There's something else," he said. "I think Adrian held a grudge against Dean. Resented his success, maybe. I think the Hawkins saw him. I think he pushed Dean. He's been hiding behind his affliction the whole time."

He stopped at the open front door and stared out into the night, hoping to see the flash of blue lights as the uniformed team drew near. But there was only an empty, silent darkness.

"What do you need me to do?" she asked.

George hurried through into the kitchen. The boxes of unpacked appliances were still stacked against the far wall. With the phone to his ear, he pulled the topmost boxes from their place, letting them crash to the floor. The others, he shoved to one side, allowing the contents to clatter and break on the kitchen tiles, caring only about what lay behind them. And when it was done, when the wall behind had been exposed, he stepped back.

A large section of wall had been recently plastered and not yet sanded and painted. He ran a hand over the flat surface and felt the telltale lines where plaster met solid wall.

"Guv, are you still there?"

"Bear with me," he said quietly, and taking the phone from his ear, he held it up to shine the light on the exposed wall. "I've got it. It's here. I know it is."

"Got what?" she asked, her tinny voice moving as he shone the light over the outline of an old doorway. "Guv, what is it you've got? Do I need to come there?"

"Just hang on, will you?"

George rested his head against the plaster and closed his eyes as though listening for the trauma held in those walls. He tapped in various places, confirming his suspicions.

He took a single step back, raised his right foot, and then lunged forward. His heel, which connected with the plasterboard, broke through and came face to face with the wall. Twice more, he kicked at the wall, each time enlarging the hole until it was large enough for him to crouch and lean into, shining the light into the damp and dank darkness.

"Guv, I'm coming," Campbell said, the rank stone walls amplifying her voice. "I'm calling Sergeant Hart, too."

He pulled himself free of the hole and slid down onto his backside.

"I see it," he told her, cutting her off. "I can see it all so clearly."

"Guv?"

He climbed to his feet and scrambled over the boxes and broken plaster, coming to a stop once more at the open front door. He peered out into the night, eyeing the one building in the distance that broke the horizon, jet black against the night.

"Where would you go, Campbell? Where would you go if you knew the game was up?"

She paused as though thinking hard, trying to offer a voice of reason to what was clearly a dark, adrenaline-fuelled moment for George. "Where would *I* go, guv?" she said slowly. "Or where would *he* go?"

"You'd go to where it all began," he said.

"Guv?"

"To where it all began," he said. "That's where you'd go. To where, all those years ago, you were forced to sing and pray, forced to pretend life was rosy. You'd go to the one place where you should have been given asylum. Where somebody should have listened to you. Where, under the ever-watchful gaze of Saint Leonard, you descended into madness." Slowly, he descended the front steps, his eyes never leaving that sandstone tower in the distance. "The patron saint of prisoners and captives."

CHAPTER FIFTY-ONE

George used the final ebbs of his fading strength to drag himself up the largest hill in South Ormsby. He had trekked past Samuel's unmarked grave, crossed the boundaries of Bluestone Lodge and into the South Ormsby Estate. Through the long-grass fields, he trudged, stumbled, and slipped, retracing Adrian Samson's footsteps from a few days before until finally, he came to a stile. He climbed it wearily and stepped down into the grounds of St Leonard's Church.

A disquiet loomed among the graves, as it had on the night he had first met Dean Worthing, sprawled across Richard Hawkins' car bonnet. George kept to the shadows, slinking between the headstones like a thief in the night. He peeked around the church tower, his ears pricked for the slightest hint of life. There was none.

The large inner door to the church was ajar. It creaked so loudly when George pushed it open that he doubted anyone in the church had missed his entrance. The last time George had climbed the tower's spring-like, spiral steps, he had done so slowly and thoughtfully, admiring the ritual of it – the old-fashioned practice of following a robed vicar up an ancient staircase. But this time, he ran without ceremony. Without the benefit of daylight, he stumbled multiple times and banged his shins against the hard stone, sometimes slipping and risking a neck-breaking tumble. But he held tight to those ancient walls, praying for all it was worth that he was in time.

He burst through the door, sending a dozen or more birds scattering from the nearby treetops, and time seemed to stop. It was as if up there, at the top of the tower, a whole other world existed. As if the stairs were a gateway.

The crossing point. The edge of life. The cusp of death.

The two eyed each other. One with caution, the other with a combination of pity, empathy, and disdain.

"James," George said, and that single word conveyed a multitude of messages. "I know who you are. I know what you've been through. I know why you live as you do. I know what you did. You don't have to do this."

He was sitting on the stone wall, his gaunt face a gargoyle in the moonlight.

"Leave me alone," he said.

"You don't have to do this, you know?"

"I do," he said, and he turned to stare down at the ground below. "I do."

"James, we can talk about it. There's things we can do. People to help you."

He laughed. It was an odd sight to see such a wretch raise a smile. It was fleeting, but George knew a laugh when he saw one.

"Nobody has called me that for years," the wretch replied.

"Does it bother you?" George asked after a pause. "Does it bring back...memories? Events you'd rather forget?"

James shrugged.

"It doesn't matter anymore, does it? None of it matters."

George took a step closer, and James flinched, placing his hand down on the wall as if preparing to push himself off,

"Easy now," George said, and he held his hands up to demonstrate he meant no harm as he sidestepped to the wall, not three metres from where James was perched, too far away to make a grab for him, but close enough to see his expression. And a sorry one it was. He peered down. It wasn't particularly high, and death was not a given. In fact, George thought, an unlucky soul might survive and be forced to endure a different kind of hell. Paralysis. Life-changing injuries. "I found him, you know?" he said quietly, and James' eyes glistened. "Dean was a damn fine writer. His description was spot on."

"He could always write," James replied, and he smiled fondly.

"And he could always run," George told him. "His words, not mine." He watched James digest the statement. "Is that what this is about, James? Is that why you did what you did? Because he left you. Because for one reason or another, he was able to make something of himself while you lived in squalor, never knowing where the next meal is coming from, never knowing where you would sleep each night?"

James shook his head, his eyes downcast.

"No," he said softly.

George turned his back on the view, folded his arms, and made himself comfortable. It was a sign, he hoped, that he wasn't going anywhere anytime soon.

"Why don't you tell me about that night, James?" George suggested.

"What?"

"The night Samuel died," he said. "Tell me about it."

"I...I can't—"

"You could try. Have you ever told anybody about it? About what happened? About what you did?"

James glared at him, his eyes a combination of bitterness and sorrow.

"Once," he said, referring, George thought, to Freddo.

"So tell me."

"I can't—"

"Come on, get it off your chest," George replied, and again, he turned to peer down into the darkness. "If you're going to do this, you'll be taking the story with you. There's nobody left when you're gone. Nobody to fight your corner."

"What does it matter?"

"What does it matter? What does it matter, James? It matters more than you think. It matters that your name isn't dragged through the mud..." James shrugged again. "It matters that Samuel's memory can live on. That he won't be forgotten. That we can understand who he was and what the three of you went through."

"None of that matters," James said. It was as if his entire persona had altered, George noticed. Twenty-four hours ago, the man couldn't utter a single word. Yet now, on the brink of death, he was as clear-minded and resolute as any man. "Not anymore."

He swung his legs around so both his feet hung in the air, and his hands gripped the stone wall ready, for one final shove.

"What about *them*?" George said. "Your parents."

"I had no parents."

"Your carers then. The people who housed you. The people who did those awful things. Tell me about them. Who were they? Where did they go? Do you know their names?"

"None of it matters," James said, slipping back into the man George now recognised as Adrian.

"People have died, James," he said. "For God's sake, how many people have to die? Samuel, Dean, Michael Wassall, not to mention the hundreds if not thousands of kids out there who have all been through something similar?" He paused, hoping for his words to connect, but there was little evidence James heard a single syllable. "Don't you want to change that? Don't you want to do something good? Think about it. Think of what you could do. The lives you could change with your story."

"They'll throw away the key," James snapped, then softened.

"That's what they'll do. They'll lock me up and throw away the key."

"I can...do things," George pleaded. "I can help you. Help me by identifying who did this to you; any judge and jury will see it for what it is. I can help you. But you need to help me. I need you to trust me."

"How can I trust you?" James said. "How can I trust anyone? The only two people I ever trusted are dead."

"Right, and you killed them both," George said. "You smashed Samuel's head into a doorframe, and you shoved Dean from this very tower. I'm offering you a second chance. I'm offering you a life. A life where you won't have to look over your shoulder in case they pop up one day. I'm offering you a chance to tell your story. To tell Dean's story and Samuel's." He stared at the doorway into the tower and what lay beyond. "I'm offering you a chance to do good. For the first time in your life, James, you've got the chance to turn this around. To turn your life around. Where's the manuscript? What have you done with it? I'll dig up every field and ditch between here and Bluestone Lodge if I have to." He stepped over to James and tapped his chest and back to see if he'd stuffed into his shirt.

"I'll do it," James cried out, and he pushed himself up onto his hands so that all he had to do was let go, and all his suffering and torment would be over.

Slowly, George backed off. There was no way, even if he could grab onto him, that he had the strength to hold him, let alone pull him to safety.

"Ah, sod you," he said, turning his back on the wretch and striding towards the door, where he stopped, not quite done. "You know, if I had a second chance, do you know what I'd do? If I had the opportunity to right all the wrongs I've done, I'd bloody well change it. I'd make a difference. Maybe I wouldn't be here now. Maybe I would have made DI. Maybe I'd never have moved away from here. Eh?" he said, hearing the crack in his own voice.

"Maybe my wife would know who I am. Maybe, and it's a big maybe, if I hadn't put her through what I did to be where I am, she'd know my bloody name. So yes, if I had the chance, I'd make it right. You couldn't stop me. And here's me now, giving you a second chance. A chance that nobody gets, eh? Life isn't filled with chances. And what do you do? You throw it away. Chuck it back in my face. Well, I tell you what, James or Adrian, whatever you want to be called, I don't care anymore. Alright? I just don't care." He stared at the wretch on the wall. The gargoyle. "So jump," he said. "Go on. Jump. Let go. The world will be a better place without you."

George sneered once more at James and found himself repulsed by what he saw. He turned away, and without a second thought, he stepped back into the tower and descended the first few steps.

And then he stopped and listened for the sound of James' clothes scraping against the stone. Maybe a light scream as he fell. And a thud. The crack, maybe, of broken bones. He wondered if he would find what he sought. Death. Or if he would be one of those unfortunate souls.

"You're wrong, you know?" was all he heard.

"I don't care, James. Just let go. Go on. Get it done. I'll take care of it. At least I now know the truth. At least I can put something in my report. At least I'll know I was right all along. He didn't jump. But his killer was a coward to face up to what he'd done. So go on. Do it. Maybe we can all move on. I've had enough of being stuck in the past." He paused, giving time to think of Grace. "I've had enough of it all, if I'm honest."

"I said you're wrong," James said again, closer this time. He heard the sound of rubber soles on the tower's stone floor, and he ascended. Slowly, unsure of what he might find. He stepped into the moonlight, where James Adrian Samson stood in the centre of the space, tall and with his chest filled in defiance. George studied him. For the first time, he wasn't cowering or hunched up. There was a pride to him. In him. About him. Something worth saving.

And then George saw them. His shoes. The shoes he had searched for in the house not thirty minutes before. They were on his feet, and just as George's shoes were, after his sprint across the fields, they were caked in mud.

"I didn't kill Samuel," he said softly. "And I didn't kill Dean."

George waited, hoping that perhaps he might embellish the statement. But that was all he was going to get. And that was better than the alternative.

"I think I'm beginning to realise that," George said. "Are you ready to make a difference, James? Are you ready to tell me who did this to you?"

James gazed into the night, his mouth ajar, revealing his foul teeth. George closed the gap between them. He stepped up close to the miserable wretch. So close he could smell the foulness from his body, from his breath. So close he could study the man's expression and see the suffering as if those days were being relived, right then, right there. So close he could see the pain in his glistening eyes, like flames dancing in the night.

And then George saw it. A fire burned in his eyes. Like a demon.

Slowly, he turned and followed that hollow gaze out into the night. Across the field and over the hill to where Bluestone Lodge stood, no longer idle in the darkness, no longer an empty house of horrors. It was ablaze. Flames danced from its rooftop like tortured souls, from its windows, and from that old front door in brilliant hues of topaz and amber and reds. Vivid red. Ruby red.

"James, I'm going to ask you one question, and I want you to answer me honestly," George said quietly as they both witnessed the ruination of the Bluestone Lodge in the distance. "Did you know what Dean was going to do?"

Slowly, James nodded, and he tore his eyes from the blaze to stare at George.

"Not until I read the dedication page. I tried to stop him, but I was too late," he said softly. "I don't think I could have stopped him, anyway."

"What makes you say that? He obviously loved you. He might have listened-"

"It had to be then. It couldn't wait," James said, cutting him off. "It had to be exactly then."

CHAPTER FIFTY-TWO

"Campbell?" George said into his phone, straining to hear a single word, buzz, hiss, or crackle. "Campbell, are you there?" He snatched his phone away and held it up, searching for a signal, but the screen only displayed a single bar and even that disappeared. He raced to the top of the staircase, then paused and looked back at James. "Will you-"

"I'll be fine," he said, and there was something in his tone that suggested sincerity.

"All right," George said, nodding. "All right, but don't go anywhere. I'll have someone pick you up. But you stay here, okay?"

A feeble smile rose and fell on James' face like the gentle swell of the turning tide. But there was little time for George to waste on the man. He'd done all he could.

He bolted down the steps as fast as he dared and burst into the night, nearly knocking Campbell off her feet.

"Guv?" she cried out as the two regained their balance. "Oh, thank Christ. I thought..."

"You thought what?"

"I don't know," she said. "I don't know what I thought."

"Where's your car?"

"Just here," she said. She hit the fob on her keys, and the graveyard glowed like fire for a moment. "You know it's burning, don't you? The house, guv. You can see the flames for miles."

"I know," he told her. "Get me there, will you?"

They ran to the car, and he climbed into the passenger seat, not bothering with his seatbelt.

"I've requested an ambulance and the fire brigade," she said while she started the car. She slammed the car into reverse, placed one hand behind the passenger seat, and sped backwards. George had just enough time to lean forward and peer up at the tower. He thought, for the tiniest of moments that he saw James there, and he prayed he would stay up there until help came.

"What about the uniformed help I requested?" George asked. "Dragging their heels, aren't they?"

"Haven't they turned up? For God's sake," she replied as they exited the church grounds. She slammed on the brakes, spun the wheel, and the car slewed to a stop, facing the bright orange glow that was lighting the night. "I called it in, guv. Duty Sergeant said he'd get straight onto it."

"I have no doubt you did," George said. "However, I'm inclined to think that any requests mentioning my name, Campbell, have been rerouted. Via Tim Long."

"What?"

"Not to worry," George said. "It's all part of the game."

"The game?"

"Just...just drive," he said. "And ease off, eh? I'd like to roll onto the driveway on all four wheels if possible. How did you know I was here, anyway?"

"Oh, erm..." She faltered and feigned concentrating on the winding lane despite her obvious driving abilities.

"Campbell?"

"Sorry, guv," she began. "But after our last call, I was a bit worried about you."

350 JACK CARTWRIGHT

"Worried about me?" he laughed. "You?"

"Yes. Is that so unbelievable? You had me scared, being out here on your own," she explained. "I called Sergeant Hart. Apparently, she can see where you are. She can see where we all are."

"So Ivy knows," he said. "Great. That's all she needs."

"I didn't know what else to do, guv. Sorry. Was it the wrong thing to do?"

He sighed and caught a flash of blue in the side mirror.

"No," he told her. "No, you probably did the right thing."

"She's having problems, isn't she?"

"I think that discussing Sergeant Hart's private life may just be venturing into dangerous waters, PC Campbell," he said as she slowed the car and pulled over to let the fire engine pass. Ahead of them, the blaze was out of control. The lane at the end of the driveway might as well have been in broad daylight.

"Jesus, is that your car?" Campbell said, and George tore his eyes from the blazing roof.

"Never mind my car," he said as he shoved his door open and climbed out. "I'm more concerned about that car."

He pointed to a blue Vauxhall Astra parked beside the front steps. The doors were open, but there was nobody inside.

The firemen were already in full flow, six of them, at least. None of them noticed him approaching the house and the car. He walked up to the downstairs window and peered inside. It was the kitchen, and the mess he'd made earlier was how he had left it, and the fire had yet to devour it.

He ran to the writing room, shielding his eyes from the heat and the bright light. Where he, Ivy and Juliet Shaw had been standing during their last conversation, was engulfed in flames. Even as he watched, the bottom the curtain took flame. Seconds later, the entire thing had gone up, flames licking at the ceiling above it, reaching out to Den Worthing's old writing desk with testing tendrils, tasting the air.

And then it succumbs to the heat. It smoked at first, as the moisture was pulled from the wood before the flames simply appeared.

George stepped back. It was a sad sight. To have read that terrible story that a troubled man had typed on the old underwood, and then to witness it burn in what George could only describe as the fires of hell.

"Guv?" a voice called, and a figure ran towards him. "Guv?"

Ivy appeared out of the smoky gloom, ran at him, and for a moment, he thought she was going to hug him. But she stopped short, shaking her head.

"What the bloody hell have you done?"

She dragged him away, but he resisted, preferring to finish the scene as if it was some kind of ceremony. A pyre for Dean Worthing.

"Guv, get away from there. The windows could go."

"I found him," he said, which was enough to discourage Ivy from dragging him away.

"You found who?" she said, to which he stepped back and pointed towards that old oak at the far edge of the property.

"Samuel."

"Oh, Christ."

"Have Campbell call Katy Southwell and her team in, will you?"

"Right," she said, staring at him as if he belonged in a home with his wife.

"And you might want to call Tim Long. I think we've grounds to request some kind of uniformed assistance."

"What? Don't tell me he's blocked-"

"Just..." he said, holding up a hand. "Just do as I ask." He smiled to convey that no harm was meant by his bluntness. "When you've done that, we're going to need the coroner and Doctor Saint," he said as the underwood fell through the burning desk onto the floor.

"Oh, God no," she replied, staring up at the top floor, where the bedrooms were. Every window was glowing. "Don't tell me... Adrian?"

"Adrian? No, he's at the church. Which reminds me. Get some uniformed officers up there, will you?"

"On what charges?"

George considered his response.

"No charge," he replied. "Call it a duty of care." He turned away to walk over to Samuel's unmarked grave. She would follow. There were too many questions for her not to.

"Guv, you're not making sense."

"I've heard that a few times tonight."

"The coroner. If Samson is at the church, then-"

"The car. Recognise it?"

"Should I?" she asked, then it struck him that she hadn't attended the scene when Dean Worthing had ended his life.

"Blue Vauxhall Astra?" he said, to which she shook her head. "Okay, what if I told you it probably has a new windscreen, new bonnet, and very likely new suspension?"

"The Hawkins?" she said. "But-"

"It was them all along," George told her. "It was them in Dean Worthing's memoir. The carers."

"The Hawkins?"

"Do you remember what they said in their statement?" he asked, then gave her the answer before she had time to recall it. "They were invited to their ruby anniversary. To the place where they were married."

"Juliet Shaw? She posted the letter?"

George nodded.

"It was his final move. He'd written the book. He had everything in place to name and shame them. All he had to do was get them here."

"So why kill himself?" Ivy asked.

"Because his story was out there," George explained. "He'd fought his demons long enough. He wanted them to suffer.

He wanted them to see what they'd reduced him to. He wanted them to panic. He was going to do it. He was always going to do it. But this way, he could make things right. Had he just killed himself without writing the book, without getting them here, then he'd have just been another body. Another suicide."

"Christ," she said, for want of anything else to say. "And the manuscript?"

He paused, thought of James, and then smiled.

"Maybe it's inside. Fancy popping in and having a look?"

"Guv, come on. You're not telling me that the only copy of that book is in there."

"It could be," he told her. "The Hawkins certainly thought so." He took two steps towards Samuel, then turned again and jabbed an index finger at the night. "Personally, I think it's out there. That's what I'd like to think. I think that whatever was in that letter to them from Dean Worthing, was anything but an invitation to a party. He told them about the book. He arranged to meet them."

"So it's not their anniversary?"

"I don't know," he said. "Maybe it is, maybe it isn't. That's what they told me the night Dean died. What else were they going to say? That one of the boys they had abused had written a detailed account of the abuse and had named them? Oh, and by the way, we also beat one of them so badly that he died, and we forced the other two to bury him in the garden."

"What?"

"That's right," George said, waving a hand as if presenting Samuel for the first time. "Care of James Adrian Samson and Dean Worthing."

"They were forced to bury him?"

"I found him, and I heard someone smash my window. By the time I got here, the manuscript was gone, as were my car keys, and a car was speeding off. I checked the house. Adrian was gone.

His shoes were gone. The only place he could have gone was the church."

"So you went cross country?" she said, eying his muddy shoes.

"Yes, I did. I found him on top of the tower, ready to follow in his brother's footsteps."

"But he didn't?"

"No, he didn't," George said. "Thank God. His shoes were muddier than mine."

"Eh?"

"He didn't drive there, Ivy. He took the same route I did."

"So the Hawkins were here. You chased them off-"

"They must have seen us at the church. They came back to get the manuscript."

"But they couldn't find it," Ivy said. "They knew the game was up. If the manuscript was out there, it was only a matter of time before we caught up with them."

"There was nowhere to run," George added, and he looked up at the burning building. "So they destroyed it." He took a few steps away from the growing heat and looked up at the upstairs window. "So you were right all along," he said. "Dean Worthing killed himself. It wasn't a murder."

"Oh, come on, it's not like you were wrong, guv. You called it. You said there was abuse going on, and look. We've got more bodies than Pippa bloody Bell."

"Funny how it works out, isn't it?" he muttered, turning away.

"Where are you going?"

"To see Samuel," he called back. "Somebody needs to say a few words. He deserves that much."

"Guv?" she called, but he kept on walking. "Guv, wait." Irritated, he stopped but didn't turn. "You said that Adrian or James, or whatever his name is, was on the tower?"

"It's okay. I talked him out of it."

"I'm sure you did, guv?" she said, and he glanced back at her. "Who unlocked the door?"

As always, Ivy was insightful and inquisitive, and her penchant for detail only raised George's smile, lifted his spirits, and restored his faith.

"Maybe it was Saint Leonard," he said, nodding at the church on the far side of the village. "The patron saint of captives."

With the fire raging behind him, he walked slowly across the paddock, where the cool evening breeze licked at the sweat on his back, and the remains of a poor young boy lay waiting for a prayer.

CHAPTER FIFTY-THREE

Bluestone Lodge may been little more than an old derelict house on a large plot. But now, with most of the roof gone, nearly every window broken, and with a coating of thick black soot, it wasn't even a fixer-upper.

As Dean Worthing had envisaged, the house would need tearing down.

The fire had just about been brought under control. Smouldering beams issued giant plumes of smoke that drifted across the landscape like freed souls.

And the oak tree under which Samuel had been buried was aglow from fluorescent lights on tripods. And the silence? That had long gone. The grave site was a hive of activity. Katy Southwell and her team to and froed in their white suits, rummaging through tuff boxes, bagging samples of soil, and then finally fetching the white polystyrene boxes in which they would cart Samuel off, piecemeal.

It was Katy herself who had elected to climb into the hole, and she had painstakingly trowelled the surrounding dirt from those bones that were visible. And as George had thought, the femur was the first bone that she extracted.

"Early teens," she said as she placed it into one of those nondescript thermal boxes with the utmost care. "I want to say male, but we won't know for sure until I've got them all out."

"It's male," George told her, to which she studied his expression and continued in her objective and professional fashion.

"We're going to be a fair while," she added. "I'd like to find every bone if we can. It's all too easy in this environment to miss a carpal or a tarsal. Not to mention the ossicles. And to make the task even more challenging, I can see there are at least two broken ribs, maybe more when I get a little deeper."

"I understand," George replied. "And if it helps, I tend to agree."

Again, she studied his expression, then lifted her goggles to her forehead.

"Do you know what happened here?" she asked, to which he nodded.

"If you don't mind, I think it's a tale best left alone," he replied. "At least, for the time being. One day, somebody might tell the world, but for now. I'd rather just let it be."

"Well, I don't know how much a pathologist will be able to help you-"

"I don't need help," he said. "I know what happened. Needless to say, this poor lad suffered beyond what you or I could even begin to imagine. Let's just get what we can of him, and I'll see to it that he's given a proper burial. He deserves that, I think."

She placed her trowel down on the ground, which was waist height to her in the hole.

"Am I to assume that you have the culprits in custody?" she asked. "With a full and signed confession?"

"No," he replied, then looked back at the house. "But I don't think they'll be ruining any more lives."

She followed his gaze to the house, eyebrows raised.

"They're inside?"

"With any luck, all you'll need to scoop *them* up is a dustpan and brush, Katy," he said. "Just drop them in the wheelie bin."

She laughed and then saw that his expression hadn't altered, so the laugh faded.

"You know, most victims of house fires are found huddled in a corner. They die of smoke inhalation, as a rule."

"Well, first of all, they aren't *victims* of anything but their own cruelty. And secondly, rules don't apply to this particular couple."

"You want them to have suffered?" she asked, appearing surprised at such a bold statement.

"No, not necessarily," he replied. "But somebody did. And it pleases me that they got what they wanted."

"You couldn't be any more cryptic if you tried, Inspector Larson."

He grinned at her. She wasn't judgemental. She was what he liked to call a safe pair of ears.

"Guv?" Ivy called out from the far side of the paddock. "Guv, you're needed."

"Apologies if my mood is a little...melancholy," he told South-well. "It's been a long day. Lots of ups and downs, if you know what I mean."

"I'll forgive you," she replied, pulling her goggles back over her eyes. "Now, if you don't mind, I have an incus and malleus to find."

Ivy was hot-footing across the grass, and she came to a stop a few metres from him.

"Guv, the Fire Officer needs a word with you," she said. "Said he's got something for you."

"Alright," he replied, joining her in the walk back to the house. "Thanks for coming, by the way. I know it wasn't exactly convenient."

"Can you think of a time when anything we've done is conve-nient, guv? I mean, wouldn't it be nice to go into the station on a

Monday morning, have a coffee, and do the crossword, and then get a call to say that somebody has been murdered and the killer left DNA, fingerprints, and a calling card?"

"I'm not sure it would be nice for the victim."

"Oh, stop it. You know what I mean. You can't have a social life in this game, can you? You can't make plans."

"Oh, I don't know. You should always make plans," he said. "But you should always be prepared to cancel them."

He winked at her, as they rounded the corner, where three firefighters were rolling heavy hoses, two more were sweeping up debris, and the Chief Fire Officer was waiting for them.

"Detective Inspector Larson," George said, holding out his hand for the man to shake. But the fire officer merely looked at his hand and presented his own grubby mitt.

"Graham Chance," the man replied, then sucked in a deep breath. "SIO, are you?"

"I'm leading an investigation," George explained. "This house features prominently in that investigation."

"I see," Chance replied. "Well, the fire's under control we're just hosing it down now. It'll smoulder for a day or so. Our forensic team is in there now doing a preliminary report." He looked up at the sky. "With any luck, we'll have that rain we've been promised. Else, this lot will be up again if the wind gets up."

"With any luck," George agreed.

Chance opened his notepad and clicked open his pen.

"Right then. I'll need the owner's name," he said. "Are they about?"

"The owner..." George started. "He's...elsewhere, right now."

A frown formed on Chance's forehead, and when it faded, the sweat on his brow had cleaned three horizontal lines in the layer of smoky grime.

"I'll take your word for it," Chance replied. "Suppose you'll be wanting to know the cause, eh?"

"Amongst other things," George replied.

"Aye, well. It was fuelled. That's a certainty. Looks like it started in an old boarded-up basement."

"A basement?"

He felt Ivy's stare boring into the side of his head.

"Yeah, looks like it was boarded up. Whoever did it kicked a bloody great hole in the stud wall, filled the space with fuel, most likely petrol, forensics will confirm that, and then torched it. Bloody weird, if you ask me."

"How so?" George asked.

"Well, we had to tear the wall down," he explained. "In that scenario, you'd expect to find charred remains of furniture, or paper and the like." He shook his head. "Just an empty room. Nothing in there to burn, aside from an old blanket."

"A blanket?"

"We think that's what it was. Not much left of it, mind."

"Well, perhaps that was fortunate," George suggested.

"Aye, I mean, God knows what went on in there. The walls are all scratched, and the concrete floor is stained. It's like somebody kept animals in there. Half expected to find chains bolted to the wall, I did."

"That would have been something," George told him.

"No. Like I said, forensics will confirm, it but my guess is that the cellar was filled with petrol, lit with a lighter."

"A lighter?"

"If there had been a match, we'd have found it. You'd think they burn, wouldn't you?" He shook his head again. "No. Once that fire gets going, it's looking for food. Won't find owt to eat on a concrete floor. Shot straight out the hole they kicked in the wall and caught a load of old cardboard boxes on the floor."

"And from there, it just continued through the house, I suppose?" George said.

"Aye, that's right. Old place like this," he said, eyeing up the house. "Flames would have torn through in under two minutes. Three at the most. Lucky whoever did it got out..."

"I'm sorry?" George said.

"I said, it's lucky whoever did it managed to get out."

"They got out?"

"Aye," he said. "Ain't nobody in there."

George eyed Ivy, who looked equally as devastated.

"You're sure?" he asked. "Nobody was hiding in a cupboard or in a bath or something?"

Chance gave a loud and hearty laugh.

"Listen, we've been through that house three times. There's not a single soul in there."

The news hit George in the chest, and he took a step back to collect his senses.

"You okay, Inspector?" Chance asked. "Sorry, I was under the impression you knew."

"Yes, I'm fine," George said. "It's just that you mentioned your forensics team being inside."

"Aye, they'll take some samples to confirm the fuel type. As I said, my guess is petrol. Has a certain whiff about it, you know?"

"Guv?" Ivy said quietly but with enough conviction that George knew what she was going to ask.

"Where's your car, Ivy?"

"Something I said?" Chance asked.

"Thank you, erm..."

"Chance," the fire officer said.

"Right. Chance," George repeated as he and Ivy backed away as politely as they could. "Thank you. I'll look forward to your report."

"Guv, what the hell is happening? I thought you said they were inside?"

"I thought they were," George hissed. "Their car is there. The bloody front door was wide open, with flames spewing out of it. It was like the bloody gates of hell."

"Well, where the hell could they have gone on foot?" Ivy said, and they both turned to the one place that broke the otherwise immaculate horizon.

"Oh no. No, no, no," George said. "Adrian's up there."

CHAPTER FIFTY-FOUR

"Here," George said from the passenger seat of Ivy's car. He jabbed a finger at the side of the road. "Here, Ivy."

"Guv, I can't stop here. It's in a bend."

"Just stop the bloody car," he said, and she took the hint, pulling the car to the side of the road and onto the verge as much as she dared. "Kill the lights."

"Guv?"

They were one hundred yards from the entrance to the church driveway, and all around them, appeared still and calm.

"Kill the lights, Ivy," he hissed, but she just stared at him, bemused by his hysteria. "Ivy, I said-"

"Alright, alright," she replied, and she clicked the lights off. Quietly, he opened his door, climbed out, and pressed the door closed before starting towards St Leonard's.

"Guv?" Ivy hissed as she too climbed out. "Wait for backup."

"No time," he muttered, but he doubted she heard him. He was focused. Dialled in on the church and its surroundings. He used the grass beside the road to prevent his shoes from clicking on the tarmac. Only when he was directly opposite the church did he cross the road as quietly as he could. Then, keeping to the line of trees that led to the church, he made his way further into the church grounds, his eyes zeroed in on the tower.

He half expected to find James' body sprawled on the ground beneath the tower or to hear the Hawkins and James battling it out. Not that the battle would be too tumultuous, given what James had done to his body over the years. A light breeze would have blown him from the top.

"Guv?" Ivy hissed. She was half a dozen steps behind him.

"Ivy, get back to the road," he told her. "I want whatever uniformed support you can get. Talk to Tim Long if you have to. Explain the situation."

"Guv, you are not going in there-"

"I am not going to have this argument with you, Ivy."

"Right, so I'm supposed to let you walk in there on your own?"

"Yes," he said. "Trust me. Just...for once, just trust me, okay?"

Her hand suddenly glowed bright green. She stared down at her phone, and the light lit the dark bags beneath her eyes.

"It's Byrne," she said.

"Well, you'd better get it then, hadn't you?"

He didn't wait for a response. He made his way to the church door, keeping as close as he could to the walls. The wire-meshed bird porch was closed, but the church's inner door was wide open and a soft glow emanated from inside, along with the gentle tenor hum of a male voice.

George took a breath, held it, and then slowly released it.

There was a time to be quiet. A time for stealth and surprise. But when those options are closed, the best option, no, the only option, George thought, was to make an entrance.

He stepped into the church, his hard rubber soles connecting with the stone floor with an inevitable click. His shadow from the light beside the door stretched across the pews and the aisle and came to a stop as if it was looking down at the lectern, where a figure was hunched over a book.

"Ah, Inspector Larson," the voice said, and Stephen Cross rose to his feet. His shadow dwarfed George's. "What a nice surprise." George scanned the church, the pews, and all the nooks and crannies he could see from where he stood. "Is there something I can help you with, maybe?"

He stepped down from the plinth and set his book down on the nearest pew, being sure to mark his page.

"I'm looking for..." George began. "I'm looking for somebody. I was supposed to meet him here."

Stephen glanced around the room.

"There's nobody else here," he replied. "Only us three."

"Three?"

Stephen grinned, and he nodded up at the cross behind him.

"He's always with us."

"Stephen, I was here a while back. I was with...somebody. A friend. He's...that is...I think he might be in trouble."

"Well, he's in the right place," Stephen said, and George, not one to disrespect others' beliefs, turned away and started towards the tower door. But it was closed.

He turned again and found Stephen, his head cocked, staring after him with a look of genuine concern on his face.

"Do you want to sit down?"

"That door," George said, ignoring the offer of a seat and pointing directly at the tower door. "I left it open."

"Oh, that was you, was it? I did wonder."

"Stephen, this is urgent. I think there's somebody up there." He ran to the door and tried the handle, finding it locked. "I left him up there."

"Why don't you join me?" Stephen said.

"Open the door, Stephen."

"There's nothing to worry about," Stephen replied, with a little laugh designed to put George's mind at ease. He waved his arm to the front of the church. "I keep a little bottle of something up here. Keeps the chill off, if you know what I mean."

"Stephen, I'm going to ask you one more time," George said.

"Open this door." He eyed the vicar, hoping that if his words had failed to convince, then the look in his eye might convey the gravity of the situation. "Now!"

Realising that his best efforts to distract George had failed, Stephen's smile faded. He gestured to the little alcove where the key was stored.

"I'll fetch the key."

"Now!" George repeated.

The vicar made no show of hurrying. He disappeared out of sight, leaving it just long enough that George was beginning to think he'd escaped through another door.

But then he returned into view, the large brass key in his hand.

"Here it is," he said. "Little devil. Always hiding."

"The door, Stephen," George said.

He walked with little urgency, seeming to glide rather than step. He hesitated at the door to study George's expression. Then, eventually, he turned the key, clicked the latch and shoved the door open.

"Care to join me?" George asked.

"Not tonight," he replied. "But by all means, feel free."

There was something about his expression. A tautness to his forehead when the rest of his face was cool and calm.

George removed the key from the door, held it up so Stephen could see it, and then pocketed it.

"I have trust issues," he said, to which Stephen smiled.

"I'll be waiting for you right here. Perhaps I can get you that drink after all. It's a Talisker. Good whisky."

"It is," George told him. "Another time, maybe."

Slowly, George climbed the stone steps. Round and round, he went, feeling the mud that he and James had deposited earlier crunch beneath his feet. He ran his hand along the cold stone wall, finding crevices to dig his fingers into to aid his ascent. Then, finally, he was faced with the door. Moonlight shone around the edges, and the only sounds were the night birds darting to a fro - bats catching flying insects, and an owl hidden in the crook of a tree branch, calling to its young.

But no voices. No shuffling of feet on the stone floor, not like he had heard before.

He reached out, touched the door, and then applied just enough pressure to move the slab of old oak.

The door opened half-way. George's push was too feeble for its weight.

But it was enough. More than enough. In fact, he didn't need to open it further. He knew to whom the feet belonged.

But open it, he did.

Richard and Sarah Hawkins stared up at him. They were seated on the floor holding hands, leaning against each other and the parapet wall. They had taken their last breaths together after forty years of marriage, with the hands of their last surviving victim fixed firmly around their bruised throats. Their deathly gazes were frozen in time, directed at the door, at George...

Or the individual who had made their escape.

He left them there as carrion for the birds that circled the night sky. He closed the door, stood tall and straight, and somewhere deep inside of him, a smile beamed warm and hearty.

It was during these dying moments of an investigation that fatigue often set in. It was the adrenaline. It was the long nights and days and endless walking. It was the hope and disappointment. It was as if he'd spent four days digging. Not for treasure. Not for the bones of some poor child who hadn't even had a chance at life. Just for the truth. When his theories come together so convincingly that he could cast the spade to one side and dig his hands into the soil. That's when he would find a flaw, and the dirt and mud and the lies and deceit would filter through his fingers, leaving him no option but to dig some more.

But he was there now. He had dug as much as he could dig. He had drawn blood, and his body could take no more.

"Tell me, Stephen," George called out as he stepped from the last step and onto the floor of that little space he had not so long ago thought to be where Dean and his brothers had been abused. He stood in the doorway, not surprised in the slightest to find Stephen still standing there like a loyal Labrador. At that moment, Ivy burst into the church, but before she could speak, George raised his hand to silence her, his eyes never wavering from Stephen's. "How was it that you managed to escape Blue-stone Lodge, yet the others didn't?"

Stephen grinned once more. It was the grin of a righteous man daring George to convince him otherwise.

"That's easy," he whispered sadly. "I had God on my side."

CHAPTER FIFTY-FIVE

"And here he is," Tim said when George knocked twice and entered his office. He pulled out the guest chair and eased himself into it with a heavy sigh. "Aren't you supposed to be somewhere?"

"Here, you mean?" George said.

"Don't be coy, George."

"Don't pretend you haven't called Detective Superintendent Granger already," George replied. "In fact, if I know you as well as I think I do, you made the call last night when you finally realised that I had been right all along."

Tim shrugged with his eyes and a slight cock of his head as if verbalising his response would somehow show his rank.

"Dean Worthing," Tim began. "Murdered or...?"

"Suicide," George said.

"Ah. And..." Tim referred to the open file in front of him. "Michael Wassall?"

"Suicide," George said.

"I see. And how is it you're inferring that you were right in any of this?"

"Samuel."

"Samuel, what?" Tim asked. "He has a surname, I presume?"

"No doubt he did," George said. "What he didn't have was a chance. He didn't have a proper go at it. At life."

"I see, and the individuals responsible for his death. They're in custody, are they?"

"You know full well they're not."

"Ah, that's right. They were found murdered at the top of St Leonard's. I remember now." He slammed his hand down on his desk, a move designed to startle George. But George was beyond startling. When the vestiges of coffee in his system had been consumed, he would most likely find a quiet corner or even a cell to lay in and rest his weary bones. "This is a mess, George."

"This is an investigation, Tim," George told him. "I told you from day one there was more to this." He jabbed a finger at his boss. "And you. Yes, you. You held me back. You wanted the whole investigation closed down, Tim. You put a time limit on it."

"It's called resource management."

"It's called *limiting my ability to do my job*," George countered. "You even blocked the uniformed support I requested."

"I did no such thing–"

"Oh come on. You blocked it. How would it have turned out if they had come, eh? If I had the help I needed? We could have got to them in time. We could have prevented two murders."

"I assume you have a lead on this Samson chap, do you?"

"A lead? A bloody lead? The man has no fixed abode. The house he inherited from his dead brother, Dean Worthing, went up in flames last night. That was the one chance he had of making something of himself, of joining society. And you know what? When we failed to stop him from murdering the Hawkins, we took that opportunity away from him." George sat back in his seat. "And that's the truth, the whole truth, and nothing but the truth."

"So help you God?"

George nodded.

"So help me, God."

Tim mirrored George's move and sat back in his seat, both of them lowering their voices to something far more conducive to their relationship.

"So help me, God."

"What about this manuscript, George? As far as I can see, it's the only piece of evidence you have."

"Had," George said. "It was stolen. And word of warning, I'll be claiming for a new window for my car."

"Ah," Tim said. "Falling apart at the seams, isn't it?" He peered down at the file again. "Okay, let's have one last stab at getting a conviction on what has been four days of work for four officers, with multiple murders, suicides, and an arson incident." Tim looked up at him. "Stephen Cross."

"Stephen Cross committed no crime."

"Is that right? According to the reports the uniformed team took down, he was instrumental in the Hawkins' murder. He opened the door to the church tower, did he not?"

"Does that make him culpable?"

"I don't know, does it?" Tim asked.

"He unlocked a door. What do you want me to do? Prove he unlocked it for Samson? How do you suggest I go about that?"

"Who is he? Why is he now involved? And why, considering you spoke to him at the beginning of this debacle, have you not even interviewed him?"

"He's a bloody vicar, Tim. Dean Worthing jumped off his church. James Samson collapsed during the Sunday service. What should I have done, interrogate him?"

"You could have brought him in for questioning."

"I could have brought the whole congregation in if that's the case. They could have all sung hymns in the waiting room. A chorus of Jerusalem, maybe? That would have cheered the place up."

Tim laughed. It was one of the benefits of having known

somebody for so long. The heated debates were just that. He was still a friend, and he was still a human being.

"How is he involved? And before you say he wasn't, it's blatantly obvious he is, even if you haven't a shred of evidence to support it."

George contemplated where to begin, then settled on the beginning.

"He was one of them," George said, and he smiled at the idea of there once being four brothers who all cared for each other. "He got away."

"He ran away and joined the church? And he didn't say a word about the abuse?"

"It was the seventies and eighties, Tim. You remember what it was like. Kids didn't stand a bloody chance."

"And what, he and Dean came up with a plan?"

"No," George said. "No, it was Dean's plan all along. He wrote the book, he came up with a plan to out the Hawkins, and he paid the ultimate price for justice."

"And Cross? Where does he fit in?"

"I've been thinking about that," George told him. "I believe he returned to South Ormsby to make amends."

"For running? For leaving his brothers?"

"He saw an opportunity to make things right," George said. "And he took it."

"But you can't prove it?"

George shook his head.

"No. Without the manuscript or James Samson, I can't prove a thing," he said as he rose from his seat. He reached for the file in front of Tim. But instead of picking it up as Tim was expecting him to, he simply closed it and tapped the front cover. "There you go," he said. "Case closed."

"George, we have two unsolved murders. We can't just leave it."

George stopped at the door, and an idea struck him.

"I tell you what," he said. "Why don't you put it in a drawer for a few decades? Then, some future team dealing with cold cases can look into it." Had Tim been twenty years younger, with a full head of hair, his eyebrows would have reached his hairline. "Now, if you'll excuse me. It's been a long night, and we're not as young as we used to be."

"George?" Tim called out in a warning tone. George stopped halfway through the door, not to listen to what Tim had to say but to make a final demand.

"One more thing," George said. "Campbell and Byrne."

"What about them?"

"I want them out of uniform," he said. "I want them on my team for good."

CHAPTER FIFTY-SIX

He walked with confidence. As if he belonged there. Like he was welcome. Known. Accepted. His shoes clicked on the concrete floor and echoed off the tall ceiling, and seemed to ring on in that cast space.

The air was cold inside, yet the pungent aroma of urine, pigeon droppings and a hundred years of industry prevailed.

He found the room at the back of the main hall and noted the whites of the eyes that saw him, tracked him, distrusted him and all he stood for.

Yet there was one whose eyes lit up in recognition when he saw George. He dragged his sleeping bag from his legs and stood to greet him, not like an old friend, but still, there was a respect there; of that George was certain.

"Freddo," he said, holding out his hand for Freddo to shake, and shake it he did, with all the confidence of a wealthy businessman greeting a rival in the corner office of a penthouse property overlooking the Thames. "How have you been?"

"Ah, not too bad," Freddo, his Birmingham accent stretching the words, and the thousands of cigarettes he'd smoked driving the tone to gutter height. "Keeping myself busy, you know?"

"I won't ask how," George said.

"I wouldn't tell you if you did," Freddo said, flashing his jaundiced teeth. "How's our boy?"

"James, you mean?" George said. "Last time I saw him, he was doing okay. Better than the first time I saw him, anyway."

"Ah, well, that's something, eh? Back on the gear, is he?"

"I don't think so," George told him. "In fact, I think that part of his life is over. At least, that's what I hope."

Freddo nodded.

"Good for him. He's the one who got away, is he?"

George paced a few steps away, avoiding the scrutinous glares from the edges of the room, doing his best to ensure they knew he was no threat to them.

"Has he been to see you, Freddo?" he asked.

"Who? Has who been to see me, Inspector?"

"Don't be coy. James. Adrian. Whatever you want to call him. Has he been?"

"Here? No. Like you said. He's moved on, eh? Onwards and upwards, and good luck to him."

Despite the open communication and general pleasantries, there were lines that George wouldn't cross. Had they been discussing the matter in an interview room with reliable witnesses to hand, George might have questioned Freddo, and probed deeper, testing his responses. But they were not in an interview room. They were in Freddo's world, in his corner office overlooking the Thames.

"When we spoke last, you mentioned that he had told you his story. I wonder if you could tell me. Now that we know he's okay and he's moved on to better things."

Freddo screwed his face and looked sideways up at the ceiling.

"I don't recall him ever telling me a story," he said, rubbing his chin.

"That's what you said, Freddo," George said. "And if it helps, he told me that he told you."

"He told you? That he told me his story?"

"You, and only you," George said. "You must feel quite privileged. Knowing somebody's secrets."

"Ah, you know how it is. I've a brain like a sieve. He could have told me."

"Perhaps I can jog your memory?" George suggested. "He and his brothers were abused. They were in a care home, in the loosest sense of the word. They were mistreated."

Freddo shook his head.

"Not ringing any bells, Georgie."

"Okay, how about this? The two individuals used to lock them in a cellar for days on end, whipping them and thrashing them for nothing more than kicks."

"Sounds like my story," Freddo said. "Are you sure you haven't read my autobiography?"

He grinned at his own joke and fished a dog end from his pocket. To light it, took more than a dozen attempts before the old disposable lighter sparked into flame.

George reached into his pocket and withdrew a fifty-gram pack of rolling tobacco, papers, and a new lighter. He held them out for Freddo, then pulled them out of reach.

"Let's have one last go at ringing those bells, Freddo," he said. "Samuel. His brother." The corner of Freddo's eye twitched. It was enough for George to probe further. "The one they buried in the garden. No, let me correct that. The boy they were forced to bury in the garden."

Freddo ran his tongue across those vile teeth and cast a glance around the room.

"Now you mention it," he said, "he did say something about that once."

George handed him the lighter, which he accepted, tested, and then pocketed.

"What about another brother?" George asked. "Not Dean, not Samuel. Somebody else."

"Does this other brother have a name?"

"No," George said. "I only know that he got away one night."

"Ah," Freddo replied, grinning. "You mean the lad that escaped and made their lives even worse?"

"Did he seem bitter about it?" George asked. "Did he resent the boy running away?"

"No. No, resentment isn't really a part of his makeup. He's not a bitter man, George. I mean, given what he's been through, nobody would question it if he was. But he isn't. Not that I saw, anyway."

George separated the rolling papers and the tobacco, handing him the former.

"I wonder if he ever gave you a name."

"A name?" Freddo shook his head and hissed through his teeth like a mechanic evaluating a crumpled bonnet and a shattered windscreen.

"Nobody is in any trouble," George said.

"So, why ask?"

"Because..." George began thoughtfully. "Because there are times, believe it or not, when the right answers mean more to me than securing a conviction." He shoved his hands into his jacket pockets, along with the tobacco, and paced back and forth a few steps. "I recently made a decision," he said. "It's a big decision. And what you tell me might just convince me to see through the law of the land and be led by morals."

"Morals? You? A copper?"

"The name, Freddo," George said, and Freddo hesitated. If only George could see into the man's mind. He wondered what other gems might lurk inside.

"And he's not in any bother, you say?"

"No bother at all," George said. "Think of it as tying a bow around a gift. It'll package things up nicely."

"It sounds to me like you already know the name."

"I do," George said. "But I want to be sure. I need to know."

"His name was Stephen," Freddo said. "That's all I know. That's all Adrian ever told me."

"Stephen?"

Freddo held out his hand.

"Your dues, Georgie."

George withdrew the tobacco again and placed it into Freddo's grubby palm.

"Thank you," he said. "Thank you for being honest with me. If you hear from him-"

"I'll be sure to let you know," Freddo said, which had less truth to it than the Hawkins' initial statement.

George turned on his heels and started towards the door. He wanted to look back. He wanted to speak more about Adrian. He found himself in need of answers. As if some part of him had connected with the man at the top of St Leonard's tower.

But some things were best left unsaid. There exists a need in a world for wonder and intrigue, however abrasive it might be to George's inquisitive mind.

He had taken just three steps into that giant hall, where the rich odour of ammonia assaulted the back of his throat.

"Oh, George," Freddo called, then followed him out of the room. In his hand was an A4 manilla envelope, bursting at the seams. George eyed the package and then Freddo, who seemed to study George's eyes, making a difficult decision. Eventually, he held the envelope out, and George noted his own name had been scrawled on the front in large, inconsistent lettering as if written by a five-year-old. "This came in the post for you."

"In the post?" George said, accepting the package and its weight was a joy to grasp. "No return address, I suppose?"

Freddo grinned at the playful back and forth.

"I'll see you around, Georgie," he said, returning to his bed, his home, his world, in that corner office overlooking the Thames.

When George stepped into the fresh air, his first thought was to check his surroundings. To search every little corner and nook and cranny where Adrian could have hidden.

But he would be long gone by now, off to someplace new to live a life. He likened the fresh start to a man being born middle-aged. To see the world as if for the first time. To have the weight of history pulled from his shoulders, so he could walk upright with his chest out.

"Good luck to you," George said aloud. "Good bloody luck to you."

CHAPTER FIFTY-SEVEN

Mablethorpe had been their home. His and Grace's. Sure, they had begun their lives together in the Wolds, but the coast had been their home. Yet, he drove towards it as a young bird might perch upon the nest edge for the very first time, with trepidation. He felt a sense of exposure. Like the walls had been torn down, and the world could see him for all he was.

But the open fields and distant horizon brought with it a perspective. He wondered if he would ever meet James Samson again, and even more, he wondered if he would pursue the matter as his role depicted, or if he would let him go. Let him enjoy that freedom.

There were arguments both for and against. Had James been charged and convicted, he would have undoubtedly received two life sentences. However, in light of the circumstances and the decades-long ordeal James had suffered, the judge might offer him parole after a minimum of twenty years. People had been known to get far less for worse crimes, but twenty years was a fair estimate.

In light of The Unholy Truth, however, James had already served his sentence and more.

But the law was the law, and being so close to retirement, George pondered on the matter. Did he really want to spend his retirement regretting his decision? Or would his decision bring him some sort of peace? Some kind of nod to all those individuals he had charged and processed, however dubious their guilt.

The wind off the North Sea was gusting, and it carried with it tiny grains of sand and salt that peppered George as he strode towards the entrance to Grace's nursing home.

He straightened his old, forest-green tie beneath his best sweater. If she failed to recognise him today, he at least wanted her to think him a decent, well-dressed man she might be happy to chat with for a while.

It was then that he came to a decision. A final decision. It should be her who decides. Grace. She always had a strong sense of right and wrong.

As always, inside, he was greeted brightly by Miss Dowdeswell, who manned the reception desk like a weathered custody sergeant. She wore her hair up, pinned in a bun, and her lipstick often reminded George of the women depicted in old wartime movies.

"Now then. Good morning, Mr Larson," she trilled. She opened the guest book and slid a pen across the desk.

"Good morning," he replied, finding a mental hole in which to stuff his thoughts. "And how are you today?"

"Better than some, not as good as others," he said, in that way that he recognised in the locals of her generation. The comment was designed merely to convey an answer more interesting than a simple 'I'm okay thank you'. But there was more to it. There was a strength in those words that youngsters these days just seemed to lack.

"In her room, is she?" he asked.

"She's in the garden today, would you believe?"

"In the garden? In this wind?"

"Don't worry, she's wrapped up warm. Says she likes it. Besides, the building blocks the worst of it."

He handed her pen back and then reoriented himself, and took a slow stroll through the glass double doors that led out to the garden.

And there she was. The woman who, even in the midst of dementia, could set his heart alight at a single distant glimpse.

She was sitting on a white, iron chair, her eyes closed against the weak sun. Thin wisps of grey hair danced around her face, and he was sure she was smiling.

Today might just be a good day.

The disease which had claimed the latter years of her life was an unpredictable beast. To call out to her, to wake her, might have roused that sleeping demon. And so he remained as silent as could be. Savouring the peace beside her. Sharing something. A moment that he would remember even if she did not. And only when the burning desire to hear her voice overwhelmed him did he step before her so that his shadow touched her face, something he so longed to do.

It took only a few seconds for her to sense the shift in temperature, and she opened her eyes as he had seen her do a thousand times before, on those lazy Sunday mornings when he would bring her tea and perhaps a slice of fruit toast - well-buttered, of course.

He waited, not daring to utter a single word.

And then a smile spread across her face, brighter than the sun.

"George?" she said, her voice cracked and weary.

George's chest soared with relief, and the tension that built during the journey deflated.

He thought that might be the most exhausting part, the first few seconds of seeing her again, the moment just before she recognised him – or didn't.

"Hey, sweetheart," he replied, stifling the emotions in his throat. He wiped his eye before the tear betrayed him. "You're...

you're looking great." He gestured at the spare chair beside her. "Can I?"

She followed his gaze, wearing the childhood smile he recognised from the photos her mother had shown him all those years ago. There was an innocence to it. A naivety that belied her years.

"Have you been out here long?" he asked once he was seated.

"All morning," she said. "I like it out here. There's no television."

"You'll never guess where I've been," he said, and she stared at him, not even trying to engage her mind. She simply shook her head. "Bag Enderby."

"Bag Enderby?"

"The Wolds," he said.

"Bag Enderby," she repeated as though she was trying to place the name. "We had a house there, you know? It was a lovely old house. Just opposite the church."

"That's right. St Margaret's," George said.

"St Margaret's, yes," she replied and then peered at him quizzically. "How did you know that?"

Words failed him, and he couldn't even bring himself to look her in the eye.

"Mum and Dad bought the place before I was born," she said. "Oh, we did have a lovely time. The summers were the best."

"They always are," he added, hoping to coax her on.

"We used to pick..."she started. "Used to pick...in the garden. We had..."

"Blackberries?" George said, thinking of the large bramble in the rear garden that he had been putting off tackling.

"No. Apples," she said. "We picked apples."

"Oh," he said, but for the life of him, he couldn't recall an apple tree on the property. "Did your mum used to make her crumble?"

"Crumble? No." She turned away for a moment. "Tell me," she

said, squinting up at the weak sun. "Do the moles still burrow there?"

George laughed. "Oh, yes."

"Could barely walk across the bloody garden without breaking my ankle on a molehill, remember? I remember this one time, my dad..." she started, then faded again. "My dad..."

"Stayed up all night trying to catch them?" George suggested, having heard the story from her mother many moons ago.

"That's right," she said. "Oh, he was a card, my dad. You would have liked him. You would have got along, you would."

George opened his mouth to tell her that he had known her father and that the two of them had rarely seen eye to eye. But he opted for silence.

"Maybe you could come with me sometime," George said.

"Where, dear?"

"To Bag Enderby," he said. "You could see the molehills again for yourself."

She opened her eyes and peered at him as if he'd suggested they walk there.

"How was your day, anyway?"

"My day?" he said. "Oh, you know? It was better than some, worse than others." She smiled at his response. "Actually, there's something I'd like to ask you."

"Ask me?" she scoffed.

"Yes, dear," he said. "I was wondering...you see, I'm a little torn."

"Torn?"

"Yes, torn. Undecided. Caught between a rock and a hard place."

"Oh, dear."

"You see, I've made a decision. It's important. I know what the right thing to do is, and I know what my heart says." She stared at him, listening intently, as she always had. "But the two things aren't the same. One answer goes against every fabric of my existence. Of my career. And the other...well, the other will help me sleep at night."

"Right," she said, tugging her blanket a little tighter. "And you can't decide."

"No. Well, I have decided, but I'm doubting myself. I never doubt myself."

"No, that's the sign of a strong man. Confident."

"Well, a few years ago, I might have agreed."

"My husband would know. He's good like that. Very decisive."

"Sorry?"

"He's a policeman, you know?"

"A policeman?" George said, and the tear he had been holding back broke free.

"Yes, he would know."

"Grace?" a voice called from behind them, and George turned to find Miss Dowdeswell strolling across the grass, pulling her cardigan tight with one hand to stop the strong breeze from taking hold, and with the other hand, she pushed a wheelchair. "The doctor is here. It's time for your appointment, I'm afraid."

"Oh, is it Friday already?" she called back weakly.

Miss Dowdeswell helped Grace into the wheelchair, raising a hand to stop George from helping, or more likely, interfering.

"Tell you what," Grace said, leaning closer as she was wheeled past. "I'll ask him next time he comes to see me." She gave him a wink. "He'll know what to do."

"Wait," George said, shoving himself from the seat. Miss Dowdeswell brought the chair to a stop, and he smiled apologetically before crouching before Grace. "The next time you see your husband, I want you to do something for me."

"Oh?"

"Give him a kiss, will you? Tell him you love him."

"Well, I-"

"Because if there's one thing I know about your husband, it's that he loves you very much." He winked back at her. "I reckon you'd make his day if you told him that. Gave him a little peck on the cheek."

Grace smiled at the idea. Perhaps she was imagining the scene. He wondered if she was picturing his face.

"I won't forget. He'll have the answer, you know?"

"I'm sure he will."

"We really must be going. We don't want to keep the doctor waiting, do we?" Miss Dowdeswell said apologetically.

"And if my husband doesn't know," she said, as Miss Dowdeswell leaned into the chair to get it moving on the grass, "you could always flip a coin."

He watched as she rolled across the grass, oblivious to the wind as they rounded a corner. Perhaps that was for the best. Perhaps there was a benefit to being oblivious to the world. He let his head fall back and stared up at the clouds for a few moments.

He wondered if he should wait for her to finish. If she would be disappointed to find him gone when she returned. He paced across the grass to the mulched flower bed, and stared out at the coastline in the distance.

Then, he found his mind wandering to memories—of those awkward dinners with her family and her father. Her mother had been fine, great, in fact. She'd been lovely, and it wasn't hard to see where Grace had got her big heart from.

He pulled some change from his pocket and fished out a fifty pence piece, then laughed at the prospect of making a decision like that on the flip of a coin.

But he found himself bridging his thumb and finger with the coin. And with one final glance back at the home, where through the glazed doors he could see Grace being wheeled to her doctor's appointment, he closed his eyes, thought of her the way she had been when they had met, when they had married, and when they laughed.

And he flipped.

The End.

UNTIL DEATH DO US PART - PROLOGUE

Deadly Wolds Book Three

She had waited her entire life for this day. It would be a day she would never forget. A day she *could* never forget. Yet for all the wrong reasons.

Her skin tingled with the significance of the day, her body alive to every sensation, from the wind caressing her half-up-half-down hair, to the goosebumps stirred by nerves that fluttered like a caged bird in her chest. Today was the most important day of her life. Since she was a little girl, watching princess films on a Saturday morning, she had waited for every second of it. Now, finally, *finally*, it was happening.

It wasn't quite everything she'd dreamed of. But it was close enough.

The sky oscillated between a brilliant azure and lingering white clouds. Her dress was a simple gown with a long-sleeved, plunging lace bodice. At the time, it had seemed an elegant and sophisticated choice, but the lace was beginning to scratch at her wrists. She would get through the day, regardless. Nothing could spoil it.

The man in front of her, her lovely Lucas, was not quite the tall, gallant prince that had romped through her childhood dreams, but his large, brown, puppy-dog eyes stared down at her, awash only with love, as the officiant announced the promises of marriage.

Nancy felt the weight of every eye in the field on her, standing at the front of the aisle, beneath the ornate, wooden wedding arch. She made a conscious effort to lift her chin and to stand on the right side for the photographer to capture her best features. Mixed in with the birdsong, unaware of the significance of their melodies that morning, was the occasional sniffle from a family member or close friend. Sure, it had been Nancy's dream to marry inside a grand, stately home with chandeliers aplenty and decorative balconies, or even a castle, which would not have been unreasonable, considering Lucas's family money. But she had to admit that the smell of freshly mown grass and the subtle scent of wildflowers created a deep sense of peace and comfort that she had always associated with her soon-to-be husband.

The rustic mill, with its ancient water wheel, was far more suited to their wholesome and grounded relationship. Lucas had brought so many things into her life that she had never expected. But they had turned out to be exactly what she needed. And as she gazed back at him without a single doubt as to her decision, the officiant declared them man and wife.

"You may now kiss the bride."

Lucas's face broke into a wide smile that seemed to ease the tension of the formalities. Like a wave breaking, their audience spilt into a chorus of applause and whistling as Lucas bent to plant a gentle, loving kiss on Nancy's lips. She turned to face the crowd and threw her right arm into the air, holding up her bouquet in triumph. Everybody bent as one to collect their packets of biodegradable confetti, and hand-in-hand, Lucas and Nancy skipped down the aisle of garden chairs in a flurry of red, green, and blue snowflakes.

While the guests prepared to follow the newlyweds back to

the watermill, Nancy and Lucas shared their first private moment as a married couple.

"No backing out now, Mrs Coffey," he whispered into her ear, pressing his cheek against hers.

"That's fine with me, Mr Coffey," she replied.

"You're mine now," he said, planting a kiss on her forehead.

At this, Nancy pulled away sharply. It was more of an involuntary twitch than a purposeful movement, a reaction to some long-lost memory she had tried to forget. But it had surfaced, just for a second, just in that moment of playful possessiveness. She swallowed and touched away a bead of sweat on her brow.

Lucas looked at her, concerned. "You okay, love?"

She shook her head dismissively, and the laugh she emitted was empty. "I'm fine."

"I didn't mean to—"

"It's fine," she said. "Honest."

He shook his head and bit down on his lower lip. "Pinch me."

"What?"

"Pinch me," he said again. "Tell me I'm not dreaming."

She placed a hand on his chest and leaned into him for one more kiss.

"It's not a dream, Lucas," she whispered.

"And this place. Is it what you wanted?" He took her hand gently. "I know you probably wanted something more like Lincoln Cathedral—"

"It's perfect," she insisted and squeezed his hand with a reassuring smile, appreciating the warmth of his body against the dampness of the grass from yesterday's storm. "I wouldn't change a single thing."

"Come on, you two," said her father from the end of the aisle, clapping as if he were herding his sheep across the field. "Lead the way. You can talk all you like after today. And trust me, the novelty wears off."

"I'll tell Mum that," she called out, then smiled up at her new husband. "Shall we?"

Nancy and Lucas Coffey led the wedding party along the small path from the ceremony field to the converted outbuildings where the wedding breakfast would be held. It was their first act as a couple, and she was in no rush to let the day pass.

They had chosen Stockwith Mill for its romance, its history, and its timelessness. With strong links to Lord Tennyson, who penned the poem *The Miller's Daughter,* the venue was everything they needed and more. Nancy and Lucas had even included the line, 'Her heart would beat against me, in sorrow and in rest,' in their wedding invitations.

But they had chosen the venue too, for its one proud guarantee: *to make your wedding day truly memorable*.

And memorable it would be.

Nancy and Lucas led the way along the path as though leading a swarm of bees. Conversations buzzed behind them, natterings about the ceremony, the touching vows, the moment the sun had broken through the clouds just as Nancy had walked down the aisle. Now, they were all looking forward to the next thrills of the day — the speeches, the wedding breakfast, and the toast to the bride and groom.

"After you," Lucas said as they reached the narrow bridge beside the water wheel. Despite the serenity of the scene, the river raged beneath them, frothing and gargling as it entered the mill pond. And just like the water's journey, the excited guests passed over the wooden bridge one by one, then spewed into the open courtyard where the catering staff were waiting with trays of champagne, and calm was once more restored.

The photographer, a ferret-like man who clearly refused to succumb to hair loss and had opted for a combover, had run ahead to snap the couple as they crossed the bridge. He scuttled around, capturing moments, planned and candid, and somehow never seemed to be in the way. Nancy, for one, could have done without the click of a camera every three seconds during the ceremony. But nothing could spoil her day. Not today.

"Nancy! Nancy, over here," he called from behind the camera, like paparazzi calling to a celebrity from the other side of the street.

She smiled politely and caught Lucas offering her a wink to diffuse her frustration. That was why she loved him. One look at Lucas could dissolve any negative emotion in her heart. He held her hand, kissed it once, and together they turned to face the ferret. With Lucas by her side, she was invincible. She beamed a bridal smile, uncompromised, honest, and a true reflection of the day.

The master of ceremonies, Ethan St Clair, had come to stand at the doors to one of the outbuildings, a long stablelike structure.

"Ladies and gentlemen," he called. "Might I invite you all to take your seats?"

He was a jovial man. The sort who seemed born to bellow announcements at guests unruly and otherwise.

As the guests began to filter inside, the photographer pulled Nancy and Lucas aside.

"Just a few photos beside the water?" he said. "While your guests take their seats?"

"Lovely," Lucas said cheerfully, and he led Nancy to the mill pond bank. He put a loving arm around her waist and turned their backs to the pool so they faced the photographer, and Nancy summoned that smile that seemed never to be far away.

Had she known the smile would be her last, she might have refused.

"Beautiful," the ferret said as he changed between two cameras, crouching, standing, and even using a small step to gain height. "Gorgeous," he said between clicks, hopping between feet as though standing on hot sand. "Now turn to face each other, if you will."

Nancy turned to face Lucas, raising her arms to his neck as though they were dancing. "Today has been the best of my life," she said honestly.

"It isn't over yet," Lucas replied with a grin. "Let's get this lot fed and watered, then you and I can slip off to—"

Playfully, she slapped him, then feigned being shocked at the very idea.

"Lucas!"

"What? I'm only saying what every newlywed husband thinks," he said. "Anyway, if you don't drag me away from the bar at a reasonable time, it'll be days before I'm capable."

She laughed and reached up to kiss him, noticing, for the first time that day, an uneasy quiet had fallen upon the place. A single moment without birdsong, without the rush of wind through the leaves, as though nature itself had silenced, or the world had stood still.

The guests had been ushered inside, their constant chatter stifled by the heavy barn doors. Even the photographer's incessant clicking had ceased.

She turned to face the ferret, wondering why he wasn't capturing photos. But there was a look on his face that just wasn't quite right. His finger had stilled above the shutter button and his pale skin was revealed as, slowly, he lowered the camera.

Nancy's first reaction was to check her dress for wardrobe malfunctions, but everything was as it should have been.

She turned to her new husband, only to find that he too had followed the photographer's gaze between them to the mill pond.

And then she saw it, and that wonderful silence she had savoured moments before was broken by her own shrill scream.

ALSO BY JACK CARTWRIGHT

The DCI Cook Murder Mysteries

A Winter of Blood

A Secret to Die For

The Wild Fens Murder Mysteries

Secrets In Blood

One For Sorrow

In Cold Blood

Suffer In Silence

Dying To Tell

Never To Return

Lie Beside Me

Dance With Death

In Dead Water

One Deadly Night

Her Dying Mind

Into Death's Arms

No More Blood

Burden of Truth

Run From Evil

The Deadly Wolds Murder Mysteries

When The Storm Dies

The Harder They Fall

Until Death Do Us Part

AFTERWORD

Because reviews are critical to an author's career, if you have enjoyed this novel, you could do me a huge favour by leaving a review on Amazon.

Reviews allow other readers to find my books. Your help in leaving one would make a big difference to this author.

Thank you for taking the time to read *The Harder They Fall*.

Best wishes,

Jack Cartwright.

COPYRIGHT

Printed in Great Britain
by Amazon

57362732R00233